KT-179-989

This book should be returned/renewed by the
latest date shown above. Overdue items incur
charges which prevent self-service renewals.
Please contact the library.

Wandsworth Libraries
24 hour Renewal Hotline
01159 293388
www.wandsworth.gov.uk   Wandsworth

Why YOU love Nancy Revell

'A cracking saga set in the North East of England during World War 2. I LOVED it and became totally immersed and involved in the story. Can't wait to read the next book in the series'

'It's a gut-wrenching and heart-warming tale of Sunderland women that's true to life. Absolutely cannot wait for the next instalment'

'What a brilliant read – the story is so good it keeps you wanting more … I fell in love with the girls; their stories, laughter, tears and so much more'

'Omg I really couldn't put this story down. I have loved getting to know the Elliott family and the girls that work in the ship yard. I can't wait to read the next chapter in their lives'

'How wonderful to read about everyday women, young, middle aged, married or single all coming to work in a man's world. The pride and courage they all showed in taking over from the men who had gone to war. A debt of gratitude is very much owed'

'Marvellous read, couldn't put down. Exciting, heart rendering, hope it will not be long before another one. Nancy Revell is an excellent author'

'I absolutely loved this book. I come from Sunderland and knew every street, cafe, road and dock. Have already ordered the sequel'

'This is a book that lets the reader know the way our ancestors behaved during the two world wars. With strength, honour and downright bravery … I for one salute them all and give thanks to the author Nancy Revell, for letting us as readers know mostly as it was'

'What a truly inspirational book. I love all the shipyard girls … What can you give? Only 5 stars will do for a wonderful author x'

'Yet another outstanding storyline! Can't wait for Shipyard Girls 4 coming out. Just hope that this is a saga that carries on and after the war!'

What the reviewers are saying...

Shipyard Girls
in Love

Nancy Revell

arrow books

1 3 5 7 9 10 8 6 4 2

Arrow Books
20 Vauxhall Bridge Road
London SW1V 2SA

Arrow Books is part of the Penguin Random House group
of companies whose addresses can be found at
global.penguinrandomhouse.com.

Penguin
Random House
UK

First published in Great Britain by Arrow Books in 2018

www.penguin.co.uk

A CIP catalogue record for this book is available from the British Library

ISBN 9781787460218

Typeset in 10.75/13.5 pt Palatino
by Integra Software Services Pvt. Ltd, Pondicherry

Printed and bound in Great Britain by Clays Ltd, St Ives Plc

To the seven hundred women who worked in the
Sunderland shipyards during World War Two.

Acknowledgements

As the Shipyard Girls series continues, so does the incredible support and enthusiasm I have received from so many people and organisations:

John Wilson and his lovely staff at Fulwell Post Office, researcher Meg Hartford, Jackie Caffrey of Nostalgic Memories of Sunderland in Writing, Beverley Ann Hopper of The Book Lovers, Linda King, Norm Kirtlan and Philip Curtis of the Sunderland Antiquarian Society, journalist Katy Wheeler at the *Sunderland Echo*, the Sunderland and Gateshead libraries, The Word in South Shields, Suzanne Brown and members of the Sunderland Soroptimists, book blogger Amanda Oughton, Pat Robinson for the loan of her father's book: *The Barbary Coast: The Story of a Community* by J. Gordon Holmes. As well as 'Team Nancy' at Arrow: publishing director Emily Griffin and editor Cassandra Di Bello, my wonderful literary agent Diana Beaumont, and, of course, my parents, Audrey and Syd Walton, husband, Paul, and walking companion, Rosie.

Thank you.

*Faith is the bird that feels the light when
the dawn is still dark*

– Rabindranath Tagore

Prologue

East End, Sunderland

July 1918

'I just don't *understand*, Mam.'

And it was true. Sixteen-year-old Gloria Turnbull simply did not understand.

'I thought we would be together for ever.' Gloria spoke her words quietly, as though more to herself than for her mother's benefit. 'We *promised* each other we would.'

Quiet tears were now rolling down Gloria's cheeks as she turned her forlorn gaze to her mother, who was perched on the edge of her daughter's narrow wooden-framed bed.

'There'll be someone else out there for you,' Peggy tried to console her daughter as she started to get up off the bed. It was nearly six o'clock and she knew Clifford would be back soon. If there wasn't a plate of something hot, filling and tasty waiting for him, there'd be another war on.

'Trust me,' Peggy said, gently pushing her daughter's curly brown hair away from her eyes, 'there *will* be others after Jack.'

'There won't be! There won't be anyone else, Mam!' Gloria's voice was thick with emotion. 'Not like Jack – I know!'

Peggy opened her mouth to rebuff her daughter's comments, but closed it again. Gloria was not far off her seventeenth birthday. She had only ever had eyes for Jack, and Jack had only ever had eyes for Gloria, or so Peggy had thought. Everyone who knew the pair had presumed they'd be engaged before long. Even Clifford had been saying to her just the other night that it was 'about time' young Jack came to ask for his daughter's hand.

'I'll bring you some supper in after I've sorted yer dad out,' Peggy promised as she left the bedroom and closed the door quietly behind her.

Only when she heard her mother shooing away her younger brothers and sisters, who had been milling around in the hallway wondering what was going on, did Gloria allow her tears to come freely.

Why, Jack? Why? Gloria wanted to scream. She wanted – *needed* – an answer.

Gloria smothered the sound of her heartache in the bunched-up pillow she had pressed hard into her face, and she coiled her body up tighter, as if by doing so she might disappear and become nothing, feel nothing. At the very least she hoped to barricade the world and all the hurtful feelings that came with it away from her being.

Deep down, though, Gloria knew that it was too late to ring-fence her heart. It had already been shattered into hundreds of pieces. And like a mirror that had been dropped, the shards of glass had been flung far and wide and there was no way it could be pieced back together.

Jack's sudden decision to end their courtship had come like a bolt out of the blue. There had been no warning, no falling-out, no gradual dwindling of feelings. Far from it – they had been as mad about each other as when they'd first met when Gloria was fourteen and Jack fifteen. And they were certainly as passionate about each other, although Gloria, of course, was saving herself for marriage.

They'd only ever really had one major falling-out in all the time they had been together and that was a few months back, when they'd argued over Gloria having a ride home from work on the back of a lad's motorbike. The green-eyed monster had showed itself in Jack and they'd had an almighty bust-up. Neither of them would back down, with Jack declaring Gloria shouldn't have accepted the ride, and Gloria standing her ground and saying there was nothing wrong in it – that the boy was just a workmate. It had been the first time their stubborn natures had clashed so force-fully and it had taken a few weeks before they'd kissed and made up.

When they did, though, they'd seemed closer than ever before, talking about getting married and even joking about how many children they'd have. Jack hinted that he intended to ask Mr Turnbull for permission to marry his daughter on the day of Gloria's seventeenth birthday next month.

But then, without any kind of warning, their lives together came to an abrupt halt when Jack came to meet Gloria after work at the ropery and told her he was 'really sorry', he was ending their courtship.

At first Gloria thought it was some kind of wind-up, but when he told her he was serious and she asked him 'Why?' – a question she would ask herself for a long while after – Jack seemed unable to give Gloria an explanation, but instead just kept on apologising.

When Gloria kept on demanding an answer, tears had formed in Jack's eyes, which alarmed Gloria even more. She had never seen Jack cry. Not once.

'Something's not right!' Gloria was beside herself. 'Yer don't just love someone one minute and turn yer back on them the next!'

But that was exactly what Jack did.

'You deserve better than me, Glor. Much better,' he said before he turned and walked away.

3

Away from Gloria and away from the future they could have shared.

In the weeks following their split, every time Gloria thought of her life without Jack, which amounted to just about every spare minute she had of every day, her whole body would well up with the most terrible feeling of panic. It was as though she was falling, like Alice down the rabbit hole, with no idea where she would land, all the while the question *Why?* spinning around in her head.

It took a month to find out the answer. Her friend Violet sat her down one lunch break at the rope factory and pushed the *Sunderland Echo* under her nose, with the words, 'Sorry, Glor, but I think you should see this.'

Never a strong reader, Gloria used her finger to follow the article Violet had directed her to look at. She saw Jack's name and her heart foolishly leapt, before her eyes darted back up to the subheading: FORTHCOMING MARRIAGES.

Again and again she read the words:

MR J. CRAWFORD AND MISS M. I. HAVELOCK
The engagement is announced between Jack Crawford, son of Irene and Edward Crawford, and Miriam, daughter of Catherine and Charles Havelock, both families of Sunderland, County Durham. The wedding will take place at St Andrew's Church, Roker, Sunderland, on Saturday, 5th September.

At first Gloria's mind seemed unable to process what she was reading, until, finally, a great wave of realisation drenched her.

Violet put her arm around her friend, who was sat stock-still, staring down at the newspaper. She couldn't imagine what Gloria was feeling. Not only had she been dumped by Jack, but she had been replaced by one of the town's most well-known beauties, who was also one of the richest. Everyone in the town knew the Havelocks. Mr Havelock probably owned or had substantial shares in a good 50 per cent of the town's businesses and shipyards. His wife, Catherine, and daughter, Miriam, were often photographed at various highbrow events and were known to go to the launch of every ship built on the Wear, which was where, Violet presumed, Miriam must have met Jack.

'And talk about a shotgun wedding,' Violet said quietly.

Gloria turned quickly to look at her friend. 'You don't think …?' Gloria left the question unfinished. It was as though she was reading about a complete stranger, as if she had never known Jack at all, as if the love they had shared had meant nothing. But worst of all, if Violet was right and this was indeed a 'shotgun' wedding, it could mean only one thing – Jack had betrayed Gloria in every way possible.

Over the next few weeks Gloria tried her utmost not to become obsessed with the Havelocks and, especially, Jack and Miriam. Jack would be turning eighteen just a few days before the marriage ceremony, meaning he would not have to get permission from his parents to walk down the aisle. Not that Gloria thought his mam and dad would have offered up any objections. They'd probably be waiting cap in hand, and palms turned skywards, as Jack walked out the church.

And from what Gloria had heard, Miriam was at least a year older than Jack. There had been speculation that she was in fact approaching her twenty-first birthday, which meant that if her own family had been against their coupling, she was of an age where she could do what she wanted, whether they liked it or not. And, if it *was* a shot-gun wedding, she had clearly been doing exactly what she wanted well before now.

In the run-up to the wedding, Gloria's emotions seemed to be in constant motion, swinging like a pendulum – one moment hate-filled, the next heartbroken. She cried herself to sleep most nights, but quietly so none of her other siblings with whom she shared a room could hear. Her father had told her in no uncertain terms that he didn't want to see Gloria's face 'tripping her up' over the trifle of some failed romance – not, he said, when every day 'our boys' were being killed on foreign fields.

Over the next six months Gloria became an avid news-paper reader, scanning the back pages every day. At first for an article on the wedding, which she had been surprised to see was just a few words with no photograph, then to check out the 'Births' section for an announcement that Mr and Mrs Crawford had had either a son or a daughter.

Gloria knew her family and friends thought it was time for her to dry her eyes and get on with her life, especially as the Great War had finally been won and people saw it as a time for new beginnings. But Gloria's heart was still raw with grief and she honestly believed it was a wound that would never heal.

'Perhaps they didn't *have* to get married, after all?' Gloria asked Violet just under a year after Jack had become Miriam's husband.

Violet looked at her friend and sighed inwardly. Gloria had to stop obsessing about Jack and his new life – with his new wife.

'Mm,' Violet agreed, before nudging her friend and add-ing playfully, 'but what I find odder still is that my best mate hasn't even been out, let alone gone on a date since that lying toerag did the dirty on you. Which is why ...'

she paused, keeping a steady hold of the huge bulk of raw fibres they were combing out, a technique known as hatchelling, ' ... you're coming out with me and Dickie tonight.'

Violet failed to mention that her Dickie was also going to bring along a friend of his who had recently been demobbed, having served most of the war out on the North Atlantic.

When Gloria turned up that evening, she was furious with Violet, but she had been brought up to be polite and not cause a scene, so when Dickie introduced her to his mate, a former Royal Navy petty officer, she forced a smile on her face.

'Gloria, this is my good friend ...' Dickie turned to the serious-looking young man, who was wearing a smart new suit that Gloria guessed must have been bought with the money he had been given after being demobilised, ' ... Vincent Armstrong.'

'And Vincent,' Dickie turned with great ceremony towards Gloria, 'this is Violet's very good girlfriend – Gloria Turnbull.'

The young man stepped forward and held out his hand to Gloria.

'Please,' he told Gloria, 'call me Vinnie. Everyone calls me Vinnie.'

Chapter One

'And Dor ... Thanks for the cake!' Gloria had to shout to be heard above the piercing squeals of a passing tram.

Dorothy and the other women welders had just left the warmth of the Elliots' mid-terrace home, where they had been for a little, low-key party to celebrate baby Hope's christening, and were now standing on the pavement of a bustling and noisy Tatham Street.

'It really was the "biggest cake ever"!' Gloria added, her voice shaking a little with emotion.

Dorothy's face lit up and she tottered back to the front door as speedily as she could in the heels and figure-hugging black dress she was wearing. Her face was full of compassion as she flung her arms around Gloria and gave her a tight hug.

Dorothy had promised Gloria 'the biggest cake ever' if she finally got round to having Hope baptised. There had been much ribbing and banter over the promised cake and how it was going to be the centrepiece of Hope's party. But, after the unexpected and very dramatic events of the day, the wonderful three-tiered Victoria sponge – a marvel in these times of rationing – had paled into insignificance.

'We're all here for you,' Dorothy whispered in her ear. 'Night or day ... And I mean that!'

For once Gloria didn't chide her workmate for her open display of affection and, much to Dorothy's surprise, actually hugged her back.

As Dorothy turned to join the group, Gloria forced back the tears welling up inside her as she looked at the women welders, who were all wearing the same look of concern on their faces.

'Thank you!' she managed to shout out above the cacophony of street sounds to the four young women who not only were her workmates, but had become her closest friends this past year and a half.

Dorothy, Angie, Hannah and Martha all waved back at Gloria before they joined the gurgling stream of shoppers who had brought the east end alive this afternoon following the morning's torrential rainstorm. The dark, thunderous clouds had gone, leaving behind a clear blue sky. Even the sun was now starting to show itself.

'Blimey,' Angie said, as they hurried down the street, 'that was a christening and a half, wasn't it? With Jack just turning up like that?'

'And did you see the look on the vicar's face?' Dorothy chuckled. 'Bet you he won't forget Hope's christening for a long while!'

'I'm still a little confused.' Hannah tried to raise her voice so she could be heard over the excited screams and shouts of the neighbourhood's children out playing, glad to be free after the storm had forced them to stay indoors for an entire morning. 'Do you think Jack has got his memory back?'

'He looked like he knew Hope,' Martha said, equally puzzled.

'Which is odd,' Hannah said, looking up at Martha, who was towering above her, 'because he's never seen Hope before today.'

'I know,' Dorothy agreed. 'I think he only knew who we were from when he was in the yard the other week. I don't think he remembers us from before he went to America.'

As they passed St Ignatius Church, where they had just been a few hours previously, the crowds started to thin out a little.

'Heavens knows what's going to happen now with Gloria and Jack – and, more worryingly, with Miriam and *Vinnie*.' Dorothy's voice dropped at the mention of the man they all detested.

'Yeh,' Angie agreed. 'Really worrying.' She'd seen the mess he'd made of Gloria's face earlier on in the year.

When she'd finally chucked Vinnie out, there'd been a collective sigh of relief, although they all knew she had done it because she was worried about the safety of her unborn child, and not for her own wellbeing.

As the four women started walking up Villette Road, Hannah suggested going somewhere for a cup of tea.

'I'd invite you all to mine, but it's the Sabbath and my aunty Rina won't even be able to put the kettle on, never mind make us a cuppa.' Hannah was a Jewish immigrant whose parents had sent her to stay with her aunt before Hitler claimed their beautiful city of Prague as his own.

'Eee, listen to Hannah here, "cuppa" now, is it? You'll be speaking like Angie if you're not careful,' Dorothy joked.

'There's nowt wrong with how I speak,' Angie said, putting on an even stronger north-east accent than the one she already had.

'Not much right with it either,' Dorothy said, purposely speaking in her best King's English.

'The café on Villette Road then?' Hannah interrupted.

The women all murmured their agreement but when they reached the little tea shop sandwiched between the butcher's and a hardware shop, they could see through the taped-up windows that it was full to bursting with customers.

'Come to mine!' Martha perked up. 'My mam and dad have been dying to meet you all properly for ages.'

'Are ya sure that's a good idea?' Angie said dramatically. 'They might meet us and decide we're not suitable company for their "little" girl ... Or that we don't speak proper.' She cast a dark look across to Dorothy.

Martha chuckled and gave Angie what she considered to be a playful shove, but nearly ended up pushing her over.

'Eee, Ange.' Dorothy gave her friend a mock scowl. 'You've got a right low opinion of yourself. And us.'

Within a few minutes the four had turned into Cairo Street, which was made up of a long row of terraced cottages.

'Here we are!' Martha said as they approached a little single-storey red-brick house that had a knee-high stone wall at the front and the remains of a hinge where there used to be an iron gate.

The front door, like many on the street, was wide open. Martha led the way, stepping over the brass doorstep and announcing, 'Mam ... Dad ... I'm home! And I've brought Dorothy, Angie and Hannah with me.'

Within seconds a tall, skinny woman with short, dark brown hair came hurrying from the back kitchen and into the hallway. She was drying her hands on the floral pinny she had tied around her waist.

'Oh my!' she exclaimed. A big smile spread across her face, showing teeth that looked too perfect to be real and Dorothy guessed they must be false.

'William!' she shouted back over her shoulder. 'Martha's back and she's brought her friends with her.' Martha's mother was clearly over the moon at her unexpected company.

'At long last,' she said, stretching out a long, very slender arm to shake hands with Dorothy, who had been first through the door after Martha.

'Hello, Mrs Perkins,' Dorothy said, 'it's lovely to meet you!'

'Oh, likewise, my dear,' she said. 'And I'm guessing,' she added, peering behind Dorothy, 'that you are Hannah?' She certainly could see why Hannah, who looked much younger than her nineteen years, had been given the nickname of 'little bird'. She was quite tiny, with perfect olive skin and the most amazing dark eyes.

'And, that must make you Angela,' Mrs Perkins said to the pretty young girl with the shoulder-length strawberry blonde hair, who was wearing what looked like an identical dress to Dorothy's, only in red.

Within minutes they had taken off their coats and dumped their boxed-up gas masks and bags, and were all sat round the dining-room table while Mrs Perkins poured out cups of tea and placed a plate of freshly made oatmeal biscuits in the middle.

'Ah, at last,' a loud, slightly gruff voice sounded out from the doorway. 'It's grand to meet you all properly,' William, Martha's father, said.

Martha's mother and father had met the women welders very briefly one night two weeks earlier when they had turned up on the doorstep to see if Martha wanted to join the search for their friend's mother, Pearl, who had gone missing. It had been a bitterly cold night and they had all been so well wrapped up that – coupled with the darkness of the enforced blackout – their faces had barely been visible, while the urgency of the search had prohibited any kind of formal introductions.

'Hello, Mr Perkins!' Dorothy's voice sang out. As usual, Dorothy had taken it upon herself to be the group's main spokesperson.

'So,' Mrs Perkins asked, 'how was the christening? Did everything go off all right?'

The women all looked at each other, not quite sure what to say. Nor were they sure how much Martha had told her parents about the intricacies of Gloria's complicated love life – or the truth about Hope's paternity.

'Well, it was certainly different,' Hannah said, sensing that, for once, Dorothy and Angie seemed at a loss for words. 'But then again, I wouldn't really know what was "normal". This was the first christening I have ever been to.'

Hannah looked at Mr and Mrs Perkins, who were listening intently, and thought they seemed like really good, honest people and that it was probably not appropriate to tell them that Gloria's lover had suddenly turned up at the christening and met his baby daughter for the first time.

'In my religion,' Hannah continued, 'we don't have a christening but something called a "bris", but it's only for the boy babies.'

'How interesting,' Mrs Perkins said, taking a sip of her tea. 'Tell us more.'

'Well,' Hannah said, 'it's when the baby is given his Hebrew and secular name.' She paused for a moment, unsure whether to go into any more detail. Deciding that it was better than talking about the christening they had just been to, she continued.

'And it's also when the baby boy is ... how do you say it in English ... "circumcised"?'

The table suddenly fell quiet. Mrs Perkins blushed and Mr Perkins decided he needed to go to the 'little boys' room'. Dorothy squirmed uncomfortably in her chair and put her half-eaten biscuit back down on her plate. Martha and Angie, however, just looked puzzled.

'Blimey, Hannah, for someone who could barely speak a word of English you know some pretty fancy words.' Angie laughed.

Martha wiped some crumbs away from her mouth and agreed, 'Yeah, you do, Hannah. What does "circum—"'

'*Circumcised,*' Hannah said the word again. 'Well, how do I put it?' She checked that Mr Perkins was not about to re-enter the room, then dropped her voice. 'It's when the baby boy is cut … you know – ' she looked down at her lap ' – down there …'

'Urgh!' Angie couldn't contain her shock and disgust. 'Blimey, Hannah, that's terrible. Why would they do something like that?'

'I think,' Mrs Perkins said, 'if I'm right,' she looked at Hannah, 'it's an important part of the Jewish religion. In the Old Testament it says that every male child should be circumcised.'

Hannah nodded her agreement, but Angie looked even more perplexed and was just about to ask another question when Dorothy kicked her under the table.

'So, then,' Mr Perkins said as he came back into the room and sat down. He looked at his daughter and the friends he had heard so much about. 'Martha here tells me you are all working on a new ship, a screw steamer – *Empire Brutus*, I believe she's called?'

Jumping at the chance to steer the topic of conversation towards something more suitable for tea and biscuits with your friend's parents, Dorothy leapt in with enthusiasm and regaled her workmate's father with how they were indeed working on a cargo vessel called *Brutus* and that she was the latest commission from the Ministry of War Transport.

'The launch date's still a way off, but when she's finished she's going to be over four hundred and twenty

foot long, and over thirty-five foot from keel to bridge!'
Dorothy boasted proudly.

Mrs Perkins had to suppress a smile as the women all
joined in telling her husband about the problems they'd
had and how the future of shipbuilding was welding and
not riveting. She marvelled at how the lives of women in
general had changed these past few years since war had
been declared.

Above all else, though, she felt such a huge relief
that their daughter – their very special girl – had found
not only a job that it was obvious she had been born to
do, but these young women who had also become her
friends.

It was no coincidence that Martha's sociability and her
speech had come on in leaps and bounds since she had
started at Thompson's. She and William had been loath to
admit it, but for Martha the war had actually been a blessing in disguise. The work she was doing as part of the war
effort, as well as the voluntary work she was doing on an
evening for the town's civil defence service, had really
brought her out of her shell.

It had been a joy to see for them both.

Half an hour later, after the biscuits had all been
devoured, and Dorothy, Angie and Hannah had thanked
Mr and Mrs Perkins profusely for their hospitality, they
bade their farewells, shouting back at Martha as they left
the house that they'd see her on Monday.

As the women headed back along Cairo Street and then
on to Villette Road to the home Hannah shared with her
aunty Rina, Angie turned to their little bird.

'Eee, Hannah, I don't know about this religion of yours.'
The perplexed look Angie had worn earlier on at the table
had returned. 'I really can't get me head around what you
said your lot did to little boys' you-know-whats.'

16

As she spoke, a couple of elderly Jews, with long beards and curls of silver grey hair, passed them on the street; not an unusual sight as they were now in the centre of the town's Jewish community.

Angie shook her head in continued disbelief.

'I will never be able to look at a Jewish man in the same way ever again.'

Hannah smiled but she seemed distracted. Dorothy looked at their little friend with her black hair, cut into a short bob, and thought the dark circles around her almond-shaped brown eyes seemed more noticeable than normal.

'Everything all right with you?' Dorothy asked.

'Olly hasn't said or done anything to upset you, has he?' Angie asked, cottoning on to Dorothy's concern.

After being transferred to the drawing office, Hannah had become friendly with a young lad called Oliver. 'Young Olly', as he was known by the women welders, had started to accompany Hannah to events outside of work, and had been to the christening with them in the morning.

'No!' Hannah said, defensively. 'Olly would not do anything to hurt me.'

'Well,' Dorothy said, 'I'm no mind reader, but I can tell something's bothering you.'

Hannah let out a long sigh. 'I didn't want to say anything, you know, with today being the christening and everything. It's meant to be a happy day, isn't it? Celebratory. And I feel so glad for Gloria that Jack was able to be there too ...' Her voice trailed off.

'Spit it out, Hannah!' Angie commanded.

'Well,' Hannah began, 'my aunty Rina heard last night that there was the possibility that my mother and father may have been put into the Theresienstadt ghetto.'

Now it wasn't just Angie who looked puzzled, but Dorothy as well.

'You'll have to explain what this *whatever-you-call-it* ghetto is,' Dorothy cajoled Hannah, as gently as she could. Hannah wasn't like the rest of them. She was so fragile, both physically and mentally. She hadn't talked about her parents, who she knew were still stuck over in what was now Nazi-occupied territory, and no one had wanted to ask her if there had been any kind of an update as she seemed so happy since starting her apprenticeship as a draughtsman.

'Well,' Hannah took a slightly shuddering breath in and tears started to pool in her eyes, 'from what my aunty has heard from our local rabbi, the Germans have been herding all the Jews into an area of the city which has been ... how do you say it ... seg ... segregated ... made into a kind of huge, walled prison. It's meant to be terrible there. People are dying of disease and starving to death ... The Germans are trying to make out it is a nice place to be, but they are lying.'

Hannah and Dorothy had slowed their pace and were concentrating hard on what Hannah was telling them. As they took in her words, they exchanged a look of outrage and anger.

'Bloody hell!' Angie couldn't stop herself. 'How can they get away with doing something like that? What have your people done to deserve that?'

'*Nic!*' Hannah said, reverting to her native tongue. 'Nothing. Absolutely nothing! It is simply because they are Jews.'

Dorothy had to bite her lip to stop herself letting rip. She had been brought up living alongside the town's Jewish population. To her, seeing a man with a skullcap or with a prayer book in his hand had been no different than see-ing some bloke wearing a flat cap and smoking a pipe. She knew that they were by no means an evil race. On the contrary, they always came across as very calm, very polite people.

Dorothy, Angie and Hannah slowed down and stopped as they reached the corner of Manila Street opposite the Barley Mow Park, which had recently been divided up into allotments. There was now fruit and veg where there had once been pretty flower beds and a bowling green.

Dorothy gave Hannah a big hug, followed by Angie.

'Try not to worry, Hannah,' Dorothy said, giving her friend a reassuring smile.

'Yeah,' Angie added, 'we'll beat the bastards and before you know it yer mam and dad will be out of that ghetto place.'

'Yes,' Hannah said, her spirits lifting a fraction at her friends' hopeful words and determination, 'and what is more is that we will help "beat the bastards",' she said quoting Angie. 'We will make the ships "to beat the bastards".'

Angie and Dorothy chuckled at Hannah's repeated use of a swear word.

'We will, Hannah!' Angie and Dorothy said, glad not to leave their friend in total despondency.

'*You'll* design the ships and *we'll* build the buggers!' Angie shouted as they left.

'Poor Hannah,' Dorothy said as they hurried across Ryhope Road and into the wide, tree-lined residential road known as The Cedars where most of the town's affluent families lived.

'I know,' Angie agreed, staring at the row of huge houses. It never failed to amaze her how magnificent these homes were.

'You know, Dor, I really just can't understand it. I don't even know why Hitler hates the Jews so much? My dad says it's because he's a nutter and thinks everyone should have blond hair and blue eyes.'

Dorothy looked at her friend in her red dress with her light blonde hair and blue eyes.

'You'd be all right then,' she said, 'but I'd be for the chopper.'

Angie looked at her friend's thick, raven-coloured hair and dark eyes.

'You know, you look a bit Jewish,' she said, as if seeing her friend for the first time. 'What was yer da like? Yer proper da, I mean.' Angie knew Dorothy's mother and father were divorced, but it was not something her friend liked to broadcast.

'I'll show you a photo when we get home. I've just got the one picture of him. He was dark, but I reckon he looks more Italian than Jewish.'

By now the women had almost reached Dorothy's home, a large Victorian house that looked out on to the massive natural arboretum known as Backhouse Park.

'Martha's mam's really dark as well, isn't she?' Angie's head was now swimming with all the happenings of the day.

Dorothy laughed.

'Honestly, not everyone with black hair and dark eyes has Jewish heritage, Ange!'

They walked up the long crunching gravel driveway that led to a large white front door.

'They both seem really nice though, don't they?' Angie added, looking at her friend.

Dorothy knew Angie would have been happy to stay at Martha's all afternoon, chatting away and eating Mrs Perkins's warm biscuits. She certainly couldn't see Angie's mother and father making polite conversation over a cup of tea. The few times Dorothy had been at her friend's it'd been pandemonium. There were kids of every age running around, either fighting with each other or screaming with excitement. Her mam always looked run ragged and rarely even acknowledged either of them. And just one look at Angie's father, sitting there in his armchair next to the fire, in just his trousers and vest, still covered in coal and dirt from the colliery, had you inching towards the front door.

'Yes, Martha's mum and dad seem really nice. She's lucky,' Dorothy agreed, thinking of her own mother and stepfather and how they would have barely batted an eyelid if Dorothy had turned up with her friends out of the blue.

'Eee, but I tell you what,' Angie said puzzled, 'Mrs Perkins isn't a bit like Martha, is she? Neither is her dad, come to think of it.' Angie was thinking about her own mam. She had inherited the same light reddish blonde hair as well as her mother's big boobs and wide hips. And her little brothers all looked like mini versions of her dad.

'Mrs Perkins is more like Olive Oyl.' She chuckled at her comparison. 'And I reckon her dad's old enough to be her grandda.'

'I know, Martha's not like them at all. Not one little bit. Makes you wonder, doesn't it?'

'About what?' Angie asked.

'Well, you know,' Dorothy said, 'whether Martha is their *real* daughter?'

She saw a look of comprehension make its way across her friend's face.

'Eee, yer might be right there, Dor,' Angie said. 'Bloody Nora,' she said, blowing out air, 'it's been a right ol' day today, hasn't it?'

As Dorothy opened the front door, she turned to Angie.

'And it's not over yet. You still up for going out tonight?' she asked.

'Too bloody right!' Angie couldn't get the words out quickly enough, before they chanted their well-worn mantra in unison: *'You only live once!'*

Chapter Two

After Gloria waved Dorothy, Angie, Hannah and Martha off, she shut the front door of the Elliots' Victorian terrace and stood for a moment in the long, narrow hallway. The mosaic floor tiles seemed more colourful than normal, and the intricate patterns seemed to dance around her feet. She didn't feel like this was really happening. In fact, she would not have been at all surprised if she had blinked and suddenly found herself back in her bed at home having just woken up from the strangest of dreams.

Had today really happened? In the space of just a few hours her world had yet again been turned upside down. In fact, it had flipped so many times this past year and a half, she didn't know which way was up. But, at least this time the outcome was good. More than good. It was a dream come true. She had been given back something she thought had been taken from her for ever.

She had the love of her life back.

It had been the last thing on earth she had expected to happen – and today of all days.

These last few weeks she had been desperate to tell Jack that he had a baby daughter, but how could she when he didn't even recognise her, let alone know they had been lovers before he had gone to America?

She had forced herself to accept that Jack was firmly back in Miriam's clutches, and had decided, for now at least, that she had to let Vinnie believe Hope was his. If he got to know the truth, she was under no illusion as to what would happen.

'You all right, Gloria?'

Gloria looked up to see Agnes Elliot in the doorway to the kitchen, her little granddaughter, Lucille, clinging to Agnes's long skirt, a thumb stuck in her mouth and her hand clutching her beloved raggedy toy rabbit.

Gloria realised she must have looked odd simply standing there, staring at the floor, lost in her own world.

'Why don't you come in and sit down and have a cuppa,' Agnes beckoned, her Irish lilt soft and reassuring.

As she came back into the kitchen – the heart of the Elliots' home – Gloria saw Arthur sitting quietly in his armchair by the big, black range.

Tramp, the Border-collie cross that had followed Agnes home one day and not left, and Pup, the runt of the litter that no one wanted, were sniffing the threadbare carpet around the old man's feet, scavenging for crumbs or any other edible titbits.

The room was calm now that all of the guests had gone. Gloria looked across at Jack sitting at the large wooden table. Hope was cradled in his arms, and he was looking at her with unadulterated love. By the sound of her daughter's gentle snuffles, she was sleeping soundly.

Gloria looked at her lover's worn face. Jack may have risen through the ranks to eventually become a yard manager, but his impoverished upbringing and the years he'd spent working out in all weathers had left their mark.

Everyone who had been at the christening and had come back for tea and cake had been sensitive enough not to stay for long. They had all made pleasant conversation, oohed and aahed over baby Hope and made a fuss of Lucille, who had revelled in the attention.

They had cut up the huge Victoria sponge that Dorothy had got delivered to the house earlier that morning, and all had relived the drama of Hope's birth at Thompson's, making great comedy out of Hope's impromptu arrival in the world.

Jack had sat and listened, mesmerised by the story of how Gloria had gone into labour at the exact moment the town had been hit by a midday air raid; how they had all been frantic, none of them ever having witnessed a birth before, never mind helped deliver a baby. As the bombs had rained down on the town, they'd managed to create a make-do-and-mend delivery suite in the paint- ers' shed.

Dorothy, he heard, had been the unexpected heroine of the moment, the one to roll up her sleeves and bring his little daughter into the world. She had been rewarded with the honour of being appointed Hope's godmother, a role she had clearly taken very seriously. Jack could see the story had been told many times these past three months as each of the women had their own retelling down to perfection.

After the cake had been consumed and the tea drunk, the women welders as well as their boss, Rosie, and her friends, Lily, George and Kate, made their excuses and left; all of them more than aware this was the first occasion that Gloria had been able to spend any time with Jack since he'd come out of his coma.

The party's host, Agnes, also knew that Jack and Gloria needed time to talk about the consequences of their rekindled love. When the truth came out it was going to be a huge scandal, especially when it became known that their adultery had resulted in an illegitimate baby.

'I'm going to pop next door to see Beryl and I'll take cheeky Charlie here with me.' Agnes glanced down at Lucille, who was being surprisingly quiet, perhaps sensing the enormity of what had taken place – and was presently going on – in her home.

'Aye,' Arthur's low voice agreed, causing Jack to drag his gaze away from Hope and look at the old man now getting to his feet from his chair near the range, 'and I'll get out o' both yer hairs. I'm sure Albert would appreciate a bit o' help at the allotment. He's probably out there now, happy as owt that we've just had that huge downpour, though I'm sure his broad beans will have taken a bit of a hammering in that storm.'

Gloria looked at Arthur and thought that they weren't the only things that had taken a battering in the storm this morning. The old man had turned up at the church with Jack, drenched to the skin and looking like he was on his last legs.

'Arthur,' Gloria asked, 'would you mind staying with us for a little while before you go? It would be good to have a chat.'

What had happened this morning had been wondrous, something Gloria never thought could happen in a million years, but for now she needed to concentrate on what they should do next.

Arthur eased himself back into his chair, inwardly thankful as he didn't think he had the strength to make it out the door, never mind trek across to the Town Moor; he'd thought he was going to take his last breath under God's roof right there at St Ignatius.

'Aye, course I will.' Arthur spoke in such a way that Gloria knew he understood why she wanted him to stay.

Agnes stepped towards Jack and baby Hope. 'It's been lovely meeting you, Jack.'

'Aye, and you too,' Jack said, reaching out and shaking Agnes's hand. 'And thank you. For everything.'

Jack had realised on returning to the Elliots' house after the christening that Agnes had already played an important part in his little girl's life. He had learnt that not only had she and her daughter-in-law, Bel, been looking after Hope during the day while Gloria went to work, but they loved this little mite, now asleep in his arms, as though she was one of their own.

'Ah, it's my pleasure.' Agnes touched Hope gently on the cheek. Then she looked at Gloria, whom she had come to know well these past few months, and gave her a smile that somehow conveyed the empathy she felt.

After Agnes left, having given in to Lucille's demands that she be allowed to keep her new yellow pinafore dress on, Gloria moved her chair nearer to Jack. As she did so, Jack looked at her and took her hand.

His head felt like it was going to explode with everything he had learnt today, and with all that had happened. As soon as Arthur had explained to him that he had been spending time with Gloria before he'd gone to America, and that his marriage to Miriam was far from what his wife had led him to believe, Jack knew he had to talk to Gloria himself. He'd raced to the church, driven by the knowledge that something momentous was about to happen. And it had. As he'd walked down the aisle, he hadn't been able to take his eyes off Hope. It made no logical sense, but he had known straight away that the child was his.

'I'm so sorry I can't remember anything from before I nearly drowned. God, I'd give anything to have my memory back.'

Gloria squeezed Jack's hand and kept hold of it.

'You know, I think you will remember in time. The doctor I spoke to said there was a good chance your memory would come back.' Gloria forced herself to sound more optimistic than she felt.

'Yes, of course,' Jack said. 'You came to the hospital, didn't you? Not long after I'd come out of the coma?'

Gloria would never forget that afternoon in September when she had rushed to the hospital in such excitement after Rosie told her Jack had come out of his coma, thinking that at last she and Jack would be reunited and live happily ever after with their baby daughter. She should have known it was all too good to be true. Her joy that Jack was back in the land of the living had been snatched away almost as soon as it had been gifted to her when she had seen the look on Jack's face and he had smiled at her with blank eyes. The nice young doctor had then taken her to his consultation room and explained that Jack had amnesia.

Gloria looked at Jack and realised she had a lifetime of memories to give him, but now wasn't the time. Too much had already taken place today. If *she* felt as though her head was spinning, Jack's must have felt like it was in the middle of a tornado.

Besides, the present was more pressing. Arthur had told Gloria on the way back from the church that Jack had taken the morning off work but was expected back after lunch. They had managed to buy more time as Polly had gone to Crown's to tell them that Jack had got held up and wouldn't be in for the rest of the day. But there would be questions asked if he wasn't home after the end of the day shift.

'Jack,' Gloria began, 'there is so much to talk to you about, but we can't do it all in one go. I'm not even sure how much you know.' Gloria looked at Arthur with a questioning face, 'How much Arthur has told you already?'

Arthur sat up and perched himself on the edge of the armchair so that he was looking at Gloria and Jack.

'Well, we didn't have that much time to chat before the service. We went for a walk along the river yesterday and I told Jack a bit about his younger days, when I was working at the yard for the Wear Commissioner.'

'I did get a memory back,' Jack interrupted. 'A man dressed in all his diving gear – you know, massive twelve-bolt helmet, big canvas suit with tubes coming out of it, and great big steel boots.'

Gloria was listening intently, a faint shard of hope breaking through that Jack might actually manage to retrieve at least some of his memory.

'But I couldn't remember anything about my mam and dad or anything about growing up,' Jack said.

'I didn't pull any punches,' Arthur admitted. 'I told Jack that his ma and da, like many back then, were very poor, and their situation wasn't helped by the fact Jack's da wasn't far off a total waste of space and when he wasn't doing piecework, he was drinking every penny he earned. I told him he started at Thompson's as an apprentice plater as soon as he left school, and that if he wasn't at the yard, he'd be with me – and Flo and our Tommy, of course – at the Diver's House.'

Arthur thought for a moment. 'And I told him that you two met when you were really just bairns, and that he courted you for, well, I reckon a good couple of years?'

'That's right,' Gloria said, flashing a look at Jack, 'two and a half to be precise.' An image of Jack as a young lad with an unruly mop of thick, dark hair and dancing grey-blue eyes suddenly struck her.

'But,' Arthur continued, 'you two split up and Jack married Miriam not long afterwards.'

'It sounded to me like there was a reason for our getting married so quickly ...' Jack looked at Gloria for an answer.

'That's what you told me, not long before you went off to America.' Gloria paused. 'That you married Miriam because she told you she was in the family way, and that later she admitted to you she had lied, but by then she'd got pregnant for real.'

When Jack had told Gloria the truth about why he had ended their courtship all those years ago – how he had gone out on a few dates with Miriam when he and Gloria had fallen out over her ride on the back of her workmate's motorbike, and how a while later Miriam had come to him and told him she was expecting – it was clear he still felt terribly ashamed.

He had told Gloria there hadn't been a day since when he hadn't regretted that one night with Miriam: 'That one massive mistake I feel like I've been paying for ever since. But worst of all, I feel like you have paid for it too.' She would never forget those words, nor the look of despair in Jack's eyes when he had spoken them. But they had brought Gloria a sense of relief. An understanding. She had always known there was more to it. Finally she knew why.

'God!' Jack's frustration suddenly came to the fore, causing Hope to wake up. 'I just wish I could remember. Miriam told me that we were love's young dream.'

Gloria got up and took Hope from Jack, knowing that her whimper would turn into a wail if she didn't soothe her.

Jack stood up and walked over to the kitchen window, which looked out onto the backyard.

'The strangest thing is' – he spoke to Gloria and Arthur but kept looking out of the sash window patterned with criss-crosses of brown tape – 'I recognised Hope even though I'd never seen her before. Hadn't even known of her existence.'

He turned round to see Arthur watching him from his armchair and Gloria standing with their baby girl in her arms by the stove.

Jack looked at them both.

'This may sound completely mad, but I saw Hope when I was drowning, and I've seen her in my dreams these past few weeks.'

Gloria felt a shiver go down her back.

'I can't remember my own past and yet I've been able to remember a daughter I never knew existed!' Jack let out a big sigh. 'You'd be within your rights to have me carted off to the local nuthouse.' He tried to laugh.

'Jack,' Gloria said, sitting back down on her chair by the kitchen table, 'you're perfectly sane. Your mind's just all in a muddle. It just needs un-muddling, and that's going to take time.' She was quiet for a moment before adding: 'It pains me to say this, Jack, but I think, for the time being, we should keep things the way they are, and you should stay with Miriam – just until we've had time to think about the best way forward. There's a lot to be considered.'

Gloria knew that Miriam would not take the news lying down. Nor would she go off and lick her wounds quietly. No way. Miriam would be beyond angry. She would be out for revenge and she had the power and the money to get it in full.

She felt herself shudder at the thought. They needed to be prepared for whatever Miriam decided to do when she found out. And with Jack the way he was, with a mind devoid of all memories of their love and the time they had spent together, an appropriate strategy was all the more vital.

Arthur nodded his agreement as he leant down to stroke the puppy.

'Aye, I think Gloria's right. Miriam's not going to react kindly to being told that you two were seeing each other before you went to America … And that you've had a child together.'

'*And*,' Gloria said with a tight smile, 'there is your other daughter to think of.'

Jack nodded. While holding Hope he had been hit by another vague memory. As he had stared at her perfect skin, rosy cheeks and rosebud mouth, he'd had a flash of holding another baby in his arms. A baby with a mop of thick, black hair, not unlike Hope's.

'Aye, Helen,' Jack said. 'This is going to be hard on her and she's going to need to know she's got a little sister.'

Gloria felt her stomach turn over at the prospect. Not only would they have to deal with the wrath of Miriam, but also with Helen – a pale imitation of her mother in her manipulative ways and her need to always get what she wanted, but still a hard, calculating and vindictive young woman. She had shown her true colours when Polly and Tommy had fallen for each other last year, and she'd done everything in her power to split them up because she wanted Tommy for herself. And when she hadn't succeeded, she had taken her anger and resentment out on them all and tried to break up their squad of all-women welders. Thankfully, she had failed, but it had been a hard-won battle.

Thinking about her reaction to finding out that not only was Jack going to leave her mother for one of those women welders, but had fathered a baby – well, it just didn't bear thinking about.

Jack sat back down heavily in his chair. 'I don't know … There's a part of me just wants to go back today and tell Miriam everything. Get everything out in the open.'

On hearing his words, a burst of panic shot through Gloria. This was so like Jack. So impulsive. Gloria took hold of his hand.

'Not yet, Jack. We need time.' Her face was serious. 'I promise we'll be open about everything soon. But not just yet. Not today.'

Jack nodded, and squeezed Gloria's hand. He had the sudden urge to hold her and kiss her. It was the complete opposite of the way he felt about Miriam, *his wife*.

He had beaten himself up about his lack of feelings, romantic or otherwise, for the woman he knew he had been married to for the past twenty-odd years. He had convinced himself that it wasn't just his memory that he had lost when he'd nearly drowned in the North Atlantic, but his ability to love as well. As soon as he had seen Gloria today, though, standing next to the font with Hope in her arms, he had become overwhelmed by the most incredible surge of love.

And sat here now, holding her hand, simply touching her, he wanted to move closer to her, kiss her, feel her next to him.

As if sensing Jack's feelings and knowing that they both now needed some time alone, Arthur pushed himself out of his armchair.

'Well, it's been quite an exhausting day for this old man,' Arthur said, 'so I think I'm gonna disappear upstairs for a little nap. Get my energy back.'

Both Gloria and Jack immediately stood up. Gloria, still cradling Hope in her arms, gave him a gentle hug.

What Arthur had done for them these past few days went beyond thanks.

'I'll be seeing you and the bab first thing Monday morning,' Arthur told Gloria, his eyes resting on Hope, who was still sound asleep.

He then turned to Jack and the two men shook hands vigorously as if to make up for the words neither of them were able to express.

'I'll pop round Crown's next week,' Arthur said. 'We'll have our bait by the quayside and have another trip down memory lane, eh?'

'Definitely!' Jack said, still holding the old man's hand. 'Definitely!'

When Arthur left the room, Gloria and Jack sat back down in their chairs by the kitchen table. There was a moment's awkward silence. This was the first time they had been on their own together, and they were both very much aware of it. They started to speak at the same time.

'Jack—'

'Glor—'

'Go on,' Gloria insisted. 'You go first. I feel like I've done enough talking for a whole week, never mind a day.'

'I just wanted to say ...' Jack hesitated, trying to work out how to put his feelings into words. 'I just want you to know that I mightn't be able to remember much – if anything – of our past together, but I do have a sense of how I felt, how I *do still* feel for you.'

Gloria looked at him and the tears started building up behind her eyes again.

Jack moved his chair so that it was right next to Gloria. 'Tell me more. About you. How we met – for the second time.'

Gloria could see that he was desperate for information but knew she had to keep it simple. Purposely avoiding the years she had spent with Vinnie, particularly the violence and abuse she had been subjected to, she instead kept it brief, telling Jack that she too had married and had her own family, but that her marriage, like Jack's, had been an unhappy one and when they met again after she'd started work at Thompson's they had fallen back in love with each other.

'It was so strange,' Gloria told Jack, 'we hadn't even spoken to each other for more than twenty years, but it was like we'd only just parted.'

'Perhaps,' Jack said, looking down at the life they had created, 'neither of us really let go of the other.'

Gloria nodded thoughtfully, following Jack's gaze and looking down at Hope sleeping soundly in her arms. She knew now that she had always carried her love for Jack in her heart, although she had forced herself to ignore its presence.

'We both agreed that this time nothing would stop us from being together,' Gloria said, 'and after you left for America, Vinnie moved out and I started divorce proceedings, although obviously he doesn't know about you and me.'

She paused for a moment. 'I haven't told him about Hope yet either. Only those you met at the christening know the truth. Everyone else has presumed that Vinnie is Hope's dad and I've just let them think that.'

Jack sat for a moment, digesting what he had been told.

'There's so much I want to ask you,' he said, 'that I want to know ... But, more than anything I just want to hold you in my arms. Would that be all right?'

'Oh, Jack,' Gloria said, blinking away tears, 'that would be more than all right.'

And so Jack put his arms around the woman he could not remember loving, but whom he knew he loved all the same.

And as he did so, Gloria rested her tired head on the man she thought she had lost. A man she knew she was going to have to say goodbye to again, but whom she now had hope that she could soon be with for ever.

Just like she had always dreamed they would be as youngsters.

Chapter Three

'Hello there, Stan!'

Polly shouted out her greeting to the old ferryman she had come to know well this past year and a half since starting work at Thompson's.

Polly travelled on the old screw steamer to and from work every day, and as Stan rarely took a day off, it was unsurprising that the two had become friendly. They'd become closer still since Polly had learnt that Stan knew Tommy well and had been giving him a free pass on the ferries since he was knee-high.

'I've got a present for you!' Polly raised her voice to be heard over the sea of flat caps as Stan, who she noticed was getting unsteady on his feet, weaved his way through the surge of passengers piling on-board.

When he reached her, Polly stretched out her hand, which was holding a large triangle of cake that had been carefully wrapped up in greaseproof paper and tied with a piece of string.

'It's from Hope's christening – you know, Gloria's baby?'

Stan's face immediately lit up. He had been guiding the ferry across the river the day Hope was born and she'd taken her maiden voyage on this very boat when she was just hours old. Stan had been one of the first people to clap eyes on the miracle of life born at the exact same time that others had lost theirs during the air raid attack just half a mile away.

'Cake!' Stan declared. 'Cor, 'n a greet big slice by the looks of it!'

Polly laughed.

'Well, it was quite a large cake, and there was some left begging that I thought you might like.'

'Ta, pet. That's really kind o' yer.' Stan held the parcelled-up cake as though it was precious treasure.

'I'm guessing yer not gannin' across the river to do any overtime.' He nodded down at Polly's tweed skirt peeking through her best coat, and the flat leather shoes she was wearing instead of her normal boots.

'No,' Polly said, grabbing hold of the side of the boat as a passing ship heading back out to sea caused a large wave that made the ferry seesaw. 'Just running an errand to Crown's.'

Polly had suggested to Jack and Gloria that it might be a good idea if she went to Crown's and told them that Jack wouldn't be back at work today. They'd all agreed it would be best for Polly to keep the reason for his no-show as vague as possible so as to avoid having to tell an outright lie.

'Any more news from that fiancé of yours?' Stan asked. It was a question he never failed to ask, and Polly never got tired of answering. Speaking about Tommy to those who knew him seemed to keep alive her hopes and dreams that he would return to her one day when this damnable war was won.

'I'm waiting for a letter. He will have got mine last week, so I should be getting one back soon.' As Polly spoke she subconsciously touched her ruby engagement ring.

Once the ferry bumped onto the quayside on the north side and everyone piled off, Polly waved her goodbyes to Stan and made her way up the embankment, past Thompson's and on to Jackie Crown's. The yards stood shoulder to shoulder and looked out across the wide, winding expanse of the River Wear.

Polly was relieved she didn't have the added worry of seeing Helen, who had been off work while her father convalesced. They'd heard she'd gone on a short break to see relatives in Scotland, but would be back at work on Monday – news that had caused all the women to groan. They'd groaned even more loudly when they'd heard she was to continue as yard manager. The position had only been given to her as a temporary measure while Jack was in America, but after Miriam had put a stopper on Jack's return to Thompson's it had looked likely that Helen would be given the position permanently.

After Polly slipped unnoticed past the timekeeper's cabin at the side of the Crown's entrance, she started walking across the yard, ignoring the wolf whistles from the men working overtime this Saturday afternoon. About a hundred yards away from the main admin building, though, she stopped dead in her tracks. The Vivien Leigh lookalike now sashaying across the yard towards her in impossibly high heels, and clearly enjoying the catcalls from the older workers, was none other than Helen.

What the hell was she doing here?

Polly's initial reaction was to turn and run back out of the yard, but she knew she couldn't. Helen had her eyes trained on her and was plainly determined to speak.

'My, what a surprise to see you here.' Helen's wide smile belied the condescension dripping from her voice.

Polly and Helen had barely exchanged two words in all the time they had known one another, yet they knew just about everything about each other. They had been love rivals, after all. And it was hard to know who hated the other the most. At a push, it would probably be Helen. After all, Tommy had chosen Polly, not her.

'And you too!' Polly replied, trying to keep the panic out of her voice.

Helen let out a shot of laughter.

'Well, you're obviously not here to work.' Helen looked Polly up and down. She had to stop herself sneering at Polly's old winter coat, and what looked like a hand-me-down tweed skirt. *And those flat, brown leather shoes! Could she have found a more hideous pair?*

'No, no, I'm not ... you're right.' Polly tried to stop herself stuttering. 'I mean, you're right, Helen, I'm not here to work. As you know, I work at Thompson's ...' She paused before quickly adding, 'Which is where I thought you also worked?'

Helen stared daggers at Polly, not gracing her question with a reply.

'And,' Polly rushed on, her mind working nineteen to the dozen, 'I didn't think you were back at work until Monday?'

'I'm not!' Helen snapped back. Looking at Polly, she was still at a loss to know what it was that Tommy saw in her. What did this plain Jane from the east end have that she didn't? She could feel the jealousy rising quickly to the surface.

'I've actually come to see my father,' Helen said, 'but he doesn't appear to be here.'

Polly started to move as if she was eager to get on her way.

'Well then?' Helen demanded. 'Why are you here, Polly? Got yourself a new bloke? What with Tommy being away. Out of sight, out of mind, is it?'

Polly felt her hackles rise. Helen would love that. She wouldn't even put it past her to spread a rumour, like she had before when she'd tried to split her and Tommy up.

'No, Helen, I'm not here to see some other bloke. As you well know, I'm engaged to be married.'

Helen's eyes automatically dropped to Polly's left hand and she felt a burst of anger when she saw the engagement ring.

'So why are you here, Polly?' Helen demanded. 'You know you're not supposed to be in the yard without proper authority.'

Now Polly was cornered. She had to say something. And quickly. *Why was she such a hopeless liar?*

'Actually, it's about Jack,' Polly said. 'I've been asked to pass on a message.'

Helen stared at her. 'It's *Mr Crawford* to you,' she said, her steely gaze now fixed on Polly's face. 'So?' She paused, waiting for an answer. 'What's the message, Polly? I am his daughter after all. I shall pass on the message myself.'

'Oh, yes, of course,' Polly stalled. 'Well, it was just to say that he won't be in for the rest of the day. Something's come up.'

Now go! a voice in Polly's head ordered.

'Oh gosh, is that the time?' Polly raised her eyes to the huge clock at the front of the main offices. 'Must dash!'

And with that Polly turned on her heels and hurried off. She had to stop herself breaking into a run and hurdling some of the huge chains that were curled up like snakes in the middle of the yard.

Watching Polly's retreat, Helen felt more than a twinge of annoyance. She had wanted to ask why her father wouldn't be in for the rest of the day. What had come up? And why had he asked Polly, of all people, to relay the message – especially when she didn't even work at Crown's?

Helen turned to go back to the offices. She had actually come here to forewarn her father that her mother had organised a surprise party for him to celebrate his return. She knew her dad hated surprises, and parties.

Well, it looked like he was just going to have to deal with both when he got back from wherever he was and from whatever it was he was doing.

As Polly hurried home, she cursed her shoes, which she didn't wear very much these days and which had been rubbing against her heels. She just hoped she got there before Jack left. He needed to know this simple errand had all of a sudden become anything but. Helen was bound to question him when he got home and tell him that she had seen Polly. And Helen wasn't stupid. She would think Polly had been acting oddly.

As Polly half walked, half jogged home, she kept thinking about Jack and Helen, and how Jack evidently had no idea how awful his daughter was. The way he had talked about her after the christening had taken them all aback. Dorothy had cheekily whispered to her that she thought there might be something wrong with her hearing – was Jack *really* talking about the Helen they all knew and hated?

As Polly limped the last stretch along the Borough Road, Jack was a mere hundred yards ahead of her, but after deciding to cut down Foyle Street, he disappeared from view, causing Polly to miss him by a matter of seconds.

Chapter Four

Borough Road, Sunderland

'I love you, Rosie Thornton. You *do* know that, don't you?'

Rosie's head was resting on DS Peter Miller's bare chest and she was luxuriating in the feel of his arms wrapped around her and the closeness of their naked bodies gently pressing together, every part touching. It was cold in her basement flat, even though she could see that the sun had come out after the storms earlier on that day, but Rosie and Peter were as warm as toast as they snuggled together under the freshly laundered sheets and heavy patchwork quilt covering the single bed.

'I know you do, Peter,' Rosie murmured into his chest with its sparse covering of soft dark hair.

Rosie wanted to tell him that *she* also loved *him*, but couldn't. She had never before told any man that she loved him because she had never loved another man, but she *did* love Peter.

The words she wanted to say, though, seemed to get stuck in her throat, so instead Rosie raised herself up on her elbow and looked down at Peter, the man she had known for almost exactly a year, and with whom, until this morning, she had only ever held hands. She slowly lowered her head and kissed him, hoping that he would feel the love she felt for him and that it would say the words she seemed unable to speak.

After a little while, Rosie sat up, holding the bedclothes close to her, partly for reasons of modesty and partly because, having moved away from the warmth of Peter's body, she realised just how cold it was.

'Let me make us a nice cup of tea,' Rosie said, relinquishing the sheets, sliding her body out of the narrow bed and walking over to get her thick cotton dressing gown hanging from a hook on the back of the bedroom door.

Peter watched Rosie's naked body move across the room. This woman had caused him untold angst, had made him plummet to the lowest of the low, but she had also taken him to the most wondrous heights. She had fascinated him from the very first moment they had met – and still did. Probably more so.

Their love affair had – until today – been a chaste one, but all the same it had been a rollercoaster of a ride. They had met in an official capacity in November last year, but it hadn't been until February this year – on Valentine's Day of all days – that they had bumped into each other by the ferry landing after he'd been transferred to the Dock Police.

They had met almost every week thereafter for tea and cake, but then he had tried to kiss her, and in doing so had scared her off. She had ended their courtship and he had been bereft.

But something had nagged away at him. Something hadn't felt right. They'd seen each other again and Rosie had agreed to meet with him, but it was only to tell him once and for all that she did not want to be with him. He'd had the gut feeling that she was lying, and he'd been proved right. She *had* been lying, and not just about her feelings. She had been lying about what he now knew was her 'other life' – running a high-class bordello in the upmarket part of town called Ashbrooke.

That had been just two weeks ago and he had been in torment ever since. It had been a choice between the law or love and he had chosen love. He had waited for Rosie to return to her flat after the christening at midday today, and when he had seen her, he had gone to her, taken her in his arms and kissed her, and his heart had soared when she'd kissed him back.

Peter sat up in the iron-framed bed and listened to Rosie as she put the kettle on and got out her china tea cups and put them on a tray. If he could stay in this moment, feeling the way he did for ever more, he would be a very happy man. He couldn't remember ever feeling the way he did now. He knew that it was wrong to think that, almost a slight on the memory of his wife, Sal, whom he had loved very much, but theirs was a different kind of love and it had taken place in very different times.

'Here we are.' Rosie came back into the room, holding two cups of tea. She looked at Peter, sat up in the bed looking dishevelled, and she noticed how relaxed his face was, and how his deep blue eyes never once left her.

'I was just thinking how, if I died at this very moment in time, I would do so being the happiest man on earth,' he said, moving over in the bed so that Rosie could once again be by his side.

Rosie smiled, handed him his tea and carefully sat on the bed next to him so as not to spill any of her own.

She could not quite believe the joys this day had brought. Like all the women welders, she had been overwhelmed with emotion and so happy for Gloria when Jack had turned up at the christening and taken his baby daughter into his arms. It was quite a surreal moment, and they had all had to hold back the tears as the vicar baptised Hope and told her to go out and bestow light upon the world – something, Rosie thought, Hope had already done.

And then, a short while later, as she returned home after tea and cake at the Elliots', dodging puddles left over from the thunder and lightning they'd had earlier on, Peter had stepped out of the shadows and called her name. She'd stood transfixed as he strode towards her, his trilby in one hand, his black woollen coat, as always, flapping open, and when he'd reached her they'd both stood still, looking intently at each other. And then Peter had gently taken her hand in his, and kissed her.

The past few hours had been magical, but Rosie also knew that they would have to break the spell and talk about the reality of their everyday lives.

'You know,' Rosie said, her face turning more serious, 'there's so much we need to speak about.'

Peter took a sip of his tea and nodded gravely.

'I know we do. I feel like we've chatted so much over the past year – we know all about each other's jobs, each other's friends – but there's so much we don't know about one another.'

As he spoke Peter looked at Rosie's profile and touched the side of her face. The skin on Rosie's body might be perfectly smooth and unblemished – untouched even by the sun – but her face told a different story. Her face was quite beautiful, but she had been left with a smattering of tiny scars from a weld that had 'gone wrong'.

He would never forget meeting her for the very first time when he had gone to inform her as next of kin about her uncle Raymond's death by drowning. Of course, he had noticed the scars that were then still quite fresh on her face. He had asked her about them and she had told him that she'd had an accident at work. He had believed her, but now, knowing what he knew, he wasn't quite so sure. Now he needed the truth. About everything.

'Can you remember when I first came to see you?' Peter asked.

Rosie could. Seeing him at her door immaculately attired in a smart black suit, starched white shirt and blue tie, she had thought him the epitome of professionalism.

'Like it was yesterday,' Rosie said. 'Although,' she added, 'it also seems like years ago.'

'I hope you don't mind me asking,' Peter took hold of Rosie's hand, 'but did you know about your uncle's past? That he'd just been released from prison?' Peter hesitated, looking at her face for a reaction. 'About what he had done?'

As he spoke, Peter could feel Rosie's body stiffen next to him and he sensed that she was already pulling up the drawbridge to her emotions.

Rosie put her cup of tea on the bedside table and looked at the man with whom she had just made love. The only man she had ever made love with. She might have lain with many men, but it had not had anything to do with love.

'No, I didn't know that he had committed those awful crimes,' Rosie said. 'How he had raped those poor women. It came as a complete shock to me. I did think it odd that I hadn't heard from him for years. But, like I told you back then, we had never been close. My mother never mentioned him when we were growing up.'

Peter looked at Rosie. He had been a copper for too many years not to know when someone was keeping something from him.

'God, Rosie! We've just made love. Surely you must know that you can trust me! You have to be honest with me!'

Rosie swung her legs off the bed and stood up, wrapping her gown tightly around her body as she glared at her lover.

'What's all this? Some interrogation? Are you being DS Miller now? Or Peter?' Rosie's face was flushed and anger sparked in her eyes.

Peter followed suit and put his cup down on the bedside cabinet. Tea sloshed into the saucer. He pulled himself up so that he sat ramrod straight in the bed.

'No, Rosie, I am not interrogating you, but I am demanding that you be honest with me. Just as I will be honest with you. Is it not enough that I told you I love you? I would never say such a thing were it not totally and utterly true. I have only ever told one other woman that in my life and it was my wife. This is not some passing affair. Surely you must know that? Surely you must know you can trust me?'

Rosie continued to glare at him. It surprised her that her emotions could go from love to fury as if at the flick of a switch.

'No, I don't know I can trust you, Peter! I have just spent the past week preparing to spend a good while in jail myself after you told me in no uncertain terms that you knew about Lily's and that I had put you in an "untenable" situation. I mightn't have known what "untenable" meant, but I knew enough to guess that you were unsure whether or not to report me, and Lily, and our business, to the authorities – so please forgive me if I'm not falling over myself to trust you.'

Peter let out a heavy sigh. It was true. He had tossed and turned every night for the past two weeks since he had found out that Rosie part-owned a high-class brothel, and that she had been a working girl there herself not so long ago.

'Come here,' Peter implored. He threw back the bedcovers next to him.

'Come here,' he repeated. 'I want you here next to me. For as long as possible. And as much as possible.' He stretched out his hand to Rosie, who was still standing statue-like by the side of the bed, although the anger in her eyes appeared to be dwindling.

She slowly took hold of his hand and allowed herself to be gently drawn back in to the warmth of the bed.

'I'm going to tell you this now,' Peter gently took Rosie's face in his hands, 'and again and again – as many times as I need to for you to believe me when I say that you can trust me. With your life. I will never betray you. And that means I will never tell a living soul about Lily's. So, let's get that one straight first of all.'

Peter saw Rosie's body wilt slightly and he put his arms around her and held her tightly as if to reiterate his point.

'But,' he said gently, 'we need to be totally honest with each other. No more lies. No matter how unpalatable the truth may be.'

Rosie found Peter's hand and held it tightly. 'All right. Agreed.'

'Good,' Peter said, squeezing her gently.

Chapter Five

Over the next hour, Peter and Rosie talked and talked. Peter told Rosie about his life with Sal, a subject they had always steered clear of in the past during their meetings at the café.

Since his wife's death Peter had never so much as looked at another woman, never mind wanted to be with one. Until he'd met Rosie.

It was the first time he had admitted to anyone that those memories of his wife that had stayed resolutely in his head were of when she was dying. Her English-rose looks overtaken by the ravages of the cancer that had relentlessly eaten away at her. He had tried to erase them and replace them with remembrances of the few short years they had been happy together, in love and, moreover, healthy. But, he confessed, it had been hard to keep them at the forefront of his mind and to stop them from being swamped by the memory of the gradual degeneration of his wife's mind and body as the cancer worked its way through every part of her being.

'I buried her five years ago,' Peter told Rosie, who was listening intently, feeling both the sadness and the anger that Peter was unable – or did not want – to disguise. 'I changed after that.' He turned his head to look Rosie in the eyes, knowing that if he demanded the truth of her, he had to give it in return.

Rosie sensed there was more. That his wife's death had affected him in a way he had not disclosed to anyone else.

'In what way?' she asked.

'Well,' Peter said, trying to choose his words carefully, 'I'd always known from a young age that I wanted to be involved in some kind of law enforcement – I was always intrigued by our justice system.' He sighed, thinking back to the innocent days of youth, when everything seemed so black and white, so clear-cut.

'After I started working for the police and began climbing my way up the career ladder, I couldn't help but feel a bit let down. Disappointed that justice often wasn't even *seen* to be done, never mind *actually* done.' There was another pause.

'Am I making sense?' He looked again at Rosie, who he could see was listening intently.

'Yes,' Rosie said simply, thinking about the lack of justice not only in her own life, but in the lives of those around her.

'When Sal died,' he continued, 'something inside of me changed. It was as if something just switched. Perhaps it was my perspective on life, I'm not sure. Whatever it was, the feeling that sticking to the rules wasn't always the right thing to do seemed to grow. I tried to ignore the thoughts I was having, rationalising to myself that it was a part of the grieving process and that I'd revert back to the person I'd been before Sal was taken from me, but I didn't. And after a while I began to realise that the change was permanent. That there was no going back, and that the conviction I felt about the scales of justice needing a little balancing out every now and again was right.'

Rosie's interest was now piqued and she sat up straight. Peter sensed her movement and looked at her.

'Go on,' she urged.

'I suppose,' Peter said, 'if I'm honest, I just got fed up with seeing society's bad apples getting away with infecting those near to them. I was frustrated that the law often could not simply take those rotten apples out of the barrel and stop them destroying perfectly healthy ones.'

There was a moment's quiet. Then the sound of a car horn blaring out could be heard on the street outside, followed by a man's angry shout.

'Are you telling me,' Rosie said, continuing the analogy, 'that you sometimes get rid of those rotten apples yourself?'

'Yes,' Peter said simply. 'But, just so you understand, I don't permanently dispose of those bad apples. I just try to make sure they don't somehow find themselves back in the barrel.'

'Like Vinnie?' Rosie asked, her eyes wide with comprehension. It was something that had puzzled her. She'd had her suspicions. Now it looked like her intuition had been right.

Peter nodded.

Rosie's mind spun back to the end of April that year when she had confided in Peter about the beating Vinnie had given Gloria. They had discussed her going to the police, but it had been clear that they were both of the opinion nothing would have been done because Gloria and Vinnie were married. The general rule of thumb when it came to 'domestics' was that what happened behind closed doors stayed behind closed doors.

Rosie could still remember the way Peter had looked her in the eyes and asked, 'Is there anything you think I could do?' She had felt there was more to his question than appeared on the surface, but she had dismissed it. It was when she heard a week or so later that Vinnie had been 'mugged' that she began to wonder if Peter had given Vinnie a taste of his own medicine. But when Rosie had mentioned what had happened, Peter had simply said it had sounded like 'divine intervention'.

'What I do, off the clock as it were,' Peter said, 'well, it's not something I'm proud of, and, obviously, if it ever came out that I occasionally took police matters into my own hands, I'd be for the chop. I'd probably not get done for it – too much of a scandal – but I'd be quietly "let go". It'd be brushed under the carpet.'

Rosie nodded again, unsure exactly what to say.

'I do have something, though, that I have to tell you,' Peter confessed.

Rosie put her hand over Peter's.

'You can trust me, you know?' she said.

'I know,' Peter said.

'It's about Vinnie,' he started to explain. 'He's not had the misfortune to be mugged again, but he has found himself behind bars. For a short while at least.'

'Really?' Rosie was intrigued.

'You see,' Peter continued, 'I knew he'd go to the christening. I've known enough "Vinnies" to realise that he wouldn't pass up the chance to go there and cause trouble, and sure enough, I caught him charging down Suffolk Street.'

Rosie was listening with bated breath, imagining how awful it would have been had Vinnie made it to the church.

'He actually played right into my hands and made very loud and very definite threats against Gloria, so I was perfectly within my rights to arrest him and take him back to the station.'

'Thank God you did!' Rosie said. 'I hate to even think what would have happened had he turned up at the church. Especially with Jack there.' She shivered involuntarily. 'So, is that where he is now?' she asked. 'Locked up in a police cell?'

Peter nodded. 'He'll be kept in overnight. But they'll probably have to let him go tomorrow.'

53

'Oh, Peter!' Rosie said, giving him a kiss on the cheek. 'I think it's fair to say you saved the day. At least Gloria's got to enjoy this one day with Hope and Jack without that nutter ruining everything. Shame they couldn't lock him up for good and throw away the key.'

'I agree,' Peter said. 'Unfortunately, it's just a temporary solution.'

Rosie sat quietly for a moment and digested everything Peter had just told her.

'I don't know what to say, Peter.'

And she didn't.

'How about another cuppa?' he suggested, taking her hand and kissing it.

Rosie smiled.

'Sounds like a good idea.' She pushed herself out of the bed and put the kettle on.

'I'm afraid I haven't got much to offer in the way of food,' she shouted through to the little box bedroom. 'I might be able to rustle up a cheese sandwich if you're hungry?'

She appeared back in the bedroom doorway.

'Actually, if we're going to be totally honest with each other ...' A smile played on her lips. 'I have my own confession to make ...'

Peter looked at Rosie, her blonde curls in disarray around her face; the make-up she'd had on when he had caught her returning home after the christening now just about all gone, bar a few smudges of mascara.

'My confession to you is, I'm a hopeless cook. I barely even shop. And I have absolutely no aspirations to become the perfect housewife.'

Peter laughed as Rosie turned her back on him and padded back into the kitchen just as the kettle was squealing for attention.

When she came back with their cups of tea, Peter was wearing his trousers and pulling his shirt on.

'I'm down for Home Guard duty in a little while.' He reached to take the tea from Rosie, who then sat down next to him on the side of the bed.

Rosie knew that Peter had shared all this with her not because he felt the need for a confessional, but because he wanted to show her that he trusted her, and that she could trust him.

'Well, now we're being so open with each other ...' She hesitated. 'You were right.'

Peter looked at her in puzzlement.

'About my uncle,' she explained.

Peter nodded, took a sip of hot tea and waited for Rosie to continue.

'It's true what I said about my mother and father not ever mentioning him. I actually thought Mum had been an only child. I only really became aware of his existence after my parents were killed in a hit-and-run accident.'

Rosie had never talked about her family to Peter during their courtship, although he had found out, almost by chance, about her parents' death. The police had carried out a half-hearted investigation into who might have been driving the car that ended up orphaning Rosie and her little sister, but it hadn't even produced any leads, never mind suspects.

'He turned up out of the blue, the day before the funeral,' Rosie continued. 'At the time, I didn't think about how he'd got to know about the accident.' She spoke calmly but also unemotionally, as if relaying something that had happened to someone else.

Her mind snapped back to when she'd first clapped eyes on her uncle and how he had repulsed her from the off.

'At first he pretended to be full of concern. That was until he found out that my parents had left everything to me. That's when he showed his true colours.' Rosie pulled her dressing gown around her body as if suddenly cold.

Peter listened, letting her speak without interruption.

'Anyway,' she continued, 'he decided to stay on for another night, said it was to look after me and Charlotte as we had no other family ...' Rosie's voice trailed off as images of that night flashed across her mind's eye. She hesitated.

Peter could feel his fists clench and a surge of fury instantly rose to the surface. He had read the files on Raymond Gallagher. Knew all about his crimes. Knew that the man was a sick and twisted pervert. A rapist who had attacked at least five women.

He took Rosie's hand and held it tightly.

Rosie knew that Peter was well aware of the type of monster her uncle was.

'It was either me or Charlotte,' she said simply.

Peter understood that no more words were needed. The few that had been uttered had said it all.

The thought of her as a fifteen-year-old being violated in such a way, by such a man, was almost too much for Peter to bear. Rosie had been forced to make a deal with the devil in order to save her sister that night. He could not imagine any woman – let alone someone who was still really a child – having to make a more heinous sacrifice. He knew the effect such malevolence had on a person. In his time as a police officer, he had seen many young women who had been forced to endure such perversions because of some man's twisted needs, and he knew that it was something that never left them.

'And Charlotte?' Peter asked. 'Was she all right?'

'Yes, thank God,' Rosie said, 'but I knew I had to get her somewhere safe. Somewhere she would be cared for. Somewhere that would give her a future. There was no way I could really look after her. And there was no way she was going to end up in some godforsaken children's home.'

Peter's mind flickered to Rosie's old school friend Kate, and how she had ended up on the streets after her time at Nazareth House, the care home run by the nuns in town, after she too had been orphaned.

'So where did she go?' Peter was intrigued.

'I spent what money had been left to us on her first year at an all-girls boarding school in Harrogate. She's still there now.' Rosie's voice lifted. 'She's doing really well. She can swim and she can even speak French.'

Peter could have cried on hearing the love flooding into Rosie's voice as she spoke of her little sister. But the tears he felt welling up inside were also because he was astute enough to realise just how Rosie had been able to keep her sister at the boarding school – and it wasn't down to her wages at Thompson's.

'Lily's?' Peter asked.

Following his train of thought, Rosie simply answered, 'Yes.'

'But there's more, isn't there?' Peter said gently. 'Your uncle came back, didn't he?' Peter had done a quick calculation. If Rosie's uncle had served a five-year sentence for the rapes he committed, that meant he must have been arrested and sent down very soon after turning up for Rosie's parents' funeral.

'He did,' Rosie said. 'I think a part of me knew I hadn't seen the back of him. People like him don't just disappear. When you told me he had been in prison, it made sense. *That* was why I'd never been bothered by him.'

'Until he came to find you again, after being released?' Peter guessed.

Rosie nodded. 'He told me I had to hand over all my wages every week otherwise he would tell every man and his dog that I was working at Lily's.'

'And you did, didn't you?' The penny was starting to drop. This evil man had once again forced Rosie into a corner. And once again Charlotte was his pawn.

'The money we found in his bedsit. It was yours all along?' Peter asked.

Rosie nodded. 'How was that for irony?' She let out a sad laugh. 'He was blackmailing me because he was convinced he should have been given the money I inherited. Money he didn't get when his parents disinherited him and left everything to my mother. In his warped mind, he was getting back what he thought was rightfully his, and at the same time getting revenge on his sister.'

Peter pushed a hand through his mop of greying black hair.

'Dear God,' he said quietly as he took hold of Rosie's hand. 'You don't have to tell me any more if you don't want to. I would understand if you had done something ...' He let his voice trail off.

Rosie looked at Peter and smiled. It actually felt good to get everything out in the open. To talk about what had happened during that awful time last year.

'No, I *want* to tell you,' Rosie said, 'but don't worry, I didn't get rid of the rotten apple, if that's what you're thinking. Although I wanted to! Believe you me. But I just couldn't. I just couldn't take another life, no matter how evil that life was. But all the same, I was pretty desperate. I was working just about every minute of every day and on top of it all, he insinuated that he knew where

58

Charlotte was, which terrified me … No,' Rosie took a big gulp of her tea, 'in the end I like to believe fate gave him his comeuppance.'

She took a deep breath.

'Raymond came to see me at the yard at the end of a shift. It was dark and there was a thick fog. The place was just about empty. He'd found out that I'd been keeping some money back – had conned his way into my bedsit and found a little box stuffed with pound notes and wage slips – boy, was he mad. *Really mad.*' Rosie unconsciously touched her face and felt the small pits of the scars in her soft skin.

'He had a knife to my throat and had my head over a live weld.' Rosie spoke quite matter-of-factly, unaware of the look of outrage and disbelief plastered across her lover's face.

'He said he was going to kill me, like he'd killed my parents. I couldn't believe what I was hearing. *It had been him who'd knocked over and killed my mum and dad.* By this time, though, I had nothing left. Not an ounce of energy to fight back. My only thought was for Charlotte. I could barely breathe through the fumes of the burning metal and all I could see was white light from the weld, and then there was his voice – his horrible, snidey, sickly-sweet voice – hissing in my ear, telling me that after he was finished with me, he was going to go and do to Charlotte what he had done to me all those years ago …'

Rosie took another deep breath. 'And then, through the mist and the fog came my squad of welders. They'd got tired of waiting for me at the Admiral and had come to find me and tell me to get a move on!'

Tears came to Rosie's eyes and she smiled at the memory. 'They were all stood there – Polly, Gloria, Dorothy, Hannah and Martha. Of course, Raymond was all mouth. He let go of me and backed off.'

Rosie looked at Peter. 'And as luck would have it, he stepped back and stood on a welding rod that hadn't been put away. He went flying backwards ...' Rosie paused, ' ... and straight over the quayside.'

'And a week later,' Peter finished the story quietly, 'his body was found at the bottom of the Wear.'

Rosie nodded.

Peter berated himself inwardly. He should have realised from the off that Raymond Gallagher had played a much more important part in Rosie's life than she had originally let on. Someone as sadistic and evil as Raymond always tried to defile those closest to him.

Rosie stood up. She felt lighter for telling the story that had hung heavily on her the past year.

'Well,' she sighed, 'you know what they say – every cloud has a silver lining and all that.'

'It most certainly does,' Peter agreed sadly. 'I just wish there hadn't been such a dark and threatening cloud over your life for so long.'

'Well, it's gone now, for ever,' Rosie said. She didn't feel sad. If anything, she felt unburdened. Relieved. She turned her head to look at her little clock on the bedside table.

'And it's time for you to go now,' she said. 'The Home Guard needs you.'

Peter stood up and pulled Rosie close, wrapping his arms around her.

'Not for long though,' he said between kisses. 'I want to take you out tomorrow night. On a proper date.' He stroked her cheeks and thought that in Rosie's case she wore her scars well – those on the outside as well as those on the inside.

'So, that's a date then?' he asked.

'Yes,' Rosie replied. 'It is! Now go and do your duty – *official or otherwise*,' she told him, a cheeky smile playing on her lips.

Chapter Six

Park Avenue, Roker, Sunderland

'Darling, you're back home!' Miriam came bustling out of the dining room where she had been checking the table settings and positioning an elaborate floral display she'd had delivered that day. She had also just been yelling at the cook, Mrs Westley, to get a move on as the guests would be arriving soon and the hors d'oeuvres weren't prepared.

'I've organised a bit of a surprise party for you, darling,' Miriam purred as she kissed Jack lightly on the lips, before taking hold of his hand and guiding him into the large reception room at the front of their grand Victorian end-of-terrace home overlooking Roker Park.

'You know ... a party to celebrate your return,' Miriam explained, as she went over to the drinks cabinet. 'Oh, darling, you look so confused. Here, let's get you a drink before the company arrives.' Miriam carefully poured a large measure of single malt into a thick crystal whisky glass. Jack knew his wife had already had a drink herself as he could smell mints on her breath.

'You know, Jack, you don't have to work overtime,' Miriam chided. 'It *is* Saturday, after all. And you were meant to be easing yourself back. It might have been nice for us to spend some time together.'

As she spoke Miriam was walking around the room, giving the place one last inspection, fluffing up cushions and moving ornaments into position. She checked the top of the large marble mantelpiece. She felt a stab of annoyance when her perfectly manicured finger collected a smudge of dust. The little cleaning girl would get what for when she came in tomorrow.

'Anyway, how *was* work today, darling?' Miriam asked.

Jack opened his mouth but didn't say anything. His mind was all over the place.

Should he admit that he hadn't actually been at work today?

Or simply lie and say that work had been fine?

Thankfully, the doorbell went before he had time to reply.

Miriam gave a little jump.

'Oh, blast, I bet you that's the Bellamys – they always arrive early.'

And with that she was gone, leaving Jack in peace and glad that he'd managed to evade the question about work.

He sighed and took a large glug of his whisky. This was not going to be easy. That much he knew. Just speaking to Miriam had made his brain go into overdrive. She appeared to be all sweetness and light, yet what he had learnt today told him that his wife was quite the opposite. If he was to believe what Gloria and Arthur had told him, and he saw no reason not to, then he had been conned by Miriam since coming out of his coma. She had fed him a load of lies, painted a completely false picture of their marriage.

Jack heard the front door open and the loud greetings of the guests he either didn't know or knew but couldn't remember. He hated parties. And he particularly hated dinner parties. Miriam had told him that he had loved entertaining, which had surprised him. In light of what he had learnt today, it would seem this was another lie that was being used to construct Miriam's new version of their life together.

Jack took another gulp of whisky. This evening, though, he was glad that the house would be full of people and that Miriam would be too busy with their guests to pay too much attention to him. He felt as though the confusion going on inside his head was there for all to see, as clear as day. The party would, at least, act as a temporary shield.

After all, how could he hold any kind of superficial conversation when all he could think about was what had happened today?

My God, he had a child – another daughter! And a lover!

'Jack, old boy! How are you doing?' Jack looked at the rotund man and his equally rotund wife as they bustled into the reception room. He knew they were Mr and Mrs Bellamy, not because he had any recollection of them, but because Miriam had jokingly referred to them as 'Tweedledum and Tweedledee'.

As Jack shook hands with the couple he'd been told he had known 'for donkey's years', it occurred to him that since coming out of his coma, he had been blindly led by Miriam. He had trusted her, had believed every word that came out of her mouth. And why wouldn't he have? But now that he knew she had lied about so many important things, there wouldn't be another word uttered by her that he didn't question. He would have to rely on his intuition. Something he should have done before now.

'How's Crown's?' Mr Bellamy asked.

'Busy,' Jack said, as Mrs Bellamy was gently guided away by Miriam to mix their drinks.

'I hear you're just about to lay down a frigate. What's her name?' Mr Bellamy asked.

'*Ettrick*. HMS *Ettrick*,' Jack said. If he could just talk about shipbuilding all night, he would be happy. And if he could just work around the clock, he would be happier still.

*

Shortly before they all sat down for their first course, Helen joined the party, looking stunning as always, and as her mother expected.

As usual, though, Miriam made sure she found fault with her daughter's appearance.

'I thought you might have worn your other dress,' she whispered quietly into her daughter's ear as the guests started to take their places at the long, oval-shaped dining table.

'You know, the one with the pussy-bow collar.' She smiled at her daughter as she spoke, as if they were exchanging pleasantries. 'I've told you before, this one makes you look too wide on the hips.'

Miriam took another sip of her gin and tonic before adding, 'I think your Aunt Margaret and Uncle Angus have been feeding you too much haggis and those potato pancakes they're so fond of up there. It's a good job you didn't stay any longer, otherwise you'd have needed a whole new wardrobe.'

As Helen listened to her mother's criticism the chirpy mood she had been in dissolved, leaving her feeling deflated. Try as she might to ignore her mother's usual putdowns, she couldn't let them simply go over her head. Instead, she found herself subconsciously pulling at her dress, which, when she had been getting ready for the party and looking at herself in the mirror, she had thought showed off her hourglass figure perfectly. Now, however, it felt as though it was too small. Too tight.

Helen, of course, didn't look any different from when she had left for the break with her aunty and uncle, but Miriam was determined to make sure she didn't get above herself. Well, that was how she rationalised denigrating her daughter so. If Miriam was honest, though, she would admit to being jealous of her daughter, of her stunning looks, her shapely figure and the way everyone admired her – men and women, young and old.

'What awful weather we've had today.' One of the guests was making small talk as they all settled down around the table and a harried-looking Mrs Westley started to bring in the first course. 'Like a tornado, then all of a sudden it just cleared up.'

As the elderly guest continued to prattle on, Jack thought of how he and Arthur had battled to the church, getting soaked to the skin in the process. At the time he'd simply been going there to speak to Gloria and had no idea that Arthur was, in fact, taking him to attend his own daughter's christening.

As the chatter swirled around him, Jack caught snatches of conversation, some discussing the latest broadcasts by the BBC, some bemoaning the hardships of rationing – not that he would have thought anybody around this table did without. He knew through his work by the docks that the black market was thriving; if you had the money, you could get just about anything you wanted. And most people around this table had the money.

'And do you like Jack's new wedding ring?' Miriam was asking one of her guests, a middle-aged woman who had her hair styled into victory rolls that looked as though they had been glued into place. 'Jack lost his ring somewhere between the middle of the North Atlantic and the Sunderland Royal. I personally think it may have gone walkabouts when he was in his coma.'

Jack felt himself bristle. This wasn't the first time Miriam had insinuated that one of the medics who had looked after him had stolen his ring. If they had, they would have been welcome to it – they'd saved his life, after all.

By the end of the three-course meal, Jack felt weary, his energy now completely depleted.

'So then, Father ...' It was Helen's voice. She had sat down in the chair next to him, which had been left vacant when one of the guests had excused himself. 'Where did you get to today?'

All of a sudden, Jack felt wide awake. He had not thought anyone, other than those who worked at Crown's, would be aware of his absenteeism. Jack looked at his daughter's pretty face and was relieved that it looked more curious than accusatory.

'How did you know I wasn't at work?' Jack automatically countered her question with another as his mind scrabbled around, forcing itself to recall that it had been Polly who had gone to the yard, saying she would be vague and make out that something had come up that prevented him from returning to work.

'Well ...' Helen looked across at her mother, thinking that she was now well on her way to being more than just a little tipsy and that she would have to try to get shot of the guests soon to save the family any embarrassment. 'I went there to warn you about your surprise party,' she said, lowering her voice and adding sarcastically, 'knowing how much you love this kind of do.'

Jack nodded and smiled. Helen had been such a support. He and Miriam must have done something right to produce such a loving and caring daughter.

'And that's when I bumped into Polly. She said you'd got held up. I tried to ask her what it was, but she scurried off before I had a chance to ask.'

Jack looked at Helen and hated himself for having to deceive her.

'Well,' he said, 'I spent the afternoon with Arthur.' Jack argued with himself that he wasn't really lying, just telling a half-truth. 'He came to see me at the yard and we ended up chatting about old times. Or rather, *Arthur*

67

chatted about old times and I listened, hoping that perhaps I might remember something.'

Normally a mention of Arthur would have caused Helen to think of Tommy and her failure to make him hers, but instead of thinking of the love she had lost, she felt hopeful that Arthur might in fact help to restore her father's memory. If anyone could, she knew it would be the old man. He had played such an important role in her father's life, and they had always stayed close.

'And did you?' Helen asked hopefully.

'Did I what?' Jack asked.

'Remember anything?' Helen repeated with a slight gasp of exasperation. Her mother's voice was getting louder and sounded more slurred.

'Actually,' Jack said, 'I did recall something.'

Helen's eyes widened.

'It was an image of Arthur when he was working at Thompson's, all kitted out in his diver's suit and massive copper helmet.'

'Well, that's brilliant news, Dad,' she said, giving him a big hug. 'Your lovely consultant Mr Gilbert said you might start remembering things and if you did, it would more likely be "remote memories" that your brain, for some reason, finds more easily accessible than more recent events.'

Mr Matthew Gilbert, whom Helen had developed a little crush on despite his marital status, had said that although there was no simple cure for what he referred to as 'retrograde amnesia', he couldn't stress the importance of 'jogging' the victim's memory enough. And that exposing a person to anything related to his past would often speed up any chance of him getting his memory back.

'Aye,' Jack nodded, 'I guess they work on the premise that the older the memories, the more ingrained they are ...'

As Jack's voice trailed off, their attention was drawn to the sound of Miriam's forced laughter as she regaled her guests with the same story he had heard a number of times about how he had dramatically resurfaced from his coma, grabbing hold of her hand and trying to speak incomprehensible words.

'I think I'll start rounding the guests up,' Helen said. 'It's getting late. Why don't you get yourself off to bed? You look tired.'

'You're right,' Jack agreed. 'It's been a long old day, to say the least.'

As Helen watched her father make his excuses and say goodnight to his guests, she couldn't shake the thought that it was odd Polly hadn't said her father was with Arthur when she had bumped into her at the yard.

'Are you all right there, Mrs Cromwell?' Helen said loudly to one of the elderly guests, as she helped her out of her chair and guided her across the room.

And now she was thinking about it, Helen could only presume that her father must have ended up at the Elliots' if they'd asked Polly to go to the yard with the message.

But why had her father simply not said he had been at the Elliots'? Helen mused as Mrs Cromwell leant heavily into her.

Perhaps, she rationalised, it was because he knew how much it hurt her that Polly had won Tommy's heart, and he was saving her dented pride.

As the rest of the guests followed Mrs Cromwell's lead and slowly filed into the hallway, Helen glanced up the stairs to see the back of her father disappearing into the spare room.

Mother will not be pleased, Helen thought with a little jolt of spiteful satisfaction.

Helen knew that her mother had been working hard at convincing her father that they had been some kind of modern-day Romeo and Juliet and had never spent a night apart, when in fact nothing could be further from the truth. Before the trip to America her parents had not spent a night together for as long as she could remember.

Helen turned her attention back to the guests, who were now all getting their hats and coats and saying their thank-yous and farewells.

As she stood at the front door alongside her mother, who, she noticed, was holding on to the thick oak door to support herself, she felt a surge of happiness at the thought that her father was going to get better. He *would* get his memory back. And she was going to help him. She'd seen a change in him already since getting back from Scotland. He seemed much more like his old self. And now he was chatting to Arthur that could only be a good thing. Couldn't it?

Chapter Seven

Lily's, West Lawn, Ashbrooke, Sunderland

'*Ma chère.*' Lily looked at Kate and started shooing her away with heavily jewelled hands that also sported a huge diamond engagement ring. 'I know you're itching to get on with your latest creation, so be gone! *Allez!*'

Lily, George and Kate had spent most of the afternoon following the christening at the Holme Café. It was owned by a Mrs E.H. Milburn and, as well as being a confectioner and caterer, also laid claim to being the cosiest café in town.

Kate was now fussing about, making a pot of tea in the huge kitchen of Lily's – the magnificent turn-of-the-century terrace that overlooked the perfectly manicured grounds of Ashbrooke Cricket Club – otherwise known as the 'Lords of the North'. There was no way this patch of greenery would be desecrated and converted into a huge allotment.

On the outside, the beautiful three-storey building owned by Lily was simply one of several residential houses in the most affluent area of the town. Inside, though, it was a thriving upmarket bordello that had been designed to emulate the cultural and artistic splendour of the French Renaissance – an impression Lily tried to enhance with her faux *accent français*.

'Are you sure you don't mind?' Kate said, but as she asked the question she was already picking up her cup of tea and the latest copy of *Vogue* ready to depart to her bedroom-cum-studio on the top floor. 'I don't want to be rude, it's just that Hope's lovely broderie anglaise christening gown has given me an idea for this new dress I'm working on.'

Lily laughed. 'Now why doesn't that surprise me? You didn't take your eyes off that baby once, and I know it wasn't because of any deep-seated maternal yearnings.'

Kate was Rosie's old school friend, who had been brought to the bordello after Rosie had seen her begging in a shop doorway. It had been an act of kindness that had ended up benefiting Lily and all the working girls as Kate had turned out to be a veritable genius with a needle and thread. It was a talent that Lily and Rosie could see should not go to waste and so they had set her up in town in a little shop called the Maison Nouvelle, next door to Mrs Milburn's café on Holmeside. They had been able to kit the shop out with quite an array of fabrics and haberdashery thanks to Lily reimbursing the previous owner handsomely for his old stock.

The Maison Nouvelle, or 'New House', a name dreamed up by Lily, had just opened as a seamstress shop, but Kate's dream was that it would one day be her own boutique, selling clothes that she had designed and made herself.

'Yes, my dear,' George agreed, taking out a very beautiful and ornate oval-shaped glass bottle of Rémy Martin Louis XIII cognac. 'You get on with your dressmaking and leave Lily and me in peace.' He winked at Kate. 'We've got a wedding to talk about!'

Kate's eyes widened. 'That means a dress to be made!'

Lily, who was looking with more than a little surprise at the appearance on the table of the most expensive bottle of brandy she'd ever clapped eyes on, forced her attention back to Kate.

'*Non, ma chérie*, I don't think we're at the stage of even thinking about wedding dresses,' she said, scowling at George. 'Never mind you making another one. I think you need a rest after all the time and effort that went into Bel's, as well as into knocking up a rather spectacular mother-of-the-bride dress for Pearl!'

Kate looked thoughtful as she hurried out the kitchen, with her cup and saucer in one hand and magazine in the other.

'George, that's all that girl's going to think about now! I can see it in her face!'

George took the glass stopper out of the bottle, which had a 24-carat-gold engraved plate around its neck, and poured out two glasses of cognac.

'It'll be good for her. Take her mind off everything else that's happening at the moment.'

Lily sighed. Six days ago, Rosie had arrived at the bordello in a panic with news that her blasted copper 'friend' had found out about the business and Rosie's part in it. There was a huge and very worrying question mark over whether or not he was going to grass them all up. From what George had found out about this DS Miller a while ago, the man was as clean as a whistle, so the chances were he was likely to be blowing the goddamned whistle on them all any time now.

As a result, Lily had immediately shut up shop. The girls had all been told to have a holiday for at least a week until they sorted out what was happening – some of them had been so worried they'd left town and gone to stay with friends and relatives living out in the sticks with the explanation that they were sick and tired of being bombed by Jerry.

Their clients had been informed there was a problem with the plumbing that was going to take a while to fix.

It had been suggested to Kate and Vivian, who lived at the bordello, that they make arrangements to move out for a while, but neither had wanted to.

Kate had been surprisingly unbothered by the threat of the boys in blue knocking on their door at any time, which Rosie had put down to the fact that in her previous life as a down-and-out she had become no stranger to the pull of her collar or a stay in the custody suite.

Vivian had put on a show of bravado and told them all in her Mae West drawl, 'Well, I for one am willing to take my chances!'

Lily wasn't sure if Vivian's devil-may-care attitude was for real or, rather, due to the fact she didn't really have anywhere else to go, having no desire to return to the Wirral, from where she hailed.

Their new girl, Maisie, who had been brought on-board to head up the new Gentlemen's Club they were starting up next door, had gone to London for a week's break. Maisie, who was of mixed heritage and had caused quite a stir, both with her stunning, exotic looks as well as her dreadful behaviour at Bel's wedding, claimed the trip was so that she and her mother, Pearl, with whom she had only just been reunited, could get to know each other better. Lily, however, was pretty convinced that Maisie had definitely felt the long arm of the law previously and, unlike Kate, had no desire to feel it again.

'So,' Lily said, taking her glass of very expensive brandy from George, 'did you really want to talk about the wedding? And why the Rémy? It really is far too special to drink, never mind be consumed around the kitchen table of all places.'

'Why not?' George said, leaning down to give Lily a kiss on the lips. 'Why the hell not, my darling?'

Lily looked up at the man she had only just recently agreed to marry, and kissed him back.

'You're worried, aren't you? About Rosie and me being carted off and banged up in some grotty police cell?'

George sat down and sighed heavily. His normally bright and cheerful demeanour seemed to have deserted him.

'I am, actually,' he said. 'It makes me feel ill thinking about you both in such abhorrent circumstances ...' He took a swig of his brandy. 'But I did want to talk to you about getting married. I think we should do it as soon as possible.' He scrutinised his lover's face for a reaction.

'Well,' Lily forced a laugh, 'if it wasn't for my age, I think we'd have people talking!'

George took hold of Lily's hand, the one proudly wearing the diamond ring he had presented her with at Bel's wedding reception.

'I just think it would be more advantageous ...' he paused, ' ... should the worst happen.'

Lily looked at George, and though she was loath to admit it, the chances were that as a married woman and one whose husband was also a highly decorated war veteran, as well as a man of high-standing in respectable society, she would, indeed, be treated with more care.

'Well, we were going to wait until the spring,' Lily pondered, 'you know how this awful northern weather plays havoc with my hair. You just need to step out the door and that's it – an hour's worth of curling, coiffuring and spraying, and in the time it takes you to walk down the front path, your barnet's left looking like you've been dragged through a hedge backwards.' Lily lapsed momentarily back into her east London twang. 'It's the one real downside of living up here.' Lily spoke her thoughts before taking another sip of her Rémy and savouring it for a moment.

'Well, I hope you don't mind, but I've organised an announcement to go in *The Times* next week,' George said. 'Make it official.'

Lily was just about to express her surprise when they both heard the front door open and Rosie's voice sounding out down the hallway.

'Helloooo! Anyone home?'

Lily turned to George. 'Someone sounds incredibly bright and breezy, all things considered.'

Raising her voice, Lily shouted out towards the kitchen door, which had been left slightly ajar. 'Rosie, *ma chère*, we're in here!'

A second later Rosie burst into the kitchen.

'Goodness,' she said, 'I don't think I'll ever get used to the house being so empty. It's awful!'

Lily and George watched captivated as Rosie, whom they loved as though she were their own flesh and blood, strode over to the sink and filled a glass with water from the tap.

She took a long drink before turning round, pulling a seat out and joining them at the large wooden kitchen table.

'Are you all right?' Lily asked, noticing that the make-up Rosie had put on for the christening earlier that day had come off, and that she had changed into her favourite cream-coloured slacks, which Kate had made for her a while ago. 'You look a little ... well, how would the French put it? *Un peu folle?*'

Rosie laughed out loud. 'A little mad? I don't know about that, Lily, but I do come bearing good news for a change.' She took another glug of her water. 'I came here as soon as I could to tell you – it's the least I could do after what I've put everyone through.'

Lily and George were still staring at a flushed-faced Rosie. They rarely saw her without a light layer of foundation, which they knew she wore to hide her scars rather than for reasons of vanity.

'*He's not going to report us!*' Rosie declared.

Both Lily and George gave a jolt of surprise. Neither needed to ask who 'he' was.

'Really?' George said, shocked. 'How can you be sure?'

Lily was looking at Rosie. Scrutinising her. She didn't have to ask. She already knew. She had seen that look on many a girl's face in the past.

'I'm guessing you've seen him – today?' she ventured. 'Sometime between you leaving the Elliots' and coming here?'

'Yes,' Rosie said, forcing herself to calm down. She had said her farewells to Peter and then rushed to get ready in order to come straight to the bordello and tell Lily the news. She had felt such dreadful guilt that she had put everyone's livelihoods in jeopardy.

After she'd given her savings to Gloria so that Charlotte's school fees could be paid, Rosie had been prepared for the possibility that she could well be sent to prison, but the guilt that she might cause the same to happen to Lily, and possibly the other girls too, was crushing.

Worse still, if Kate had also been arrested and implicated in any of the bordello's wrongdoings, Rosie would never have been able to forgive herself. Kate had done nothing to deserve any of the suffering she had been subjected to her entire life, and if Rosie had caused her any more, well, she wouldn't be able to live with herself.

'Yes, I did,' Rosie started to explain. 'He was waiting for me when I came back from the christening.' She paused, unsure what to say next.

George stepped in. 'I'm guessing you both sat down and talked things through?'

Lily's eyes never once left Rosie's face and she saw her relief at not having to go into too much detail about what had been said – or, more importantly, what had occurred.

'Yes, yes, we did, George,' Rosie said, still all of aflutter. 'We sat down and talked and he told me that he would not tell anyone about the bordello.'

Rosie looked at Lily and George and realised they were not totally convinced.

'He *promised*,' she stressed, looking at both their faces, still fixed on her.

Lily sat up straight. 'Was this before – or after ...?' She didn't say the words, but they all knew what Lily was implying.

Rosie opened her mouth but nothing came out. She knew she had to tell the truth, that Lily was owed the truth.

'After,' Rosie finally admitted.

There was an awkward pause.

'I thought you would be relieved – happy?' Rosie implored. 'I ran all the way here ... It means you don't have to worry any more. We can get the girls back. Tell the clients the plumbing's sorted ... Put Kate's mind at rest.'

Lily let out a burst of laughter. 'The only thing on Kate's mind at the moment is the latest design she's working on!'

George looked at Rosie's crestfallen face. He got up and gave her a hug.

'Well, I think it's marvellous news,' he said. 'Bloody marvellous! I, for one, am massively pleased. And I have to admit – exceedingly relieved.' He walked over to the cupboard and retrieved another crystal tumbler, sloshed a good measure of the expensive Rémy into the glass and handed it to Rosie.

'A toast!' he declared, a wide smile on his face as he looked at Rosie. He raised his glass, throwing a look of reprimand in Lily's direction.

'Here's to a brighter future!' he said. 'In all ways. This damnable war included!'

The three chinked glasses and drank in silence for a moment.

'This is great news, *ma chère*,' Lily said, trying to soften the hardness in her voice. 'It really is. And everyone is going to be over the moon and, like George says, "massively relieved". They really are. *I really am* ... But,' she hesitated, trying to choose her words carefully, 'I hope you haven't done anything you didn't want to do just to get us out of this scrape. Something you may not have done otherwise?'

'No!' Rosie was shocked, which she knew was absurd. After all, she had been a working girl herself until relatively recently. But that had always been an open transaction. Money in exchange for a service. There had never been deceit involved.

'I didn't think so,' Lily admitted. 'I just needed to check.'

'So, I'm taking it that you and your detective will be continuing to see each other?' George asked tentatively.

'Yes,' Rosie said. Her heart, which had been so full of love and joy, felt as if it had been punctured by Lily's insinuation. 'I'm seeing him tomorrow after he's finished work.'

'Well, that all sounds jolly good,' George said, looking at Lily. 'Doesn't it?'

'Mm.' Lily didn't sound convinced. 'Just be careful, Rosie. Watch your back. Make sure you can trust this Peter one hundred per cent.'

Just then the front door went again. They could hear the stomp of heels across the parquet flooring before the kitchen door swung open.

'Oh, thank the Lord for that!'

It was Vivian. She was still wearing her long, beige-coloured woollen coat, but on seeing everyone sat around the kitchen table, she immediately undid the belt and shrugged it off, revealing a rather stunning knee-length burgundy dress with a plunging neckline.

'I thought I might be coming home to a house full of boys in blue!'

'Is that why you're wearing your best dress?' Lily asked, looking at her head girl, who, it had been said more than once, looked more like Mae West than Mae West herself.

'What? This little thing?' She pouted and put her hands on her hips to show off her voluptuous figure before letting out a hoot of laughter and noisily pulling up a chair and sitting down to join the impromptu get-together. She caught sight of the bottle of Rémy and let out an audible gasp of surprise.

'*My!*' she said, at the same time pulling out a box of Sobranie Russian cigarettes she had acquired that afternoon on the black market. 'What's the occasion?'

George got up and went over to the cupboard for another crystal tumbler. He knew he didn't need to ask Vivian if she wanted to partake of a drink.

'Oh, George, thank you. I wasn't expecting this when I got back. Quite the contrary.' She lit her long black cigarette and blew a stream of smoke up towards the ceiling.

'There's good news,' Lily said, shaking her head at Vivian's offer of one of her cocktail cigarettes.

'Please let it be what I think it might be!' Vivian said, her Scouse accent suddenly strong.

'It is,' Lily said. 'We're off the hook! Normal services will be resumed on Monday!'

'Ah, that's bloody brilliant news!' The sheer relief in Vivian's voice was there for all to hear. She had done a good job, as they all had, of masking her worry. It had been a tough week and she had barely slept a wink.

Vivian looked over at Rosie, thinking she appeared a little peaky before realising that it was just because she didn't have any make-up on and her mascara was smudged, making it look as though she had been crying – not that Rosie seemed at all sad.

'You spoke to him then?' she asked Rosie, who nodded in return.

'Yes, he's not going to say a word, so we can all breathe a sigh of relief. And,' Rosie said, taking another sip of her drink, 'I just wanted to say how truly sorry I am for putting everyone through all of this. I really am.'

Vivian downed the rest of her drink in one and took another long draw on her cigarette.

'No worries, doll,' she said in her best Brooklyn accent. 'It's a risk we take in our line of work.'

'I'll tell the rest of the girls tomorrow,' Lily said.

'Oh,' Vivian said excitedly, 'and I'll send Maisie a telegram to tell her the coast's all clear for her to come back.'

'I thought she was having some kind of "bonding" trip with her mother?' George asked.

Vivian looked across at George and then to Rosie and Lily. 'Well, I think it was a bit of both, you know? Get away from here for a while *and* spend some time with Pearl.'

'Vivian, *ma chère*,' Lily asked, 'can you be a sweetheart and go and get Kate, please. Drag her away from that bloomin' sewing machine so we can tell her the good news.'

George picked up the bottle of Rémy and poured everyone another drink.

This had turned out to be a good day.

A very good day.

Chapter Eight

Tatham Street, Hendon, Sunderland

Sunday 23 November 1941

Bel was sat at the kitchen table, her cup of tea in one hand and her daughter Lucille sitting on her lap, gazing up at her mammy as she regaled Agnes, Arthur and Polly with a vivid description of the splendour of the town's most exclusive hotel.

'... the food, the room, the amazing decor.' Bel sighed dramatically. 'It was incredible! It was like staying the night at Buckingham Palace – not that I know what Buckingham Palace is like inside.'

'Well,' Agnes said, stirring a large pot of vegetables, potatoes and bacon bits gently simmering on the range, 'they say they don't call it "the Grand" for nothing.'

'Grand by name, grand by nature, that's for sure,' Joe agreed as he added some coal he had just brought in from the backyard to the fire.

'Well, as long as you don't start getting used to this kind of highfalutin living.' Agnes looked over her shoulder at her daughter-in-law.

Her son Joe and Bel had just got back from what they were calling their 'second honeymoon' at the Grand Hotel. Standing opposite St Mary's Church on Bridge Street, the hotel was a well-known landmark. Not many had been inside, but everyone had seen its formidable five-storey

Queen Anne-style frontage. Nothing, it was said, could touch it for its elegance and class.

Normally, it was the domain of the rich and famous, but last night Joe and Bel had been treated to a night's stay in one of its fifty ornately decorated rooms. It had been a wedding gift from Maisie, the sister Bel had only just got to know. It had been a rather extravagant treat, a way of apologising to Bel for ruining her special day, for Maisie had tried to shame Pearl for giving her up for adoption as a baby by 'introducing' herself at Bel and Joe's wedding reception.

Maisie's retribution had not had the anticipated effect, however, for Pearl had gone on a massive bender and would have bedded down in a watery grave had Maisie and Bel not found her and stopped her wading out into the bitterly cold North Sea.

Afterwards, Maisie had learnt that the idealised image she'd had of her mother and Bel could not have been further from the truth. It became clear that Bel had been practically dragged up by Pearl and, had it not been for Agnes, would have more than likely ended up in the workhouse.

Yesterday morning, Bel, Joe and Lucille had gone to wave Maisie and Pearl off at the train station. The pair had gone to London to revisit the place where Maisie was born – at least that was the reason Maisie had given everyone.

'I wonder how Maisie and Ma are getting on?' Bel said to no one in particular.

'God only knows!' Polly laughed.

'I dread to think,' Joe chipped in.

Maisie's appearance had made a massive impact on Bel, not just because she suddenly had a sister, but after hearing snippets of information about Maisie's dad, it had brought thoughts of the father she had never known to the forefront of her mind – a father Pearl had always claimed was dead. Bel hadn't believed her mother as a small child and was no more convinced now that she was an adult.

'Right,' Agnes said, bending over her pan and taking a sip of broth from the wooden spoon she had been using to stir their supper, 'this is as good as it's going to get. Let's get the table set.'

'So ...' Bel put Lucille down and she and Polly headed into the scullery to fetch the crockery and cutlery, ' ... how did it all go with Gloria and Jack yesterday?'

'Oh, God,' Polly said, 'what a day!' She looked back into the kitchen as Joe was putting Lucille onto her special chair stacked with cushions so that she could reach the table. 'I'll tell you when little flapper lugs has been put to bed.'

'So, come on then, tell me what happened after we left?' Bel asked, savouring another slurp of her tea and adding, 'That's one thing the Grand can't compete with – there's nothing like a cup of your own freshly brewed tea.'

Lucille had been put to bed clutching her raggedy toy rabbit and sucking her thumb, and Joe had read her half of her favourite story, *The Lambton Worm*, before she had fallen sound asleep. He'd then left to do his Home Guard duties, while Agnes and then Arthur had taken themselves off to their beds, leaving Polly and Bel on their own to have a good catch-up.

Polly took a drink of her tea and chuckled. 'But I'll bet you the teacup you were drinking out of was bone china and didn't have chips in it!'

Polly was so glad Bel and Joe had come back happy and had clearly had a wonderful 'second honeymoon'. She had been mad at Maisie – not just for spoiling Joe and Bel's nuptials, but also because her shenanigans that day had thrown a great big vat of cold water on their first night together as man and wife. Finding out you had a sister you never knew about, and then seeing your mother leave your reception in a state and not come back, was enough to spoil anyone's wedding night.

On top of everything, their first overnight stay at the Grand had cost Polly an arm and a leg. But when she heard Maisie had paid for another stay at the Grand, as well as an evening meal to show how sorry she was about causing so much trouble and upset, Polly's resentment towards Bel's new-found sister had been somewhat quelled.

'So then, after the christening? After we left? What happened? How was Gloria?' Bel asked.

'Well,' began Polly, 'everyone had their tea and cake and left pretty sharpish. I think it was obvious Jack and Gloria needed time on their own.'

She took another drink of tea.

'Oh, and George's red MG caused a right commotion. I think every child within a quarter-mile radius was stood gawping at it by the time George, Lily and Kate left the party. George was a real sweetie and gave every single one of them a go sitting behind the wheel.'

Bel smiled. She thought George was a real gem and she liked Lily, even though she was well aware of how Lily made a living. She and Polly agreed that Lily was the most eccentric person they had ever met.

'And Kate?' Bel asked. 'Was she all right?' Bel had become close to Kate, which was inevitable after the number of hours she had spent in the Maison Nouvelle, having dress fittings and alterations and chatting about the design of her wedding dress over numerous cups of tea.

'Yes,' Polly said. 'As usual she was as quiet as a mouse, but she seemed happy. And she's so good with Hope. She managed to keep her entertained after you two left. No one stuck around for long, though, which was just as well. Jack looked in a total daze and Gloria didn't look much better.

I think they were both in shock.' Polly paused. 'No, Jack looked more confused and Gloria looked like you could have knocked her over with a feather, but she was happy. Really happy.'

'I can't even start to imagine what she must be feeling,' Bel mused. 'That poor woman has been through so much, I'm surprised she's still sane.'

'I know,' Polly agreed. 'She's got Hope, though, hasn't she? So I guess she has to keep it together.'

'Mm,' Bel agreed, 'especially with a nutter like Vinnie always marauding around in the background ... So, go on then, what happened after everyone left?'

'Oh my God! How could I forget?' Polly's eyes widened. She had been so excited hearing about the Grand that she had temporarily forgotten about bumping into Helen.

'What!' Bel demanded, intrigued.

'Well, when everyone was gone, I went to Crown's to tell them that something had come up and Jack couldn't make it back to work – and guess who I bumped into when I got there?'

'No? You didn't! Did you?' Bel knew there was only one person who provoked this kind of reaction in her sister-in-law.

Polly nodded her head solemnly.

'Oh, yes! I did!'

'But I thought you said she wasn't due back at work until Monday? Wasn't she supposed to be in Scotland?'

'Yes and yes!' Polly said. 'She was!'

'And what was she doing in Crown's? I thought Thompson's was her domain?' Bel asked, intrigued.

'Well, that was just my luck,' Polly said. 'I was saun- tering across the yard, thinking about the christening and about how Jack had told me to just keep it simple and tell them that "something had come up", when all

of a sudden I saw Helen coming out of the main office!'
Polly's voice rose.

Bel took a dramatic intake of breath.

'So you can imagine my complete and utter horror!'

Bel nodded. Her sister-in-law and Helen had never made any bones about how they felt about each other, even before Helen had connived and lied to try and break up Polly and Tommy.

'So what did you do? What did you say?' Bel asked, knowing full well that Polly was the worst liar ever. When the two had been growing up together Bel had often been exasperated by Polly's total inability to tell even a convincing white lie.

'Well,' Polly said, 'obviously I panicked. And obviously I must have had guilt scrawled across my face.' She paused, before adding, 'I'm loathe to say this, but I actually felt bad. I may hate Helen and all that, but I felt awful knowing that her dad is going to leave her mam and that she's got a baby sister.'

Bel nodded sagely. This was Polly to a T. Agnes had always taught them to put themselves into other people's shoes, but Polly had always gone one further and not only put on the shoes but walked in them for miles.

'Mm,' Bel agreed, 'and let's face it, she's going to find out at some stage. It's inevitable. So anyway, when you came face to face, what did you do?'

'Well, to be honest,' Polly admitted, 'I nearly turned and ran!'

Bel spluttered on a mouthful of tea. 'Honestly, Pol, you do make me laugh!'

'Thankfully, I didn't. I stayed put. Rooted to the spot, more like. Then I just asked her what she was doing at Crown's. She said she was looking for her father and *what was I doing at Crown's*? That's when I just came out with what I had originally been going to say, which was "something had come up" and Jack wouldn't be back.'

'And what did Helen say?' Bel asked, intrigued to know how the scene had played out.

'Well, she didn't get a chance. I just turned on my heels and left her standing there ... The thing is, I started to panic then ... knew I had to get back and tell Jack. Give him some warning, you know?'

Bel nodded.

'But when I got back,' Polly said, 'he'd gone – as had Gloria and Hope. Arthur was the only one left in the house and he said I'd just missed them by minutes. God, I could have screamed in frustration. And I had on those stupid shoes I hate. It was hard to run in them and now I've got two great big blisters on my heels.'

Bel chuckled, knowing which ones Polly was referring to. She knew they were as uncomfortable as they were awful-looking.

'Oh dear, Pol, what a state! Let's just hope Jack was able to cover his tracks when he got home ... So,' she asked, 'I'm guessing Jack and Gloria are going to keep quiet about things?'

Polly nodded. 'For a while at least. Arthur says Jack just wanted to get it all out in the open, but Gloria's managed to convince him to keep everything under wraps for the moment – until they work out what to do.'

Polly had become close to Arthur since she'd got engaged to his grandson, and even more so after the old man had moved in with them. Last night the pair had sat and chatted as Polly had bathed her sore feet in front of the stove.

'Well, I would say they haven't got much choice,' Bel agreed.

Polly nodded. 'God knows how Vinnie's going to react when he finds out that Hope's not his. Never mind what

Miriam'll do. I think she'd have him hanged, drawn and quartered if it was allowed.'

'Goodness,' Bel said in all seriousness, 'they're what you might call well and truly caught between a rock and a hard place.'

They were both silent for a moment, before Polly perked up.

'Anyway, enough morbid talk,' she said, 'I've got something I've been dying to show you.'

Bel looked curious.

'Follow me!' Polly commanded.

Bel did as Polly requested and followed her out of the kitchen and to the bottom of the stairs. Polly turned around and put a finger to her lips, before quietly walking up the stairs.

Bel tiptoed behind her. When they reached the first floor, where Agnes, Arthur and Pearl had their bedrooms, much to Bel's surprise Polly continued up the narrower, steeper staircase that led to the attic room that had been empty for as long as she could recall. In fact, she couldn't remember anyone ever living up there, and Bel had been a part of the Elliot family since she was five years old.

'What you doing?' Bel whispered up at Polly, who had now reached the top of the staircase and had momentarily disappeared from view. She could hear Arthur snoring and didn't want to wake either the old man or Agnes, who she was pretty sure would also be fast asleep.

When Bel reached the little landing at the top of the house, she saw Polly standing with one hand on the doorknob of the attic room.

'Ta-da!' Polly exclaimed in a loud whisper, opening the door and then flicking on the light switch.

When Bel walked into the room she gasped in awe. The room where they had often snuck up to as children to play in had always been filled with a mixture of broken tables and chairs, as well as old wooden boxes, and had been covered with a heavy layer of dust and enough spider webs to carpet the entire ground floor of the house.

But as she stared at the room now, it was unrecognisable. All the junk had gone and the bare boards had been scrubbed clean, as had the walls and ceiling. A pair of old but pretty green floral curtains had been put up, as well as the regulation blackout blinds. In the middle of the room was a small wooden table with a few wild flowers in a white ceramic milk jug.

'Is this what I think it is?' Bel could barely contain her excitement.

Polly's smile was wide as she nodded her head.

'Not quite comparable to the Grand,' she said, 'but at least you'll be together.'

Bel and Joe had been married for more than two weeks, but so far they had been sleeping in separate rooms downstairs.

'Oh, Pol! You are the best sister-in-law – the best friend anyone could ever wish for.' She flung her arms around Polly and gave her a bear hug.

'Well, it wasn't just me,' Polly said, 'it was a team effort. Even Beryl and the girls came round to help. Now we just need to get a bed up here and you're sorted. And,' she added, 'we thought, as Arthur's struggling with the stairs more nowadays, that he could move into Joe's room and we could move Lucille's cot into Ma's room, so that she's not quite so far away from you and Joe. Plus she'll have Pearl right next door too.'

Bel looked round at the room that held so many happy memories of when she was a child. Of when she had been taken in by Agnes after Polly had found her crying on her own doorstep after her mother had gone off with some spiv and hadn't come back. This house had more or less become her home and the attic had been her and Polly's playroom when the weather was bad.

Now it was to be the room where she would properly start her married life with Joe. Her second chance at love.

Bel rarely allowed herself tears, but these were happy ones so she permitted them to flow.

'Oh, Pol, thank you! Thank you so much!'

Chapter Nine

Grindon Village, Sunderland

'Where the hell have you been?'

Sarah jumped up off the sofa and stubbed out her cigarette as Vinnie let himself into the flat. *Her* flat. Recently
she'd started to regret letting him move in. Not that she'd
had a lot of choice, mind you. Vinnie had just tipped up
one night with his bag, declaring that he had left Gloria
and that it was Sarah he wanted to spend the rest of his
life with.

Of course, she wasn't stupid, and she wasn't surprised
when she'd heard the next day that it was Gloria that had
sent *him* packing, but she hadn't minded. She'd wanted
him back then. Now, though, she wasn't quite so sure.
Vinnie always seemed to be kicking off about something
or other, and it was starting to get wearing.

Last night he hadn't come home, and she'd been worried sick, imagining all sorts. She'd had images of him
lying half dead in some gutter, or a hospital bed, or worse
still, lifeless on some cold mortuary slab.

'Are ya all right, Vin?' Sarah put her hands up to her
lover's face to check for any evidence that he had been in a
fight. 'Where've yer been?' She wasn't quite sure whether
she was angry at him or just relieved he was back home
alive and well.

'Where've I been?!' Vinnie grabbed hold of both of
Sarah's hands, now lightly cupped around his face. He

squashed them in his own, before flinging them aside as though they were pieces of screwed-up paper. *'Where've I been?!'*

Sarah rubbed her hands. He had squeezed so hard it hurt. Vinnie had never been violent towards her, but lately she had felt that a part of him sometimes wanted to be. Sarah knew Vinnie hadn't been averse to giving Gloria a few slaps, but he had always made out that she had been the one to start it and she'd given back as good as she got.

'I've been banged up in town. Stuck in a soddin' police cell all day yesterday and all last night! That's where I've soddin' well been!'

Sarah was taken aback.

'You? Banged up?' she asked, her face contorting with disbelief. Vinnie, generally, kept his snout clean. Especially when it came to the plod. 'What the hell for?' Her voice rose, but just as she was asking the question, she guessed what the answer was.

'Please don't tell me it's anything to do with yer ex-missus, or that bab you keep going on and on about?'

'Bloody hell, Sarah, I've got a good right to rabbit on about the bairn! Especially with you putting it into my head that the bab mightn't even be mine! It's *your* fault I ended up stuck in a stinking cell all night! *You* wound me up a treat with yer "Have you thought it might not be yours?"' Vinnie put on a whiny voice, mimicking Sarah's. 'Bloody hell, I couldn't sleep that night for thinking about it, that's why I decided to go to the christening. See for myself.'

'Oh!' Sarah's hands went up into the air. 'I might have guessed *I'd* be to blame for this!' She walked over to the coffee table and snatched her box of fags. As she did so, she knocked the overflowing ashtray and cigarette butts spilled onto the table.

'So, come on,' she snapped. 'Tell me all the gory details. I might as well hear it from the horse's mouth rather than from chatty Cathy down the road.'

Vinnie huffed.

'Like I said,' he started to explain, 'I was going to the church. To see the bab. To see *my* daughter being christened. The christening I hadn't even been told about – never mind invited to! *My own soddin' bairn's christening!*'

'Well, why didn't yer tell me yer were going?' As Sarah spoke, a stream of smoke trailed out of her mouth.

Vinnie dismissed her question with an irritated shake of the head.

Sarah was riled now. 'So, go on, what happened? Did yer see the bab?'

'Did I hell!' Vinnie snatched the packet out of Sarah's hands, rammed a cigarette into his mouth and looked around for a box of matches.

'Here.' Sarah struck a match as Vinnie bent down to take a light off her. 'Go on.' She sat on the little two-seater settee and tried to calm herself down.

'Well, I was walking to the church – that one down Hendon, the big one on Suffolk Street?' Sarah nodded, she knew which one he was talking about. 'When all of a sudden, I felt a hand on the back of my shoulder and it was some copper asking me where I was going and – what were his words? – what my "*intentions*" were!'

'Then what?' Sarah asked.

'I told him in no uncertain terms that it wasn't any of his business and to sod off! Then I guess there was what yer might call an "altercation". The next thing I knew I was being hauled off to the cop shop,' Vinnie told Sarah, as if he were the epitome of innocence, never having done anything even remotely wrong in his entire life.

'So, how come they kept you in? What did they charge you with?'

'They said they were going to slap some trumped-up charge of "intent to commit serious bodily harm" on me. Complete bloody joke! There's a soddin' war on and they're wasting their time on people like me who only wanted to go to a bleedin' christening!'

'For God's sake, I've never heard the like!' Sarah said, although she wasn't stupid and was sure there was more to it and she'd hear it when they were down the pub, which was where they would inevitably end up this evening.

There had been a time when she would have hung on Vinnie's every word, believed everything that came out of his mouth, but since they had been living together she had seen a different side to him. His interpretation of events was often very different from reality, not that he could or would see that for one second. In Vinnie's eyes, he was always right. He would never back down. And he would certainly never apologise, because nothing was ever his fault.

'Obviously, I haven't cooked,' Sarah said, stubbing out her cigarette and looking at her packet to see how many she had left. 'I've been that worried about yer, I haven't been able to do anything.'

Vinnie let out a burst of genuine laughter. 'Pull the other one, Sar, it's got bells on.' He blew out smoke. His tone of voice was evidence that his mood was improving.

'Let's face it,' he added, walking over to the sofa and sitting down next to her, 'I didn't fall for yer cooking skills, or yer housekeeping.' As he spoke they both looked around at the flat, which was in need of a good clean and a tidy-up.

Vinnie put his arm around the woman who had been his mistress well before Gloria had chucked him out and whom he still fancied like mad, even if she drove him round the bend half the time.

'Come here, give us a kiss 'n a cuddle,' he said, pulling her close to him. 'I missed ya last night, lying there on my lonesome on a slab of cold concrete.' Vinnie's voice had softened, and Sarah knew what was coming next. Part of her couldn't be bothered but the other part of her relaxed, knowing that Vinnie's temper was being replaced with a need for intimacy.

'Let me make a sandwich, then we can go down the pub – and when we come back we can kiss and cuddle all night long,' Sarah said with a suggestive smile on her face. This was a part of Vinnie she had control over and always had. When it came to the bed department she could wind him round her little finger.

As Vinnie watched Sarah get up from the sofa and walk into the kitchen to make the sandwiches, his eyes were drawn to her pert, rounded bottom, which he knew she was proud of, considering her age, and was the reason she always wore skirts that looked just a little too small for her.

As he lit another cigarette, he knew that he had a good life here with Sarah, and that he had to be careful not to ruin it. Besides, if she chucked him out, he'd be stuffed. He didn't have a pot to piss in, never mind the money to pay any kind of rent for a roof over his head.

He had to play this one carefully, but by God he was going to see that baby if it was the last thing he did. Gloria was not going to get one over on him, and he needed to make absolutely sure that the bairn *was* his. He'd had the slightest of doubts when he'd first found out Gloria was in the family way – but only because they very rarely slept together and whenever they did, he was always careful.

Well, he'd know for sure when he actually got to see the bab. His two boys had looked the spit of him when they were born. Same deep brown eyes. Both chunky – like little barrels, they were. He just needed to find a way to do it. The custody sergeant had warned him to stay well away from Gloria, telling him in no uncertain terms that if he didn't, he'd find himself right back in police cells – and this time they'd charge him.

As he listened to Sarah clatter around the small kitchen, his mind drifted back to the copper who had arrested him. What was his name? That was it – Detective Sergeant Miller. He thought he recognised his voice. He'd sounded very like the balaclava man who'd given him a thrashing a while ago and told him he'd be drinking beer out of a straw if he ever hurt Gloria again. Could they be one and the same? And if it was the same bloke, did this mean that Gloria had him in her pocket?

'Here you go.' Sarah placed a plate of spam sandwiches in front of Vinnie. 'I've put a good lashing of mustard on there. Just how you like it,' she said.

'Ta,' Vinnie said, but his mind was still on the detective. No, he argued with himself, Gloria wouldn't even know any plod, never mind a detective, and a detective sergeant at that, would she?

But then how had this DS Miller known he was on his way to the christening? He'd thought it was just a coincidence, but last night when he'd been stewing over it all in that bloody awful cell, he'd started to have his doubts.

'Get us another beer, Sar,' Vinnie asked through a mouthful of bread and spam.

He heard Sarah walk back to the kitchen, open the cupboard door and pop the top off another bottle of Double Maxim. He watched her pouring it carefully into a pint glass.

Well, it didn't make any difference either way if the copper knew him or not, or if Gloria had friends in the force – he couldn't give a fig. He had a bloody right to see his own bairn.

And by God, he was going to, come hell or high water.

Chapter Ten

J.L. Thompson & Sons Shipyard, North Sands, Sunderland

Monday 24 November 1941

Helen stood looking out of the main office window of Thompson's on the first floor of the administration building. It was a typical, overcast November morning. The wooden venetian blinds had been pulled right up so that she could see what was happening in the yard below, as well as on the river, which, as always, was filled with an array of half-built ships, cargo vessels, trawlers and punts, all overshadowed by a northern sky that since the declaration of war had been punctuated with huge torpedo-shaped barrage balloons.

Helen never got tired of looking at this view. She had been on day trips and holidays, both further down south and in Scotland, and she had admired the stunning beauty of the lush green countryside and picture-perfect villages that seemed untainted by time or technology – but those views had never kept her attention like the one she was looking at now.

This urban landscape could not have been more different and Helen loved it with a passion. She loved the expanse of metal and concrete, and she loved the noise, the sounds of men and machinery working – *creating* – together.

Perhaps, she wondered, as her eyes sought out the women welders who today were working in the dry basin, what she loved most about this view, or indeed any view of the River Wear, was the fact that it was never the same from one day to the next. And that out of the constant chaos that seemed to fill the winding banks of the river rose the most magnificent beasts of steel. Metal monsters that rode the waves across hundreds of thousands of miles of oceans and seas. Warriors against the elements of God and Nature. And now warriors against Hitler and his army.

As a child, Helen had listened to her father talk about how Sunderland had become 'The Biggest Shipbuilding Town in the World', and how ships used to be made from wood and sail, carrying huge quantities of coal, glass and pottery around the world. She was always begging her father to take her to the yard – it had been something her mother had fought vehemently against, but it had been one of the few battles she had lost as Jack had taken his daughter to Thompson's as often as he could.

'Miss Crawford?' Helen heard a polite voice call out and she turned to see one of the secretaries standing a few yards away from her, clutching what looked like an order form.

'Can you check and sign this off, Miss Crawford, please?' The young girl was clearly nervous about approaching her boss.

Without speaking, Helen took the piece of thick white paper that was embossed with big bold black lettering: *J.L. Thompson & Sons – Shipbuilders – Ship Repairer, North Sands Yard, Sunderland*. She took a few minutes to scrutinise the order, checking quantities and pricing, before taking the pen and signing her name at the bottom. She returned the form and pen to the secretary without saying a word, then turned back to the view of the yard.

Her eyes picked out Rosie and her squad, all working on a large patch of the ship's decking, and she felt a familiar twinge of envy. Was it because they were a part of this massive army of workers building ships with their bare hands? Or because the squad of women welders were such good friends, who always had each other's backs?

It had made her mad earlier on in the year when she had tried – unsuccessfully – to divide them. She had been so furious with Polly for stealing Tommy from right under her nose, and then she'd found out that it had been the young, dippy one called Dorothy who had told Ned the plater's wife that Helen had been spreading false rumours about Polly seeing her husband. God, she'd never forget how the wife came waddling into the yard, showing off her huge bump, before publicly humiliating her in front of the whole workforce.

At the time she had felt as though that was the worst thing that had ever happened to her. But so much had changed in such a short period. After what her father had been through, her own humiliation seemed almost pitiful. When her father's ship went down, her whole outlook on life had changed. Those few days thinking that he was dead had been the worst ever, followed by the painstaking wait to see if he would come out of his coma – and praying that if he did, he would be the father she had always loved and adored and not some shell of a man, unable even to feed himself.

Helen looked at her watch just as the klaxon sounded out the break for lunch. Behind her she heard chairs scrape back as the two dozen secretaries, clerical staff and comptometer operators made good their escape from their monotonous labour. Not that they themselves particularly saw it as boring work, but Helen had done the kind of typing, filing and note-taking required of the basic office worker when she'd first started at the yard and the tedium of it had driven her to distraction.

Helen remained standing by the window as everyone hurried out of the large, open-plan office. As usual, her personal secretary, Marie-Anne, a ginger-haired girl with a wealth of freckles covering her pale face, asked Helen if she wanted anything for her lunch; as usual, Helen simply shook her head, not even deigning to look at the girl, whom she had employed not just because of her efficiency and incredibly speedy shorthand, but also for her plain Jane appearance.

Helen had been intending to go and spend her lunch break with her father over at Crown's, but he had told her that he was meeting up with Arthur again.

The rain was starting to come down more heavily now and Helen could see the mass of flat caps hurrying to the canteen. The headwear of the mainly male workforce made it easier for Helen to pick out the women welders, for in place of tweed caps, they were wearing headscarves. Everyone, that was, apart from Big Martha, who didn't need one as her trim bowl haircut was short enough not to get in the way or to risk being singed by the heat of a weld.

Helen felt her stomach rumble and she regretted telling Mrs Westley that she didn't want a packed lunch today. She had decided her mother was right and that she had put on weight. Her aunty did make the best potato pancakes – even better than Mrs Westley's, which was some feat – and Helen knew she'd been a bit of a pig when she was there.

Putting her hand on her stomach, Helen kept her eyes on the women as they all switched off their machines and started hurrying across the yard to the canteen.

Bet you they're going to have a nice hot mince and onion pie and gravy, Helen thought with a mixture of irritation and envy. Martha would probably be having double helpings. The woman must eat her parents out of house and home. And then there was Gloria, who still looked like she was eating for two.

Just then Helen's attention was diverted by what looked like a child dodging the rivet catchers and sidestepping heaps of chains and the five-barrel fires that were now burning more or less constantly to provide some respite from the bitter cold.

Of course, Helen thought, *who else could it be but Hannah?* Her short black bob made her appear much younger than her age. Now that was someone who really did look like she needed a good feed. The girl was all skin and bone.

'Ooh,' Helen exclaimed to the empty office as she saw Hannah trip over and fall flat on her face. If there was one person who was really not suited to working in a shipyard, it was Hannah.

Helen leant down to pick up her prized Schiaparelli handbag, from which she retrieved a packet of recently acquired Pall Mall cigarettes and a chrome Ronson lighter. If she was going to start smoking, she had decided she would do it with style. She'd read that a lot of the stunning and very slim French actresses lived off coffee and Gauloises, so that was exactly what *she* was going to do.

She lit her cigarette and suppressed a cough as she inhaled, then with her free hand picked up the gold-framed photo of her parents from the top of the desk.

Helen looked for a long time at the photograph of the two people who appeared so handsome and so happy, but although it was an image of a true moment in time, it was by no means a reflection of the truth. The photograph, like most of the others her mother had dotted around the house, was a lie – a mask hiding the fact that her mother and father, as far as she could remember, had never been happy, or in love.

Helen knew her mother had worked hard to snag her father when they were younger, but her carefully laid plans had come to nothing, for he hadn't turned into the husband she'd wanted.

Now, however, Miriam had been given an extra chance. Another throw of the dice. And it looked as though she had just rolled a double six, because her father had no memory of his past life and her mother could paint whatever picture she chose onto the blank canvas she had been handed. She could finally have the husband she had always wanted.

As Helen carefully tapped the end of her cigarette on the side of the metal ashtray, she thought about her father's luncheon date with Arthur Watts. If her mother found out, she wouldn't be happy.

Not one little bit.

'All right, you lot! I'm off now!' Gloria shouted through the rain that had gone from a light shower to looking as though it was going to turn into a full-on downpour. 'I'll see you in an hour!'

Rosie, Polly, Dorothy, Angie and Martha squinted through the dense drizzle and gave Gloria a wave.

'Hope it goes well,' Rosie shouted out. They all stood for a moment as they watched their workmate hurry across the yard, battling her way against the tide of workers who were heading for the warmth of the canteen.

'Come on, then! Let's gerrout of this blasted rain!' Angie said, looking at everyone's doleful faces as they watched Gloria disappear from view. None of the women had to say anything as they hurried across to the cafeteria, but they all felt for Gloria. Not one of them would have liked to swap places with her. She had told them earlier on during their short tea break that after the christening on Saturday, she and Jack had talked and she had persuaded him to go back to Miriam and carry on as normal – or as normal as could be – just until they'd worked out what to do for the best.

'Hey!'

The women all turned as they heard Hannah's distinctive chirping voice. She had broken into a jog to catch them up, having just come out of the drawing office.

As the women waited, Hannah tripped on the edge of a large metal plate that was jutting out from a huge stack piled up by one of the cranes. She immediately went sprawling.

'You all right?' Martha said, stomping across to see to her friend.

Hannah had managed to get back on her feet by the time Martha arrived.

'Any damage?' Martha asked earnestly, putting her two big hands on both of Hannah's skinny shoulders and looking her up and down.

Hannah wiped dirt off her skirt.

'No damage, Martha,' she said, letting out an embarrassed laugh. 'Just me being, how do you say? A clumsy clot?'

Five minutes later the women had settled down at their table in the canteen, which was now full of smoke and the smell of sweat, and were chattering away between mouthfuls of meat and potato pie.

'Did Bel and Joe enjoy the Grand?' Angie asked Polly, adding, 'Or is that a stupid question?' She chuckled and Dorothy nudged her. Sometimes Angie didn't realise when she was overstepping the mark. The two women got on well with Polly, but compared to them their workmate was very straight-laced.

'Yes,' Polly said, ignoring Angie's innuendos, 'they both came back happy as Larry, though Joe had to go straight back out to meet with Major Black to organise some kind of all-night exercise for their squad.' Joe had been discharged from the army on medical grounds due to what he referred to as his 'gammy' leg, but it hadn't stopped him joining the Home Guard.

'Bet you the food there was amazing,' Martha said, scraping her plate and looking behind her at the counter as if deliberating whether to get second helpings.

Polly laughed. 'Yes, Joe said he almost forgot there was rationing, it was so nice. He had all our mouths watering describing just about every morsel he ate!'

Martha pushed back her chair and headed over to see the dinner ladies.

'So, Pol, you heard owt from lover boy?' Angie's question precipitated another nudge from Dorothy. Angie turned to look at her friend. 'You not got enough room there, Dor?'

Dorothy glared at her. Tommy's well-being was a sensitive subject at the moment, particularly after the sinking of the *Ark Royal* and with Gibraltar being a thorn in Hitler's backside due to the fact that the British were able to control virtually all naval traffic into and out of the Mediterranean.

Polly, however, wasn't put out by Angie's insensitivity. She knew the most recent recruit to their squad meant well and that she was always full of it and in good spirits after she'd been staying over at Dorothy's.

'Just a postcard telling me he was all right and not to worry,' Polly said, subconsciously touching the left-hand pocket of her overalls, where she kept her engagement ring. By keeping it close to her heart, she felt that at least a part of Tommy was always with her.

'He said he'd write a longer letter as soon as he could,' Polly added, thinking of the postcard now propped up on her bedside cabinet. Every night before she switched her light off she reread her fiancé's words and smiled at the secret code he always used to tell her that he loved her. 'ILYFE' – Tommy's way of telling her 'I Love You For Ever' – was printed in bold capitals alongside his name and a kiss.

'Talking about "lover boys",' Dorothy said, focusing her gaze on Hannah, who was, as usual, spending more time pushing her food around her plate than actually eating it, 'how's young Olly?'

'I don't know why you keep calling him "young",' Hannah said. 'He's the same age as me. Actually, a bit older. He's going to be twenty soon.' There was a pause as she shuffled over to make room for Martha, who was carrying a bowlful of rhubarb crumble and custard. 'But as you are asking,' she continued, 'he is fine, thank you.'

'He's doing voluntary ARP duty now,' Martha added, causing Rosie, Polly, Dorothy and Angie to look at her in surprise.

'Yes,' Hannah said, 'Olly and Martha often end up working together.'

Everyone knew that Martha spent most of her evenings out with the town's civil defence unit. Her pure physical strength had proved invaluable to the town's rescue services, who were involved in getting the dead and injured out of bombed premises. It was an area women weren't normally allowed to work in, but an exception had been made when Martha volunteered.

'Eee, well that's a turn-up for the books, isn't it!' Angie said what everyone was thinking. Not so long ago Martha and Olly had barely been on speaking terms. It had been clear Martha had felt left out by Hannah after she'd been moved to the drawing office, even more so after Hannah became chummy with her new 'friend boy', which was how Hannah liked to describe him. Rosie had had a subtle word with Hannah and afterwards the group's little bird had made sure Martha felt involved and not cast aside in favour of Olly.

'Anyway, what about you two?' Rosie asked. 'What have you been up to this weekend?' She paused. 'Or do we really want to know!'

Everyone started laughing as Dorothy gleefully took centre stage and told the women about their Saturday night out on the town and how they had gone to the Rink and danced the night away before being treated by two high-ranking officers from the Admiralty to a hot potato from the tattie man on Bedford Street.

Rosie listened and chuckled at Dorothy's and Angie's shenanigans, but her mind kept wandering back to her own weekend – to her lovemaking with Peter on Saturday after he had surprised her following the christening. Then, yesterday, they had enjoyed a special, low-key date at Vera's café. This time they had openly held hands across the table while they chatted and Peter had told her about his mother and father, who were both now dead, and how his French mother had moved to England after meeting his father.

Rosie had commented that this explained his dark looks and she had jokingly asked him to speak a few words of French to her, which, much to her surprise, he had. Apparently, his mother's English had never been brilliant so Peter had been brought up to be bi-lingual.

Rosie, in turn, had told Peter a little about her own parents and, of course, Charlotte. She had shown him a letter she had received the day before that he had read with interest, then asked if perhaps he could meet her sometime in the not too distant future.

' … they were staying in the Grand, funnily enough.'

Dorothy's voice cut through Rosie's thoughts and she forced herself to concentrate on the conversation. She surmised that 'they' were the lucky officers who had gained her two very pretty welders' attention for the evening.

'Some of the Admiralty have been billeted there, apparently,' Dorothy explained. 'Actually, it sounds like they've taken over half the hotel.'

'But we didn't go back for a nightcap,' Angie said, looking at Polly, 'just in case we saw Bel and Joe.'

'Yeah,' said Dorothy, 'the last thing they needed was for their honeymoon to be spoilt – again.'

'Not that we would have spoilt it,' Angie said in their defence.

'Well, that's quite the sacrifice,' Rosie joked, 'hot potatoes out in the cold rather than a port in the warmth of the Grand.'

Polly joined in the banter. 'I'll be sure to tell Bel and Joe. I think they owe you one!'

'Nah, dinnit worry,' Angie said in all seriousness. 'We met them there last night instead.'

Dorothy gave her friend yet another jab with her elbow.

The women's faces all revealed their surprised curiosity.

'Eee,' Dorothy said, looking at a non-existent watch on her wrist and pushing back her chair so she could stand up. 'Lunch break's over. We best get back!'

Rosie and Polly exchanged amused looks and shook their heads. But as they all made their way back out into the rain and the wind, which was now picking up, judging by the rattling of the canteen's windowpanes, Polly snuck another look at their boss. Rosie was certainly living up to her name today. She had never seen her so jovial and relaxed. It was certainly a marked change from last week when she'd had that anxious, gaunt look that usually meant something was on her mind.

Well, whatever it was, Polly thought as they all shouted their goodbyes to Hannah as she headed back to the drawing office, *it's certainly not bothering her any more. That's for sure.*

'Oh, God, the bitch is back!' Angie hollered across to the other women after she caught a glimpse of Helen standing by an open window on the first floor of the admin offices. She was holding a cigarette, blowing out smoke and looking every bit as glamorous as a silver-screen starlet.

'Oh, bloody Nora! Watch your backs everyone!' Dorothy warned, although she was speaking more to herself as she knew that Helen realised it was Dorothy who had grassed her up to Ned's wife. Dorothy knew women like Helen never forgot – or forgave.

'She can't hurt us, you know,' Martha said adamantly, but none of the other women were quite so sure and there was not a single murmur of agreement.

'I think we're going to have to get used to the idea that she's here to stay – Harold told me she's going to remain yard manager for the foreseeable future,' Rosie warned. 'I think we're stuck with her, which means, I hate to say this and I know you're not going to like it, but we're going to have to *try* and make it work. For all of our sakes.'

Polly recalled her short exchange with Helen on Saturday when they'd bumped into each other at Crown's and thought that this might be easier said than done.

'Hey! Gloria, you're back!' Rosie shouted out as Gloria reached them just as the horn sounded out the start of the afternoon shift.

All the women looked at their workmate and tried to gauge whether it had been a successful meeting with Jack. Or more of a stressful one. They had all wondered about how it must feel to be with someone who had no memory of their past, never mind of the love they had shared.

As Rosie told the women to gather round so she could give them their instructions for the afternoon, she looked across at Gloria and mouthed, 'All right?' Gloria nodded, but it was hard to tell whether her nod meant a yes or a no.

At the end of the shift, Dorothy and Angie sang out in unison, 'Admiral?'

'I've got to do ARP duties as soon as I get back,' Martha said, swinging her boxed-up gas mask across her broad shoulders. 'And Hannah said she had to help her aunty Rina out with something to do with her work.' Hannah's aunty worked as a credit draper in the town's Jewish quarter, which, from what the women could tell, meant selling clothes and goods on tick.

'I'm afraid I'm going to have to take a rain check tonight as well. Sorry.' Rosie was all ready to leave with Gloria, who was eager to get back and collect Hope from Aggie's nursery. No one asked the reason for Rosie's 'rain check'. They never did. Rosie was the only one of their team they didn't feel comfortable quizzing about her private life.

'Looks like it's just Polly, Ange and me then!' Dorothy said.

Polly smiled. She wasn't massively keen to go to the Admiral, but she needed distracting. Whenever she was home she felt like she was hanging on every word coming out of Arthur's wireless, waiting to hear any updates from the BBC Home Service, and praying there were none about Gibraltar.

At least Dorothy and Angie would take her mind off it all.

'How was he?' They were the first words Rosie asked Gloria. She didn't want to beat about the bush as they only had their journey back over to the south side to chat, and even then they had to be careful about what they said in case there was anyone earwigging in on their conversation.

'Ah, he's all right,' Gloria sighed. 'It's just so bloody hard. My mind's all over the shop, wondering the best thing to do and say, and all the time I can see this awful look of confusion on Jack's face.'

They both stopped chatting for a moment as they handed in their board cards to the timekeeper.

'It must be incredibly frustrating,' Rosie tried to empathise, but really she couldn't begin to imagine for one moment what it must be like.

'He's admitted it's a living hell,' Gloria said. 'He said he knows he loves me, but that it's so "damned frustrating", in his words, not being able to remember anything. But he did say that he's glad he knows the truth, that he'd felt from the start that something just didn't feel right about his marriage to Miriam.'

'Sounds like he can have more confidence in his feelings and his intuition, if not his mind,' Rosie mused.

'Yes,' Gloria enthused, 'that's exactly what he said. That he can "trust his gut" now.' Her words, though, were followed by a weary sigh. 'I'm just tired of keeping everything a secret. I feel like I've been this one big ball of secrets for so long now I don't know any different.'

'I know a bit about keeping secrets,' Rosie laughed a little sadly. 'And I know it doesn't do you any good, but sometimes you don't have a choice.' She gave her friend a sidelong glance. 'Actually, I have a bit of a secret to tell you.'

Gloria swung round. 'Now that sounds intriguing. And I'm guessing by the look on your face, it's not an altogether bad one?'

Rosie paused for a moment. 'You know, Gloria, I don't think it is ... I hope not anyway,' she added, with a slightly nervous laugh.

'Go on, then!' Gloria demanded. She had thought something seemed a little different about her boss today.

'Well,' Rosie said, 'put it this way, I don't have to worry about Lily's any more.'

Gloria's face lit up. 'Oh, that's fantastic news! How come? What's happened?'

Rosie was unsure what to say. She was so unused to confiding in people. Just having friends, and ones that she could trust, was something of an anomaly for her.

'Well, after I left the party at Agnes's on Saturday, I was walking up Borough Road, the rain had just stopped and I was thinking about you and Jack and baby Hope and everything that had been said by the vicar at the christening ...'

'And?' Gloria said, nudging Rosie on, knowing that it was hard for her to speak about anything personal.

'Well, I was nearly back home when I saw Peter.'

'Really!' Gloria took a deep intake of breath.

'Mm,' Rosie hesitated again, unsure of how to tell Gloria that Peter had walked over to her and that neither of them had said anything to each other, but had simply kissed.

'Well,' Rosie hesitated. 'I guess you could say we made up.'

'Oh, Rosie,' Gloria said, 'this is wonderful news. So, does this mean ...?'

'Yes,' Rosie said, 'it means no more worries about the *business*. We can get back to normal.'

'And does this mean that you and Peter are going to be together?'

'It certainly looks that way,' Rosie said with a shy smile. 'But, you know, I'm just taking it easy. One day at a time. Everything's happened so quickly. To be honest, it all feels a little unreal.'

Gloria smiled. She knew that feeling. That wonderful feeling of falling in love.

'You just enjoy it,' she said. 'Enjoy every minute and every second.'

Rosie smiled back at her friend.

'But there's another reason I'm subjecting you to the ins and outs of my love life,' she said, looking across at Gloria, who now had a worried frown on her face.

'Why am I getting a bad feeling?' she asked.

'Well, I guess it's kind of good *and* bad news.' Rosie was keen not to worry Gloria. 'You see, Peter told me that Vinnie *had* tried to go to Hope's christening.'

Gloria felt herself tense. 'I thought it was odd he hadn't heard about it. Bet you it was that Muriel and her big gob.' Muriel was one of the dinner ladies at Thompson's who was a barrel of laughs, but an incorrigible gossip. It didn't matter how quietly the women talked, Muriel still seemed to get to know all their business.

'I don't know about Vinnie, but Peter knew about the christening because I'd mentioned it to him that awful night I took him Agnes's pie to say thank you for helping to look for Pearl.'

Gloria nodded, her face solemn. She knew all about the terrible falling-out that had followed Peter's revelation that he knew about Lily's.

'Peter guessed,' Rosie said, 'Vinnie would try and gate-crash the christening. Luckily he caught him before he made it to the church.'

'What?' Gloria asked, intrigued. 'Did he arrest him?'

'Yes,' Rosie nodded, 'banged him up in the cells overnight.'

Gloria let out a big sigh. 'Thank God he did. Can you imagine if both Jack *and* Vinnie had turned up on Saturday?'

Rosie nodded again, a grim look on her face.

'Oh, Rosie, you must thank Peter for me. I don't know what to say. Is there anything I can do to show him how much I appreciate what he's done for me?'

Rosie shook her head. 'I don't think he would have said anything, but he thinks – and I agreed with him – that you should know what's gone on.' Rosie hesitated. 'Just so you can be on your guard.'

Rosie didn't need to say any more; Peter might have been able to avert a nasty scene at the weekend, but it was by no means a solution to the problem of Vinnie.

His overnight incarceration was just a temporary fix.

Chapter Eleven

Town Centre, Sunderland

Saturday 29 November 1941

Bel had a tight hold on Lucille's little hand as they hurried past the grandiose, pillared frontage of the Municipal Museum and Winter Gardens, before crossing the wide Borough Road and heading up Fawcett Street, which had been teeming with shoppers earlier on, although the crowds were now starting to dwindle. The rain had stopped but it was still windy and as Bel looked down at Lucille to check on her, she saw that her daughter had a firm grip on her threadbare toy rabbit, which now simply looked like a dirty piece of rag. Bel had tried to part Lucille from her beloved cuddly toy, but to no avail.

As they both leant into the natural wind tunnel that always seemed to appear in the town's centre on days like today, Bel passed a newspaper stand. The boy was shouting out the day's headlines but his words were being whipped away as soon as they left his mouth. Bel sidestepped the billboard and as she did so she saw the words of the new headline the young lad was shouting out in vain: SOVIET TROOPS RETAKE ROSTOV.

Polly had been telling them the other night as they all had their supper about 'the battle on the Eastern Front' and how important it was for the Russians to hold off Hitler's army. From Bel's limited understanding, it seemed to be a case of one step forward and two steps back for both the Allies and the Axis. The Germans might take a town or city, but more often than not the Russians would then fight back and reclaim what was rightfully theirs.

And by the sounds of it the weather in Russia was deathly, which had worked in their favour as the German army hadn't been prepared for the sub-zero temperatures. It made north-eastern winters look like a walk in the park.

Bel was just glad, though, that at the moment Hitler's focus was elsewhere and that their town seemed to be having a hiatus from any more air raids. Although how long this would last was anyone's guess.

'Nana!' Lucille started half singing, half chanting as they hurried past another cordoned-off bomb site where a row of shops had once stood. Bel looked up at the town-hall clock tower, built to evoke Italian architecture of the Renaissance period. It was about to turn three o'clock. If they didn't get a move on they were going to be late.

Bel bent down and picked up Lucille, who was starting to drag. Her little legs were tiring. As Bel scooped up her three-year-old daughter, she found no resistance. Lucille happily put her arms around her mother's neck and wrapped her legs around her waist, all the while continuing her excited chant for her grandma.

A few minutes later they were turning into Athenaeum Street and Bel was breathing a sigh of relief to be out of the windy turbulence. She dropped Lucille back on to her feet and purchased her penny platform ticket from the machine by the main entrance.

Bel and Lucille slowly made their way down the wide flight of stairs that led onto platform number two and as Bel watched her daughter carefully climb down each step she thought of how many memories this station held for her. She had come here often as a child for want of anything else better to do and would sneak under the barriers when the ticket collector wasn't looking and watch loved ones waving their hellos or kissing their goodbyes as the trains came and went. It had been one of her favourite pastimes when her ma had either gone on a drinking spree or taken off with some bloke she'd just met.

Later, as a young woman, Bel had herself waved off a loved one – her husband, Teddy, when he had left for war – and like those she'd seen waving farewells as a child, she too had forced back the tears until his train had disappeared from view. That was to be the last time Bel ever saw her husband; she hadn't even been able to take one last look at him laid out in his coffin as he'd been buried in North Africa in a place she couldn't even pronounce.

In February this year, she'd returned to the station, this time with Lucille and Agnes, to welcome back Teddy's twin, Joe, after he'd been injured by a landmine whilst fighting alongside his brother. Everyone in the family had been grieving in their own way, although Bel's grief had turned to anger and that anger had found a target in Joe and was made worse by Agnes asking Bel to tend to Joe's leg wounds.

Joe had become Bel's emotional punchbag, but had taken it all on the chin; he had watched sadly as her deep-seated depression manifested itself in bitterness and resentment. As he knew it would, his sister-in-law's anger at the injustice of Teddy's death finally spilled over. When it did, he made sure he was there for her, and as the months wore on, the darkness that had taken hold of Bel was gradually replaced by the light of their growing love and care for each other.

Today, however, Bel was returning to the town's train station to welcome back her mother and the half-sister who had introduced herself in such dramatic fashion at Bel's wedding just three weeks previously.

As Bel and Lucille reached the bottom of the flight of stairs, the tannoy sounded out the arrival of the seven-fifteen train from London.

Bel lifted Lucille up again so she could see the carriages rather than just the tops of the huge metal wheels peeking up from the edge of the platform. The hissing and squealing as the black locomotive drew to a halt had Lucille putting her hands to her ears, causing her to drop her toy rabbit and cry out. They both looked down but the cloud of smoke that had enveloped them prevented them from seeing where the rabbit had gone.

'LuLu! Isabelle!'

Both Bel and Lucille looked up as they heard Pearl's distinctive gravelly voice, which had somehow cut through the sounds of the train halting. Pearl was leaning out of the carriage window, her skinny arms waving frantically at her daughter and granddaughter.

'Nana!' Lucille shouted out, her face breaking into a big smile as she was distracted from the panic of losing her toy.

A few minutes later the train was at a standstill and Pearl and Maisie were disembarking. Bel thought that they both looked tired, which wasn't surprising after an eight-hour journey, but they seemed happy. Maisie, Bel observed, seemed in particularly good spirits.

Bel was more than curious about how their 'bonding' week in London had gone. It had come out of the blue, but Pearl had happily agreed to it after Maisie told her that everything would be paid for. Over the past week Bel had wondered to herself – and to anyone else who would listen, for that matter – how her ma and Maisie were getting on.

'Look what I've got for my favourite little niece?' Maisie's southern vowel sounds, startling looks and, of course, her caramel-coloured skin drew curious glances from those who, like Bel and Lucille, had come to welcome loved ones back from their travels.

When Lucille saw what her aunty was holding in her hand, she let out a squeal of delight. It was the cutest, cuddliest – and cleanest – toy rabbit that Bel had ever seen. Maisie had never said anything outright to Bel about the piece of stuffed rag that was now barely recognisable as a cuddly toy, but the look on her face and the way she flinched from it if it came anywhere near her had spoken volumes.

Bel put an excited Lucille, now struggling to be free, down on the ground so she could go and collect her present.

'Rabbit!' Lucille called, her little arms stretching out to take her gift. Maisie bobbed down so that she was at her niece's eye level. As she did so, she spotted Lucille's raggedy old rabbit on the ground. The second she spotted it, so did Bel. The two sisters locked eyes for a split second, before Maisie grabbed hold of her niece and picked her up. As she did so, she quickly kicked her foot out to the side and flicked the rag toy down the side of the platform. As she oohed and aahed with Lucille over her new toy, she gave her sister a wink and a cheeky half-smile.

'Isabelle!' Pearl was throwing her arms open as if she was about to embrace her daughter. Bel looked horrified. She couldn't remember her mother ever putting her arms around her or cuddling her in her entire life. Seeing her daughter's frozen stance and look of shock, Pearl dropped her arms but didn't look hurt by her daughter's rebuttal of the show of affection. Instead, she looked down at her bulging holdall.

'Well then, give us a hand with my luggage – it weighs a bloody ton!' Pearl's demand, though, was said good-naturedly.

Bel did as instructed and she and her ma took a handle each and carried it between them as Maisie walked ahead with Lucille on her hip, her own, much smaller and lighter bag over her shoulder.

'Eee, Isabelle, what a week we've had! It's been quite an adventure,' Pearl said, digging into her pocket with her free hand for her packet of fags and managing to pull one out and spark it up with the new lighter Maisie had bought her. 'But,' she added, puffing on her cigarette hard to get it going, 'it's grand to be back home where I belong, eh?'

Bel looked at her ma in disbelief as they hauled the bag up the two flights of steep steps. Until Pearl had tipped up unexpectedly earlier on in the year, Bel'd had no idea where her mother was. Pearl had probably spent just as much of her life moving around the country as she had in the place she had been born and brought up.

'So,' Bel asked as she reached the top step, 'you've had a good time? I wasn't sure how long you were going to be away.' And it was true. Maisie and Pearl had left in such a flurry, neither of them had seemed sure how long they intended to stay down south. Her ma hadn't seemed to care how long she was going for, which hadn't surprised Bel as she knew that her mother would follow Maisie to the ends of the earth. She had seen how much Pearl truly loved Maisie when she had come face to face with her for the first time on Bel's wedding day – and how much it had broken her heart to give Maisie up.

'Aye, I wasn't sure myself. You know, it being Maisie's shout 'n' all. But we got a telegram a few days ago from Maisie's friend, Vivian. The one that did our hair fer yer wedding?'

'Yes, Ma, I do remember – it's only been three weeks,' Bel jibed.

'Well,' Pearl explained, 'she sent a telegram to the hotel we were staying at and Maisie said that she was needed back at work and we'd be getting the train back up today.'

Pearl started coughing and had to stop to get her breath.

'I was glad enough, though,' she said when she'd recovered enough to speak again. 'A week in the big smoke was just enough for me.'

Bel would never come out and admit it but she was dying to know what her ma and Maisie had been up to this past week, and if they'd succeeded in tracking down Evelina, the midwife who had helped Pearl give birth in the Salvation Army's unmarried mothers' maternity hospital. Bel was also particularly keen to hear if Maisie had found out anything more from Pearl about her real father, other than he was a sailor from the West Indies. Maisie had told Bel before she'd gone to London that she was determined to track him down, which Bel did not disbelieve. All their chatter about unknown fathers, though, had really started to play on Bel's mind.

On stepping out of the railway station, Bel and Pearl followed Maisie and Lucille as they went to hail a taxi.

'Tell you what,' Maisie said, turning around and raising Lucille into the air with both her hands, causing her to scream in mock fear. 'I'll do you a swap? I'll keep this little cheeky monkey and you can take that cheeky money?' she joked, throwing a look over to Pearl, who was trying to light another fag off the one she had been smoking, but was struggling because of the wind.

'I think,' Bel said, with a grim smile, 'that I'm gonna get lumbered with *two* cheeky monkeys, but Maisie, you are more than welcome to come and take either of them off my hands whenever you want.'

Maisie put Lucille down and then turned to the driver, who had just got out of his cab, and pointed to her bag. The balding, middle-aged man jumped to attention and retrieved the holdall, flinging it into the boot of his black Austin and opening the passenger door like Maisie was royalty.

'I'll get off, then,' Maisie said, stepping towards Bel and giving her a light kiss on both cheeks.

'Say "thank you" to your aunty Maisie,' Bel said, looking down at Lucille who was cuddling her new toy. She had not once enquired as to where her raggedy old rabbit had gone.

'Thank you!' Lucille beamed up at Maisie as if she was the best person in the whole wide world.

'Probably see you all tomorrow,' Maisie said, before climbing into the taxi for the last leg of her journey back to West Lawn, where she knew it was now safe to return thanks to Vivian's coded telegram, which had read rather cryptically: THE COAST HERE IS LOVELY AND CLEAR. NO MORE STORMS. Maisie had chuckled to herself when she'd seen that Vivian had signed off: LOVE MAE X.

After they waved Maisie off and watched her cab turn left into Waterloo Place, Bel looked at Pearl and Lucille.

'The walk'll do us good,' she said as she took hold of one of the handles while Pearl automatically took the other. Lucille ran round to her nana's side and grabbed hold of her hand; her new rabbit was stuffed into the top of her coat, only its long bunny ears were visible and now flapping about in the wind.

Bel had wanted to broach the subject of her father with Pearl as they walked home, but she realised that wouldn't be practical – not with the wind and the presence of her daughter, who understood more than she let on.

Bel was determined, though, now more than ever before, to find out exactly who her father was.

Maisie didn't have a monopoly on unearthing family secrets.

*

That evening Pearl lay in bed wide awake. She had thought the whisky she'd enjoyed with Bill, landlord of the Tatham Arms where she had worked these past six months, and then the dregs of a bottle of Teacher's she had drunk with her friend Ronald, who lived in the house that backed on to the Elliots', would have succeeded in knocking her out. But they seemed to have had the reverse effect.

She could possibly put it down to the fact that her mind was still churning over the last seven days. It had certainly been all go and also pretty emotional. She and Maisie had revisited Ivy House – the place where Maisie was born when Pearl herself was just a child of fourteen – only to find the original building had been demolished. They had stood and looked at the bare patch of land and Pearl had told Maisie how she had arrived there and been taken in by a nice woman called Evelina, carrying out chores in exchange for board and lodging. When she had gone into labour, Evelina had been her midwife.

When they had found the new Ivy House half a mile away on the Lower Clapton Road, Pearl had been over-whelmed to meet Evelina. She was still a 'soldier', as they liked to call themselves, and she was exactly the same as Pearl remembered, only older. Maisie had been fascinated by the charity – and Evelina – and the pair had talked for a long time while Pearl sat and listened, happy to be almost a bystander, immersed in her own private thoughts and feelings.

Near the end of their week away, Maisie had opened up a little about her own life. As Pearl had suspected, she had led a somewhat unconventional life. The parents Evelina had found for Maisie as a baby sounded nice enough, but within a year of Maisie being taken to her new home, war had broken out and Maisie's adoptive father went off to fight and never came back. 'The wife', as Maisie referred to her, had gone to pieces and returned to America, where she was originally from, leaving Maisie in the care of her relatives. Although 'the wife' had promised to return, she never did, and Maisie had got passed from pillar to post, before running away at sixteen.

Maisie had been purposely vague about the exact nature of the work she'd drifted into, saying that she had been paid to be a kind of 'companion' to men who were rich and lonely, but she hadn't gone into any more detail. Pearl was no fool, though, and knew that Maisie had heavily sugar-coated her version of reality, just as she wasn't fooled by Maisie's sudden decision to come to London. She guessed something had happened just before Hope's christening and that Maisie was doing a bunk. She'd sneaked a look at the telegram Vivian had sent and it was clear that it was a veiled thumbs-up to come back.

Perhaps in time Maisie would trust her and, furthermore, want to tell her about her true life – both the one she was living now, and the one she'd had before.

Chapter Twelve

'Where's Martha?' Rosie had thrown her welding mask onto the ground and was pulling off her long protective gloves. She looked frantically about the yard, her hand protecting her eyes from the glare of the sun, which had made an appearance despite the bitter, icy cold weather.

The women welders all stood stock-still, their faces showing their confusion as to what was happening. The deep bellow of the shipyard horn had sounded out across the yard even though it had only been half an hour or so since its short, deafening bellow had signalled the end of the lunch break. The women were on the top deck of a 300-foot-long cargo vessel that, despite having two holes blown in its hull by enemy torpedoes, had managed to stay afloat and limp back to Allied shores.

'She went to the lavvy, miss.' Angie still spoke to her as though Rosie was a headmistress. No matter how many times Rosie had told her to simply call her by her Christian name, Angie did not seem able to oblige.

'Yeh,' Dorothy added, 'think she's got a bit of a dicky stomach.'

As Rosie, Dorothy, Angie, Polly and Gloria stood and looked down at the shipyard from the upper deck of the injured ship, they could see the whole yard had come to a standstill.

'What's happening?' Gloria asked, looking at Rosie for an answer. 'Why did the klaxon just go off?'

Rosie continued to stare down at the yard. Her eyes had narrowed and were scrutinising the area where a gaggle of about half a dozen men were now crowding underneath a large crane that wasn't moving and whose driver was peering out the side of his metal box cabin.

'There's been an accident,' she said in a monotone.

There was a joint intake of breath.

'Oh my goodness – Martha!' Polly exclaimed. 'She should be back by now. She went to the lav ages ago.'

Rosie didn't look at the women but continued to inspect the yard. Her eyes, which had become overly sensitive to the sun since her 'welding accident', were now watering, making it harder for her to see what was going on. The women followed Rosie's gaze. It didn't take them long to suss out the route Martha would have taken to the women's toilet.

It passed the exact spot where the crane had come to a stop and the cluster of workers had gathered.

'Look!' Angie shouted, her arm shooting out and her gloved hand pointing in the direction of a black and white van with a blue flashing light that had just come into their vision and was making its way slowly across the yard. Its pace was snail-like as it was having to drive around the usual obstacles: stacks of huge metal sheets, fires used to heat the rivets and warm the workers, coils of ropes and rows of steel poles.

'Stay here!' Rosie told them, as she headed across the metal patchwork deck they had all been welding and across the gangplank that created a short, narrow bridge to the flat concrete of the yard. None of the women listened to her and instead followed hot on her heels.

Within minutes they were marching towards the growing throng of workers.

'Move! Gerrout the road!' one of the yard foremen shouted out. The workers immediately parted, creating a clear pathway for the St John ambulance that was kept in the yard at all times. None of the women, apart from Rosie, had ever seen it in action before.

Rosie turned to the women.

'Wait here!'

The way she said it this time made it clear there was no room for debate or disobedience. The women stood shoulder to shoulder in a line fifty yards away from the commotion.

'Polly! ... Gloria!' It was Hannah, running towards them with Olly in tow. She had seen Rosie disappear into the melee that was slowly growing in size at the foot of the crane. Her face scanned the women.

'Where's Martha?' she demanded.

There was no reply.

'Where's Martha!' Hannah was verging on tears, her voice full of fear.

'We don't know, Hannah,' Dorothy said. 'Come here,' she beckoned, stretching her arm out. The group's little bird ducked under and let her former workmate cuddle her as they continued to watch and wait.

'She went to the toilet,' Dorothy dipped her head to speak to Hannah, 'but she didn't come back.'

Hannah started speaking in her native tongue and Dorothy looked down to see that she had her hands clasped in prayer. She didn't need a translator to know what Hannah was saying.

For what felt like an eternity but was, in reality, only a few minutes, Gloria, Polly, Dorothy, Hannah, Angie and Olly stood frozen to the spot, their faces grey with worry as they waited. Then they heard the foreman's command-ing voice shout out again: 'Right, let's get him gone! Make way!' And once again the workers parted and the ambulance started to reverse slowly.

'Martha!' Hannah's high-pitched voice made Dorothy jump as Hannah ran towards her best friend and flung her arms around her waist. Hannah's head barely reached Martha's chest as she looked up and continued speaking in the language of her beloved homeland.

'Thank the bleedin' Lord!' Angie blustered.

'Hear, hear!' Dorothy said, her face a picture of sheer relief.

'I'll second that,' Polly said as they all walked towards Martha.

'You all right?' Gloria asked, looking Martha up and down. She couldn't see any injuries.

'I'm fine,' she said, looking at her friends in surprise before realising what they'd been thinking. 'It wasn't me in the accident!'

Just then Rosie appeared behind Martha.

'You feeling all right, Martha?' she asked. 'That wasn't the most pleasant of sights.'

Martha nodded. 'I'm fine. Honest.'

'Come on then. I think you need a cup of sweet tea at the very least,' Rosie said, leading the way over to the cafeteria.

A few minutes later they were all supping their tea and Hannah had treated her friend to a piece of apple pie. All eyes were on Martha.

'How bad was it?' Gloria asked, looking at both Rosie and Martha for an answer. Martha looked at Rosie to relay the news as her mouth was full of apple and pastry.

'Not good,' Rosie said. 'But it would have been a lot worse if it hadn't been for our Martha here.'

The women all waited for an explanation.

'One of the metal plates came loose when it was being hoisted up by the crane ...' She paused.

'Oh, please don't tell me it landed on one of the platers?' Polly was aghast. She had heard over the years that this was not uncommon in the shipyards. When her brothers had been working over at Bartram's before the war, one of their workmates had been crushed to death when a metal plate that was being hauled on to one of the ships broke loose.

'Just his leg,' Martha said, swallowing hard as she finished off her pie.

'Anyone we know?' Dorothy asked.

Martha shook her head.

'So, he's alive?' Angie asked.

Martha nodded.

'Yes,' Rosie added, 'but his leg was in a bit of a mess. I'm guessing he'll be lucky to keep it. And if he does, I doubt very much he'll be walking on it again.' She looked at Martha. 'It could have been a lot worse, though, if Martha hadn't been there.'

The women all looked intrigued.

'One of the men told me the second it landed on the poor man's leg, Martha got her hands under the metal plate and somehow managed to lift it up enough for a couple of the other platers to drag the man free.'

'Blimey!' Angie said, letting out a low whistle. 'Martha, you're a hero!'

'Heroine,' Dorothy quickly corrected. 'And yes she is. She's our real-life heroine!'

Martha blushed.

Rosie, who was next to Martha, squeezed her arm. 'I think you should be proud of yourself.'

Martha allowed herself a wide smile, showing off the big gap between her two front teeth.

'Ya know what my mam says about having a gap in yer teeth?' Angie had been fascinated by Martha from the first as she had never come across anyone like her before, which was unusual for Angie as she had not had a sheltered upbringing by any stretch of the imagination.

'What's that Angie?' Martha asked, genuinely intrigued.

'She says that if you can get a threepenny bit in between your two front teeth and wiggle it around, then that means you're going to be lucky!'

Everyone looked at Angie. They were starting to get used to her sudden random thoughts.

'Mm,' Dorothy said, looking at her friend as if she were from another planet, but as she looked up her eye caught two 'suits' coming through the canteen door. She gasped audibly as they were followed into the canteen by none other than Helen.

'Oh. My. God,' she punctuated each word dramatically. 'Don't look now but Helen's just come into the canteen!'

Instinctively, all the women turned to look. Sure enough, Helen was walking across the canteen – and it looked like she was coming straight to their table.

Realising that the two managers and Helen were indeed coming to see her squad, Rosie stood up to welcome them.

'Hello, Harold. Hello, Donald.' Rosie stretched out her arm to shake the hands of her superiors.

'And Helen,' Rosie was the epitome of courteousness, 'it's good to see you back.' The women shook hands.

'Actually, we're not here to see you, Rosie,' Helen said in a manner that appeared to be genuinely good-natured. 'We're here to see one of your welders. Martha. I do believe she has been quite the hero of the hour.'

On hearing the word 'hero', Angie nudged Dorothy, who nudged her friend back equally hard. Their eyes, and those of Polly, Gloria, Hannah and Olly, were glued to Helen.

Rosie stood aside and crocked her head at Martha, signalling her to stand up. Martha followed her boss's unspoken command, bumping the table as she did so and causing the teacups to jiggle but not spill over.

'Sorry,' she said, 'I'm so clumsy.'

Helen looked up at Martha. 'Well, clumsy or not, Martha Perkins, your quick-thinking actions may well have saved a man's leg – even his life. Harold, Donald and I thought it was only right that we come and thank you personally.'

Helen hesitated for a moment before she put her hand out. Martha looked down at the pale, perfectly smooth and manicured hand before tentatively taking it in her own huge paw and shaking it.

Rosie was amazed that Helen had managed to keep her face so impassive. Normally she wouldn't even look at Martha, never mind speak to her – *never mind touch her*.

Harold stepped forward to shake Martha's hand, followed by Donald.

'We're going to make sure you get an official commendation, Martha, but we just wanted to tell you in person just how much we appreciate your actions today.'

'I just hope the man's all right,' Martha said.

'Yes,' Rosie added, 'please tell him that Martha and the rest of her squad send our regards and wish him a speedy recovery.'

Harold nodded. 'I will, Rosie, but I'm not sure how speedy it'll be.'

'Still,' Helen interrupted, 'at least he's alive. We have to be thankful for small mercies.' Her words, however, lacked their usual hoity-toity quality and had a surprising hint of empathy in them.

Helen, Harold and Donald thanked Martha again and then left. The canteen, which had fallen quiet as soon as the three managers had entered, returned to its normal volume.

'Cor! Martha, looks like you're gonna get some kind of a medal!' Angie was awestruck. 'Yer mam and dad are gonna be dead chuffed when they hear about this!'

Angie had mentioned Martha's parents a few times since she, Dorothy and Hannah had dropped in for a cup of tea after the christening. She had joked more than once with Martha about doing a 'mam and dad swap'; it was a suggestion Martha had politely declined.

'I don't know what the fuss is all about,' Martha said. She seemed genuinely perplexed.

Rosie could tell their gentle giant was becoming a little uncomfortable with all the attention, so she suggested that they all head out and sit by the quayside for a short while before they started work again. She knew from experience that they had to wait for the horn to sound again before they were actually allowed to go back to work. Some legal beagle would have to give the green light that the yard was safe to carry on its work after such a serious accident.

Five minutes later they were sitting on their makeshift seats – a load of old pallets that had been half-heartedly stacked up a few yards away from the quayside. It was the women's favourite spot and somewhere that held a lot of memories for them all, both good and bad.

It was near to where they had all learnt to weld as trainees a year and a half ago; it was where Polly had first clapped eyes on Tommy being helped out of his diving helmet; it was here that Raymond had nearly killed Rosie and he himself had ended up losing his life; and it had been here almost four months previously that they had all been sitting, quietly enjoying the summer sun on their faces, when the Luftwaffe had dropped its bombs and Gloria had gone into labour.

'I used to think the shipyards were right ugly, dirty places,' Angie piped up as they all sat in their usual positions facing the river, so that they could talk while watching the live theatre that was constantly being played out on the Wear's grey, murky waters.

'And now,' she laughed, 'I *know* they're right ugly and dirty – *and bloody dangerous as well!*'

Everyone chuckled.

'Eee, well.' Dorothy looked to her left at the huge liner that was moored up and in the process of having camouflage painted onto its hull. 'That was a turn-up for the books. Helen coming into the canteen like that, wasn't it?'

There was a general assent.

'Still the same stuck-up madam, though, by the looks of it,' she added, chuckling.

There was a murmur of agreement.

'She thinks the world of her dad, though,' Gloria suddenly chipped in. 'From what Jack's told me – ' she dropped her voice, even though there was no one else around ' – she was by his bedside more or less constantly when he was ill.'

'Mm,' Rosie agreed, 'I think Helen's always heroworshipped Jack.'

The women sat in silence for a while, trying to match these two conflicting images of the woman they all hated and who had brought such trouble into their lives.

'Well, she might be nice to her own, but she's still a bitch to just about everyone else,' Dorothy said.

'Yeh, look what she did to Hannah here,' Martha said with a frown on her wide brow. 'She ground her down ... made her do all the hardest welding jobs ... tried to get her the boot.'

Olly, who was at the end of the row of women, took hold of Hannah's hand and squeezed it.

'I know, Martha,' Hannah said, letting Olly keep a hold of her hand, 'but we have to forgive people.'

'Only if they *want* to be forgiven,' Dorothy butted in. 'And all the lies she told about Polly seeing Ned the plater. And let's face it,' she looked at Polly, 'she very nearly succeeded in breaking you and Tommy up.'

Polly nodded, looking down the quayside at the diver's pontoon and thinking how that all seemed such a long time ago.

'And,' Angie took up the list of charges against Helen, 'she was trying to give Gloria the elbow just 'cos she was preggers.'

'The thing is ...' Gloria suddenly blurted out. She had been sitting quietly through her workmates' diatribe against Helen. ' ... I feel really guilty every time I see her. I keep thinking about how she's going to feel when she eventually gets to know that her father's had a child with someone else.'

The women all fell silent and turned to look at their colleague. These past nine days since Jack had come back into her life in such dramatic fashion, Gloria had *appeared* to be coping with everything incredibly well, but it was hard to tell; she'd always kept a lot to herself.

'And,' Dorothy agreed quietly, 'that "someone else" isn't just anyone – it's one of us.'

There was a moment's quiet reflection before Hannah piped up.

'Do you know what you're going to do yet?'

Gloria sighed wearily.

'No, not yet. It feels like a minefield and I don't know where to step, because wherever I do there's bound to be a massive explosion.'

'And that nutter's still not shown his face yet?' Dorothy asked, her voice angry as it always was when she spoke about Vinnie.

'No, but I feel like he's a time bomb waiting to go off,' Gloria said ominously. 'I swear I can hear him ticking all the way in Grindon.'

The women now knew all about Vinnie being arrested on the morning of Hope's christening and had agreed amongst themselves that although this had enabled Gloria to enjoy a peaceful christening, and would probably keep Vinnie at bay for a little while, it might well add oil to the fire.

They all watched for a moment as a merchant ship from one of the yards up the river made its way under the Wearmouth Bridge and out of the mouth of the river.

'Anyway, Pol,' Dorothy forced her voice to sound chirpy as she steered the conversation away from the darkness that was Vinnie, 'have Maisie and Pearl returned from their mother-daughter "bonding" trip in London?'

'Ohh ... yesss ...' Polly drew out the words, voicing them in a mock-weary manner. 'We now have the joy of Pearl back under our roof. Which means there'll be some other drama just waiting round the corner to jump out at us when we least expect it.'

Everyone chuckled.

Rosie smiled and thought the same could be said about Maisie, who had arrived back at the bordello on Saturday. Maisie now clearly felt she had done her time being remorseful about the upset she had caused at Bel's wedding, and was successfully worming her way back into everyone's good books – helped enormously by some very extravagant presents she had brought back from the capital.

Rosie looked back over her shoulder to see the crane that had been involved in the accident being driven across the yard to one of the engineering sheds. She knew it would be scrupulously checked over for any faults.

As Rosie brought her vision back to the choppy waters in front of them, she was unaware that she was being watched – albeit surreptitiously – by Dorothy and Angie.

'Go on!' Dorothy whispered to Angie. 'Now's the perfect opportunity.'

Angie pretended not to hear her friend.

Dorothy elbowed Angie gently in the side.

This time Angie shook her head vehemently and whispered back, 'No, you do it!'

Dorothy huffed her annoyance, before turning her attention to their boss.

'Hey, Rosie.' Dorothy tried to make her voice casual, but she failed, sounding unusually nervous instead. 'You know me and Ange are never ones to nose into anyone else's business—'

Her comments were met by a blustering of chuckles from the rest of the women.

Rosie looked at Dorothy and then to Angie with a look of suspicion.

'Or anyone else's *affairs of the heart*,' Dorothy said in as theatrical a manner as possible, trying to keep the conversation light-hearted and by-the-by, when in fact she and Angie had been gagging for days to say something, but hadn't plucked up the courage.

'Mm,' Rosie said. 'And?'

Angie sat back as if moving herself out of the line of fire should the woman she called 'miss' react unfavourably to what Dorothy was about to say next.

'Well, me and Ange,' Dorothy looked around and glared at her best friend, who was very obviously not supporting her in the way they had discussed, 'we were walking into town the other night, and we were passing that posh tea shop on Holmeside – what's the name?'

Again Dorothy glared at Angie, who seemed to have lost the power of speech.

'Vera's Café,' Rosie said helpfully, a smile playing on her lips.

'Yes, that's the one,' Dorothy said, encouraged by her boss's helpfulness. 'Just up from the docks on High Street East.'

Another 'Mm' from Rosie.

'And,' Dorothy said, 'I'm sure my eyes, nor Angie's – ' another glare in her friend's direction ' – weren't deceiving us, but we could have sworn we saw you in there with your policeman friend, Peter?'

'Well,' Rosie said, taking a deep breath, aware that the women were all observing her with great anticipation, 'I believe your eyes, and Angie's – ' she strained her head so that she could look at Angie, who was now practically hiding behind Dorothy ' – were telling you the truth. You did, in fact, see me and my policeman friend Peter in Vera's café.'

Rosie didn't say anything else, but trying her hardest to suppress a smile, just looked at Dorothy.

Gloria couldn't hold it in any more and burst out laughing. 'Ah, Rosie, go on, put the poor girl out of her misery!'

The relief on Dorothy's face defeated Rosie's attempt to suppress her smile.

'Yes, Dorothy, I am, indeed, stepping out with my policeman friend. The one I do believe you like to describe as "scrummy in an older type of way".'

Dorothy's face lit up in delight. Partly because she hadn't been lambasted for sticking her nose in where it wasn't wanted, but mainly because this was headline news. Rosie was courting! And what was more, she was courting a copper!

'Congratulations, miss!' Angie had suddenly reappeared from Dorothy's shadow.

Everyone looked at Angie, a little puzzled.

'Why "congratulations"?' Martha asked, genuinely puzzled.

'Yeh, ya divvy,' Dorothy said, her relief sounding through. '"Miss", as you keep calling her, isn't getting married or anything. Well, I'm presuming it's a bit early for all of that. Or ...?'

Rosie hooted with laughter. 'It most certainly is, Dorothy. Besides, I hate to spoil any hopes of another wedding, but I'm really not the marrying kind.'

'That is fantastic news, Rosie,' Hannah said. She was still holding Olly's hand. He knew better than to intrude on the women's conversations and was simply happy to be there, though even happier that he was being allowed to hold hands with Hannah.

'So that's why you've not been able to come to the Admiral with us?' Polly said, before adding, 'Does this mean we might all finally get to meet him?'

'Oh, now you're asking!' Rosie laughed as an image of Peter surrounded by her women welders suddenly skated across her mind. 'I think I need to go on a few more dates before I put him under all your scrutiny.'

Just then the klaxon sounded out.

'Saved by the horn!' Rosie declared as she jumped up from the pallet and dusted down her overalls. 'Back to work we go!'

But that didn't stop her from being bombarded by myriads of questions as they trudged back to the dry dock. She had opened the door a fraction and her women welders were enthusiastically trying to push it open as wide as possible.

'See, we was right!' Angie sidled up to Dorothy and whispered to her.

'It's "*were* right", Ange. Plural,' Dorothy corrected. 'And thanks, by the way, for the moral support! God, talk about being put in front of the firing line. Remind me never to rely on you for any kind of backup.'

Angie just laughed.

'Aye, why, you know what they say, "All's well that ends well". Shakespeare that is, did yer know?'

Dorothy look impressed.

'Well remembered, Ange! Now I just need to get you to speak properly.'

As Rosie continued to field questions from them all, including an unusually curious Martha, she looked across at Gloria and rolled her eyes in despair.

Gloria smiled; she didn't think she had ever seen her friend look quite so relaxed, or quite so happy, as she had of late.

Chapter Thirteen

When Jack had heard the emergency klaxon sound out earlier on, he'd sprinted the short distance from Crown's to Thompson's, terrified that Gloria might have been in some way involved in whatever had happened.

He was now standing at the large window of the first floor of the administration building in the exact spot where earlier his daughter had been smoking her way through the lunch break.

He watched Gloria and the women welders, as well as a small, dark-haired lad wearing thick spectacles, as they sat by the quayside. They were in a row, facing the river, their heads occasionally turning to chat to each other. He thought they all looked in good spirits.

'I take it you've got a message to Mac's family?' Jack kept his eyes trained on the yard as he spoke. 'Mac' was Jim Mackie, the unfortunate man to have had his leg nearly taken off in the accident.

'Yes, all sorted.' Helen walked over and stood by her father's side. 'I've sent Marie-Anne to go and tell his wife. She should be there now. He only lives up the road.'

'Good choice.' Jack was still keeping his eyes peeled on the scene below. 'Marie-Anne will be able to deal with Mac's wife – she's what some would call "of a nervous disposition", so a woman's touch will be needed.'

Helen looked at her father.

'Dad!'

Her eyes widened with excitement.

'You remembered!' Helen felt like jumping with joy.

Jack looked at his daughter with a puzzled expression.

'You remembered!'

Helen looked around, suddenly aware that they were in the main office and that others could be privy to their conversation.

'Come into your office!' She still wasn't used to calling it 'her' office in front of her father.

After shutting the door behind them, she gave her father a big hug.

'You remembered who Mac is – and his wife – *and Marie-Anne*! There's no way you could have known. You haven't seen any of them since before you went away!'

Feeling a little dizzy, Helen went to sit down behind her desk; missing lunch had made her light-headed.

'Yes, you're right.' Jack spoke the words slowly as if it was taking his brain a little longer than normal to digest their meaning.

He then let out a whoop of laughter.

'Looks like there's hope for yer old dad yet!'

After her father left, Helen reached into her handbag and took out another Pall Mall. Having lit it, she took the photograph of her mother and father that was taking up space on her desk and put it away in the bottom drawer. She suddenly felt a deep bitterness towards her mother. Her father had been here at Thompson's for barely five minutes, and already he had remembered people from his past! How much more would he remember if he was working here all the time?

God, she could strangle her mother with her bare hands. Why couldn't she have just left well enough alone, and let her father come back to work at the yard where he had spent almost every waking minute of his working life? But, oh no – her manipulating mother had to go and get him moved to Crown's.

Did her father not realise that it was a load of old codswallop that he was needed to help with the amalgamation of the two yards?

'Of course he doesn't!' Helen said aloud to the empty office as she ground her cigarette into the metal ashtray. *'He has no idea.'*

As Jack left Thompson's, he cast one last look over his shoulder towards the dry basin, even though logic told him it was a futile gesture. He wouldn't be able to make Gloria out at this distance.

'See ya, Alfie,' Jack shouted out to the young timekeeper, who waved back at him.

Jack marched along the cobbled lanes back to Crown's, and as he did so, he felt energised.

He'd had another memory!

He just wished he could have stayed working at Thompson's rather than have to move to Crown's. Being at Thompson's this afternoon he'd felt so at home, which made sense after what Arthur had told him about his past.

He knew the reason why he'd been given the new job. And it made sense that it would be good to have a Thompson's man already at Crown's, but the buyout was still a way off.

More than anything, though, he wanted to be working in the same yard as Gloria. To be near her.

Since the day of the christening, he'd felt a need – *almost a craving* – to be with her.

It shocked him that he could feel such love for a woman he could not even remember. But he did.

And he wasn't going to fight it.

Chapter Fourteen

'I can't believe that Rosie has got herself a bloke. And a copper at that!' Angie said to Dorothy at the end of the day's shift as they walked up from North Sands to a part of the town known as the Barbary Coast.

'I've still not forgiven you for chickening out on me,' Dorothy said in all earnestness.

'Ahh, you'll get over it!' Angie laughed out loud before dropping her voice. 'Not a bad move that, is it? Getting a boy in blue in yer pocket. Never know when you might need one. Especially in Rosie's line of work.'

Dorothy threw her friend a look of reprimand.

'Shh,' she looked daggers at Angie, before whispering in her ear, 'remember, no talking about the boss's *other job* in public.'

Angie nodded her compliance but thought Dorothy was being both overcautious and overly dramatic, as usual.

'She seems dead happy, though, doesn't she?' Angie carried on chatting as they walked along Dundas Street.

'Yes, she does,' Dorothy agreed, stopping to look in one of the shop windows at a dress that was being put on a mannequin.

'So, Ange, we won't be hanging about at yours, will we?' Dorothy always got a little tense whenever they had to 'just nip' to Angie's house, which was always full of feral-like children yelling at the tops of their voices and creating chaos. Dorothy had met Angie's parents on just a couple of occasions as most of the time she opted to wait outside. Angie's mother wasn't exactly over-friendly, but seemed all right. Angie's father, however, was a brute of a man and put the fear of God into Dorothy.

'Nah, we'll be in and out in a jiffy,' Angie said. Lately she had been spending less time at home and more at Dorothy's where it was much quieter and calmer; Dorothy's mum and stepdad didn't bother them – the house was that big they rarely even bumped into them – and there was the added bonus of an indoor toilet and a proper bathroom.

As Angie and Dorothy walked through Angie's front door, they were instantly hit by the smell of a roaring coal fire and the usual screeches and screams of Angie's younger siblings.

'All right!' Angie called out to her dad over a few bobbing heads playing chase around the house.

'Aye, aye,' he replied, barely looking up from his paper.

Dorothy had got to know Angie's parents' daily routine over the past year since she and Angie had become firm friends; she knew that her dad would do the early shift at the Wearmouth colliery and that her mam did the late shift at the nearby ropery. Lately, Angie's mam had been doing quite a bit of overtime, so she hadn't been about as much. Angie had told Dorothy that she reckoned it worked well as it meant there was less chance of her mam and dad kicking off – something that, by the sounds of it, was a common occurrence.

'Mam gone already?' Angie asked as she picked up the youngest offspring and smothered the little blonde girl in a barrage of kisses.

'Aye, she's deeing time and a half today. So,' Angie's dad nodded over to Dorothy, who was being used by the other children as some kind of slalom pole to dodge around, 'if Liz isn't back in the next five minutes, you'll have to stay with yer mate here 'n' look after the bairns.'

146

Dorothy immediately shot an anxious look over at Angie.

'Ah, Dad, I'm sorry. Me 'n' Dor's got overtime. I've just popped back for a few things before we have to get back,' Angie said without a trace of deceit.

Dorothy looked at Angie's father, who was like one of those musclemen pictured on adverts for the local circus under the banner of 'The World's Strongest Man'. His arms were like boulders. She could even see the thick veins through the smears of dirt and coal dust.

'Ah, yer a good girl, Angela,' he said with a wide smile that showed off a surprisingly good set of teeth. 'Yer a hard worker. I'll grant yer that. Go on then, get what yer need and bugger off. Yer don't want to be late. I've heard they're right tight bastards down those yards. One minute late 'n' yer docked a whole hour.'

Angie forced a laugh. 'Yer right there, Dad, "right tight bastards".'

As Dorothy quietly exhaled, Angie dumped the baby she was holding into Dorothy's arms and hurried off out the back to fill her bag with the essentials needed for her night out.

By the time Dorothy had jigged the baby up and down and made her gurgle and then giggle, Angie had reappeared with her haversack, which was stuffed full to the brim.

Angie's dad stood up and to Dorothy's shock and surprise took the baby from her and gently held her in his huge arms. The baby let rip a loud, excited cry and made a reach for her father's long moustache that curled ever so slightly at the ends. Seeing him and the baby made Dorothy think of Beauty and the Beast.

Angie pushed Dorothy out the lounge door, dodging the rest of her young siblings and shouting 'Ta-ra, Dad,' over her shoulder.

'Dinnit forget. Take care down them yards,' her dad shouted by way of a goodbye.

A few minutes later Angie and Dorothy were back on the main road.

'Bloody Nora, close call there!' Angie gasped as they hurried down the street and away from the house.

'God, Ange. You're a good little actress when you need to be.' Dorothy was secretly breathing a huge sigh of relief that they hadn't got cornered into playing nursemaids. She didn't know if she could actually have stuck it there for an entire evening.

'Lifetime of practice!' Angie was quick to reply.

As they made it to the end of Dundas Street and turned into St Peter's View, they slowed their pace.

'So where's it to be tonight?' Angie asked, but as she looked at Dorothy she saw that her attention was elsewhere – she looked captivated by something happening down one of the back lanes.

Angie followed Dorothy's stare.

'Eee, Ange, it's your mam!' Dorothy exclaimed.

Angie took one glance at her mother and then back at Dorothy, who looked like she was about to shout out a greeting and was raising a hand to wave to her.

'Dor!' Angie grabbed her friend's arm.

At that moment, a tall, young-looking bloke stepped out of one of the backyards. He slid his arm around Angie's mam's waist and pulled her towards him. The next moment the pair disappeared and the cobbled back lane was once again empty.

'You can let go now,' Dorothy said.

'Sorry, Dor, I didn't want my mam to see us.'

'And I bet you she didn't want us seeing her either,' Dorothy said quietly. 'I thought she was meant to be at work?'

'So did I,' Angie said.

'But you don't seem that surprised that she's not.' Dorothy followed Angie as she started to walk back along the main street in the direction of the Wearmouth Bridge.

Angie didn't say anything. Nor did it seem that she wanted to, either.

As they hurried to catch the tram over to the south side, Dorothy's only thought was that Angie's mother must be completely out of her mind.

You didn't do the dirty on a man like Angie's father.

No way.

Chapter Fifteen

It had just gone six o'clock and Gloria and Jack had managed to snatch a half-hour together after the end of the shift. They were huddled in the porch of the historic fourteenth-century St Peter's Church. It was within a stone's throw of Thompson's, but thanks to the blackout they could have been in the middle of nowhere.

Gloria had purposely chosen this place to meet as not only did it provide them with shelter and a modicum of privacy, it held so many memories for them both. It was where they had met as courting teenagers, and again when their love had been rekindled last year.

They'd been chatting about the terrible accident at work; Gloria had told Jack word had gone around the yard that there had been some fault with the crane pulley, which had caused the metal plate to slip.

'God, I was so worried something had happened to you.' They were both quiet for a moment. Gloria was happy simply to be in Jack's arms, but she could tell that the man she loved was unsettled.

After a few moments Jack suddenly sat forward, his hands clenched together.

'I can't keep doing this!' he said, staring straight ahead at the stone wall. 'We can't go on like this, Glor,' he implored, turning his head to look at her. 'It feels so wrong to be skulking about like this.'

A sense of déjà vu passed over Gloria as she recalled Jack saying almost the exact same words to her before he left for America.

'God!' Jack sounded exasperated. 'Why do I feel I've said all of this before?'

Gloria let out a sad laugh. 'Because you *have* said it all before. In this very church. Just days before you left for America.'

Jack had been determined to tell Miriam that he was leaving her, but Gloria had persuaded him to wait until he returned. She'd known nothing could get in the way of him going to America. He'd been chosen to be part of a special mission to help set up production of a new cargo vessel, the Liberty ship. Cheap to construct and mass-produced by the Yanks, it was to be bought by the British to replace the growing number of ships being torpedoed by German U-boats. His duty to his country came first, their love second.

Jack put his hands on his head. 'There's a part of me that can vaguely recall us being here before I left. But is that because you *told* me that we used to meet here or because I really can remember?'

'Perhaps a bit of both,' Gloria said.

Jack took hold of Gloria's hand. It felt frozen.

'This is madness. It's bitter cold. And here we are meeting up like two teenagers with nowhere else to go. I want us to go to Miriam and tell her the truth. I don't like all this lying and deceit!'

Gloria felt herself panic – she needed more time. *They* needed more time. She had worked out the practicalities – and the consequences – of revealing their love, and their love child, to the rest of the world and the future did not look at all rosy.

'Apart from everything else,' Gloria argued, 'we've got to think about how we're going to live once everything's out in the open. It goes without saying that we'll both be chucked out of the yard, and I can guarantee from that moment onwards no one else will go near us with a barge-pole. Miriam – and more so her father – will make sure of that. They've got the power to make certain that happens, which means we'll have nothing. We won't be able to even keep a roof over our heads and we'll also have a little baby to look after.'

'We'll survive,' Jack said, simply.

There was a part of Gloria that agreed with Jack. They would survive. She had felt that on the day of the christening when Jack had stood by her side with baby Hope in his arms. She'd known then that the road ahead was going to be rocky, but they had a foundation of love and could deal with anything life threw at them.

Her real concern – and one she didn't want to tell Jack about yet – was the reaction of Vinnie once he learnt the truth. Jack was what she would call 'all man' but he was no fighter. She'd rarely seen him lose his temper. Vinnie, she knew for certain, would batter him to within an inch of his life, if not more.

'Please, Jack,' Gloria squeezed his hand hard, 'just keep shtum for now. Just for the next few weeks. Until we've worked out a proper plan of action. And give yourself a little more time to recover – hopefully get more of your memory back.'

Jack looked at Gloria and knew he couldn't go against her wishes. He knew they had to be unified.

'All right,' he agreed. 'You win – this time.' He put his arms around her shoulders and pulled her towards him. He loved the feeling of them being close. 'Now, enough arguing. Tell me how Hope's doing.'

Gloria looked up at him and gave him a quick kiss. She was relieved he had capitulated. For now, at least.

'Well, Hope's being spoilt rotten, as always, by Bel and Agnes.'

Jack smiled. That was one thing he didn't have to worry about. His daughter was in good hands.

As they sat there for the next twenty minutes, Gloria talked to Jack about everything and anything she could think of that would help paint a picture of his past life. She regaled him with the story of how they'd first met down by the quayside when he had helped her up after she'd fallen flat on her face, having slipped on the icy cobbles.

'Eee,' Gloria said, starting to laugh at the memory, 'we laughed and laughed at my rather spectacular fall – and how I somehow managed not to upend the basket I was carrying.'

Jack chuckled, enjoying the story, even if he couldn't remember.

'Anyway,' Gloria continued, 'you were a proper gentleman, even then, and insisted on carrying my basket and walking me home. We chatted away and I'll never forget the feeling that I'd known you all my life.'

'So, I must have been, what, fifteen ... sixteen?' Jack asked.

'You were just days away from your fifteenth birthday, and a year into your apprenticeship. I used to wait for you outside the gates after work,' Gloria said, smiling at the memory. 'Sometimes, when you were working overtime, you'd sneak me in and, oh, you were so proud of where you worked and the job you were doing.'

'Still am,' Jack said thoughtfully.

'The funny thing is,' Gloria reflected, 'I understand it now more than I ever did. I think I might even love the place as much as you do.' She laughed. 'Which is madness, really. I mean, who would love working bloody hard, all hours, in all weathers?'

Jack gave Gloria a cuddle and chuckled.

'Aye, gluttons for punishment. The both of us.'

'Ah, darling, you look chilled to the bone,' Miriam said as she hurried to greet Jack as he came through the front door.

'And,' she said, looking down at her dainty gold Rotary watch, 'you're late. I hope they're not overworking you at Crown's?'

Miriam took Jack's face in her hands and kissed him gently on the lips. She had purposely not had a drink. She had slipped a little lately and drifted back to her old routine of having a gin and tonic in the late afternoon. She didn't want Jack thinking he was married to a lush; besides, something told her that she needed her wits about her at the moment. For over a week now Jack had insisted he sleep in the spare room, claiming he was not sleeping well and didn't want to disturb her. There was no reason to disbelieve him, but whenever she had been up during the night, she'd heard him snoring and he'd sounded like he was out for the count.

'No, no,' Jack reassured her, 'they're not overworking me. It's all hands on deck at the moment.'

'I know, darling. And I know, as everyone keeps saying, "there's a war on", as if we could possibly forget, but you have more than done your bit. It's time to think of yourself now. I don't want you working yourself to the bone.'

As Miriam took his hand into her own, Jack felt crippled by guilt.

Guilt that he had been with Gloria and not working himself into the ground as Miriam clearly thought.

Guilt that Miriam was being so loving, so caring, so concerned about him, unaware that he loved another woman and would soon be leaving this house – this life – to be with her.

Jack knew logically that Miriam had committed the most terrible deceits, but he too was being duplicitous.

As they walked down the tiled hallway and through the breakfast room, Miriam continued to hold his hand, and he could smell the faint trail of perfume as she walked ahead of him.

'Mrs Westley!' Miriam's voice sang out as they entered the large kitchen at the back of the house. 'I'm giving you tonight off!'

The cook turned around with a look of astonishment on her face. She couldn't remember the last time she'd had an evening free from Miriam's unrelenting culinary demands.

'Jack and I,' Miriam said with a little light-hearted laugh, 'are going to rough it tonight! I'm going to raid the pantry and my darling husband and I are going to eat it here – in your lovely, warm kitchen. I think we've both had enough of stuffy, boring dinner parties for a while.'

Mrs Westley's mouth slackened in sheer amazement at what she was hearing, but she didn't need telling twice and was already untying the back of her apron.

'Well, Mrs Crawford,' the cook said. 'That sounds like a wonderful idea. There's some of Mr Crawford's favourite stew on the stove. Just needs heating up. And there's a fresh batch of bread in the pantry. Just come out the oven.'

Miriam looked over at the big pot of stew and inwardly grimaced. She had never got used to Jack's taste in food. He would take a pie or a pan of stew over any kind of cordon bleu cooking that he might be offered.

'That's perfect.' Miriam looked over to Jack and noticed his face had relaxed. She'd been right. She'd been wearing him out with too many parties and posh social dos. He was drifting away from her and she needed to reel him back in. And if that meant forcing down a bowl of Mrs Westley's poor man's gruel that Jack loved so much, then so be it.

She was so close to finally having the husband she wanted, if that meant sacrificing the occasional dinner party and eating the occasional ladle of slop in this wretched kitchen, then she'd do it.

'Night, Mrs Westley.' Jack waved the cook goodbye as she hurried out the back door.

With the cook gone, the house suddenly felt quiet.

'I'll get us our drinks.' Jack stood up and left to go to the cabinet in the drawing room.

'Ah, darling, that'd be perfect,' Miriam said. The thought of a gin and tonic made the meal all the more bearable. Now she just had to get Jack back into the marital bed.

Perhaps tonight would be the perfect time.

After finishing their supper in the kitchen, Miriam suggested they go and relax in the front living room, where they could put the gas fire on and have a nightcap.

Jack's feelings of guilt had continued to plague him as they had chatted, and he had tried to push them away as he asked Miriam about their past. Still, it had been so good to simply relax and eat in the kitchen instead of being served by Mrs Westley in the dining room or, worse still, being subjected to another dinner party.

When the clock chimed nine times, Jack made to push himself out of the comfy leather armchair he had been sitting in for the past half-hour.

'Well, I think I'm going to hit the sack,' he said, stifling a yawn.

'Just one more nightcap,' Miriam said, walking over to the drinks cabinet.

Jack looked up to see Miriam was already pulling the cork stopper out of the bottle of Glenfiddich she was holding. She was pouring it before he had time to answer.

'Have you read the lovely letter that Margaret sent?' Miriam pointed to the coffee table where a thick white sheet of concertinaed paper lay.

As Miriam watched Jack leaning over to get the letter, she quickly slid her hand in her skirt pocket and took out one of her 'reds', a shiny, jewel-like capsule that the doctor had prescribed as a sleeping draught. Keeping her eyes glued on Jack, she split the small torpedo-shaped capsule open, before quickly glancing down and emptying the white powder into the tumbler of whisky.

Swishing the amber-coloured spirit around in the glass, and checking that the fine powder had totally dissolved, she walked around the cabinet and handed Jack his drink.

Returning to mix her own, she watched as Jack automatically raised the glass to his lips while he read her sister-in-law's note. It had annoyed Miriam in the past that Jack always gulped back his drink, just as he always ate as though someone was going to come and snatch his plate off him; over the years she had tried unsuccessfully to change what she saw as his working-class manners, but tonight she was glad of them.

'It sounds like they enjoyed having Helen to stay, doesn't it?' Miriam fluffed the cushion on the soft leather armchair next to Jack and sat down.

She watched with quiet pleasure as Jack took another large swig of his drink.

'Who wouldn't?' Jack said. 'She's a joy to have around. And such a bright spark. I'm surprised they didn't try and keep her there!'

Miriam had to bite her tongue.

God, the man's got no idea, she thought bitchily. Men, in her opinion, were as thick as two short planks when it came to their daughters. It didn't matter what they did, or what they were really like, fathers seemed to have some kind of innate blind spot when it came to their little princesses.

'She seems happy to be back,' Miriam said, looking across at Jack and seeing that his attention was fixed on the flickering flames of the gas fire; her 'red' was doing its work faster than expected.

'Darling, you look shattered.' She forced her voice to sound genuinely caring.

Jack turned his face to his wife but his eyelids were heavy and he was struggling to keep them open.

'See, I told you you've been overdoing it.' Miriam was up and out of her chair in a flash, suddenly worried that Jack would pass out there and then.

'Come on,' she said, linking her arm with his and gently pulling him out of the armchair.

Jack acquiesced and stood up, staggering a little as they walked towards the living-room door. He could feel Miriam guide him up the stairs and when he automatically started to head to the back bedroom, he felt a slight pull to his right.

'I think you should sleep in our bed tonight,' Miriam whispered into his ear, as she guided him along the landing and into her large, high-ceilinged bedroom at the front of the house. She had told Mrs Westley to get a little fire going and although it was now dwindling, the room was lovely and warm.

'God, Miriam, I don't think I've ever ...' Jack stopped talking as he slumped onto the bed. ' ... felt this ... tired ... in my life.'

Miriam started to unbutton his shirt. She had just managed to free his arms from the sleeves when he fell back onto the soft, thick mattress.

Miriam looked at Jack. His eyes were now completely closed. This was not the scenario she had hoped for, but at least she'd managed to get him into her bed. It was a minor victory.

'Sssor ...' Jack was now slurring badly.

'What's that, darling?' Miriam spoke softly into his ear.

'Ssssorry,' Jack managed to say.

'What have you got to be sorry for, silly billy?'

'H-hope ...' Jack managed to get the word out.

'Hope? What do you "hope", Jack?'

But Jack was out for the count before he could answer his wife. He was snoring by the time she had tugged off his trousers and managed to get him under the freshly laundered sheets.

Five minutes later, Miriam was sitting up in the bed, listening to Jack's heavy breathing getting louder by the minute. She had just taken one of her reds, so she knew she would be out like a light in no time and undisturbed by anything, least of all Jack's snoring.

As she shuffled down in the bed and turned off her side lamp, she snuggled up to Jack and placed one of his arms around her, as if he was giving her a cuddle.

Miriam started thinking about the evening and how Jack seemed to be asking a lot of questions about their past. She'd heard from Helen that Arthur had made a reappearance – *the interfering old has-been* – and when she'd questioned Jack about it over the meal she'd forced down, it was clear that the pair of them had met up a few times this past week.

Miriam started to feel the warmth and relaxation that her reds gifted her, although her mind didn't feel quite so at ease.

Why hadn't Jack told her before that he'd been meeting up for cosy little chats with the old man?

And she'd felt more than a little antsy when Jack had asked her more questions about how they'd met. At one point she'd felt as though he was grilling her. She'd said as much, albeit in a jokey way, and Jack had apologised. Had looked truly sorry. Even a smidgen guilty. He'd stopped then and told her it was just that he was so desperate to get his memory back it made him a little impatient and frustrated.

Don't be so paranoid, Miriam reprimanded herself as she felt the first wave of chemically induced sleep start to wash over her. It was natural that Jack wanted to try and remember his past.

She just had to make damn sure that he didn't, that it remained embedded deep in the bottom of the Atlantic Ocean, and that the version he did have ingrained in his mind was a version of the past that she had either created or censored.

Chapter Sixteen

Monday 8 December 1941

As Polly stomped across the yard to the rest of the women welders, she was waving the morning edition of the *Daily Mirror* in her hand.

'Have you heard?' she demanded as she reached the women, who were all huddled around their metal drum fire. They had moved it nearer to the platers' shed to protect them from the vicious winds coming in from the North Sea.

Dorothy, Angie and Martha looked at Polly, but kept their hands over the warmth of the blazing coals.

'Look!' She had to raise her voice to be heard above the blustering winds. 'The Japs have bombed the Yanks!' As she reached the women she held out the front page of the paper and read out the headline: '"Japanese Bomb US Naval Bases in the Pacific"!'

'Blimey, who needs the BBC when you've got Pol,' Angie joked.

'God! This is serious stuff,' Dorothy said, looking at Angie and then to Martha, who also clearly had no idea what Polly was going on about. Dorothy took the paper off Polly and quickly read the front-page article.

'Well, this is a turn-up for the books. I can't believe they've done that!'

'I know!' Polly said, pulling her flask out of her holdall and unscrewing the top.

'Says they're gonna declare war on Japan.'

'Will one of you explain to Angie and me what's happened?' Martha interrupted.

Dorothy looked up at Martha and then back at the newspaper.

'Well, it says here,' Dorothy began, then started reading, '"Japan last night started the war in the Pacific by bombing the United States naval and air bases in Manila, in the Philippines, the Hawaiian base at Pearl Harbour ..." It says that the attack happened while a couple of Japanese diplomats were trying to negotiate a "farce" of a peace settlement—'

'Why was it a "farce"?' Angie asked.

'Because,' Polly interrupted, 'they obviously had no intention of trying to keep the peace as they'd already planned this attack.'

'Oh,' Angie said, but she still didn't look terribly enlightened. 'Anyway, where's Gloria, Pol? She normally comes in with you.'

'She was a little late with Hope and I wanted to get a paper early before I came in. She should be here any minute.'

'Talk of the devil,' Martha said, looking over her workmate's head and seeing Gloria fighting against the winds to reach them.

'Eee,' Gloria said, 'we'll be blown away if we're not careful today, that's for sure.' She took one look at the women. 'Why the serious faces?' She did another quick scan of the area, before adding, 'And where's Rosie?'

'She's not got in yet,' Dorothy said.

'Probably having a lie-in with her dishy copper,' Angie piped up.

Dorothy gave Angie one of her stares that told her she had yet again overstepped the mark and said something very inappropriate.

'And,' Dorothy continued answering Gloria's initial question, 'we've all got serious faces because Polly's been telling us all the latest – that the Japanese have attacked a couple of American airbases.'

'*Hi everyone!*'

The women all turned to see Hannah hurrying towards them. She was dressed as if she was about to embark on a trip to Siberia, with matching hand-knitted hat, scarf and mittens, along with an oversized blue woollen coat that her aunty had purchased for her in one of the second-hand shops in the east end.

'Have you heard the news?' she asked as she reached the fire, immediately pulling off her mitts and sticking her two delicate white hands out to catch some warmth.

'Dorothy's just been telling us what the paper's saying,' Martha said.

'But I'm still not sure what this means for us?' Angie asked.

'It means,' Hannah said, 'that the Americans will join the war. And most importantly, they're going to be on *our* side.'

Hannah paused.

'*They're going to help us win the war!*'

Polly nodded in agreement. 'Let's hope so, eh? About time they stopped sitting on the fence. They've got no choice now. This is really shocking because you're meant to declare war on someone before you attack them and the Japanese didn't.'

Dorothy looked at Polly in surprise. 'When did you become the fountain of wisdom on all things war-like?' she asked.

Polly blushed. She had never been very good at school, although her ma had always made sure she could read and write and do her maths, but since Tommy had been sent

163

over to Gibraltar she had wanted to know and understand as much as possible about what was happening, not just over in Europe, but throughout the whole world.

'So, then,' Angie asked, 'where's the Pacific when it's at home?'

Dorothy's reply was interrupted by the klaxon sounding out.

'See you all in the canteen at lunchtime?' Hannah asked as she turned to leave for the drawing office.

Everyone agreed and waved Hannah off before turning back to Gloria.

'Rosie's still not here,' Dorothy said.

'What'll we do?' Martha asked.

'Yeh, what'll we do?' Angie asked, looking about the yard to make sure Rosie wasn't on her way over to them.

'Well,' Gloria barked, 'we can't just stand about here like lemons. Come on, get your gear and we'll pick up from where we left off last week.'

Leading the women across the yard and over to the dry basin, Gloria checked behind her. There was still no sign of Rosie, although something told her that there was nothing to worry about. In fact, she had a sneaking suspicion that Angie's presumptions as to why 'Miss' was late might well be not far off the mark.

As the women settled themselves down at their table in the canteen, Rosie apologised yet again to her troop of welders.

'I can't say enough how sorry I am,' she said, looking guiltily at them all. 'I don't think I've ever overslept like that in my life ... I can't even remember the last time I was late.'

Martha laughed. 'Probably never!'

'Yeh, probably never!' Angie repeated, adding, 'Anyway, it's nice to know you're not perfect, miss.'

Rosie smiled. 'Far from it, Angie! As long as I'm forgiven. I'll make sure it doesn't happen again. Promise,' she
said.

The women all looked in slight amazement at their
boss. Rosie had never – not once – been late for work in
the eighteen months they had all worked there. Of course,
they had not dared enquire as to why Rosie was late, but
what was all the more intriguing was that their boss was
still wearing her make-up from the night before.

None of them had said anything, but they would have
all pooled their week's wages and laid a bet that Angie's
supposition was spot on: Rosie had indeed been out with
her 'scrummy detective' last night and had not made it
back to her own home.

As Rosie picked at her lunch, she felt extremely self-con-
scious, as if she were an open book for all to read. If anyone
had wanted to take a peek, they would have learnt that
Peter had taken her out for a drink and then persuaded her
to stay the night at his. The last thought on her mind had
not been to set the alarm.

She had been in such a panic when she'd woken up and
seen the time, Peter had forced her to calm down, telling
her that being half an hour late for work was not the end of
the world. He'd managed to talk some sense into her, but
still she'd been in a right tizzy and had run the whole way
from Peter's lovely terraced house in Brookside Gardens in
the west end of the town to her flat on the Borough Road
in the east end.

She'd not thought to wash her face, instead had just
climbed into her overalls, pulled on her boots and overcoat and run out the door and down to the ferry landing.
She had no idea she was sitting there still sporting a good
amount of make-up – it had stayed on remarkably well,
with only her mascara slightly smudged.

'So, tell me all the latest,' Rosie said, now determined to push the attention away from herself.

'The Japs have bombed somewhere called the Pacific and now they're going to help us win the war,' Angie said knowledgeably. 'Hawaii to be specific – that's in the Pacific,' she added with a chuckle. 'Which if you didn't already know, miss, is left of America if you're looking at a map.'

Rosie looked at Angie and had to suppress a smile. She knew now that for ever and a day she would be 'miss' to her most recent recruit.

'So sorry I am late,' Hannah said, squeezing herself between Martha and Polly, and putting her home-made sandwiches down on the table.

'Looks like it's the day for being late,' Polly said, deadpan.

'You off somewhere nice after work, Rosie?' Hannah said as she started to unwrap her packed lunch.

Rosie shook her head and looked puzzled.

'Only you've got your make-up on today,' she said in all innocence.

Rosie went bright red.

'So,' Gloria said, seeing Rosie's obvious discomfort and kindly moving the spotlight away from her and back on to the latest war news, 'one of the drillers was saying in the queue that the Yanks are going to officially declare war on Japan later on today.'

'Yes,' Polly said, 'I think that's a cert, especially as there were so many casualties. I heard one of the dinner ladies say there'd been at least *a couple of thousand* killed. And loads more injured. A lot of them civilians as well.'

There was a thoughtful break in the conversation before Hannah spotted the newspaper that Polly had brought into the cafeteria.

Polly handed her the paper, but didn't speak as she had a mouth full of food.

'Oh, that's good,' Hannah murmured, 'Hitler has not succeeded in taking Moscow. They are retreating.

'You know – ' she looked up at the women and her face looked uncannily serious ' – the Nazis killed ten thousand Jews last week in Riga. That's not far from Russia,' she explained. 'They were marched from the ghetto, taken to a forest and shot dead.'

The women all stopped eating. They were shocked.

'That's not the ghetto your mother and father are in, is it?' Dorothy asked, remembering what Hannah had told Angie and her on the day of the christening.

'No, *díky bohu*,' Hannah broke into her native tongue, 'thank God. The one they're in is in Czechoslovakia, but how long before he does the same there?'

'How do you know this?' Polly asked. She now listened to the BBC world news religiously with Arthur every night. It had become their ritual. They sat there in front of the range's open fire, both wanting and not wanting to hear news about Gibraltar.

Martha looked down at her friend. 'Rina?'

Hannah nodded.

'Her aunty Rina,' Martha told the women by way of an explanation. 'She hears things from the rabbi.'

'So ...' Hannah forced herself to perk up. 'This is good? About the Americans? Yes?'

'Yes,' Dorothy and Angie said in unison.

'They're going to help us win this war,' Polly said in earnest.

'And moreover,' Gloria said, her heart going out to Hannah. The worry the poor girl must be going through. '*We're* going to help win this war. Aren't we?'

'Too right,' Polly added. 'Every ship Jerry sinks, we'll make damned sure we're building another one to replace it.'

'Yes, with your brains,' Dorothy said to Hannah, 'and our brawn,' she leant over and felt Martha's biceps, causing them all to chuckle, 'bloody Jerry doesn't stand a chance!'

At the end of the shift everyone made their way to the bottleneck that always formed at the timekeeper's cabin.

'Thanks for taking charge this morning when I didn't show,' Rosie said to Gloria. The pair were walking together, their shoulders practically touching due to the surrounding throng of workers all eager to get home or to the pub. Martha, Hannah and Olly were a few heads in front of them. Angie, Dorothy and Polly were just behind, chatting away nineteen to the dozen about some new film that was just about to come on at the cinema.

'Any time,' Gloria said. 'If you ever want a bit of time off, you know, I'm more than happy to stand in for you. It's not as if I need to do much. You've done such a good job at training us and they're all hard workers. I wouldn't have to get the whip out on them.'

Rosie nodded. They had all worked like Trojans this afternoon. No one had said anything but the conversation over lunch and thoughts of what had happened in the Pacific and in Riga had affected them all.

'Thanks, Gloria,' Rosie said, 'but that really was a one-off.'

'You off out tonight with Peter?' Gloria asked tentatively.

'God no!' Rosie laughed. 'I think Lily'll sack me if I do. I'm falling behind with the books as it is. How about you? How's things with ...?' Rosie didn't need to say Jack's name.

'It's difficult,' Gloria said. 'Very difficult.' She sighed slightly. 'He seems really tired lately, which I suppose isn't surprising.' She paused as she thought about Jack and how he had told her that these days as soon as his head hit the pillow, he was out like a light.

'But,' she added, 'at least he managed to see Hope over the weekend and spent a little time with her at Agnes's, which was lovely. He really does adore her.'

'I know,' Rosie said, thinking of the look of pure, unadulterated love she had seen in Jack at the christening. 'And,' her voice dropped to almost a whisper, 'how's he managing with Miriam?'

'Well,' Gloria said, her face suddenly becoming harder, 'she's apparently been really nice. She's not dragged him out once this week to any kind of dinner party or social. Looks like she's playing happy families, with just the two of them cosied up together on an evening.'

Rosie could feel the anger and jealousy coming off Gloria.

'She's even,' Gloria said as they both handed in their cards and allowed themselves to be carried down to the ferry in the slow-moving sea of workers, '*got him sleeping in her bed.*'

The image of Jack and Miriam lying together in some big, comfy bed had been goading her relentlessly since Jack had told her, rather innocently, that he and Miriam shared the same bed, although he had been quick to reassure her that it was just the bed they were sharing and nothing else.

'Oh no!' Rosie was genuinely alarmed. 'But I thought you said before that the pair of them hadn't shared a bed for years. That the marriage was dead in the water – in all ways?'

Gloria leant into Rosie as they were jostled about near the ferry landing.

'It *was*,' she said, as she fished out a penny from the top pocket in her overalls, ready to pay the ferryman, 'but Miriam's made out to Jack that they never spent a night apart in all their years of being blissfully married.' Gloria's words dripped sarcasm.

'Jack doesn't believe her, though, does he?' Rosie was becoming a little anxious that Miriam might well be doing a good job of making fiction into fact.

'No,' Gloria hesitated, 'I don't think so.' She stopped speaking while they both handed over their fare and stepped on to the ferry that was bobbing about, the boat's paddles throwing up water in anticipation of the return journey across the Wear. 'I just think it's a lot for him to take on-board at the moment.'

'It must be hard,' Rosie said, looking at her friend and wondering how on earth she was managing to stay so calm and in control. 'And Vinnie?' she asked.

'Mm, all quiet. A bit too quiet. I'd like to think his night in a cell put the willies up him, but I think that might be wishful thinking. It's been weeks now since the christening and if I know Vinnie, he'll be stewing everything over in that sick head of his. Plotting something. The question being – what? It's either that or I'm being totally paranoid and he's finally giving up the ghost and is just enjoying life with that Sarah woman.'

Rosie felt herself bristle. She knew Vinnie, and was pretty certain he would be making a reappearance in the not too distant future.

'I'm guessing you've not filled in Jack's memory regarding Vinnie being handy with his fists?' Rosie asked.

Gloria shook her head.

'I was going to,' she sounded weary, 'but I know as soon as I do that he's going to go mad and the cat will be well and truly out of the bag. And I'm just not ready for that at the moment. I need a plan of action and to be honest, I haven't got one yet.'

'Oh, Gloria, I do feel for you. I wish I could do something to help. You know we're all here for you, don't you?'

Gloria squeezed her friend's arm as they looked behind to see the rest of the women waiting for the next ferry as this one was chock-a-block with workers.

Gloria waved to the women welders as the seagulls circled and screeched above.

'I know you are,' she said, with a sad smile. 'I don't know what I'd do without you all, I really don't.'

Chapter Seventeen

As Rosie hurried up the steps from her basement flat and onto the Borough Road, she pulled the belt on her grey mackintosh tightly around her waist and tucked the large lapels across her chest to keep out the bitterly cold wind that showed no signs of tiring. She pulled out her little torch from her pocket to guide her way through town across to Ashbrooke.

Normally she would walk, but this evening she was exhausted. She felt as though she had been running around all day trying to grab back the time she'd lost by sleeping in. Seeing a tram squealing to a stop on Toward Road, she ran, or rather trotted as fast as she could in her heeled shoes, to catch it before it pulled away. Grabbing the pole and pulling herself on-board, she found the tram practically empty and sat on the first seat she saw, paying her fare to the young, fresh-faced clippie.

As the tram trundled its way past the bomb site where the town's Victoria Hall had once stood, Rosie tried to reprimand herself for feeling so happy when she was surrounded by such devastation. Especially after what they had all heard today. On the way home she had seen the latest headlines that America had declared war on Japan and Germany as predicted. This was a world war in the truest sense. Yet, in complete contradiction to all this darkness – all this death and destruction they were being faced with on a daily basis now – she had never felt so light, so excited and so alive.

Since the afternoon of the christening over a fortnight ago, she and Peter had managed to see each other almost every other evening, which had not been easy. Peter had his civil defence work to do after his policing duties, and Rosie had Lily's, which had been busier than normal following its reopening after the sudden 'plumbing emergency', and because they were almost ready to officially open the Gentlemen's Club.

As Rosie put her purse back into her shoulder bag, she unzipped the side pocket and looked at the shiny silver key Peter had given her when she left that morning. She had been in such a panic, but as she had rushed out his front door, he had grabbed hold of her arm and pressed what had felt like a piece of metal into the palm of her hand and pulled her back for one final kiss.

'So you can come whenever you want,' he'd told her.

Now that she had a moment to think, she realised the importance of his gesture. He had already told her that he loved her, and she believed him. But this was showing her that he trusted her and wanted her to be a permanent part of his life.

She felt her heart start thumping as her mind wandered to the time they had spent together last night. She even felt herself blush as images of their lovemaking flashed wantonly across her mind. She looked at the elderly couple who sat adjacent to her and was relieved they were staring somewhat forlornly out the window and were paying her no heed.

Rosie reprimanded herself. It was so dark in the tram – the Ministry of Defence regulations allowed only the smallest sliver of light as guidance through the enforced blackout – Rosie would have had to be glowing like a beacon for the old couple to have even noticed her, never mind read her thoughts. Still, she couldn't help but feel exposed and she forced back those very private images, replacing them with ones from the earlier part of their evening when they had sat close together in the corner of the Victoria Gardens, holding hands under the table and chatting away, immersed in their own little world.

When they'd left they'd practically been blown off their feet by the winds that had worked themselves up into a frenzy while they'd been having their drinks. When they'd arrived at the little private road where Peter lived, Rosie had gasped in delight. Despite living and working in the town since the age of sixteen, not once had she ever stumbled across this little gem of a residential street that was gated at both ends and consisted of a row of thirteen immaculately kept Victorian terraced houses.

'Mowbray Road!' the young clippie's voice sounded, bringing Rosie back to the here and now.

This was her stop. She jumped up, smiled at the conductress and stepped carefully back into the darkness of the blackout. As she hurried down the quiet, tree-lined street she passed the Sunderland Church High School, which she knew was the all-girls private school where Helen had been educated. As Rosie regarded the grand, slightly Gothic-looking building that she presumed must have at one time been the home of some town dignitary or other, the slightest wisp of resentment managed to skirt around her feelings of love and joy.

Helen was one of those women in life who just seemed to have had everything handed to her on a plate. She'd had a stable, happy home life – admittedly, Miriam was probably not the best mother anyone could wish for in the world, but Jack wasn't far off the best dad a girl could have – on top of which she had never ever done without. But most of all, in Rosie's opinion, she'd been given the greatest gift of all – a top-notch education.

As Rosie hurried across the Ryhope Road and on to a long, wide residential road called The Cloisters, which was also home to the magnificent Christ Church, Rosie started thinking about her conversation with Peter the other day. They often talked about Charlotte and she had told him about how she had found the single-sex school in Harrogate. It was one of the few state-funded boarding schools in the country, which meant that Charlotte's education was paid for by the government, but all her living expenses – her board and lodgings – were financed by Rosie. When she had found out about the school all those years ago after her mum and dad were killed, she had been over the moon. She had looked into the Sunderland Church High School, but it had been too costly, and Rosie had also felt the need for her little sister to be somewhere their uncle Raymond wouldn't easily find her, should he try.

But now, Rosie mused as she turned left into West Lawn, she didn't have to worry about anyone knowing where her sister was, and her present income far exceeded what she had been earning back then.

As she reached the front gate of Lily's and walked up the short gravel pathway, the beginnings of an idea started to form in her head. Could she bring her little sister back home to live?

All of a sudden, Rosie didn't feel so tired as she hurried up the steps.

When Rosie reached the top and got out her key, the familiar whine of the air raid siren started up, and by the time she let herself in, Rosie was just in time to hear the house mantra, which, as always, was vocalised in true Mae West fashion by Vivian.

'Come on, y'all.' Vivian's very convincing American accent was emitted in an almost growl. She stood with her hand in the air, demanding everyone's attention and beckoning them to the cellar door.

'And remember ...' She put her other hand behind her ear to show she was expecting a response.

'Keep calm ...' she repeated the house mantra.

' ... *and party on!*' the rest of the girls and their 'guests' sang out as they slowly made their way down the steep stone steps and into the extravagantly kitted-out basement-cum-air-raid-shelter.

Rosie shook off her mac and hung it up on the coat stand by the doorway, then followed everyone down to the cellar.

Lily, she noticed once her eyes had adjusted to the darkness, had added more rugs and also hung up some old oil paintings that had been gathering dust in the attic. There were also candles in every nook and cranny.

Rosie saw the slender back of Maisie as she moved from candle to candle, lighting them. She might have been full of herself since coming back from London, but she had also been eager to please, and had ingratiated herself even more with Lily by checking on La Lumière Bleue, Lily's second business. Modelled on the Parisian 'blue light' brothels, it catered for a higher class of clientele.

Within just a few minutes everyone was settled, a record had been put on the portable gramophone and the drinks cabinet opened up. Milly, more or less a permanent fixture at Lily's as both cleaner and cloakroom girl, was presently taking on the role of bartender and mixing and serving drinks on demand. Rosie wouldn't have been surprised if she was on the verge of asking Lily to become a live-in employee.

Rosie greeted Lily, who gave her the usual light kiss on both cheeks, but was distractedly looking about the room. Rosie was just about to start saying something to her when Lily huffed dramatically and walked back up the stairs.

Poking her head into the hallway, she bellowed out: 'Kate! *Ma chère. Descends!* Now!'

A few minutes later a sheepish-looking Kate came scurrying down the steps and into the cellar. As usual she made a beeline for Lily. True to form, Kate, who would never come down to the shelter empty-handed, had a piece of embroidery in her hand.

Rosie went to get herself a brandy before returning to Lily, who had now commandeered the chaise longue. She had been chatting to the Brigadier but he was now being enticed away by Vivian, who knew that Lily's patience was limited at times like this. She didn't like to be stuck talking to clients for too long, especially the Brigadier, who was what Vivian deemed a 'sweetie' but had the annoying habit of spitting when he talked.

'Lily.' Rosie sat down on the chaise longue. 'You all right?' she asked.

'*Oui, oui, ma chère*, I'm good. Just been a bit of a day of it. We haven't had an air raid for weeks now – it lures you into a false sense of security, doesn't it? You forget what a disruption they are. Never mind. Shouldn't complain. There are worse things.'

Lily put her hands up to check that her oversized updo was still more up than down. Satisfied, she clasped her hands together. She looked at Rosie, who she could tell wanted to say something. Lily had known Rosie long enough now to know what she was thinking before Rosie herself did.

'Well,' Rosie began, 'I've been wanting to chat to you – now that things have calmed down a bit.'

Lily gave a sharp gasp. 'Calm! It certainly doesn't feel like that. I'm being run ragged at the moment! I've had so much catching up to do since that unexpected week off we had!' Seeing the instant look of guilt on Rosie's face, Lily squeezed her hand.

'*That* week,' she added, 'was actually quite nice in a strange kind of way. No work, just enjoying every day as it came.'

'Mm.' Rosie wasn't remembering it quite through such rose-tinted glasses. 'Like living every day as though it was your last, more like.'

Lily gently slapped Rosie's hand before reaching for her Gauloises.

'Remember, no smoking in the cellar!' George's voice warned as he made his way down the length of their underground sanctuary.

'Force of habit,' Lily said, putting the packet back down.

George came and sat next to Lily.

'So, then,' Lily asked, 'what is it you wanted to chat to me about?'

'Well,' Rosie said, 'you know before the "mass panic"?' That had become Rosie's way of referring to the night they'd had to shut up shop for fear of being raided by the police.

'You mean,' Lily said somewhat harshly, 'when your copper "friend" found himself in – what did he call it? That "untenable" situation? – and couldn't quite decide whether to grass us up or not?'

Lily might have forgiven Rosie for landing them in it, but her charity had not stretched as far as Peter, and she still couldn't bring herself to absolve him for putting Rosie and the rest of the girls through a week of hell while he made up his mind whether to lock them all up.

'Yes,' Rosie said through pursed lips. Lately, whenever she chatted to Lily she felt her bubble of love and happiness start to deflate.

'Before then,' she continued, 'we had started to talk about the possibility of legitimising the business, hadn't we?'

'Mm,' Lily said. George had leant forward a little to hear what Rosie had to say as she had dropped her voice in order to keep their conversation private.

'Well, I was wondering, because of everything that has happened, whether we should start looking at that seriously?'

Both Lily and George guessed that this wasn't just a casual question. And they were right, Rosie *had* been giving it an awful lot of thought. From the moment she knew that Peter had found out about the business – the very illegal business she was involved in – she had been thinking of ways in which they could somehow become legitimate.

When she had been under the threat of exposure – and of imprisonment – after Peter had rumbled her 'other life', Rosie had vowed that if she managed to keep her liberty, then no one – especially not a man – would ever be able to have such control over her ever again. Her uncle Raymond had managed to screw her into such a tight vice she'd hardly been able to move; then Peter had come along, and although he was by no means in any way comparable to her uncle, her future had, for a while at least, been dependent on what he decided to do or not do. She knew now that Peter would never use her life at Lily's against her, but what had happened these past few weeks had stoked her desire to make her life as normal and as legal as possible.

'Well,' Lily began. She seemed unexpectedly at a loss for words. 'Yes, we can certainly start looking into that. I suppose it's been so hectic lately, I haven't really given it much thought.'

Lily looked at Rosie's expectant face. She looked as though she was on a different planet – a happy one – and Lily didn't want to spoil it for her. Rosie had had enough awfulness in the past without Lily dragging her back down to earth, much as she might want to.

'Yes.' Lily looked at George, who was wearing a blank expression on his face, making it impossible to know what he was really thinking. 'We'll definitely get our thinking caps on, won't we, George?'

Rosie looked at them and smiled. 'Thank you. Both of you!'

The excitement in her voice was painful for Lily and George to hear, but they beamed back at her.

'In the meantime, though, you just concentrate on those ledgers of yours. Business is booming at the moment, so you just keep us right with all those balance sheets and whatnots of yours,' Lily added.

Rosie gave them both a hug, which took them by surprise.

'We just need this damned raid over with,' Rosie said, but with no trace of real annoyance in her voice. 'Next time I'm going to do a Kate.' She flashed a look over at her old friend, now sitting in the corner hunched over her sewing, squinting to see what she was doing by the meagre light of the candle burning next to her.

As Rosie meandered over to chat to Milly, and when she was safely out of earshot, George whispered to Lily, 'Darling, I feel awful. I feel like some deceitful old scoundrel.' His voice sounded so down and dejected.

Lily looked at him and picked up her packet of Gauloises again and started rotating it in her hand.

'Don't be silly, George!' she reprimanded him, but she too looked guilty.

'We should have just come straight out and said it.' George leant in again to speak into Lily's ear. 'I feel like we're stringing her along.'

'It would have been unwise to say anything to Rosie at the moment,' Lily said, forcing a smile on to her face so that if anyone was looking at the pair of them they would think they were having a perfectly harmless, light-hearted conversation. 'She's flying high as a kite due to that bleedin' copper of hers.' Lily took a deep breath. 'I hate to say it—'

George immediately butted in and finished her sentence off for her: '—but you don't trust him as far as you can throw him.'

George had lost count of the number of times that Lily had told him this over the past couple of weeks since Rosie had coyly admitted that she and Peter were together, and quite clearly lovers at that. Neither of them had ever seen Rosie even a little in love, never mind totally and utterly head over heels.

'Bloody typical of Rosie,' Lily lamented. 'She never as much as goes on a bleedin' date – ever in all the time I've known her and I've known that girl since she was sixteen – and now, aged... how old is she? Twenty-two? ... *now* she decides to fall madly in love. And with a copper! And not just some lowly boy in blue, *but a bloody detective.*'

As George looked at the woman he loved and whom he hoped to marry sooner rather than later, he realised she was right in not being entirely forthcoming with Rosie. He just hated not being upfront and truthful with anyone – let alone Rosie.

'We have to keep our heads well and truly screwed on,' Lily said quietly, still making sure she had a wide smile on her face, 'as Rosie is very obviously losing hers to Detective Sergeant Whiter-than-White.'

She took George's hand. 'You and me both know there is no way we can go legit. Not completely. Not with the bordello. It's impossible. And if Rosie was thinking straight, which she plainly isn't, she would see that too. Yes, we might be able to make the Gentlemen's Club a bona fide, above-board business – but the bordello? Never. It doesn't matter how we dress it up, it's always going to be what it is

'... Gawd, I need a fag,' Lily muttered, looking at her packet of cigarettes.

'I think,' George said, 'we will have to explain to Rosie that when we originally talked about going legitimate, it was more to do with the Gentlemen's Club, and that we'd not really meant the bordello. The bordello will actually be keeping the club afloat until it gets going and becomes self-sufficient, which is going to take time.'

'I know,' Lily said. 'I wish we'd never breathed a word about it. Besides, this is the only business I know, and Rosie may hate to admit it, but the same's true for her too.'

As Lily and George chatted on the Regency settee, Rosie was standing next to Milly, nursing a brandy and looking around her. The faces she caught in the flickering candle-light were either deep in conversation or animated with laughter. Rosie thought how wonderful it would be to make all of this legal. She had no idea how, but she was sure Lily and George would find a way. George had his friend Rupert who was a lawyer. Surely he could work something out?

She and Peter had never once discussed the bordello. It was about the only subject they had not talked about, but she started to imagine how she would tell him that her 'other life' was now totally legal. That she was a proper businesswoman. An accepted part of society.

And there was another huge advantage in going legit – with nothing to hide, she could bring Charlotte back home for good.

Chapter Eighteen

Friday 19 December 1941

Vinnie sat up in bed, lit a cigarette and gave it to Sarah before pulling out another and lighting one for himself. He put the heavy glass ashtray on top of the bedspread between them. Sarah looked at Vinnie in surprise. He wasn't normally so considerate. Especially first thing in the morning. He'd even been unusually considerate during their lovemaking last night.

Sarah inhaled on her cigarette, then blew out a long stream of smoke and felt happy. Happier than she had done for a while now. Perhaps things were finally starting to settle down.

It wasn't far off a month since the christening fiasco, and since then Vinnie had rarely mentioned Gloria or the baby. Perhaps Vinnie's stopover courtesy of the Sunderland Borough Police had instilled some sense into him, and made him get over this obsession with Gloria and the bab.

'Let's do something nice today, eh?' Vinnie asked, tapping his cigarette on the side of the ashtray and taking another drag. 'It's not very often we have a day off together. And it's nearly Christmas. Might as well make the most of it, what do you reckon?'

Sarah looked at Vinnie with complete surprise for the second time in as many minutes. Things really were looking up.

'Ah, I'd love to, Vin,' Sarah said. 'What do you reckon? A trip into town and maybe a drink in the Londonderry for a change?'

'Sounds good to me!' Vinnie stubbed out his cigarette and swung his legs out of bed. 'Bloody hell! It's brass monkeys!' he said as he hurried to put his clothes on.

'I'll get a nice pot of char on the go,' Sarah said, getting out of the bed and pulling an old woollen cardigan around her before padding into the kitchen. 'And I think we'll treat ourselves to a fry-up this morning.'

This was going to be a good day. It wasn't very often she got into town of late. She might even persuade Vinnie to go to the flicks after they'd been to the Londonderry – perhaps even treat themselves to some fish and chips on the way home.

Vinnie and Sarah finally made it out of the flat at eleven o'clock and by the time they got the bus into the town centre it was gone half past.

'I've got an even better idea,' Vinnie said as they got off at the Park Lane depot. 'Why don't we head down to Hendon for a change?'

Sarah looked at Vinnie.

'Ah, it's a bit of a walk, Vin?' she said, trying to keep the disappointment out of her voice. She didn't want anything to spoil today, but still, she'd had her heart set on going to Jacky White's market, maybe even picking up some cheap Christmas presents, and then over to Joplings – even if she couldn't afford anything, she could at least window-shop.

'Come on, yer lazy cow.' Vinnie gave Sarah a playful shove. 'Let's do something different. Anyways, the girls at work are always saying that there's some great shops along the Hendon Road – and some even better pubs.'

Sarah could tell that Vinnie had made his mind up and that it didn't matter what she said, they were going to the town's east end. Seeing Vinnie check his watch, she assumed he was thinking about opening times.

'All right, you win,' she said, forcing herself to sound more enthusiastic than she felt.

'Come on then.' Vinnie grabbed Sarah's hand as he hurried down Holmeside. 'Look, there's a tram,' he said, grabbing Sarah by the arm and pulling her along a little too forcefully. She was struggling to keep up due to her three-inch heels and her gas mask, which was bobbing about annoyingly by her side.

'God, Vinnie, what's the dash? The shops aren't gonna shut anytime soon,' she said as they jumped on-board the wooden platform of the number 7 tram just as it was starting to pull away. 'And neither are the pubs,' she added, trying to sound jokey.

The tram was more or less full but there was one seat free, which Vinnie gave to Sarah.

As they trundled down the road, Sarah looked out the window and saw the bomb site where Binns, the town's top department store, had once stood. She'd loved that shop as a young girl, loved walking around it and gawping at all the elegant clothes and posh pieces of furniture. It was a peephole into how the other half lived.

A few minutes later they were getting off at the top of Tatham Street. It was busy today. It was just six days before Christmas and although few people had any money, and there wasn't even that much in the shops, the entire town seemed buzzing with anticipation. Perhaps that was what she was picking up from Vinnie. He seemed buoyed up and excited.

'I tell yer what,' Vinnie said, rubbing his hands to keep them warm. It might have been a clear day and the sun was out, but it was still bitterly cold. 'There's a really nice little pub two minutes from here. Why don't we go for a little snifter, bolster me up before you drag me round all the shops?'

Sarah squinted down the road, which was busy with trams and bicycles. The pavements were spilling over with shoppers, old women wrapped in shawls and mothers with their children. Halfway down the street Sarah could see a sign for 'Vaux's Maxim Ale' painted in huge letters on the side of a pub.

'What, that one on the corner ?' Sarah asked.

'Nah, it's a bit further down, follow me.' And once again Sarah found herself being pulled along a little too force- fully. After dodging a few prams and old fishwives selling their wares from large wicker baskets, they arrived outside the pub.

'Here we are,' Vinnie declared. 'The Tatham Arms … After you.' He swung his hand forward as if he were the epitome of a true gentleman, allowing his lady to go first.

As Sarah stepped over the pub's threshold, she didn't see Vinnie checking out a house just across the road – a Victorian three-storey, mid-terrace home that had a gleaming white front doorstep and a polished brass plaque bearing the number 34.

'What can I get ya, pet?'

Sarah was standing at the bar, which was still fairly quiet as it had just gone midday, although a few men were hurrying in, heralding the start of the Saturday-afternoon rush.

'I'll have a pint of Vaux for his lordship.' Sarah glanced over at Vinnie, who had gone straight to the table by the window and seemed engrossed by what was happening in the street outside. 'And I'll have a port and lemon, ta.'

Sarah observed the barmaid and thought that she looked like a woman you didn't get on the bad side of. Probably had to be tough working here. It wasn't exactly a dive, but it wasn't the Grand either.

As usual, Sarah paid for the drinks and took them over to Vinnie, who still had his eyes glued to the window.

Why was she getting the feeling that there was more to this day out than Vinnie was letting on?

'Here's yer pint,' Sarah said, staring at Vinnie's profile. 'Did yer want me to put it to yer lips fer fear of yer missing the action?' Sarah tried to sound funny, but her voice had an edge to it that she hadn't been able to disguise.

Vinnie glanced back at Sarah and then down at his pint. He put his hand around the straight pint glass with the red and gold Vaux Brewery logo on the side and took a large gulp.

'Sit down, Sar. Yer making me nervous,' Vinnie said, turning his head back towards the window.

'Vin, what's going on?' Sarah demanded. Her voice came out louder than she had meant and she caught the mutton-dressed-as-lamb barmaid look over at them both. She sat down and took a sip of her drink.

'Come on, then,' Sarah leant across the table and whispered. 'What're we doing in the east end, and in a pub that's no better than any round our way?'

'All right, all right.' Vinnie spoke in hushed tones, his eyes darting between Sarah and the view outside. 'I didn't want to tell ya before we left, 'cos I knew you'd play war.' His voice was low and had a rare hint of meekness. 'But I've got a favour to ask.'

He looked at Sarah's puzzled face as she took a drink of her port.

'It's about the bab,' he said a little sheepishly. 'I've got to see her.'

'*Ah, please, Vin!* Not this again!' Sarah let out a loud lament. She'd been kidding herself to think that just because Vinnie hadn't mentioned the baby in a good while, it was a sign he'd put the whole debacle behind him.

Sensing the barmaid and a few of the regulars were looking over at them again, Sarah glared back and snapped. 'You all had a good enough look?'

Sarah saw a big fella who must have been the landlord grab the barmaid's skinny arm as she made to come over to them.

Vinnie realised they were creating unwanted attention and glowered at Sarah.

'For God's sake, Sar, keep yer knickers on.' He looked out the window.

A few seconds later he jumped up out of his seat.

'Come on!' he demanded.

'I've not finished my drink!' Sarah was angry, but kept her voice low. She'd seen how the barmaid had been keen to have a word and she didn't fancy her chances if anything kicked off.

'Neck it down,' Vinnie told her, before pouring the rest of his pint down his own, swallowing it in two large glugs.

They both put their empty glasses down on the small wooden table and made for the saloon door that led out into the long hallway. As Vinnie reached the pub's main entrance, he turned to Sarah.

'Just follow my lead.' He squeezed her hand. 'I'll never ask you for anything else again if you can just do this one thing for me.'

Sarah knew this was as close to a plea as Vinnie would ever make and that she couldn't turn him down, although God only knew what he was up to.

As they stepped back onto the street, Sarah saw a pretty young blonde woman manoeuvring a big Silver Cross pram from the doorway of a house just across the road. The woman checked on the baby before heading along the street in the direction of town.

And that's when Sarah realised what was really going on.

As she looked at the back of the woman now walking away from them, she would bet what little money she had that nestled up in that pram was a little baby girl called Hope.

On seeing the man leave with the gobby woman in the skirt that was too short and a pair of heels that made her legs appear even longer than they already were, Pearl hurried from behind the bar and over to where the couple had been sitting. She nudged one of her regulars out of the way in order to get right up close to the window.

Bill had gone down to the cellar to change a barrel and the pub was starting to fill up fast. There were now customers waiting at the bar.

'Come on, Pearl!' one of them shouted out good-naturedly. 'Has a man got to die of thirst before he gets a drink round here?'

Pearl stood stock-still as she kept her sight on the middle-aged bloke with thinning hair and the beginnings of a bald patch, and his bit of stuff that looked like a right tart, as they hurried across the road. Something wasn't right about the pair.

'Hold yer horses, Georgie,' Pearl shouted back, but kept her eyes looking straight ahead.

She stared at the couple as they started to cross the road.

Then she saw Bel taking Hope out in her pram.

For a split second Pearl felt a wave of panic. The man and woman looked like they were headed straight for her Isabelle and the baby. Something told her to run out of the pub and shout a warning to her daughter, but just as she started to move, the man and woman veered to the left and started hurrying off in the opposite direction.

What's up with ya, ya daft mare! Pearl reprimanded herself. *Yer going loopy in yer old age.*

'I'm coming!' Pearl shouted out to her impatient regulars. 'I think yer barmaid needs a little tipple to keep her on an even keel this afternoon.'

Vinnie looked behind one last time to see Bel steer the pram left into Murton Street.

'Come on, then!' Vinnie said. 'We're gonna have to run if we want to catch her.'

'Run?' Sarah was now shouting. She'd practically knocked her port back in one and it had gone straight to her head. 'Have you tried running in heels like these?'

'This way.' Vinnie pulled Sarah immediately right so that they were hurrying up Maeburn Street. It was quieter than Tatham Street, so they weren't slowed down by pedestrians or gaggles of old women taking up the pavement as they stood idly chatting.

'Why are we going in the opposite direction?' Sarah asked as she felt Vinnie pull her right again and onto Northcote Avenue, hurrying straight across the road and up Winifred Terrace. The street was pretty much deserted, apart from a few children playing out on the street or sitting on their front doorstep.

Vinnie didn't answer. He looked like a man possessed.

When they turned right into Laura Street, Sarah worked it out. They were doing what amounted to a sprint around the block so as to meet the young woman and Gloria's baby head-on.

'What yer gonna do when we meet them?' Sarah rasped. She was struggling to get her breath.

Vinnie slowed down.

'Not me. *You!*' Vinnie said. 'You're gonna act yer socks off 'n' coo over the baby like you women always do. And then yer gonna somehow get hold of her 'n let me have a good look.'

Sarah opened her mouth to voice her objection – *you couldn't just lift someone else's baby out of a pram, for God's sake!*

But before she had a chance to say what she was thinking, they turned the corner onto Murton Street and ran slap bang straight into the pram.

Vinnie nearly landed on top of it and would have risked crushing the baby had the grey canvas hood of the pram not been up.

The sudden clash caused a long wail to start up.

'Oh my goodness!' Sarah said. 'I'm so sorry!' The shock of crashing into Gloria's babysitter was genuine, as were her words of apology.

Bel stared at the couple in front of her, who were now blocking the pavement.

Hope was screaming her head off and Bel looked into the pram to see a reddening, scrunched-up face peeking out of her little bed. She reached in to pick her up.

'No need for an air raid siren when this little one decides to exercise her lungs.' She sounded jocular, but was actually trying to keep under wraps her annoyance that they had set Hope off.

'I'm sorry, pet,' Vinnie said.

Bel looked up at the man and felt an instant dislike.

'Don't worry,' she said, a little harshly. 'Don't let me stop you getting on your way,' she added, jiggling baby Hope around as she spoke. Thankfully her cries were starting to die down.

'Oh,' Sarah said, stepping nearer and craning her neck to have a better look at the babe in arms. 'She's adorable, isn't she?' Sarah looked at Bel and then at Vinnie, who was staring at the baby unashamedly.

'And what beautiful blue eyes she's got.' Sarah went to touch the baby's cheek, now wet with tears. Bel got a whiff of alcohol and moved to the side.

'What's her name, then?' Sarah kept on, putting on her poshest voice. She could tell the woman was feeling uncomfortable and that their time was running out.

'Hope.' Bel reluctantly gave up the baby's name, adding, 'I'm sorry, I don't mean to be rude, but I'm in a bit of a dash.' She leant forward to put Hope back into her pram and as she did so the baby's little white hat came off, revealing a mop of jet-black hair.

Vinnie bent down, quick as a flash, to retrieve it, but rather than give it back to Bel, he fumbled to put it back onto the baby's head, causing Hope to start crying again.

Vinnie stared at the child. He took in her sea blue-grey eyes and her shock of black hair. Vinnie's own eyes scoured the baby's delicate features – and it was then he knew that the child was not his.

'Don't worry,' Bel said, panicking a little and snatching back the hat. She could smell beer and fags on him as well. 'I'll get her moving and she'll calm down.' She gripped the handlebar of the pram and pushed it forward, almost ramming it into Vinnie and Sarah. They had no choice but to move out the way.

'Oh, sorry,' Bel said, but it was obvious she wasn't at all apologetic as she pushed the pram determinedly past them both, banging it down the pavement and hurrying across the narrow residential road and along Laura Street. She only started to breathe properly when she had Toward Road and the Winter Gardens in her sight.

She cast a look back and saw the couple staring at her as she and Hope made good their escape.

*

Vinnie and Sarah stood watching Bel's back as she hurried away. It wasn't until she disappeared from view, merging with the crowds on the busy main road, that they turned to each other.

'Well! That's a turn-up for the books! Isn't it?' Sarah said, trying hard not to sound as happy as she felt. This was better than she could have wished for. It was well worth being dragged to the east end, having to more or less down her drink in one and then sprint around the block in her high heels.

'There's no way that bairn's yours!' she said. Vinnie's face was a mix of shock and confusion. 'I mean, that thick black hair! And those big blue eyes!' Sarah looked at Vinnie with his thinning, tawny-coloured hair and his brown eyes.

'What colour eyes has Gloria got?' Sarah asked. She was starting to feel excited. This could mean the end of this whole bloody baby saga. Once and for all.

'Brown,' Vinnie said.

'Well, brown and brown do not make blue!' Sarah declared. 'That hair!' she gushed. She had been genuinely taken aback by how stunning Hope was. Sarah wasn't normally one to slaver over babies, and she certainly didn't think all babies were adorable little cherubs, but this baby was really quite beautiful.

Vinnie was nodding in agreement, but still looked shell-shocked. In his mind's eye he could see his two sons, Gordon and Bobby, as babies. Bald as coots, the pair of them. Thickset, like little boxers, they were. And deep brown eyes. Just like his own.

'Actually, if the babysitter hadn't said her name, I would have thought we'd got the wrong baby.' Sarah spoke her thoughts aloud.

'Aye,' Vinnie agreed.

'Come on,' Sarah cajoled. 'I think this calls for a celebratory drink. The Burton is just a few minutes away.'

They started walking, Sarah's mind replaying the unexpected turn of events.

'So, how did yer know where the bab was?' she asked.

Vinnie gave his one-word answer: 'Muriel.'

Sarah nodded, knowing that Muriel worked in the canteen at Thompson's and that her best mate, Elsie, worked with Vinnie in the ropery. Sarah had commented in the past that it was like the pair of them were in some kind of competition to be the town's number-one gossipmonger.

'And how did you know the childminder would be out with the bab this afternoon?' she asked, intrigued that Vinnie seemed to have orchestrated the whole accidental meeting with such precision.

'Apparently she's as regular as clockwork. Goes up to town the same time every day,' Vinnie said. His voice was expressionless and his eyes were still staring straight ahead as though he was in a different world.

'You all right, Vinnie?' Sarah asked. She gave him a sidelong glance as they turned right onto Toward Road. 'Yer look a million miles away. I've never heard yer so quiet.'

'Aye, aye, I'm all right. Nothing that a drink won't sort out.' Vinnie said the words through habit rather than with any real meaning.

Sarah's mind started galloping ahead. 'And this also means,' she said excitedly, 'yer won't have to pay a penny towards it. Not if it's not yours.'

Vinnie nodded, but didn't say anything.

'So, you were right,' he said at last.

'What do yer mean?' Sarah asked as they hurried right onto Borough Road. She could see the Burton House pub. In a few minutes they'd be enjoying a drink and thinking about their future. One without Gloria and the baby in it.

And with the divorce under way, they could start planning their wedding.

'When you said that night that Hope mightn't be mine,' Vinnie said. His voice sounded uncannily calm. Neither of them had really believed Gloria would ever be unfaithful, never mind have another man's child. The only reason Sarah had tried to put doubts into Vinnie's head was to get him to drop his obsession with the child.

How wrong they had both been. Gloria had *been off the side!*

'That's why she never wanted me to see the bab,' Vinnie said, but his words were drowned out by a passing tram.

'What's that, Vin?' Sarah was aware Vinnie had said something but not sure what. 'Tell us when we get inside,' she added as they reached the pub.

Once they were through the door, Sarah went straight to the bar and ordered a pint of bitter and a brandy. This time she had no resentment about paying for the drinks. She'd be happy to spend what money she had in her purse today. It was worth it. And besides, once all of this was done with, she would sit Vinnie down and they could talk about their future together, including their finances. This was a clean sheet. After what they had found out today, they could start afresh. No Gloria and no baby hanging on, ruining everything for them both.

'Get this down yer,' Sarah said, as she put their drinks on a table near the back of the bar.

Vinnie looked at Sarah and smiled. 'Ta, pet,' he said, putting his hands round the glass of frothy beer and taking a big mouthful.

'I'll be back in a jiffy,' Sarah said. 'I just need to go to the little girls' room and freshen up.'

As she walked away she smoothed down her short skirt, knowing that Vinnie always liked to watch her and have a cheeky gawp at her backside. Today, though, if she had glanced behind she would have seen that Vinnie's eyes were focused purely on his pint and that her bottom was the last thing on his mind.

A few minutes later, after Sarah had spruced herself up, tidied her hair and redone her lipstick, she strutted out of the ladies. Halfway across the busy bar, though, she stopped in her tracks. The table Vinnie had been sitting at was empty. She looked around but he was nowhere to be seen. She looked back at the table and saw her brandy was still there, untouched. Next to it stood Vinnie's pint glass. It had been drained.

Sarah looked around again, in case she had missed him and he was waiting to be served at the bar, but there was no sign of him.

She went to sit down at the table and took a sip of her brandy, thinking that perhaps Vinnie had gone to the gents, but after a few minutes and a few more sips, it was clear he wasn't answering a call of nature.

When there was still no sign of Vinnie fifteen minutes later, Sarah realised he'd gone.

He'd just up and left.

Sarah's heart sank.

This did not bode well.

Chapter Nineteen

As Gloria hurried back to the yard at five minutes to one, she knew she was cutting it fine. She and Jack had lost track of time today. Instead of staying within the confines of St Peter's porch, they had enjoyed a stroll around the cemetery. It had been a risk worth taking, though, as there hadn't been anyone else in the grounds of the church.

As Gloria hurried towards the main gates with a few other stragglers who, like her, were pushing it to be in time for the one o'clock horn, she smiled at Alfie, the young timekeeper. Gloria breathed in the icy air and blew out a stream of vapour, but the cold didn't bother her today. The weather never bothered her after she'd been with Jack. She always felt so happy whenever they managed to snatch some time together – happy that Jack was alive, that they had been reunited – and so very happy that the love they had shared before Jack had lost his memory was also very much alive.

Gloria decided to make a quick detour to the women's toilet just along from the main entrance when all of a sudden she felt a thump on her back as if someone had just tripped up behind her and pushed her. She felt her body fly forward with such force that she ended up landing on all fours. Feeling an instant sting on her hands and her knees, she knew she'd grazed them badly.

As she was finding her feet again, Gloria felt a pair of hands lift her up by the back of her overalls.

At first, she thought that the person who had rammed into her was simply helping her up, but when she felt herself being spun to the right and propelled forward again, she knew that wasn't the case.

Stumbling into a little side alley that ran along the side of the timekeeper's cabin, she clattered into a line of bicycles.

Finding her feet again, she managed to turn her body around slightly.

As she did so she came face to face with her assailant.

She shouldn't have been surprised when she saw Vinnie's distorted, snarling face just inches from her own.

'She's not mine, is she?!'

Gloria felt Vinnie's spittle hit her face, and she automatically went to wipe it off. As she did so, he smacked her hand away.

'Am I right?'

He paused before raising his voice.

'Am I?'

Vinnie towered over her, his shoulders hunched up and his hands by his sides, his fists in tight balls.

Gloria forced herself to stand tall. Not to back down. She knew what was coming. Should have expected it really. Now it was time to face the music. And this time she wasn't going to shy away. This time there was no baby in her belly to protect so she wasn't going to be doing any kind of cowering.

Gloria took a deep breath.

'No, Vinnie, she's not!' Her words were spoken with defiance, yet she could feel her body starting to shake with fear.

The moment had arrived. The moment she had kidded herself could be put off. The moment she had fooled herself could be dealt with in some way that would not lead to any kind of upset or harm.

Somewhere inside of her she let go of the fear.

And for the first time, she didn't care any more.

Let him do what the hell he wanted!

But before he did, she was damned well going to have her say.

'And you know what, Vinnie?' Gloria spoke the words calmly, as if she was genuinely asking a question.

Vinnie looked at her. A slight expression of confusion showed on his red, twisted face.

'There is not one day – no, not one hour, not one minute of every day – that I don't thank God that that gorgeous, perfect little girl is not yours.'

Gloria just managed to get the last word out before she felt a jarring thud across the bridge of her nose and everything went black.

Chapter Twenty

The afternoon shift had just started and Helen was eager to go and see her father over at Crown's. She needed some advice on an area of production that she didn't feel all that confident about, but it was also an excuse to go and see him and have a cup of tea and a chat. Nowadays, that was about the only chance she got to see her father, never mind spend any time with him. Every evening her mother dominated him – from the moment he got in from work to the minute they went to bed.

Helen thought of her mum, and as much as she hated her at times, she had to hand it to her – she was a clever woman. She had ditched all the dinner parties for now and was playing the perfect home-loving housewife. Helen's jaw had nearly hit the ground the other night when she came in to find them tucking into one of Mrs Westley's shepherd's pies, which they were actually eating at the kitchen table!

As Helen approached the wide metal gates of Thompson's, partially shut to keep out the blustering winds that seemed to be unrelenting of late, she stopped and opened her handbag to fish out her packet of Pall Malls. As she did so, something caught the corner of her eye – some kind of movement in the bike alley. She squinted. The overhang from the timekeeper's cabin and the adjoining stockroom made it difficult to see.

She stepped forward and that was when she saw the back of a man.

He looked quite tall – and was that his hand raised in the air?

Helen stepped forward.

What was he doing?

Helen moved towards the darkness and that's when she heard the man speak. Or rather, shout – his voice was so loud she could hear it over the din and clatter of the yard.

'Yer sneaking, lying, conniving bitch!'

She heard the man's words clearly and they shocked her. What the hell was going on? Who was this man? And who was he speaking to?

'Yer slag!'

Helen took another tentative step forward. The vitriol in the man's voice frightened her.

'Trying to fob the bastard off as mine!'

She walked further into the darkness. Something – curiosity perhaps? An instinct that something was wrong, very wrong – propelled her forward.

And that's when she saw the whole sickening scene.

A man was crouching like an animal over his prey.

Each sentence he spoke was punctuated with his fist.

'Make a laughing stock of me, will ya?'

Punch.

'Thought you'd get away with it, did ya?'

Punch.

Helen felt sheer panic. Whoever was on the floor was going to get beaten to death. The man was clearly deranged.

'Stop!' she screamed out, but the man was like a runaway train. Unstoppable.

Helen looked about her. Frantic. *There!* She spotted a shovel that was propped up against the wall. Without thinking, she grabbed it.

Holding it as though it was a rounder's bat, she strode towards the man as his fist once again thudded down into the overall-clad figure curled up on the ground.

She heaved the shovel back.

And then with all her might she swung it forward.

The metal pan of the shovel wacked the madman on the side of the head and for a moment it stopped all movement. Then the man staggered a few steps to the left and smacked into the side of the prefab cabin.

Helen held her breath as she watched the man crumple to the ground. Flinging the shovel aside, she ran to the heap on the floor.

'Are you all right?' Helen's voice was shaking.

She heard a faint murmuring.

Helen knelt down. As she did so she gasped in horror. *It was a woman.* Her face was bloodied. It took a moment for Helen to recognise who it was.

'Oh my God, *Gloria!*' Helen gasped in shock. 'Are you all right?' she asked.

Gloria blinked and moved her head forward to nod.

Helen heard a noise behind her, and swung her head around, expecting more violence, but thankfully saw only Alfie's worried face hurrying towards her.

'Call for help, Alfie!' she shouted. 'Ambulance – and police.' She looked over at Vinnie.

The bastard needed locking up and the key thrown away!

Five minutes later Vinnie was being dragged out of the cycle alley by two burly drillers. His head was bobbing on his chest and his feet were trailing the ground. He was semi-conscious and letting loose the odd profanity. The two workers, who must have been nearly six feet tall, chucked him down onto a stack of wooden pallets and stood guard over him with their arms folded. Gloria was still with Helen, but she was now sitting up and being seen to by the two St John Ambulance first-aiders.

'Honestly,' Gloria said, 'I'm fine. Really I am.'

Helen was leaning against one of the parked-up bicycles, looking down at Gloria as she was checked out by the two medics. Helen ignored Gloria's reassurances and instead directed her question to the two men who were tending to her.

'How is she?'

'I can't see any serious damage,' the younger of the two said, looking up at Helen, 'but I'd feel happier if she was checked out up at the hospital, just in case.'

The older one, who had been inspecting Gloria's hands and arms, smiled reassuringly at Gloria before looking at Helen and saying, 'I think this brave lady has had a lucky escape.' He looked back at Gloria. 'Am I right in saying that you managed to protect your head with your arms?'

Gloria nodded. She couldn't really remember much, but she must have automatically curled up into a ball when she'd hit the ground. Vinnie's punches had not, thankfully, been able to hit their target, but only the shield of her arms.

'Well, I agree with you.' Helen looked at the younger medic. 'I think Gloria here should at least be given the once-over up at the hospital. Just to be on the safe side.'

As the two men got their patient to her feet, they slowly helped her walk out of the alleyway and into the back of the St John ambulance.

'*Gloria!*'

The distraught, high-pitched voice belonged to Dorothy, who was sprinting across the yard. The rest of the women welders were just behind her. They caught a glimpse of Gloria being helped into the back of the ambulance and saw her bloodied face. Dorothy pushed through a small gaggle of workers who had drifted to the scene to see what was happening.

'Oh my God.' Dorothy tried to hold back her shock and horror as she climbed into the back of the van despite objections from the two first-aiders.

'And there was me hoping for a bit peace and quiet,' Gloria said. She had just put her head down on the soft pillow on the stretcher, and had her arms resting across her stomach.

'Are you all right?' Dorothy said, amazed at her mate's capacity for backchat at such a horrendous time. She perched on the edge of a large white wooden box. The van was so small, she was practically hunched over Gloria. As she spoke she inspected her friend's face. She could see a good deal of blood, but from a cursory examination she didn't look like she'd had her nose broken, and there were no immediate swellings on her face.

'Come on, out of there,' the older medic ordered Dorothy.

Dorothy looked at Gloria, whose face suddenly became deathly serious.

'Dorothy ...' Her voice was a whisper. 'Don't tell Jack. Promise?'

Dorothy looked at her battered workmate and wondered how she could think of such a thing at a time like this.

'No worries,' she said. 'I'll keep mum,' she reassured Gloria, before reluctantly leaving the van.

As she clambered out, she was met by five worried-looking faces.

'She all right?' Martha asked.

Dorothy nodded. 'I think so.'

'Can I go with her?' Rosie asked the older St John officer. 'I'm her immediate boss. I'd like to make sure she's all right.' The man nodded, and Rosie ducked into the van.

But a few seconds later Rosie got back out of the ambulance and, peering over the women's heads, called out.

'Helen!'

No one had noticed that Helen had been standing by the side, smoking a cigarette. If anyone had looked closely they would have seen that her hands were shaking.

Helen raised her head to look at Rosie.

'Gloria wants a quick word,' Rosie explained.

As the words registered with the women welders, they glanced at each other. A question on each of their faces.

Helen chucked her cigarette and walked through the small crowd that parted to let her through. They watched as Rosie moved to the side to allow Helen to climb into the back of the ambulance.

'How're you feeling?' Helen asked. Her voice was soft and full of real concern. She had never seen such violence up close. Never seen any kind of violence in her life, really. She'd seen a few scraps between some of the workers in the yard, but that was all they were really, scuffles – a load of flailing arms, wildly thrown punches, most of which missed their target, and a lot of pushing and pulling. What she had just witnessed down the bike alley was real brutality. And it had shocked her to the core.

'I'm all right. Honestly,' Gloria reassured Helen, whose face was as white as a sheet. 'I just wanted to say thank you. Thank you for helping me. For doing what you did.'

'God!' Helen blew out air. 'I'm just so glad I passed when I did.'

Neither of them said anything, but they were both thinking that if she hadn't, Gloria would certainly not be capable of having a conversation like she was now. Vinnie had been totally out of control – more than he had ever been before. Gloria shuddered at the thought of what might have become of her had Helen not intervened.

'Right,' said Helen. She could feel herself becoming emotional and would have been mortified if anyone had seen her looking like she might be even remotely on the verge of tears. 'Best get you off to the Royal. Take as much time off as you need,' she said, climbing out of the ambulance van as daintily as she could, considering she was wearing heeled shoes and a skirt that did not have much leeway in it.

As Helen exited, Rosie jumped back in and the younger medic slammed the doors shut, hurried around the other side and got into the passenger seat. Everyone watched in silence as the ambulance drove away.

'Right, everyone back to work!' Helen forced out a voice that sounded commanding.

When her gaze fell on Vinnie, still under guard, his hand on the side of his head, a pained expression on his face, she shouted across to the two drillers.

'And I want *him* out of this yard. Now!'

The women stared as Vinnie was hauled back on to his feet and dragged out through the main gates before being chucked out like a piece of rubbish. As if timed to perfection, they then heard the sound of a police siren approaching from down the embankment.

'Come on, you lot!' It was Jimmy, the head riveter. The women looked around. 'We need a hand with this frigate that's just been hauled in. Don't think just 'cos the boss's gone you can waste the rest of the afternoon yapping to each other.'

His words might have been harsh, but they were spoken with compassion.

*

Halfway through the afternoon shift, Rosie was back.

'I'll take this lot off your hands now, Jimmy,' Rosie smiled. She had caught them on their tea break and they were all standing, looking unusually sombre, around the riveters' fire.

Jimmy laughed. 'They've been as good as gold! Send them my way whenever yer want. Especially Martha. She's been doing a bit of riveting for us this afternoon.'

Rosie opened her mouth to speak.

'But dinnit worry,' Jimmy said, 'I'm not gonna steal her from you. Unless, of course,' he looked across at Martha, who was picking up her haversack and gas mask, 'she wants to jump ship?'

'Nice try!' Martha piped up.

The banter over, they all followed Rosie back across to the dry dock to continue their work on SS *Brutus*. The noise of the shipyard was at its normal deafening level, so they were only able to catch a little of what Rosie told them, but it was enough to know that Gloria was going to be all right, although it sounded as if the doctors were going to keep her in overnight as a 'precautionary measure'.

At the end of the shift, when they could all speak without having to shout, Dorothy asked the question they were all dying to know the answer to.

'What was all that with Helen?'

'Yeh, why did she gan in the back of the ambulance?' Angie added.

'Well,' Rosie said, 'it would seem that Helen actually saved the day. Or should I say, saved Gloria.'

'How?' Martha asked, intrigued.

'From what Gloria told me, she clobbered Vinnie round the head with a shovel.'

The women all looked gobsmacked.

'And then,' Rosie continued, 'she got Alfie to get the first-aiders and call the police.'

'Blimey!' Angie said. 'Hey, Martha, looks like you've got competition in the "heroine" department.'

Angie cast a look at Dorothy, who ignored her friend and asked, 'So that's why she wanted her in the ambulance. To thank her?'

'Yes,' said Rosie, 'it would seem so. Anyway, you can hear it all from the horse's mouth yourselves this evening. You all up for a visit to the Royal?' There was agreement all round, with Martha hurrying off to tell Hannah about what had happened.

Rosie asked Polly if it would be possible for Bel and Agnes to look after Hope until Gloria was discharged. Polly replied that she was sure Bel would be over the moon to have Hope overnight, as her sister-in-law loved the little girl 'like she was her own'.

As Rosie, Polly, Dorothy and Angie made their way to the main gates, a few of the platers and riveters who knew the women welders asked after Gloria – some adding that they hoped her ex got a taste of his own medicine.

'What do you think's going to happen now?' Polly asked Rosie when they were on the ferry.

'God knows,' Rosie said. 'Gloria asked Dorothy not to say anything to Jack. She seems to think he's not going to find out about this, which is highly unlikely.'

Polly agreed. 'Yeh, gossip goes around the shipyard faster than the speed of light. It won't take long before it reaches Crown's.'

Rosie looked out at the rough, agitated waters of the Wear.

'Mm, and if he's not heard about it by now, I think there'll be more than a good chance Helen tells him when they both get back from work.'

Chapter Twenty-One

'Yer *do* think Gloria'll be all right, don't ya?' Angie asked Dorothy.

'Yes, she's as tough as old boots,' Dorothy said as they jumped on the bus that would take them from Thompson's back over to the south side. 'Remember that last beating he gave her, just before you started welding?'

Angie nodded. The image of Gloria's battered face as they sat and ate cakes after work in a little tea shop on Dundas Street would always be imprinted on her mind's eye.

'Well,' Dorothy said, as they each paid the bus conductor their fare, 'I reckon that was much worse. The only reason she got taken to the hospital was because this time it happened in public rather than behind closed doors.'

Angie looked around her to make sure there was no one she knew as they sat down in the seats at the front of the double-decker that was now trundling along Dame Dorothy Street.

'It made me think about my own mam,' she said quietly. 'Not that she's had someone else's bab, though!' Angie kept her voice low as she whispered into her friend's ear.

'What?' Dorothy hesitated. 'You mean, if your dad found out ...' She let her voice trail off.

Angie nodded.

Neither of them had said anything since the day they had spotted Angie's mother down the back lane with another man.

'My dad's not like that Vinnie, ya know,' Angie said. 'He's not as bad as he looks.'

Dorothy wasn't sure if she believed her friend or not.

'Sometimes he doesn't mean to hurt ya,' Angie continued, 'I just don't think he knows his own strength.'

Dorothy thought Angie might well be kidding herself. She had seen a few examples of Angie's dad's inability to 'know his own strength' on her friend's face when he'd cuffed her or given her a backhander.

As the bus drove across the Wearmouth Bridge, they were both automatically looking out down the river when Angie suddenly let out a loud laugh.

'God, who am I kidding! He'd go bloody ballistic and – ' Angie's voice was back to a whisper ' – God only knows what he'd do if he found out any of us weren't his! Not that any of us aren't Mam and Dad's! Well, I hope not anyway!' she added as an afterthought.

'Well,' Dorothy said, 'I think if I was your "mam", for starters I wouldn't be doing anything I shouldn't.' She dropped her voice, even though the bus was now full and everyone was immersed in their own loud chatter. 'And secondly, if I *was*, I'd make damn sure I never got found out.'

Angie nodded. 'Yeh, yer right. Luckily, my dad's not the brightest.'

As they stood up to get off at their stop, Dorothy warned: 'And if I was you and your dad ever did find out, I'd make bloody sure I didn't get caught in the crossfire.'

They walked down Fawcett Street and crossed over to Burdon Road in silence before Angie asked, 'What do ya reckon *yer* stepdad would do, if he found out yer mam was having it off with someone else? And worse still, had had another bloke's bab?'

Dorothy shrugged. 'He'd probably either pretend he didn't know and turn a blind eye, or just leave.'

Angie made a face that intimated this was far stranger than getting a beating. 'What, even though he's got four bairns with yer mam?'

Dorothy shrugged again.

As they continued to walk up the road they were silent for a short while, both immersed in their own thoughts.

'I don't think I've ever known anyone who's got a step-dad,' Angie said out of the blue.

Dorothy looked at her friend and laughed. 'I don't think I have either. Mind you,' she added thoughtfully, 'I reckon there's plenty out there. People just don't let on.'

Dorothy had never been exactly forthcoming herself about the fact that the man her mother was married to was not her biological father. And even though her step-father wasn't her most favourite person ever, when people assumed that he was her real father, she didn't correct them.

'Ya never say much about yer dad, Dor.' Angie looked at her friend. 'Yer *real* dad, I mean. Can yer remember him?'

'Bits and pieces,' Dorothy said, sounding unusually vague. 'I was only young when he left. My memory of him is a bit of a blur. He left one day and never came back. I do remember that Mum seemed happier afterwards. Like she was relieved. She used to tell people that he'd died.'

'Really?' Angie said. 'That's a bit naughty.'

'Well, I don't think she wanted the stigma of being classed as a divorcee. It's still frowned upon now, but back then it was quite scandalous.'

Angie thought for a moment before chirping up: 'Yer know, I don't think I have ever known anyone who's got divorced either.'

Dorothy looked at Angie and was going to say something but stopped herself.

'Anyway, enough about boring parents,' she said, grabbing her friend's arm, forcing them both to hurry across the Mowbray Road and on to the start of the long stretch of Ryhope Road. 'On to more important things,' she said theatrically, 'like where're we gonna go after we've seen Gloria at the hospital? Shall we see what's on at the flicks? Or do you think we should have a little drink somewhere?'

'Both!' Angie said, linking arms with her friend as they both hooted with laughter.

Chapter Twenty-Two

When Helen had raced round to Crown's just after the attack and told Jack what had happened, he'd been seized by the worst panic imaginable. He had asked Helen repeatedly if any serious harm had come to Gloria, but his daughter had reassured him that the St John Ambulance crew seemed to think she was going to be just fine. No serious or permanent damage.

Jack had seen the state his daughter was in and held back his surprise when she pulled out a packet of Pall Malls and lit up a cigarette. He'd had no idea his daughter had started smoking, but didn't say anything; instead he simply gave her a big hug and told her that he was incredibly proud of her and that she had been so brave. By the time she'd left his office, she'd looked happier and some colour had returned to her cheeks.

As soon as Jack was on his own, though, he opened his top drawer and did something he rarely ever did – he poured himself a stiff drink.

He felt the burn and with it came a cascade of thoughts and scattered memories. Disjointed memories, but as he finished his drink, pulled on his overcoat and made his way to the hospital, those memories started to become more cohesive.

Fragments of conversations between him and Gloria started to swim to the forefront of his mind: her telling him about Vinnie and their marriage – and that violence had been a constant in her life for many years.

When he arrived at the hospital and hurried up to the Observation Ward, he felt a surge of relief to see that Gloria was sitting up in bed and looked relatively unscathed.

'Are you all right?' he asked as soon as he reached the side of her bed.

'Yes, Jack, I'm fine, honestly.' Gloria spoke through the tears that had come out of nowhere on seeing the man she loved. 'I don't really need to be here,' she added. 'I really am perfectly fine.'

Jack brushed a piece of Gloria's curly brown hair away from her eye and inspected her face. It looked unmarked, which surprised him after what Helen had described of the attack.

'It looked so much worse than it was. There was a load of blood on my face from a nosebleed.'

She didn't tell Jack that the nosebleed had been caused by Vinnie headbutting her, and the damage was minimal as she'd instinctively jerked back.

Jack leant in to kiss Gloria, who kissed him back, their exchange of love gentle and slow.

Jack stood back up and looked down at Gloria.

'You *really* shouldn't be here.' Gloria's face was angled up at Jack as she reprimanded him in a whisper, although she doubted the old woman to her left and the even older woman on her right would be able to hear; the nurse had to bellow at them every time she wanted to ask them anything, or give them their medication.

The only reason Gloria wasn't shooing Jack back out straight away was because it was highly unlikely anyone else would visit her. Not only was it out of normal visiting hours, but the only people she knew who were aware of what had happened to her were the women welders, and Rosie had told her they would see her that evening.

'Wild horses weren't going to stop me,' Jack said, and he took her arm and squeezed it. As he did, Gloria flinched.

Jack glanced down to see both her arms looked red and sore. He felt his face flush with anger. At that moment, if Vinnie had been standing in front of him Jack thought he would have killed him with his bare hands.

'I swear—' he started to say and stopped himself.

'Jack,' Gloria said, seeing the murderous look on his face, 'don't even think about it. Promise me?'

Jack was silent.

Gloria saw the nurse walking towards her bed. She'd been sitting at the little desk by the entrance when Jack had come in and had stood up to reprimand him for coming outside of visiting times – it was just after five o'clock and visiting wasn't until seven – but when she saw the two embrace and the tears that had spilled down Gloria's face she'd decided to turn a blind eye for a few minutes.

'You're just about to get kicked out,' Gloria told Jack with a smile. 'Now go. You've taken enough chances already coming here like this.' But Gloria was glad he had; it had made her feel so much better than any of the painkillers she had been given.

'Yes, I'm gone!' Jack said to the young nurse now just a few yards away, who was tapping her wrist and frowning.

He turned back to Gloria and gave her a quick kiss. 'I'll see you tomorrow.'

Before Gloria had time to argue, he'd turned and disappeared through the heavy swing doors of the ward.

'No more secrets,' Jack said out loud as he hurried out of the hospital. Tomorrow, he resolved, they were going to have a serious talk. Gloria had not been entirely honest with him. He knew it was because she'd wanted to protect him, but he didn't want protecting.

It was time he knew everything – the good *and* the bad.

Chapter Twenty-Three

When Helen had gone to see her father at Crown's she had been in a bit of a state to say the least. She'd even had to have a smoke in front of him. Never before had she witnessed such savagery waged against one person, let alone a woman.

She knew there were plenty of battered wives about, but she hadn't thought about the reality of what being a 'battered wife' meant. And she had certainly never *seen* that reality with her own eyes.

And, to top it all, she herself had never before in her life committed such an act of violence. Not that she had any regrets about doing so. It had been a knee-jerk reaction. She was just relieved that the spade had been to hand, and that she'd managed to make the man she now knew was called Vinnie stop.

When her father had commended her on her bravery and had clearly been as proud as punch of her, Helen's mood of shock and upset had quickly morphed into one of joy and happiness. She had proved herself to her father. He was proud of her. She felt worthy. Validated. Loved.

It wasn't until Helen had been relating the horror of seeing Vinnie's rain of punches on Gloria and the poor woman's bloodied face that she remembered her father had once dated Gloria many moons ago. It had been the way her father kept asking if Gloria was all right – the way he said her name – that had made her recall his previous romantic history with her. How close they'd actually been back then, she had no idea. From what she had gathered, they'd just gone on a few dates before her mother had decided he was the one for her.

When she'd returned from her trip to Crown's to see her father, she'd been met by a uniformed police officer who had asked her if she would kindly give a statement as to the events of the afternoon. It seemed to have taken ages, and the young constable's handwriting was laboriously slow to say the least, but they'd got there in the end, and Helen had felt a certain amount of satisfaction that she was playing some part in bringing justice to this despicable man, who obviously thought he could walk into one of the most important shipyards in the country and try to beat a woman half to death.

It was her father's words of praise, however, and not the giving of the police statement, that were at the forefront of her mind as Helen arranged for a chauffeur-driven car to take her up to the hospital at quarter to five.

'The Royal,' Helen commandeered the elderly driver as she climbed into the back of the car.

She knew she would be visiting Gloria outside the permitted hours, but she felt as though the hospital had become her second home after the amount of time she'd spent there by her father's bedside. Also, she knew as soon as she mentioned her name and who she was – and that her grandfather was one of its main benefactors – any objections would be silenced.

The main reason she was going now, though, was because she knew that Gloria's women welders would, without doubt, be descending en masse that evening and would stay from the minute they were allowed in to the moment they were told they had to leave. There was no way she wanted to be there when they were. No way.

Helen got out a cigarette, lit it and wound down the window in the back seat of the little shiny black Austin that was now making its way over the Wearmouth Bridge. As she blew smoke out into the cold, late-afternoon air, she felt as though life really was on the up.

As they drove up the New Durham Road, Helen spotted a little florist and asked the driver to pull over. You couldn't arrive at someone's bedside empty-handed.

Five minutes later she was hurrying up the stairs to the ward on the first floor, where the young girl at reception had told her a Mrs Gloria Armstrong had been taken on arrival at the hospital.

Helen smoothed her skirt and was pleased to feel that it wasn't as tight on her as it had been. Her cigarette lunches were having the desired effect.

She could hear the sound of her heels on the shiny tiled floor of the windowless corridor and smell the now familiar odour of disinfectant as she approached the clearly signed Observation Ward.

Having a quick smell of the rather extravagant bunch of yellow chrysanthemums she had bought, she pulled open the heavy swing doors.

What Helen saw next stunned her far more than what she had been a witness to earlier on in the day.

She hadn't quite made it into the actual ward – one hand was still keeping the door partially open, the other clutching the bunch of flowers – when she stopped dead.

Her father was leaning over Gloria and *kissing her*!

And it was not a quick kiss on the cheek.

Nor was it the kiss of a friend.

No, this was most definitely a kiss exchanged between two lovers.

Helen watched, her face set in a look of sheer disbelief, as her father straightened up again.

She saw him say something to Gloria and then he touched her arm and she jerked it back in pain.

Helen's vision was then blocked by the sight of the ward nurse, who had been tending one of the other patients and was now walking slowly across the ward towards her father and Gloria, tapping her wrist.

Helen took one step back and let the swing doors close in front of her.

Taking another step back, she turned around and walked down the corridor, down the staircase to the ground floor, and out of the main entrance.

When she realised she was still clutching the bunch of chrysanthemums, she dropped them instantly, as if they were poison.

Chapter Twenty-Four

'I'm back!'

It was Polly's familiar call whenever she stepped over the threshold of her home. Her words were always met with relief by Agnes, who still worried about her daughter's safety even though she had now been working at the yard for over a year and a half. Agnes had accepted that she would never stop worrying. How could she? Not only were the yards hazardous places to work, they were now also the Luftwaffe's primary targets – the price the town paid for its revered ability to build ships. Agnes prayed this war would end soon so that Tommy would come home and he and Polly could get married and start a family – and, above all else, put an end to her daughter doing a man's job.

When Polly walked into the kitchen she found the usual mess left by Aggie's nursery being cleared up by Bel. Baby Hope was asleep in Lucille's old crib, which they had found amongst various bits and pieces they'd come across while clearing out the attic. Agnes was hanging out the laundry, helped by Lucille and the new toy rabbit she had refused to be parted from since the day Maisie had given her it at the station.

Polly looked at Bel and saw how carefully she was trying not to make a noise, and then across at Hope, who looked in a deep, blissful sleep.

'God,' Polly dropped her voice to a near whisper and sat down at the kitchen table, 'you wouldn't believe what happened today.' She carefully put her holdall and gas mask on the floor and took off her boots.

Bel looked at Polly with interest. 'Really? Looks like it's been a bit of a funny day all round.' She went over to the stove, moved the kettle back on to the hob and then checked on Hope.

'I think I'll move her into the back room so she doesn't get disturbed and wake up. I've had a hell of a day with her. She's been so upset and just won't settle. I've only just got her off.'

Bel disappeared into the little back bedroom that could probably be better described as a walk-in cupboard. It had been Polly's bedroom, but since the household reshuffle she had moved into what had been Bel's room.

'Right,' Bel bustled back into the kitchen and sat down heavily on one of the kitchen chairs, 'tell me all!'

As Polly began to relate the awful events of the day, Bel's face changed. 'That man needs to be strung up! He's not right in the head – can't be, doing that.'

'I know. I just thank God Gloria's all right. I don't think anyone can believe she got away with so few injuries.'

'Mm, she's probably got some kind of innate self-defence mechanism now, after all the years having to put up with all of this.'

Polly nodded in agreement.

'Did you get a look at him?' Bel asked.

'Who? Vinnie?'

Bel nodded.

'Actually, I did catch a quick look at him as he was being hauled out of the yard.'

'What did he look like?' Bel asked.

'Quite tall,' Polly said, thoughtfully, 'broad ...'

'What colour hair did he have?'

'Oh, he wasn't bald, but he wasn't far off either. A few wisps of light brown hair. I didn't really get a good look at his face, though.'

'I knew it!' Bel said. 'I knew there was something off about them.'

Polly looked puzzled. 'What do you mean? Who're you talking about?'

Now it was Bel's turn to regale Polly with the odd events of her day. How she'd had a strange couple bump into her as she was walking into town with Hope in the pram. There had been something about them – something not good – and they'd stunk of booze.

'Oh, they were all over Hope like a rash. I swear they would have tried to hold her if I'd let them. Normally blokes stand there bored to tears while their missus oohs and aahs, but not this one. Something inside of me told me I had to get away from them as soon as I could. I practically ran into town. Poor Hope screamed all the way.'

'Eee, honestly, Bel, I can't believe it! The man's got a screw loose. And more than one! And getting his fancy bit involved like that? She sounds just like Gloria's described her. A right hard cow. It makes sense, though – why Vinnie's realised Hope's not his. Polly started to get up.

'Right. I better get myself out of these scruffy overalls and cleaned up. I'm meeting the girls up at the hospital for visiting hours,' a look of mortification suddenly appeared on her face. 'Gosh, Bel, I'm *so* sorry – I haven't asked you if you're all right about having Hope for the night? If it's any bother I can have her in the room with me?' Polly was sincere in her offer, even though she was not the best with babies.

'Of course I don't mind.' Bel couldn't reassure her quickly enough. 'It's no bother at all. You know how I feel about Hope. Don't tell Gloria, but I sometimes feel she's half mine!'

Chapter Twenty-Five

'Mum!'

The chauffeur-driven car had just brought Helen home after she'd fled the Royal twenty minutes earlier. She was now standing in the hallway, both hands on her hips, trying to catch her breath. Her heart felt as though it was going to explode.

'Mother!' she shouted again, louder this time, making her head throb even more than it was already. She sounded desperate and her breathing was heavy, as if she couldn't quite get enough air into her lungs.

'Whatever's wrong, pet?' Mrs Westley's voice could be heard before she was seen coming out of the breakfast room where she had been polishing the silver cutlery and having a general tidy-up. She stopped dead in her tracks when she saw Helen. As always she looked stunning, in her deep olive-green tailored skirt and cream cashmere cardigan, but her face told another story. The poor girl looked in bits. She had rivulets of watery black tears spilling down her face, and she was bent forward as if she either had a stitch or was about to throw up.

'Come here,' Mrs Westley said, automatically going to Helen and putting her arms around her. The cook had been with the family since Helen was a baby, and although Mrs Crawford had always stressed there should be no fraternising with the 'help', Helen had spent much of her childhood when she wasn't at school at the kitchen table, doodling or chatting away to Mrs Westley as she baked, cooked and cleaned.

As the cook felt Helen's whole body juddering, letting loose great, heaving sobs, she was genuinely worried. She had never seen 'young Helen', as she called her, so upset. So heartbroken. If Helen had been courting, she would have presumed it was 'boy trouble', but Mrs Westley knew that wasn't the case. There were only two loves in her life – her father and the shipyard.

'There, there, pet.' She gave Helen a gentle cuddle. 'Whatever it is, it can't be that bad.'

Her words only seemed to make Helen cry more, though. 'It *is* "that bad",' she mumbled into the starched cotton fabric of Mrs Westley's apron top.

'Whatever it is,' Mrs Westley said, 'it'll come out with the wash. It always does.' They were words of reassurance she still offered up to her own children, even though they were now adults.

Standing there, in the wide, grandiose hallway, feeling Helen's arms wrapped round her girth so tightly it was as if she was afraid she would collapse if she let go, the cook was taken aback by just how distraught Helen was. Helen might have been brought up with a silver spoon in her mouth and been spoilt rotten, but she'd never been a 'cry baby'.

Mrs Westley continued to cuddle her charge and mutter reassurances that all would turn out all right, but it was as though the more comfort she gave, the more overwrought Helen became. Even if she had wanted to tell the cook what it was that was causing her so much grief, her words would have been incomprehensible.

'Come on, petal,' she said, bending down and talking to the top of Helen's head. 'Let's go and sit down in the kitchen and get you a nice cuppa.' She gave her a big squeeze and rubbed her back. 'I've just taken a batch of your favourite gingerbread biscuits out of the oven.'

Hearing the large front-porch door slam shut, Mrs Westley turned to see Miriam walking into the hallway.

'Helen!' Miriam's voice was high-pitched and full of reproof at seeing her daughter sobbing in Mrs Westley's arms. 'What *are* you doing?! Pull yourself together. That's no way to be going on!' Miriam poured scorn on her daughter. 'And stand up straight!'

Helen did as she was told while Miriam put her handbag and gas mask down on the little oval-shaped console and quickly checked herself in the mirror hanging above it. She turned away from her reflection and her eyes narrowed as she looked at her daughter. Miriam couldn't believe what she had come back to. She'd just had a lovely afternoon at the Grand with her best friend, Amelia. They had allowed themselves a little afternoon tipple and taken a few nibbles out of some salmon and cucumber sandwiches, but the highlight of their little tête-à-tête had been the attention they'd received from some of the Admiralty billeted at the hotel. It had made up for all the wretched pies and puddings she was having to pretend to enjoy eating in the kitchen with Jack of an evening. Now, though, it looked like her perfectly good mood was about to be ruined. What an embarrassment to see her daughter in such a state. It was a good job it was just Mrs Westley who was witness to Helen's hysterics.

'Thank you, Mrs Westley. I'll take it from here.' Miriam made it clear that the cook should make herself scarce. 'Helen,' she glowered at her daughter, 'I'll speak to you in the dining room.'

As Helen looked at her mother she wished more than anything in the world she could run to her and seek solace. But hearing her mother's clipped words and the disapproval written all across her face, she knew no kind of comfort would be forthcoming. It never had been. Nor likely ever would be.

Helen had accepted many years ago that her mum would never be like other mothers she knew. She had learnt as she had grown older that she existed purely to boost her mother's standing in society, so that she could bask in a kind of reflected glory. If Helen was beautiful, or successful, or made a good marriage, it was her mother who was revered.

Helen walked past her mother, wiping the tears from her face.

Miriam followed her daughter into the large dining room and went straight for the mahogany drinks cabinet. 'What the hell's the matter with you?' she snapped as she sloshed a good measure of gin into her crystal tumbler, adding just a splash of tonic.

Helen pulled out one of the heavy upright oak chairs that were positioned around the dining table in the centre of the room and slumped into it. The shock of what she had seen – the gravity of the terrible secret just revealed to her at the Royal – had sapped all the energy from her. Helen opened her mouth to speak, but nothing came out. Instead, she just looked at her mother.

'For goodness' sake, Helen!' Miriam stood upright, drink in hand, staring at her daughter. 'Stop looking so gormless and spit it out,' she barked. 'What on earth's the matter?'

She had never seen her daughter so upset. Helen was no softie. She'd taught her as a child that tears would never get her anywhere. Even when Tommy Watts had proposed to that common welder girl, she had not been *this* upset. Angry, perhaps. Frustrated at not getting what she wanted. But there had not been any tears.

Miriam had a rare stab of concern. 'No one we know has died? Have they?'

What else would affect her daughter so much?

'It's Dad,' Helen said simply, still staring straight ahead into space, her mind replaying the heinous scene she had witnessed just half an hour previously. Her brain was still taking its time to process not only what she had seen at the hospital, but the far-reaching implications of what she had unknowingly stumbled across.

'What do you mean, "It's Dad"?' Now Miriam was starting to feel anxious. Logically she knew that if anything had happened to Jack in the yard she would have been the first to have been informed, or at the very least someone from Crown's would have accompanied Helen back to the house as the bearer of bad news.

Helen managed to shift her gaze so that she was now taking in the vision of her mother as she stood there just a few feet away. Her face was hard, her eyes angry, and her tone one of pure irritation. Helen watched as her mother's lips moved and her brow furrowed questioningly, but she didn't hear the words. It was as though the volume control of her life had suddenly dropped to zero. All she could hear were her own thoughts buffeting their way into her consciousness. Forcing her to accept the terrible, heartbreaking truth:

Her father was having an affair.

With Gloria.

Who had just had a baby.

A baby who had not been fathered by her husband.

Which could only mean one thing ...

Helen suddenly felt a short, sharp slap across her face. Miriam had crossed the room and struck her daughter to snap her out of her trance. She was now standing there, looking down at her.

'Stop staring like some imbecile!'

Helen's hand went to her stinging cheek. She looked up at her mother – her cold, harsh, unloving mother – and at that precise moment all the shock, sadness and heartache she was feeling were replaced by another deep hurt. A hurt that her mother could not do the one thing she had ever wanted of her. And that was to give her some love. To comfort her. To ease her pain.

It was then that the need to give back some of that hurt ploughed to the fore.

Helen looked at her mother and her eyes shone with her need for retribution. A need to strike back at this woman who stood before her.

'It's about Father.' Helen spoke the words coldly. There was not a hint of any kind of emotion.

Miriam took a slight step back, a little unnerved by both her daughter's look and the tone of her voice.

'Well, is he all right?' Miriam countered. The last thing she needed now was any more drama. The past few months had been a complete nightmare, not knowing whether Jack would live or die, or if she'd be landed with a retard of a husband for the rest of her life.

'Oh, Dad's *fine*, Mother,' Helen said. Her eyes had gone hard and were now free from any more tears. Her words were no longer laced with child-like sobs, but with a heavy dose of sarcasm.

'*More* than fine,' she added, pushing her chair back and standing up. She was taller than her mother by just an inch or so.

'Well then, why the waterworks?' Miriam demanded, puzzled now, but still a little concerned by her daughter's increasingly bizarre behaviour.

'I'll be back in a minute. And then I'll tell you everything … But if I were you, I'd get myself another drink …' she paused ' … and I'd make it a big one.'

*

228

When Helen returned to the dining room she found her mother staring at herself in the large mirror above the mantelpiece. In keeping with the blackout regulations, the lush, crimson velvet curtains had been drawn, whilst the Tiffany lamp on the side table had been switched on.

Picking up a heavy glass ashtray from the sideboard, Helen walked back to the dining table and sat down. This time her back was straight and Miriam noticed, as her daughter lit a cigarette, that she had wiped away the mascara that had smudged down her face.

'I didn't know you'd taken up smoking?' Miriam said.

As she watched Helen exhale, she thought how much smoking suited her daughter. It gave her an air of sophistication. She had tried it herself many moons ago, but it had only made her feel sick and so she had given up trying.

'Well, Mother, it would seem that there are a number of things you don't know,' Helen said, tapping the end of her cigarette into the ashtray. 'Many more things. *Far more* interesting things than me "taking up" smoking.'

Helen sat for a moment without saying anything. She had managed to pull herself together out in the hallway. She had heard Mrs Westley moving around and the clash of pans and cutlery in the kitchen, so she wasn't worried that the cook would hear what she was about to disclose to her mother.

'Spit it out then,' Miriam said, taking a slightly nervous sip of her gin and tonic. Her daughter had a disturbing look about her. She couldn't quite put her finger on it, but it made her uneasy.

'You might want to sit down, Mother,' Helen suggested. She needed to hurt her mother as much as her mother had hurt her. Helen had come here straight from the hospital and had craved nothing more than comfort. For someone to listen to her as she poured her heart out. For someone simply to be there as she let loose the onslaught of thoughts and feelings that had been spinning around inside her, making her feel dizzy and nauseous.

Her father.

An affair.

A bastard.

A sister.

Her *sister!*

But her mother, as usual, was unable, or simply didn't want, to give her only child any kind of love or understanding. As usual it had been Mrs Westley who had given her a maternal cuddle, just as it had been Mrs Westley to whom she had gone as a child when she had fallen over or hurt herself.

'I'm fine standing, Helen,' Miriam said, annoyance clearly evident in her voice. 'Just tell me what you've got to say. I'm sure my legs will be perfectly capable of supporting me, whatever this shocking news is.'

Helen took another drag and let out a plume of smoke. Well, now it was payback time. If her mother broke down, *she* would enjoy being the one to tell her to 'pick yourself up' and 'get a grip'.

'Mother ...' Helen paused. 'I'm afraid your husband – my father – has been having ... no, sorry, is *still* very much having ... *an affair.'*

Miriam looked at her daughter as if she was totally insane.

'What on earth are you talking about? Of course your father's not having any kind of affair.' She almost laughed it off as she went back to the drinks cabinet and added a touch more tonic water. She had been rather overgenerous with the gin.

'Oh, but *he is*, Mater,' Helen said, her eyes scrutinising her mother, waiting to see her reaction when she realised that what her daughter was telling her was true.

'And the reason I *know* he is having an affair is that I have seen it with my own eyes. Just today. In the last hour. Which was the reason for "the waterworks".'

Miriam put her drink on the table.

'What do you mean you saw it with your own eyes? Where? What did you see?' she demanded, her cool exterior starting to crumble.

'I saw Dad. Together with another woman. Kissing her. They were obviously very much in love. It was rather touching actually.' Helen had to force the words out, and it cut deep to have to say them.

'But, really, that is by the by,' Helen continued, looking at her mother's stunned face.

Now who was looking gormless?

'Perhaps,' Helen said slowly, 'you should really be asking "*With whom* is my husband having an affair?"' Helen was speaking in her best King's English, the way she had been taught in her elocution lessons.

Miriam had her hand, claw-like, on the back of the tall dining-room chair and was leaning across to her daughter, who, she observed, was being infuriatingly calm, smoking her cigarette.

'Well, this is where we get to the shocking part, Mother,' Helen said. 'But I have to add that this is not the *most* shocking part of what I have to tell you.'

She had just about finished smoking her cigarette. Helen felt her stomach rumble. She had hardly consumed a thing all day, but lately she had begun to enjoy the feeling of light-headedness that came with not eating.

'*Who?*' Miriam was now tired of playing this sick game.

Helen crushed her cigarette in the ashtray and looked up at her mother.

'Gloria,' she said simply, 'Gloria Armstrong ... You know *Gloria*, don't you, Mum? One of the women welders at the yard ... the one you snatched Dad from all those years ago.'

The room was silent. Miriam's face had gone white as a sheet.

'G-Gloria?' she stuttered. 'Gloria Turnbull?'

'That might have been her maiden name, but yes, that's the one. She's called Armstrong now – although I'm not sure for how much longer. Not after what I saw today.'

Miriam shook her head, as if trying to free herself from the words her daughter had just spoken. Words she was struggling to understand.

'Are you seriously telling me, Helen, that your father is having some sordid affair with Gloria? *Frumpy, poor as a church mouse, plain ugly Gloria?*'

Helen thought it was a tad harsh to call Gloria 'ugly'. She might be carrying a little extra weight, but she wasn't *ugly*.

'That may be your opinion, Mum, but clearly Dad doesn't think Gloria is either "frumpy" or "ugly".' Helen was sticking the knife in and knew it. 'Nor does he seem to mind that she is as "poor as a church mouse".'

Miriam drew the chair she was leaning against out from under the table and sat down. Helen stopped herself from commenting on the ability of her mother's legs to keep her upright. Lighting up another cigarette, she watched as her mother took a large gulp of her drink.

'But I'm afraid the worst is yet to come, Mum,' Helen said, creating a mist of smoke around them both.

'It would seem,' she said, her eyes searching her mother's face, 'that Dad and Gloria have had – what do people like to say? That's it! – *a love child*. They've had an adorable little "love child" ...

We, of course, would call it a "bastard" ... But that's all semantics. It doesn't really matter, does it, Mother? The fact of the matter is, your husband and one of the women welders have recently welcomed into the world a daughter. *Their* daughter.

'Their *very own* baby girl.'

Mrs Westley nearly dropped the fine china gravy boat she was drying when she heard the most blood-curdling cry come from the drawing room.

'Nooo!'

The cook stood stock-still, gravy boat in one hand, tea towel in the other.

She had worked for the family long enough to know that the scream that had just pierced the air, was Mrs Crawford's.

Chapter Twenty-Six

Vera's Café, High Street East, Sunderland

'Bloody hell!' Peter said.

He had been listening aghast as Rosie told him all about what had happened that afternoon at Thompson's. 'And you're sure she's all right? No kind of concussion or head injury? Sometimes these things don't show themselves until a while later,' he said, desperately trying to keep his anger at bay, but thinking, *That bastard! Wait until I get my hands on him!*

Reading his mind, Rosie took hold of Peter's hand, which had formed itself into a tight fist during the telling of the attack.

'She's got a bad bump on her head, which is why I think they're keen to keep her in overnight, but honestly I think she's going to be fine.'

She paused and looked at Peter in earnest.

'But,' she whispered across the table, 'I'm not telling you this because I want you to do anything ... you know?' They hadn't spoken any more about Peter's 'out-of-hours' policing since the afternoon they had become lovers and had shared their secrets with each other.

Peter nodded, but didn't say anything. Just then Vera came bustling across to them with two plates of apple and plum pie.

'Get some meat on yer bones. The pair of ya!' She plonked the plates down in front of them.

Since her favourite customers had clearly worked out their differences and were now open about being a proper courting couple, Vera enjoyed clucking about them. She had decided that they both needed 'feeding up', in her words, and so they could no longer simply come in for a pot of tea without being given a slice of whatever speciality Vera had baked for that day's trading. The way Vera rationalised it was that Peter might as well get something for the five-bob note he always left at the table regardless of what they ordered.

'Ah, Vera,' Rosie said, gently taking hold of Vera's arm, 'can I be a real pain and ask if you could box this up for me? I'm going to see a friend in hospital and I know this will cheer her up no end.'

Vera cast Rosie a look of reprimand. 'I will do, but – ' she looked tellingly at Peter ' – you need to get some more good meals down this one.' She looked back at Rosie. 'She's wasting away!'

Peter chuckled and nodded his compliance. 'I will do, Vera. I promise.'

Pleased at Peter's response, Vera picked up Rosie's plate and padded back to the counter, where there was, as usual, a queue of customers.

Rosie looked at Peter. 'And will *you* promise *me* that you won't do anything foolhardy regarding the *Vinnie situation*?'

Peter nodded as he pushed his plate of pie to the middle of the table.

'Providing,' he bartered, 'you help me eat this.'

Rosie forked a piece of pie and popped it in her mouth. The mix of apples, plums and Vera's melt-in-your-mouth pastry tasted gorgeous. Since she and Peter had been seeing each other, she seemed to have totally lost her appetite and was having to force food down just to keep up her energy.

'God, that's nice,' she mumbled.

'So,' Peter said, taking a big sup of his tea, 'it sounds like Helen saved the day.'

'Indeed,' Rosie said, 'and thank goodness she did, as I really don't think anyone else would have seen what was happening.'

'I'm guessing you went with her to the hospital?' Peter knew Rosie would have insisted on being by Gloria's side after such a violent and traumatic event. Especially as he knew they had become even closer these past few months.

Rosie ate another piece of pie, washing it down with a good swig of tea. 'Once they'd got her all cleaned up and settled on the Observation Ward, she actually seemed quite relaxed. More relaxed than she's been for ages. You know, all that worry about Vinnie finding out and wondering when to tell him and what he'd do when she did. It's like she's actually happy – no, *relieved* – that the decision has been taken out of her hands. She's wanted to tell him for so long now. She's hated lying, but not really had any choice.'

'And at long last the truth is out,' Peter said.

'Well, I guess half of it,' Rosie added. 'Although I don't think it'll be long now before the whole truth is.'

'At least then,' Peter dropped his voice, in case anyone was earwigging next to them, 'Gloria and *Hope's father* can be together properly.'

'Exactly,' Rosie said. 'And from what Gloria's been told by George's friend Rupert – you know, the solicitor from Gourley and Sons in John Street?'

Peter nodded. He knew most of the town's lawyers and legal beagles, even if they didn't work in the criminal sector.

'Well, it looks like the divorce is making good progress.'

'And,' Peter said, thinking of some family cases he had been involved in over the years, 'at least there won't be any wrangling over custody.'

'Mm ...' Rosie mumbled her agreement as she ate the last bit of thick-crusted pie. 'Not that Vinnie would have really wanted Hope, even if she had been his. But you can bet your bottom dollar that he would have used it as a way of continuing to try and beat Gloria down.' Rosie looked at her watch. 'Sorry, but I can't stay long. I said I'd meet the girls in about an hour up at the hospital, so we can catch visiting hours.'

'Of course,' Peter said, 'I didn't realise that was the time. Will you tell Gloria I was asking about her? I know I've not even met her yet, but I feel like I've known her for ages.'

Rosie laughed. 'She says the same about you.'

Peter suddenly leant forward in his seat. 'I saw an old friend of mine today called Toby. He dropped by—' Peter started, but was interrupted by Vera's reappearance.

'That's what I like to see,' she said with a satisfied look on her face. She dumped the boxed-up pie next to Rosie. 'Sharing,' she said simply, before turning around and hurrying back to her customers, who were now huffing their impatience.

'God,' Rosie said, glancing at her watch again, 'I really better get going, otherwise I'll be late.'

'Yes, yes, of course, get yourself away,' Peter said, standing up and going round to pull Rosie's chair out for her.

'I'm going to give up arguing with you about paying the bill,' Rosie laughed, turning and giving him a quick kiss on the lips.

She grabbed the boxed pie and hurried out of the shop, turning at the door to look for Vera. She managed to catch her eye as she was pouring hot water from her copper urn into one of her big brown ceramic teapots. Rosie mouthed the words 'Thank you' and Vera responded in her usual fashion by frowning and waving Rosie away with her free hand.

After Rosie left, Peter paid up and made his way into town to the police headquarters. As usual, his mind was churning over. He had wanted to tell Rosie about his old school friend Toby, who had popped by out of the blue to see him the other day, but it looked like that would have to wait.

He sighed. It seemed like the time he and Rosie managed to scrape together was never long enough. Whenever they parted there were so many things they had not had time to chat about. They both always seemed to be in a rush. Sometimes they only managed a quick cuppa at Vera's before they went off to their respective evening jobs. Only occasionally had they managed to crib a night off so they could do something special – something 'normal' couples did. Not that, as they had discovered, they particularly enjoyed doing what 'normal' couples did. They had both admitted that they didn't have the urge to go dancing; neither were either of them that keen on going to the cinema. They'd been the once, but had whispered to each other all the way through the film and had been tutted at more than once.

All Peter wanted was Rosie's company, and lots of it. And he was sure Rosie felt the same. This past week she'd voiced her concerns about her little sister, Charlotte, who, judging by the tone of her letters lately, didn't seem as happy as she normally did. Peter had suggested that it could well be her age. She had just turned fourteen, after all. He'd had to suppress a chuckle when he had seen the thunderous look Rosie had given him for daring to suggest her little sister was not really that little any more.

'But I don't want her to grow up!' Rosie had declared, and they had both laughed.

'I *know*,' she'd admitted. 'I'm like one of these awful mothers who refuse to let their children grow up and keep mummying them all their lives.' Peter thought that it was certainly true that Rosie was more like a mother to Charlotte than a sister.

Although Peter hadn't shown it, he'd been gutted when Rosie told him that she was going to spend Christmas with Charlotte and the Rainers in Harrogate. Mr and Mrs Rainer were old friends of the family who looked after Charlotte during the holidays. Peter had hoped that Rosie's sister would come to Sunderland for Christmas, not just because he was keen to meet her, but because he wanted to spend Christmas with Rosie. She'd told him, though, that she didn't feel it was safe enough for Charlotte to come to Sunderland. There had been too many air raids, in her opinion.

And it was true. Just the other evening two high-explosive bombs had been dropped near the Hendon gasworks. Luckily, no one had been killed, but the town was getting a regular bashing from the Luftwaffe. It was making Peter increasingly unsettled. And that feeling had been exacerbated by Toby's visit. They'd talked a little about their misspent youth at Bede Grammar, but most of the afternoon had been taken up in chatting about more present-day matters, in particular Churchill's most recent plans and military strategies.

As Peter reached the front entrance of the police headquarter he forced his mind to concentrate on the task at hand.

'Peter!' the desk sergeant shouted out on seeing his old colleague step through the double-fronted glass door. 'Good to see you!'

Peter shut the door behind him as his entrance had already allowed a gust of cold air into the warm reception area.

'And you, too, Neville. Do you ever go home?' Every time Peter came to the station, his old colleague always seemed to be there behind the front desk.

'Do *you*?' Neville shot back.

Peter laughed.

'I'm after the custody sergeant. Who's on duty tonight?'

Neville looked down at his rota.

'Gregson.'

Peter made his way along the corridor and down a flight of steps to the bowels of the building where the police cells could be found.

When he pushed through the swinging doors that led to DS Gregson's desk, Peter didn't even look over to the cell where Vinnie was presently residing, although he could hear him snoring loudly.

'Aye, aye, there, Pete. What brings you down to these parts?' DS Gregson asked.

'A favour,' Peter said, nodding in the direction of Vinnie's cell. 'How long were you going to keep this one for?'

'Well ...' DS Gregson looked at some paperwork. 'He should get dealt with either tomorrow or the next day at the latest.'

'Can you make it "the latest"? I need to sort something out and it might take a little while.'

'No bother, mate,' DS Gregson said. 'I'll tell you what. I'll go one better. I'll wait for you to give me the nod. From what I've heard about this one's shenanigans today, I'm in no rush to give him back his liberty.'

Peter thanked Gregson and left the custody suite just as Vinnie woke up and started shouting for his 'brief'.

Chapter Twenty-Seven

'So, will Vinnie now go to jail?' Hannah asked Rosie and the women welders as they headed out of the main hospital entrance and made their way back onto the New Durham Road to catch a tram back into town. They had just spent the last hour with Gloria, although the strict ward nurse had only allowed them to see their friend two at a time.

'Mm,' Rosie said, 'these things are hard to predict. They're not always straightforward.'

Hannah looked puzzled.

'It depends if they have enough evidence to charge him,' Martha interrupted. She had asked her mum and dad the same question earlier on. 'But,' she continued, repeating her father's words verbatim, 'sometimes they just get what is called a caution, which basically amounts to a slap on the wrist.'

Now Hannah was looking even more puzzled as they all crowded into the bus shelter in an attempt to protect themselves from the cold wind. It didn't look like they were going to get a white Christmas, but it would most definitely be a windy one.

'I don't understand,' she said. 'They slap him on the wrist rather than send him to jail?'

'Nah,' Angie said, 'it just means they do nowt about it.'

'What? He might not receive any kind of punishment for what he did to Gloria?' Hannah asked incredulously.

'It's possible, Hannah,' Rosie said. 'Gloria'll know in a few days if he's going to go to court for what he did to her.'

The conversation was interrupted by the arrival of the number 15 bus that would take them into town.

Once they were on-board and had paid their fares, Hannah continued her questioning.

'But what will happen if they don't send him to court?' Her pale face was full of concern. 'Won't he just do it again?' she asked anxiously.

None of the women had an answer to Hannah's question. If they'd had to guess, they would have said that Vinnie would most likely lie low for a while before something would stir up his ire again and he would go looking for the woman who had, over the past few decades, become his reliable punchbag.

A few minutes later they arrived at Park Lane.

'A pre-Christmas drink everyone?' Dorothy suggested.

No one needed asking twice as they all hurried across to the Park Inn on the corner of Olive Street.

As Helen climbed the stairs to the top of the house, she felt a little dizzy, as though *she* had been the one blindsided by a shovel and not Vinnie. And it was not just her body that felt off-kilter, but her mind too. As she reached the third floor and went into her room, she shut the door firmly behind her before flopping in a heap on top of her bed. How could one day bring so much horror and fear, followed by joy and happiness, and then end in such a terrible betrayal?

Her stab at her mother and the retelling of her father's infidelity had given her a temporary reprieve from the deep-seated grief she had been hit with. But it had been only the very briefest of reprieves.

Now she was on her own, there was no escaping her true, very raw pain. At least here, in the privacy of her own room, knowing that no one could hear her, she could allow the gut-wrenching sobs to steamroll their way out of her. Alone she could finally unleash all the feelings that had been bursting to break free from her all day.

Her mother's coldness had enabled Helen to harden her own heart and relay her father's indiscretions in a way that gave her a perverse sense of revenge. If her mother could be insensitive to the point of being downright cruel – then so could she.

It had brought Helen a sliver of satisfaction to see that she had been able to push her mother to such an extreme that not only had she been unable to keep a stiff upper lip, she had actually lost control of herself in such an ear-splitting fashion.

Her revenge, however, though sweet, was also short-lived. Helen should have known that her mother's emotional depths were actually quite shallow, and within a few minutes she had composed herself and was back to normal, pouring herself a fresh gin and tonic and sitting down to cross-examine her daughter about every aspect of Jack's infidelity. And, of course, anything Helen knew about the said 'love child'.

It had dawned on Helen, slowly at first, but then with gathering momentum as she answered Miriam's questions, that the vocal expression of her mother's torment had not been brought about by her husband's betrayal, but from a kind of childish frustration. It was a toddler's tantrum. A stamping of the feet. A spitting out of the dummy. Her mother was not getting what she wanted. It had nothing to do with her husband loving another woman, but everything to do with the humiliation she would be subjected to if – *when* – her husband left her.

Helen had not been able to offer up much more than what she had already told her, and once that was clear, her mother had suggested that Helen retire to bed early as she had clearly had quite a day of it and needed to get some rest.

Her mother's words had sounded sincere, but Helen had been left with the feeling that she was being dismissed.

Just as Helen was leaving the room, however, Miriam had called her back.

'Darling,' she'd said, her voice unexpectedly soft, 'go to work as normal tomorrow, but obviously I don't need to tell you that you can't breathe a word of this to anyone – absolutely no one.'

It was not a request but an order. Her mother was back in charge. She would deal with this in whatever way she saw fit. Like she always did.

As Helen lay curled up on her bed, she felt as though she was drowning in her own salty tears. Hearing her mother's bedroom door close below, she looked at the clock and saw it had just gone eight. It looked like they had both had enough of this day.

Helen forced herself to get up off the bed where she had been lying fully clothed, crying for what felt like an eternity into her silk eiderdown. She quickly changed into her favourite winceyette nightdress and slipped under the covers. Her feet found the warmth of a hot-water bottle, which Mrs Westley must have put in there, probably guessing that Helen would head off to bed early after all the upset.

Helen switched off the side light and was glad to be immersed in complete darkness. As her mind reran the events of the day for what felt like the hundredth time, the tears came once more. This time they were steady and constant.

Her world had been turned upside down in the space of just a few hours. But worst of all, she knew it could never be righted again. Ever. This wouldn't come out with the wash as Mrs Westley had promised her it would. No, the stain that had appeared in her life today was indelible. It would be there for evermore.

Over the next few hours, until sleep finally offered a respite, Helen cried on and off. Random thoughts pinged in and out of her brain. The image of Gloria's bloodied face kept flashing across her mind's eye. She had felt so sorry for her. Such compassion. In the back of the ambulance she had even felt a kind of camaraderie towards her. There'd been a connection there. She had nearly cried in front of her, she'd felt so overwhelmed with emotion!

Then came the anger as she thought of her father's praise and how he had told her she was so 'brave' – when all along it was just a smokescreen. All the while, he had only been thinking of one person. Gloria. Was likely just desperate for Helen to leave so he could race to see his lover. The mother of his child.

God, she felt like shaking herself as she remembered actually thinking on the way to the hospital that perhaps she could even become friends with the rest of the women welders.

Helen tossed and turned in her bed as if trying to shrug off the sting of humiliation.

They must all be laughing at her now.

But this wasn't just about her father having another woman. God knows, it happened plenty, especially in the circles in which her family socialised, where a blind eye was always turned, providing, of course, the marriage was not put in jeopardy. Providing the bit on the side remained just that. A side dish and not the main course. The problem arose when the status quo was threatened. When the two lovers wanted to leave their old lives and start a new one together.

Helen might only have caught a glimpse of her father and Gloria together, but she had seen the way they had kissed one another. She had never seen her mother kiss her father in such a way. That one kiss had spoken a thousand words. Her father and Gloria were in love. And in that moment Helen knew she was going to lose her father.

He had not only a woman he clearly loved, but a new baby – *a whole new family*.

Another batch of soul-wrenching sobs broke free from Helen. Her heart felt as though it was slowly being ripped to shreds.

Downstairs on the second floor, Miriam sat at her dressing table. To her right was her gin and tonic, to her left a bottle of her red 'gems'. Tonight she was going to indulge in two little gems rather than just the one. She needed the escapism of sleep and her bottle of pills afforded that. Lately they hadn't been quite as effective as they had been when she'd first been prescribed them, so tonight she intended to double her dose, guaranteeing at least ten hours' respite from the nightmare she'd been plunged into. But before she allowed herself this release into oblivion, she had some thinking to do. Lots of thinking. And lots of planning.

She had left a note downstairs for Jack, telling him she had been struck down with one of her ghastly 'heads' and had gone to bed early to try and sleep it off. She had worded the note carefully and asked him if it wouldn't be too much of an imposition for him to sleep in the back bedroom. It was imperative he didn't get a sniff of a suspicion that she was on to him, so she had written it in such a way as to sound totally genuine and believable that she just needed silence and bed rest.

In truth, if Jack graced her bed with his presence tonight she might just end up stabbing him to death with the sharp end of her metal comb. Doing so would bring her immense satisfaction – but the consequences would be unpalatable. And besides, it would mean the whole world would get to know of her humiliation.

No, she had to calm down and work out a real solution to this hellish scenario she now found herself in. And what was absolutely paramount was that no one could ever find out about Jack's infidelity, and definitely not about his bastard child.

Miriam took another sip of her gin and then started to take off her make-up with a generous amount of thick face cream and cotton balls. As she inspected her reflection in the mirror she congratulated herself on maintaining her good looks despite her age. Unlike Gloria. God, when she had seen her that time at Thompson's she'd looked dreadful. Tired, worn out, pale and plump. Although now Miriam realised why she had looked so frazzled. What she had put down to middle-aged spread was obviously baby fat. Although Miriam doubted she would ever lose it. Not at her age. She'd just get fatter and fatter. And older and older. And Jack would rue the day he ever became involved with her again.

What on earth had made Jack go back to Gloria, she had no idea. If he had been having an affair with some young starlet, or even with someone who was the same age as herself but more beautiful, Miriam would have understood. *But not Gloria.*

As Miriam inspected the tautness of her skin in her magnifying mirror, and checked out her profile for any sign of the beginnings of a wattle, she knew it would have destroyed her if Jack had been having an affair with a younger or better-looking woman than herself. At least that was one minor blessing in this whole debacle. Gloria was no match for her in any shape or form. No one would ever believe he was having an affair with her, which, Miriam mused, she could work to her advantage.

The real problem was Jack and Gloria's bastard daughter.

After her momentary breakdown when Helen had told her about the 'love child', she had pulled herself together and carefully questioned Helen, eking every tiny detail out of her.

Now she knew everything, or at least everything that her daughter knew.

She knew Jack was having an affair, and that he had been seeing Gloria before he had left for America.

She knew that Gloria had given birth to Jack's baby sometime back in August and had been passing the child off as her husband's, but that she had finally been rumbled this very day.

And she knew, from what Helen had imparted about this afternoon's drama at the yard, it was unlikely that this Vinnie character knew who had fathered Gloria's baby – only that the baby wasn't his.

It was a start.

Now she needed ammunition. For this was war. And the more ammunition she had, the more chance she stood of winning the battle. Or at least of saving her dignity, her reputation, her standing in society – her life as she knew it.

So, how did she go about getting the ammunition with which to destroy both Jack and Gloria – and thereby save herself?

As she plucked a stray hair from her already thin eyebrows, her mind idled over other bits and pieces of information that Helen had divulged.

Gloria had worked at the yard since they had started taking on women in August last year, and she had become very close to her squad of women welders.

Gloria's gang included Rosie, whom she'd known for years, and Polly, whom Miriam already knew about because of the Tommy fiasco.

Then there was the young, pretty girl called Dorothy, her best mate, Angie, and, of course, there was Martha, whom everyone knew.

Finally, there was the little Czechoslovakian refugee, Hannah, who was now working in the drawing office.

Thinking about what Helen had told her about Gloria and how close she was to her fellow welders, the beginnings of an idea started to form in Miriam's mind. A very good idea, if she said so herself. Of course, it was just a fledgling idea at the moment, but it wouldn't take much to find out if it could be developed to provide her with the weaponry she needed.

Miriam smiled to herself and unscrewed the top of the bottle of her little red gems.

She congratulated herself on her ingeniousness, took out two capsules and swallowed them back with a good swig of gin.

Chapter Twenty-Eight

Saturday 20 December 1941

When Miriam got up the next day her head felt thick and her mouth dry. She had slept right through until eight o'clock. Pulling on her warm dressing gown, Miriam padded down the carpeted staircase and into the breakfast room. There was now just the one place setting, which told her that both Jack and Helen had already had their breakfasts and had left for work.

She'd told Helen to go into work as normal, but not to give anything away. Not a word to anyone. It didn't matter what Helen felt like doing, or saying, she *had* to put on a show that she knew nothing. Miriam knew it would be relatively easy for Helen to avoid Gloria and the rest of the women welders, but she realised she should also have stressed that she had to steer clear of her father. Jack was the potential spanner in the works. Helen had been using any excuse to go and see her dad at Crown's since he'd started back at work and she was worried that her daughter would get overemotional and blurt out that she knew about Gloria. And the baby.

Helen adored her father, which might well mean that she would either spill the beans or, worse still, take Jack's side. And that would truly be a disaster. Miriam needed her daughter on-board. There was to be no jumping ship, which could well be a possibility. After all, Helen now had a half-sister. Even if it was a bastard half-sister.

Miriam realised she would have to ingratiate herself with Helen as much as she could. With hindsight she wished she had been a little more sympathetic to her daughter when she had arrived home and found her in a state yesterday. But, Miriam reflected as she sat down and looked out into a side garden that was looking rather sorry for itself having been battered in yesterday's winds, it was no use crying over spilled milk. She'd work her way round Helen. She knew how. Had done it enough in the past.

'Morning, Mrs Crawford.' Mrs Westley bustled out of the kitchen and into the breakfast room. She was careful to use the tone she always used to greet her employer of a morning. There was to be no hint of last night's upset.

'Just a pot of tea, Mrs Westley. I don't feel that hungry this morning,' Miriam told her cook.

As Mrs Westley headed back to the kitchen, Miriam looked at the clock on the mantelpiece. She had an hour to get herself ready, and then she would start putting her plan into action.

Jack had been relieved coming back last night to find the house quiet. When he'd read Miriam's note that she had taken to her bed with 'one of her heads', he had breathed an even bigger sigh of relief. He didn't think he had it in him to pretend that everything was normal.

He'd woken surprisingly early, and without the usual feeling of grogginess that he seemed to be suffering from of late, and had left the house before anyone else was up. He'd hurried to the Royal, but when he walked onto the ward and saw that Gloria wasn't there he panicked.

'Sir.' Jack felt a tap on his shoulder and turned to see the same nurse who had been on duty yesterday evening. 'Mrs Armstrong has just been discharged, but if you hurry, you'll catch her down the pharmacy on the ground floor. She's collecting a prescription.'

Jack didn't need telling twice and ran along the corridor and back down the flight of stairs. He was looking for signs to the chemist when he saw Gloria walking towards him.

'Jack!' she said, her face a mixture of surprise and reprimand. 'You shouldn't have come here,' she whispered as she reached him.

Jack put both hands on her shoulders and inspected her before planting a kiss on her lips.

'How are you feeling?' he asked, still scrutinising her face. He noticed a bruise the size of a penny had developed on the bridge of her nose.

'I'm feeling fine, honestly.' Gloria looked about her, anxious that someone they knew would see them. 'Just got some painkillers, not that I need them.'

Jack caught her worried look and took her arm. 'Gloria, I don't give a damn who sees us any more. Now come on, I've got a taxi waiting to take you home.'

Gloria was just glad to get out of the hospital and into the black cab that was waiting at the bottom of the steps to the main entrance. Her concern about being seen dissolved as she climbed into the back of the car. Jack climbed in the other side.

'Number fifty-six Fordham Road, please,' Jack instructed the elderly cab driver.

Gloria looked at Jack with a half-smile on her face. 'Did the girls tell you where I live, or did you remember?' she asked.

Jack took hold of Gloria's hand and squeezed it.

'I remembered.' He looked as pleased as Punch. 'And what's more, I've started to remember lots of other things too.'

A few minutes later they were pulling up outside Gloria's home. As Jack paid the driver and gave him a generous tip, he looked around him.

'God, I remember this when it wasn't quite so nice,' he said, suddenly hit by the memory of squalid tenements and open gutters.

'You mean when it was a slum,' Gloria said. The estate had been built just a few years previously after the decision was made by the Corporation to raze all the town's poorest areas and replace them with new housing estates.

Once indoors, Gloria went straight into the kitchen and put the kettle on.

'That hospital is lovely. I even had a bath there last night *and* they washed my clothes. But,' she added, her face deadpan, 'their tea's like dishwater.'

Jack stood and stared at the woman busying about in her little kitchen. He had started to remember so much these past few days – images, thoughts and memories. He realised that this woman he loved, the one now hunting around in her cupboards for some biscuits, was different to the one he'd known, and it wasn't his memory that was amiss. Gloria had changed. She was different from the woman he had left a year ago, when they had said their farewells in the unlit porch of St Peter's Church.

Jack carried the tea tray into the lounge.

'You've changed a lot, haven't you?' Jack put the tray on the coffee table and sat down in a slightly worn-out, but very comfortable armchair. Gloria smiled. Never in a million years would she have thought that Jack would be here in her home, and that he would be sitting in what she had always secretly called 'Vinnie's throne'.

'I have, but then I think we all have. This war's changing us all in so many different ways.' Gloria poured the tea and as she did so, the sleeve of her overalls rode up her arm slightly, exposing a sleeve of bruised skin.

Jack felt himself wince. Then he felt the familiar flood of anger as he thought about Vinnie. He couldn't wait to get his hands on the bloke.

'Do you know what's happening with Vinnie?' he asked.

Gloria looked up at Jack to see that his face had gone stony-hard; as she looked back down again, she saw her exposed, discoloured forearms. She pulled her denim cuffs so that they were covering the visual reminder of yesterday's beating.

'Well,' Gloria said, knowing exactly what Jack was thinking, or, rather, planning on doing. It was exactly the reason why she hadn't wanted it to come out that Vinnie wasn't the father. It was like a bloody line of dominoes – you knocked the first one and there was a chain reaction.

'From what the police told me yesterday, the impression I got was that they were going to keep him in custody for a good few days. Maybe even a week. I think they wanted to keep him in until they'd got him in front of a magistrate.'

Gloria looked back down at the tray, then picked up the plate of shortbread and offered some to Jack. She hoped he hadn't picked up on the slight flush she'd felt come to her face. A flush she always got when she told a lie. Not that it was a lie as such – more an exaggeration. The police officer who had come to take her statement had told her that Vinnie would be kept in the cells overnight, but was unsure as to how they were going to proceed thereafter.

'So, they're going to charge him?' Jack asked, trying to keep his voice even.

Gloria nodded, although she had no idea if they would or not. It was still a domestic. And she was sure that once Vinnie had calmed down and told them his tale of woe about being lied to by his conniving wife – who, he had just found out, was not only having an affair but had also had another man's baby – he might just end up walking out of the custody suite a free man.

Jack pushed himself out of the armchair and stood up. 'We have to come clean about everything now.' He started pacing the small living room. 'Enough secrets.'

Gloria had known this was coming. She had lain awake most of the night in the hospital, her mind turning over what to do, and what not to do.

She knew Jack and Vinnie well enough to have a good guess at what was going through both their minds. Vinnie would be sitting in his cell, becoming increasingly wound up. He was probably just simmering at the moment as the beating he had given her had probably taken his temper off the boil. He'd also be worried about what the police were going to do with him. But she knew it wouldn't be long before he'd find himself back at boiling point. Gloria had learnt a lot these past few months. She had been working long hours, and had her hands full with Hope, but she'd still had time on her own to think, and she had come to realise just how controlling Vinnie had been. Or rather, how controlled *she* had been by him. And if there was one thing that got Vinnie's temper piping hot, it was the fact he wasn't in the driver's seat any more.

'I agree with you,' Gloria said, taking a sip of her tea and savouring it. It had been a long night and it was looking as though she had another long day ahead of her.

'That's good.' Jack was visibly relieved. 'I thought I'd have an argument with you on my hands.'

Gloria took another sip.

'I agree. It's inevitable we have to tell everyone about us, and, of course, about Hope.' She took a deep breath. 'But I really think we have to choose our timing well.'

Jack looked at her and was about to object. If it was up to him, he would march right back to the home he shared with Miriam and tell her everything.

'I know you just want to go straight back to Miriam and tell her everything,' Gloria said, as if reading his thoughts. 'And so do I,' she stressed, her arms stretched out as she gently took hold of Jack's large hands, gnarled and scarred from his early years at the yard.

'It's going to be wonderful to finally be free of all these secrets and lies.' Gloria looked around her front room, which was spick and span and homely. 'We can live here together, or better still, find a new place that we can make our own.'

Jack nodded, thinking how lovely it would be to come back to a place they could call their own and simply enjoy being a family.

'But,' Gloria added, her voice becoming more serious, 'this isn't just about us. I did a lot of thinking last night.' She took a deep breath. 'Obviously, I don't give a fig about Miriam. You know that already. She's the most heartless person I know, just out for herself.' Jack nodded his agreement. Since he had started to get his memory back, he'd had flashes of his former life with Miriam and they had not tallied with the picture his wife of twenty years had painted – in any shape or form.

'It's Helen I feel awful about.' Gloria's voice changed; the guilt she was feeling could be heard in her voice and seen on her face.

'She was so brave saving me from Vinnie. No one's ever stood up for me like that. She came to see me in the back of the ambulance and I felt terrible. It was far more painful than all the beatings I've had off Vinnie. I felt so guilty. There she was, risking getting battered to a pulp herself—'

Gloria broke off. She'd been lying on the ground, her arms shielding herself from Vinnie's fists, when she'd caught a glimpse of Helen, her face contorted with fear as she'd swung the shovel round and knocked Vinnie flying.

'That girl was terrified. But she protected me all the same.' Tears had now come into Gloria's eyes. How wrong could you be about someone. They had all demonised Helen for so long now, she had become a two-dimensional figure. A caricature. But she wasn't. She was a young woman who had problems, just like they all had. And, just like the rest of the women welders, she'd stuck her neck out when required and put her own safety on the line to help another woman in need.

'I want you to give her one last Christmas before this scandal breaks. Because it *is* going to be scandalous, no matter how we go about it. Her life is going to change, just as ours is. And I know how much she adores you – how she was by your side while you were in the coma and how determined she's been to help you get better.'

Gloria had now started to cry. She hated hurting people. And she knew Helen was going to be devastated when she found out.

Jack got out of his chair and sat down next to Gloria on the sofa. He wrapped his arms around her and let her cry out her tears. He knew Gloria was right. And he realised that he had been pushing thoughts of Helen to the back of his mind, convincing himself that she would take it all in her stride – that she'd be fine. But he knew he was kidding himself.

'You're right,' Jack said when Gloria had stopped quietly weeping.

'You're right,' he said again. 'Helen *is* going to be devastated. I've not thought it through, have I? I've been selfish. And the last thing she needs is two selfish parents.'

There was a pause as he thought about Christmas, which was just a few days away. It would be hard to keep his feelings in check around Miriam, but he'd have to. His daughter deserved it. He owed her. He would make this Christmas special. And it might also help lay the foundations for a future in which he hoped Helen would be able to forgive him, and perhaps also become a sister to Hope.

Chapter Twenty-Nine

'Come on then, darling, I'm taking you out to lunch!'

Helen jerked her head up from some order forms and invoices she was checking at her desk. She had a cigarette burning in an ashtray next to her.

'Honestly, Helen, it's as foggy in here as it is out there.' Miriam waved a hand about in a vain attempt to clear the air.

Helen stared up at her mother. She had been intending to work through her lunch break, not because there was a need to, but simply because she wanted to avoid any kind of human contact.

'Go to the ladies and powder your nose. I'm treating you to lunch at the Grand!' Miriam said, forcing a wide smile on her face. 'And put a little lipstick on. You never know who we might meet.' Miriam tried to make their luncheon date sound as though it might be fun, with the potential of meeting a future beau.

'All right,' Helen said, but her tone in no way mirrored her mother's. 'I have to be back by one, though. I've got a lot of work to do.'

Miriam had to bite her tongue and stop herself from snapping and telling her daughter to 'Cheer up!' God, the girl looked like she was dressed for a wake in that morbid black dress she was wearing. She'd nearly said as much when she'd walked into the office, but had managed to stop herself; this was no time for honesty – she had to concentrate on what she had come here to do.

She watched as Helen walked across the open-plan office, now empty of workers, and disappeared into the ladies' bathroom.

As soon as she was gone from view, Miriam hurried over to one of the tall metal filing cabinets that lined the walls of the office. She had visited Jack here enough times during his many years as yard manager to know where everything was kept.

Pulling out the bottom drawer, Miriam rifled her way through files stuffed full of paperwork until she found what she was looking for.

'Yes!' she said triumphantly to herself.

She was in luck. The women's employment records had been kept separate from the men's; probably because they were only considered to be temporary. Once the war was over, it was expected that the men would return and reclaim their jobs.

Taking the file and laying it open on the desk, Miriam looked up quickly to check Helen wasn't coming back. Confident she had at least a few undisturbed minutes to find out what she needed, she quickly thumbed through the file. Every now and again she pulled out a thick sheet of paper embossed with the Thompson header and put it to one side.

When she'd been through the whole file, she counted the number of documents she had put in a separate pile on Helen's desk.

'Perfect,' Miriam muttered to herself.

As she folded the six single sheets of paper, she heard a noise and looked up to see Rosie coming through the main doors by the top of the stairs.

Quick as a flash, Miriam stuffed the hastily folded documents into her handbag and snapped it shut. She was just returning the file to the cabinet by the time Rosie reached the doorway of the office.

'Ah, Mir— sorry, Mrs Crawford,' Rosie said, surprised, 'I'm looking for Helen.' She looked around as if Helen might be hiding in a corner.

Miriam let out a small laugh. 'Well, Rosie, as you can see, she's not here.'

There was a pause.

Rosie's eyes strayed from Miriam to the cabinet she was standing next to and that she could have sworn she'd seen her closing.

The silence was broken by the sound of Helen's heeled shoes clip-clopping across the linoleum floor.

'Ah,' Rosie turned and smiled at Helen, 'I just wanted a quick word while I had the chance.' She looked at Miriam, hoping she would leave her to speak in private with Helen.

'Well, make it quick,' Miriam butted in. 'I'm taking my daughter out to lunch today. And we're already running late.' Miriam felt like giving Helen a shake. She looked like a rabbit caught in a driver's headlights.

Rosie purposely turned her back on Miriam and gave her full attention to Helen.

'It was just to tell you that Gloria is back home and feeling much better. There doesn't appear to be any serious damage. Thank goodness. And she'll be back at work tomorrow. She told me that you kindly told her to take as much time off as she wanted, but she really does feel fine. And well enough to return to work.'

Helen continued to stare at Rosie.

'Is that it?' Miriam interrupted.

Rosie stopped herself from looking around at Miriam and instead kept her attention firmly on Helen.

'And,' Rosie lowered her voice, 'we all wanted to say a big "thank you" for doing what you did yesterday. It was incredibly brave of you. And I think it's more than fair to say that Gloria would not have escaped with such minor injuries had it not been for you.'

Rosie stepped forward, grabbed Helen's hand and gave it a shake. 'So thank you, Helen. From all of us.'

Miriam stared at her daughter. *Was the girl welling up?!*

'Oh my goodness,' Miriam's shrill voice cut through the air, 'is that the time? Sorry, Rosie, but I'm going to have to cut short your little speech and drag my daughter away or we're going to have no time whatsoever for our lunch.'

And with that, Miriam slipped around Rosie and manoeuvred her daughter out of the office, practically pushing her in the direction of the stairs.

'For God's sake, Helen, get a grip of yourself!' she hissed into her ear, at the same time keeping an eye out for, and her fingers crossed they would not bump into, Harold or Donald; that was the last thing she wanted.

Especially if they started talking about Helen's bloody heroics.

When mother and daughter had made it to the main gates without seeing anyone of importance with whom they would have to converse, Miriam sagged with relief as the chauffeur who had been waiting by the side of their car quickly opened the back passenger door and they both climbed in. 'The Grand, driver!' she commanded, before turning her attention to Helen.

'My dear,' she forced herself to adopt the most compassionate voice she could muster, 'are you all right?' She went to hold Helen's hand and was surprised when her daughter let her. Reining in her impatience, she spoke quietly and gently: 'We're going to have a lovely luncheon at the Grand—'

'I'm not hungry,' Helen interrupted. She'd got used to skipping lunch and the last thing she felt like doing at that moment was eating.

Miriam pursed her lips; this was going to be harder work than she had anticipated.

'Well, we'll just have a nice drink and a chat,' she said, swallowing her irritation. 'I've got lots I want to talk to you about.'

Helen didn't say anything, but instead looked out the passenger window at the fog. A heavy fret had come in from the North Sea this morning and had clearly decided to settle.

Five minutes later, mother and daughter were seated in the Grand; Miriam had ordered a gin and tonic for herself, and a cup of tea and a brandy for Helen.

'You've had a terrible shock,' Miriam said after their drinks had arrived and she knew they wouldn't be disturbed any more, 'but we're going to have to deal with this awfulness together.'

Miriam watched Helen as she took out her packet of Pall Malls and lit herself a cigarette. As she did so, she saw that she wasn't the only one who was paying attention to her daughter. An officer for the Admiralty was chatting to another, lower-ranking naval officer, but his eyes kept flicking over to look at Helen.

'You are a very beautiful and intelligent young woman, who could have her pick of men.' Miriam put her hand over her daughter's. 'And I want you to enjoy that, because believe you me, it won't last for ever.' Miriam touched Helen's face and gently took hold of her chin so that she was forced to look her mother in the eye.

'But most of all I want you to leave this mess that your father has created to me. I'm going to sort it out.'

'How? How can you undo what's already been done?' Helen dropped her voice as she blew out smoke. 'You certainly can't undo the fact that Gloria,' Helen leant forward and whispered into her mother's ear, 'has had Dad's baby!'

Helen's words were like a slap. The news of Jack's adultery, and worse still, his baby, was still pretty raw and shocking.

Miriam took a drink of her gin and tonic to dampen her anger at this great injustice.

'That's for me to worry about,' she said, 'not you. I'll get it sorted. I promise you.'

Seeing her daughter now, and having witnessed her reaction to Rosie earlier on, had left Miriam in no doubt that she would indeed have to deal with this on her own.

My goodness, the girl needs hardening up! Miriam thought as she took another sip of her drink.

Jack had brought her up too soft, but this was not the time to try and rectify that. For now, what was important was for Helen to feel that she had at least one parent she could rely on, and Miriam had to make sure it was her mother, not her father.

'And to take your mind off things,' Miriam said, 'I thought after work we'd go to this new boutique that's just opened. It's got some French-sounding name – "Maison" something or other.' Miriam waved her hand as if dismissing the name as unimportant. 'The girl who owns it always works there late by the sounds of it, so we can go when you finish today, if you like? According to Amelia she's meant to be a virtuoso with a needle and thread.'

Miriam glanced at Helen's black dress, which was looking a little slack on her.

'I think we should go and sort you out with a nice new outfit. The girl can even design something especially for you.'

Miriam noticed Helen looked a little less glum.

'Get you something with a bit of colour in it?'

Miriam chatted on for a while, ordering another couple of drinks before finally signalling the waiter for the bill.

'So that's sorted then? This new boutique after work?' Miriam asked.

'All right, Mother,' Helen said, standing up and finding a very handsome man in the starched white uniform of the Admiralty moving her chair away so that she could leave unhindered. Miriam watched as the officer introduced himself to Helen before offering to escort her out of the building and into the waiting car.

'Of course,' Miriam said, thinking that this was the kind of match she wanted for her daughter.

'And Helen? Five o'clock. I'll come and see you in your office. I've got to go and see Harold, so I'll be in the building anyway.' Miriam smiled. She was lying through her teeth and had no intention of seeing Harold. She did, however, need to return the documents she had borrowed before anyone noticed they were missing.

Chapter Thirty

Pickering & Sons, Bridge Street, Sunderland

'You can't keep these,' Miriam told the bespectacled, grey-haired man sitting behind the large oak table, the top of which was barely visible due to piles of papers and half-opened boxes.

From where Miriam was sitting she could see that the small, frail-looking gentleman was dressed in a green and brown tweed three-piece suit that would have looked smart, even classy, had it not been for the lopsided dicky bow he was sporting and what appeared to be a gravy stain on his shirt.

'You'll have to copy what information you need. I need to get them back to where they belong by the end of the day,' Miriam explained. She sounded more confident than she felt as the old man, whom she knew to be Mr Pickering, leant forward across the desk and took the six pieces of paper that were still folded in two, having just been pulled out of Miriam's handbag.

Mr Pickering took a few moments to cast his eye over each individual document, before picking up a little brass bell to his left and ringing it.

Its tinkling was followed by the appearance of a rather plain-looking girl from the adjoining room. Miriam watched the young woman, who must have been no more than twenty years old, as she silently took the papers and left without even casting a glance in her direction.

'So,' Mr Pickering said, looking over the rims of his glasses at the woman who had turned up unannounced just half an hour ago – not that this was unusual in his business, most potential clients arrived on the spur of the moment. Those who made appointments, funnily enough, usually didn't turn up.

'We have talked through what you want. And I have explained to you what to expect and what not to expect.' He started to cough and took a drink of water. 'We have agreed a fee.'

Miriam nodded. She was feeling more than a little out of her depth, but she was just about managing to keep her head above water. She had always left anything official to either Jack or her father; her domain had always been restricted to that expected of a wife and mother.

'Yes, we have. And I'm satisfied with what we have discussed and agreed,' Miriam said, 'but I have to ask who will be doing the actual ...' she paused whilst she found the word she was looking for ' ... the legwork, as such?'

Mr Pickering took off his glasses and smiled good-naturedly.

'Well, as you've rightly guessed, I'm no spring chicken and not really up to the kind of running around this work entails.'

Mr Pickering started to stuff tobacco into a pipe that had been lying on its side next to his glass of water.

'As you probably noticed when you came in,' he waved the hand now holding the pipe towards the entrance, 'the sign on the door reads, "Pickering & Sons".'

Miriam nodded.

'It's a family business,' she volunteered. 'You have help.'

'Precisely,' Mr Pickering said, getting to his feet and making his way around the huge wooden desk. He extended a bony, arthritic hand to Miriam, who took it as she stood up.

'Come back in ten days and we'll see what we have for you,' he said, smiling.

Miriam smiled back.

Just then the young woman appeared again from the next room and gave the six documents back to Mr Pickering. She retreated to where she had come from without uttering a word. Miriam thought there was something a little unnerving about the girl's quietness.

Taking the documents from Mr Pickering, Miriam carefully folded them so as not to crease them too much before putting them back into her handbag.

Mr Pickering guided Miriam back towards the door and opened it for her. Judging by the woman's attire, she was clearly from money, although Mr Pickering would have been just as courteous had she been dressed in rags.

'So, shall we say two weeks?'

'Yes, two weeks,' Miriam agreed before she walked out of the front door and found herself back in the fog and on the corner of High Street West and Bridge Street.

She was tempted to head straight back to the Grand and have another drink. She certainly needed it, but her work for today was far from done.

As she waved her arm to a passing taxi, which saw her at the last moment and came to an abrupt halt, causing the vehicle behind it to blow its horn loudly, Miriam knew what she had to do next could only be done face to face. There were a few nosy parkers working on the telephone exchange and she couldn't risk the conversation she was about to have with her father being overheard by anyone at all.

By the time Miriam had hailed her black cab, Mr Pickering had seated himself back behind his desk and was lighting his pipe, making short puffing noises as the tobacco started to burn.

Opposite him was the young girl, who was now occupying the chair where Miriam had sat. In her hand, she had a pen and a notepad into which she had copied the details of the women welders' employment records.

'That's a lot of work there, my dear,' the old man said. As he talked he let out a billowing cloud of smoke. 'Are you sure you can manage it all?'

'Of course I can, *Father*,' the young girl smiled.

Chapter Thirty-One

Sunderland Borough Police Headquarters, Gill-bridge Avenue, Sunderland

Monday 22 December 1941

'I've gorra great big lump the size of an egg on the side of ma head!' Vinnie shouted through the small oblong hole in the middle of his cell door. He had no idea who he was shouting at, only that there had to be someone on duty.

'Ya can't keep us here for ever, ya know!' Vinnie paused and listened for any noises that might tell him he was not wasting his breath and someone could indeed hear him.

His head jerked as he caught what sounded like a door closing.

Someone had just come in, or gone out.

'I need medical help!' This time he yelled as loudly as he could. If the person was leaving, then they'd still hear him.

Vinnie turned away from the door and sat back down on the hard wooden bench that had been his bed for the past three nights. One more night spent trapped inside these four walls and he thought he might just go mad.

Not only was he gagging for a beer followed by a good few chasers, he couldn't stand being alone with his own thoughts. He'd never liked being on his own and never would. God only knew how anyone survived being locked up for months, never mind *years*, on end. It was beyond him. Three days had felt like a lifetime. He honestly felt he'd end up round the bend if he was kept in much longer.

'Vincent Armstrong.' The voice sounded deep and low on the other side of the two-inch-thick metal door. Vinnie stared at the steel panelling as he heard a key being jammed into the lock and turned.

He immediately got up and marched towards the door.

Before he saw the face that went with the voice – *a voice he was sure he recognised* – he felt two strong hands shove him hard.

Vinnie tottered backwards, and in an almost slapstick fashion his bum plopped back down on the bench.

When he looked up he saw the back of a man, dressed in a three-quarter-length black overcoat, shutting the cell door.

This did not feel at all right and Vinnie panicked. The cell was small and now there were two people in it, it felt even smaller. As the man turned around and stepped towards him, Vinnie instantly recognised the thick mop of grey-speckled hair and the slightly jaded look on the older man's face.

It was the copper from the morning of the christening! The one who had arrested him.

The one who had stopped him getting to the church in time to see the child that he now knew was not *his!*

The one who had stopped him giving Gloria what for.

Well, Mr High-and-Mighty Detective might have put the stoppers on him that day, but he'd not been able to prevent him giving Gloria her just deserts on Friday, had he?

Vinnie would have spoken his thoughts out loud had there not been something a tad menacing about the man.

'I'm afraid the "help" you need, Vincent, far exceeds anything "medical",' Peter said.

Vinnie immediately felt the familiar anger that was always lying close to the surface flare up at the audacity of the man calling him 'Vincent'.

271

No one called him Vincent! No one, that was, apart from his mother.

Vinnie made to stand up, but Peter placed two hands on his shoulders and pushed him down so that he landed with a thump back on the bench. As he did so, Vinnie clocked the black leather gloves the detective was wearing – and it was then that the penny dropped.

He *was* the mystery man in the balaclava who had beaten seven bells out of him that night down the alley by the side of his local – the man who had threatened him and told him that if he ever touched Gloria again, he would be drinking his beer through a straw.

He knew the voice was familiar when he'd been arrested last!

'You still like supping beer, Vincent?' Peter asked, as if they were just two men enjoying a bit of idle chit-chat. 'You still get down the Grindon Mill most nights?'

Vinnie felt himself grow cold. If there had been the slightest uncertainty about this being the balaclava man, then these two apparently innocuous questions dispelled any kind of doubt.

Vinnie looked nervously behind the detective at the closed door of his cell.

'Hey, Sergeant,' he shouted out, 'I want my brief.'

Peter let out a hollow laugh.

'There's just you and me, Vincent,' he said calmly. 'You can scream your head off, but no one's going to hear you down here. And the sergeant you seem so keen on has been called away on urgent business. He told me he's going to be gone for a good while.'

Peter looked down at Vinnie's face, which was becoming paler by the second.

Vinnie's head jerked towards the adjoining cell, causing Peter to let loose another mirthless laugh.

'You don't think there's anyone else down here, do you? Not with Christmas just a few days away? Looks like you've got the place to yourself.' Peter again used the same tone, as if he were simply exchanging pleasantries with an old friend.

What Vinnie didn't know was that Peter had no idea whether the cells on either side were occupied or not. And as far as the custody sergeant was concerned, he had told Peter he needed the little boys' room and asked would he mind 'holding the fort' until he was back?

'Yer can't do this!' Vinnie was now shuffling backwards on the bench so that he was up against the wall. 'It's against the law!'

'Do what, Vincent?' Peter said, his brow furrowed as if he was genuinely puzzled. 'Do you mind if I sit down?' he asked, but he had already done so before Vinnie had time to reply.

The two men were now side by side.

Peter moved his hand quickly and Vinnie flinched.

'Don't worry, Vincent,' Peter said, as he reached for the inside pocket of his coat. 'I'm not going to hurt you ...' He paused and looked Vinnie straight in the eye. 'Providing – ' he pulled out an official form and slowly straightened it out with his gloved hand ' – that you agree that the suggestion I'm going to make is the best way forward in this very difficult situation you find yourself in.'

The fearful look on Vinnie's face began to be infused with curiosity.

'First of all, I'm a man of my word, and if I make a promise I always keep it.' Peter let his words sink in as Vinnie considered a life of supping ale through a straw.

'Secondly, I've got a very peculiar gift of being able to see into the future.' Peter paused again.

Vinnie was now looking at him as if he were certifiable, which was just the impression Peter had been hoping to create.

'And when I look into my crystal ball, I see a charge of grievous bodily harm, along with another, equally serious charge of "making threats to kill" that, I'm sure you can remember, relates back to a month ago during your abortive little attempt to go to a christening in the east end.'

Another pause. Vinnie felt the anger start to bubble up again as he recalled being restrained by this man, who he now knew was actually a nut job hiding behind the socially acceptable façade of holier-than-thou detective.

'Ya bastard!' Vinnie spat the words out.

Peter didn't bat an eyelid.

'As there is plentiful evidence to corroborate these charges,' Peter continued, his face impassive, 'I see your length of incarceration in HMP Durham being a minimum one of six months to a year. And that goes alongside the unofficial punishment you will receive at the hands of your fellow inmates when they find out the man serving time on their wing is a wife batterer.'

Vinnie could feel his heart starting to hammer at the thought of being in prison, trapped in a six-by-eight cell, alone and controlled by a load of sadistic wardens. His mate down the pub had done time and in his words those in charge were 'a breed apart' – and got away with blue murder.

But it was other inmates, his drinking buddy had told him, that could do the most damage. If they got wind that you were in for any kind of crime committed against a child or a woman, you'd be what for. Men on the outside might turn a blind eye to men who abused women and children, but on the inside, well, that was a different kettle of fish. Vinnie was in no doubt that his fellow prisoners would turn on him like rabid animals and rip him apart if they found out what he had done to Gloria.

Vinnie's anger started to recede and his fear began to grow as he sat there and Peter's clearly articulated words sank in.

'But,' Peter said, his voice lifting and becoming upbeat as he raised the papers he was holding in the air, 'there is an alternative.'

Fighting a growing feeling of nausea, Vinnie watched as Peter laid the papers on his lap and smoothed them out with the palm of his gloved hand.

Now Vinnie could see exactly what they were. The heading on the form was big and bold: APPLICATION FOR ENLISTMENT.

Vinnie started shaking his head, his whole being rebelling.

'Nah, mate. No way. I did my bit in the so-called "war to end all wars".' Vinnie let out a bitter laugh. 'Anyways, I'm too old.'

'Well, that's where you're wrong, Vincent,' Peter said, now sounding like a teacher talking to his pupil. 'Let me explain.'

Peter smiled in a way that reminded Vinnie he was not dealing with a sane man.

'You see, on the eighteenth of this month the powers-that-be changed the law and created a new, second National Service Act.'

Another smile.

'They have decided,' Peter said, 'that all unmarried women aged between twenty and thirty – bar those who are pregnant or have children under fourteen – have to do some kind of war work. But of course, all of this isn't any of your concern, is it, Vincent?' The question was clearly rhetorical.

'What *does* apply to you,' Peter stressed, 'is that they also decided that all men aged fifty-one and under *have* to go into military service, unless, of course, they are in some kind of reserved occupation. Even those aged up to sixty now have to do some kind of national service – so, you see, *Vincent*, everyone has to do their bit, regardless of age.'

Vinnie sat staring at Peter, his mind working overtime.

'So, what's it to be, Vincent?' Peter asked, still in his headmaster role. 'A stay in His Majesty's Prison? With an enthusiastic welcoming committee, who will also make good my promise to you from earlier on this year. Or signing up to serve your country?'

He looked at Vinnie, who appeared to have been struck dumb.

'But, actually – ' Peter gave a look as though he'd just been struck by an idea ' – you know what, this little pow-wow we're having is rather a waste of breath because when you've served your sentence, you'll be forced to enlist anyway. And if you were thinking you'd worm your way out of conscription by getting a job in some kind of reserved occupation, then think again. With your criminal record, no one will touch you with a bargepole.'

Peter chuckled and nudged Vinnie as if they were having playful banter and just joshing around.

'So, your decision, Vincent, is absurdly easy, don't you think? It's either all of the above, or a nice change of scenery. A free train journey to Portsmouth, and food and board courtesy of the Royal Navy. You might even see a bit of the world – I hear they're doing regular trips across the Arctic to Russia at the moment.'

Peter looked at Vinnie. His expression said it all. He was in a corner and there was only one way out.

'So, what's it to be, *Vincent*?'

Vinnie could feel the panic start to swell rapidly inside him. He wanted to run, to escape, but as his eyes darted from wall to wall and then to the closed cell door, he knew this was a physical impossibility. He was trapped. Just like he would be if he was sent down. There would be no escape. He couldn't batter his way out of this problem.

He could feel sweat start to form on his forehead. His anger was now ebbing away fast. This, he realised, was one fight he wasn't going to win.

Vinnie looked at the detective sitting next to him, now calmly looking around the cell. The man was a certified lunatic, but even worse than that, he was a madman with the power to send him to his own personal hell if he so chose.

Vinnie's eyes flickered again down to the papers in DS Miller's hands. He sat for a few minutes without saying a word. His heart felt as though it was hammering like a fist inside his chest. Finally, he took a shaky breath, put out his now trembling hand, and reached for the piece of official documentation Peter was holding.

Forlorn and beaten, Vinnie flicked through the pages until he got to the end, where his signature was needed.

'Good man,' Peter said, digging around in his jacket pocket and retrieving a pen.

He watched as Vinnie signed and dated the document and handed it back to him.

'Right then.' Peter stood up, shoving the forms back into his jacket pocket. 'Let's get you out of here!' He knew that time was of the essence if he was to make his final move to push Vinnie into checkmate.

'What, *now*?' Vinnie looked taken aback.

'Of course!' Peter said. 'Unless you want me to come back for you tomorrow?'

Vinnie jumped to his feet and grabbed his jacket, which he had been using as a pillow at the end of the bench.

'No, no, now's good,' he said, desperate to get out of this cell that seemed to be closing in on him by the minute. He pulled on his coat, pushed his few remaining strands of hair back across his balding head, and followed Peter out.

'Ah, DS Gregson,' Peter said, stepping out of the cell and finding his colleague back behind his counter. 'Looks like Mr Armstrong here is eager to do his patriotic duty.' Peter reached over the counter and pulled out the large hard-backed ledger that was used to sign prisoners in and out.

'Oh aye?' DS Gregson asked, wiping some crumbs from the corner of his mouth. He had been distracted by the delivery of some complimentary pastries from a café called Vera's. The skeleton staff at the Borough Police headquarters had all gathered at the front desk as the pretty young woman who had made the delivery at exactly ten o'clock had asked to hand over the treats personally to all the coppers, one by one.

'Vincent here is joining – or should I say rejoining – the Royal Navy,' Peter explained as he signed Vinnie out.

'Well done, my man!' DS Gregson said. He had been chatting to Peter yesterday about this particular collar. The prosecutor for the Crown had looked over the case and had decided it was unlikely to make it to court.

'The usual reasons,' DS Gregson had told Peter resignedly. 'It's a domestic. And even though the victim's not living with him any more, they're still married, and if the rumour mill is true, it won't look good that she's been having it off with someone else, and worse still, has had a bairn with her bit on the side.'

DS Gregson had also told him the prosecutor had said that even if the case did manage to limp its way to court, the most Vinnie could expect would be some kind of con-ditional discharge.

'Right then!' Peter said to the custody sergeant, as he pushed Vinnie gently in front of him. 'Let's get this one out of your hair.'

DS Gregson bade his farewells to Peter and Vinnie before making his way around the counter and walking across to what had been Vinnie's home these past three days. He checked inside to make sure everything was as it should be before shutting the cell door.

As he did so, a well-known pickpocket, who had made the mistake of branching out into black-market racketeering, started shouting from the cell next door, demanding to see *his* brief and moaning that if everyone else was getting out of here why couldn't he?

'*It is Christmas, after all!*' he bellowed.

As Peter and Vinnie climbed into the police car parked at the bottom of the front steps, Vinnie noticed on the back seat a leather holdall that looked familiar.

'Is that mine?' Vinnie demanded.

'Well spotted,' Peter said. He looked at his watch and knew he had to get Vinnie to the station in no less than fifteen minutes. He was cutting it fine. He started up the engine and pulled out quickly when he saw a gap in the traffic.

Vinnie's mouth dropped open. 'We're not going straight to the railway station now, are we?'

'We most certainly are,' Peter said, 'no time like the present.'

'But I need to see Sarah! Say my goodbyes! Make sure I've got all my belongings.'

Vinnie's temporary relief at having been released and his joy at breathing in fresh air, even if it was bitterly cold fresh air, were replaced by panic.

Peter indicated right and drove down St Mary's Way.

'First off,' he said, keeping his eyes on the road, 'everything you need is in that holdall you see on the back seat, including all the relevant paperwork and details of who you have to report to when you get there.'

Peter slowed down to let a woman and her two children cross the road.

Vinnie had the sudden urge to open the door and make a run for it.

'And don't even think about not turning up at the barracks,' Peter said, as if reading his mind. 'If you're not there by midnight tonight you'll be looking at a court martial.'

He put the car into first gear and then second.

'And as regards, Sarah ...' Peter said, casting a quick look at Vinnie, who had leant over to the back seat to retrieve the bag. 'Or rather, Miss Caldwell – I believe she reverted back to her maiden name after her husband died. Anyway, Miss Caldwell has been fully informed of all your previous misdemeanours – most of which, you and I know, go back many years and were never reported to the local constabulary – as well as your more recent offences, including this last one, which, of course, *was* reported.

'She was loath to believe what her ears were hearing, so she was provided with irrefutable evidence – photos of your handiwork from the other day, and also copies of the written statements of those who witnessed the attack.

'Miss Caldwell has since changed the locks on her flat and wants it known that she never wants to see "hide nor hair" of you ever again. And, if you do ever "dare to darken" her doorstep at any time in the future, she will be straight down the station and has been told to ask for me directly.'

Fifty per cent of what Peter had just said was true. There hadn't been any pictures of Gloria's injuries as photographic paper was now being rationed, but a copy of the written statements had done what was needed, with Sarah declaring she'd had enough and would be glad to see the back of him.

Peter had embellished his visit to Sarah a little. She'd had no intention of changing her locks, nor had she made any mention of calling the police should he 'darken my door' – women like Sarah never did – but Peter needed Vinnie to feel that there was nothing left for him in the town. No Gloria, no baby, and definitely no Sarah.

If there was no Sarah, he didn't even have a home to go back to.

Peter sensed Vinnie droop in defeat into the leather-upholstered passenger seat as they pulled up outside the entrance to the railway station.

Jumping out of the driver's seat, Peter waited for Vinnie to drag himself out of the car. He hoicked his bag over his shoulder and walked with Peter into the station. There was a Salvation Army band, braving the cold, playing 'I Saw Three Ships Come Sailing In'. Peter flashed his badge at the stationmaster, who promptly let them through the barrier.

By the time they'd walked down the two flights of wooden steps to platform one, the Portsmouth-bound train was just pulling in.

Peter congratulated himself on his perfect timing.

'Your train warrant is in the side pocket of your bag,' he told Vinnie.

The two men looked at each other.

'Don't forget,' Peter said, 'you brought all this on yourself. Every last bit of it.'

Vinnie's mouth tightened. He wanted to say something, but he had no idea what.

Peter opened the carriage door to the third-class compartment and stood back. 'After you,' he said.

Vinnie looked at this man, who he now knew was beyond any reasoning, and stepped on to the train before Peter gave the door a hefty shove, causing it to slam shut.

Peter then walked back over to the middle of the main platform and sat down on one of the seats, watching as Vinnie slumped down into a seat by the window.

A few minutes later, amidst much whistle-blowing and shouting, huffing and puffing, the train pulled away and Vinnie's morose face turned to give Peter one last look before disappearing behind a thick fog of steam.

Peter stood up and breathed a big sigh of relief. He'd been juggling a few balls, but had managed not to drop any. Vinnie had played right into his hands, better than he could have expected, and the timing had been spot on – even down to the delivery of the cakes.

All he had to do now was head back to the station and call Captain Quinn to tell him that his new recruit would be arriving as discussed. The captain, an old friend of Peter's who hailed from Sunderland, had been more than happy to do his bit after hearing of Vinnie's litany of atrocities against his estranged wife.

Ten minutes later Peter was back at the station and standing behind the main desk. He brushed a few crumbs off the top of the counter and picked up the receiver of the Bakelite telephone. A few words to the operator and he was connected.

'The package is on its way to you!' Peter said.

'Great news.' Captain Quinn's booming voice came down the line loud and clear. 'I'll make sure one of my men is there to pick it up!'

'I owe you one,' Peter said.

'No worries, Miller!' the captain said. 'Rest assured, we'll take it from here. And if there's any bother, I'll keep you informed.'

Peter thanked the captain again and hung up.

That was one problem solved.

Gloria could finally wash her hands of Vinnie.

Now, Peter said to himself, *time to put my own house in order.*

As Peter took a bite of the pastry that had been left for him, he wished more than anything that his own problems were as easy to solve as other people's.

Chapter Thirty-Two

Tuesday 23 December 1941

Rosie was walking quickly up the Borough Road towards the Holme Café, where she was due to meet Peter. Her haste, though, was not because she was running late, but simply because she felt so excited. So happy. It was a buzz of anticipation that was now familiar, but it was also a feeling that had not abated in the least since the two of them had become lovers over a month ago.

Rosie might have just done a hard day's graft in freezing cold temperatures, in the usual gale-like conditions that went hand in hand with working within spitting distance of the harsh North Sea, but on the evenings she was due to meet up with Peter, she felt rejuvenated. As fresh as a daisy. It was as though the very thought of being with him instantly restored her depleted energy levels.

As she reached the bottom end of Holmeside, she spotted Peter striding down the other side of the road. She couldn't quite make out his face, but she could now recognise his swaying gait a mile off, and the way he never buttoned up his coat so that it always seemed to have a life of its own as it flailed around his legs. He'd obviously given up trying to keep his trilby on and was presently carrying it scrunched up in his right hand.

The physical effect Peter had on Rosie never ceased to surprise her. Every time she saw him, even if they had only been parted for a day or two, it was as though her body was being given a tiny jolt of electricity. It came as quickly as it went, but it always took her off guard.

Rosie waved as they neared each other.

'How's that for timing!' Peter's low, definite voice sounded out. He strode towards her and immediately wrapped one arm around her waist, so that their bodies were pressed together, and kissed her. He kissed her again on the neck and whispered, 'God, I've missed you.'

Rosie felt herself blush. It had only been a few days since she had seen him, but she too felt like it'd been an eternity. She wanted to tell him so, but of course she didn't.

Peter went to open the café door, but Rosie grabbed his hand.

'Would you quickly like to meet Kate?'

Peter took a step back. This was a bolt out of the blue. Rosie had not shown any inclination to introduce him to anyone she knew, let alone those closest to her. And he knew Kate was very special to her. The pair of them had been school friends, but after Kate's mum had died suddenly when she was ten, she'd been taken into the care of the Poor Sisters of Nazareth. It hadn't been until last year that Rosie had come across Kate begging in town and had taken her in. Not surprisingly, out of all Rosie's nearest and dearest, apart from Charlotte of course, it was Kate she was the most protective over. By introducing him to Kate, Rosie was showing Peter just how much she trusted him and also how serious she was about him.

'I'd love to meet her!' Peter said.

'Come on, then,' Rosie said, tugging him towards the Maison Nouvelle, which was just next to the café.

Kate's boutique had officially opened for business last week, although there had been a growing number of customers through the doors well before then. Word was spreading about the unique little seamstress-cum-clothes-shop that had just started up, run by a young woman who, it was said, was like Coco Chanel in both looks and talent.

Rosie pushed open the glass-fronted door of Kate's boutique, the front window of which had Bel's beautiful pastel-pink wedding dress on show, although its view was obscured by the criss-cross of anti-blast tape.

'Kate!' Rosie's voice sang out at the same time as the little brass bell tinkled above the doorway.

As Peter followed Rosie into the shop, his eyes widened.

'My goodness!' He couldn't hide his astonishment. He felt as though he had just stepped into another world – an Aladdin's cave stuffed full of a dressmaker's treasures. Rolls of fabric were stacked up against the walls, and there was a black and gold Singer sewing machine on a trestle, surrounded by baskets of overflowing ribbons and huge jars filled with buttons of all shapes and sizes. Two mannequins, swaths of silk and lace pinned to them, took centre stage.

It was only when Peter caught a sudden movement behind the long wooden workbench, which was littered with pincushions, cotton reels and what looked like samples of embroidery, that he saw, or rather heard, Kate.

'Ouch!'

Kate had been rummaging around in a basket on the floor and on hearing the doorbell she'd jerked her head up quickly and caught the underside of the bench.

'Oh, Kate! Are you all right?' Rosie hurried over to see her friend, who was now rubbing her head with one hand, the other clasping the piece of velvet she had been searching for.

'Yes, yes,' Kate said, but her eyes were glued to Peter and a genuine smile was spreading across her narrow, pale face. 'I see you have brought a visitor,' she said, turning her head back to Rosie.

'Well, I thought it was about time Peter met those who are closest to me.' Rosie looked over to see her lover stepping towards Kate with his hand outstretched. 'And I thought to myself, what better person to start with than my very dearest – and oldest – friend?'

Kate tossed her velvet scrap onto the workbench and took Peter's hand for a formal introduction.

'Pleased to meet you, Kate,' Peter said, stooping down a little as he hadn't realised just how small she was. He had quite vivid recollections of her when she had been brought in by the local constabulary for vagrancy, but had never realised just how petite she was.

'Likewise,' Kate said, shaking his hand, which felt rather huge in her own, but was also surprisingly gentle. She also recognised Peter. Not that she had ever had any direct dealings with him in the past, but she'd spent enough time in the cells at the Borough Police headquarters to have clocked most of the coppers who came and went.

Neither of them let on, however, that they knew the other. Peter out of respect, and Kate because she never allowed her old life to even take a peek out of the box where she kept it securely locked away.

'This place is amazing!' Peter said, once again looking around him and seeing a rack of clothes he had not spotted when he first came in. Seeing Peter's eyes rest on the five dresses hanging from the metal frame, Kate looked at Rosie.

'Peter's got a sharp eye,' she said with a mischievous look on her face. 'He's spotted something I was going to give you this evening, but as you're here – ' Kate stepped over various obstacles to get to the dresses that were hanging up ' – I might as well give it to you now.'

Rosie and Peter watched as Kate pulled one of the hangers off the rail.

'This, Rosie – ' she held the dress to the side so that it could be seen in all its glory ' – is my Christmas present to you.'

Rosie took a sharp intake of breath as she looked at the very beautiful, crimson rayon dress that had a loose V-shaped neckline and a thin belt around the waist.

'Oh, Kate! It's gorgeous!' Rosie said.

Kate proudly handed her the dress.

'I know you prefer trousers, but I thought – ' she looked over at Peter quickly before returning her attention to Rosie ' – that as you seem to be going out more of an evening, you could do with a nice dress to wear.'

Kate walked across to the free-standing mirror and angled it towards Rosie. She then stepped back to the woman who had given her a new life, and whom she loved so very much, and held the dress just an inch in front of her.

'See how the colour complements her corn-coloured hair,' Kate said to Peter, 'and the cut of the dress totally suits Rosie's figure.'

'I really don't know what to say!' Rosie was totally taken aback.

'Don't say anything,' Kate said, 'just wear it. And enjoy wearing it! It goes without saying that you'll look totally stunning in it.'

Not, Kate thought, that Rosie needed this dress to look stunning, especially since she had kissed and made up with her detective. This past month everyone at the bordello had commented on how Rosie was positively glowing. Vivian had said she 'radiated being in love'. And all the women had admitted to feeling a tad jealous that Rosie had very obviously found 'The One'.

Everyone, that was, apart from Lily, who was still very sceptical about the whole romance and seemed determined to cling on to her suspicions of Peter, whom she still

288

insisted on calling 'Detective Sergeant Miller'. Kate hadn't argued the point with her – everyone had a right to their own opinions – but as far as Kate was concerned, Rosie was the happiest she had ever seen her, and that was all that mattered.

Seeing Peter for herself now, and meeting him properly, Kate was confident that the man Rosie had fallen for meant her friend no harm. Kate had seen enough of life to know good from bad, and Peter, she knew, was one of the good ones.

'So, our Rosie is leaving us tomorrow,' Kate said to Peter.

'I know.' Peter looked instantly crestfallen. 'I tried my hardest to persuade her to allow Charlotte to spend Christmas here in our lovely town.' He looked over at Rosie. Kate was now carefully putting the red dress into a garment bag. 'But,' he added, 'to no avail.'

'Our "lovely" town,' Rosie retorted, 'appears to have caught Herr Hitler's attention this past year and he seems determined to keep paying us regular visits.' She looked at Peter and Kate as if ready for an argument. 'It's too risky to have her here at the moment.'

Rosie had had to contend not only with Peter's subtle attempts to persuade her to allow Charlotte to come and stay, but also with her sister's not so subtle demands that she be allowed to do so.

Kate and Peter looked at each other. Neither of them needed to say anything; it was clear they were thinking the same thing. Rosie could perhaps be accused of being a tad overcautious, and more than a little overprotective of her younger sibling.

Kate zipped up the front of the bag and handed it to Peter to carry.

'Well, as Rosie is leaving us tomorrow, all the more rea- son why I am now going to push you both out the door.'

She looked up at the large grandfather clock that she had inherited with the shop and from which she had hung a huge berry-red ribbon; it was her one and only nod to the festive period.

'It's getting on,' she said in the sternest voice she could muster, 'and you two need to make the most of what little time you have together. So, go on. Get yourselves away!'

'In fact,' she said, suddenly getting an idea, 'if you're not to spend Christmas together, why don't you two celebrate it this evening instead? It is the eve before Christmas Eve, after all!'

Peter didn't need telling twice. With his free hand he opened the tinkling shop door while Rosie gave Kate a big hug, thanking her over and over again for her dress.

'Let's ditch the café,' Peter said, once they were back on the street. Thankfully the wind had now dropped, although so had the temperature. 'Why don't you come back to mine, change into your new dress, and we'll go for a drink?'

Rosie pulled her coat tight around her and nodded her agreement.

'Bus?' Peter asked.

'No, let's walk,' Rosie said.

Peter took her hand. He was glad they were walking, in spite of the bitter cold. It would give them time to talk.

'I can't believe how different Kate is,' Peter said as they walked up Holmeside.

Rosie had guessed Peter would probably know her friend from Kate's days on the streets, but knew he would never have embarrassed her by making any kind of mention of it, unless Kate brought the subject up herself.

'How much she's changed,' he added thoughtfully.

The darkness of the enforced blackout created an intimacy between them that was partly the reason Rosie had not wanted to take public transport, despite the plummeting temperatures. Walking close together with only the light of the half-moon to guide their way made it feel as though they were in their own private world.

'I know,' Rosie agreed.

'Even her voice sounds different,' Peter added. He remembered how Kate would often be dragged off the streets into the station, kicking and screaming, out of her mind on cheap spirits. He recalled her having quite a strong local accent, but hearing her this evening, if he hadn't known better he might well have thought she hailed from the south.

Rosie laughed. 'Well, that's all due to Lily. As well as a new hairstyle and wardrobe, she also gave her elocution lessons, which is ironic as Lily is a pure-bred cockney!'

Peter chuckled. The more he heard about this Lily, the more he was intrigued. He wasn't stupid, though, and he knew that as a long-time madam, Lily probably would not be best pleased Rosie was courting a copper. 'I bet you Lily was amazed when she discovered that Kate had such a natural talent,' he mused.

'I don't think Lily could believe her luck. She was more than happy to have Kate as a live-in maid, but when she saw what Kate could do with a needle and thread, that was it. In the blink of an eye the duster got replaced with an old sewing machine.'

As they turned into Stockton Road, a car, followed by a bus, passed by, both driving at a snail's pace as the light was so limited they could just about make out the road. This was the first time Rosie had talked so freely and openly about Lily, or even really mentioned the bordello. Peter knew it was another sign that Rosie was truly starting to trust him.

'I told you her mother was the village dressmaker, didn't I?' Rosie asked.

Peter murmured that she had.

'Kate obviously takes after her, but I think there's more to it with Kate. That shop, her designs, her dressmaking – they're all she thinks about. It's her obsession – not that it's a bad obsession to have. I mean, you've seen some of her creations, they're incredible. You just need to look at Bel's wedding dress.'

Peter nodded his silent agreement. He could see that the Maison Nouvelle was just the start for Kate. If they won the war, she was going to go far. With or without Lily's help.

'Does she ever talk to you about her time on the streets? Or her time at Nazareth House?' he asked.

'No, never,' Rosie said, sadly thinking of the occasion she had seen Kate as a child, about a year after she'd been taken into the so-called 'care' of the nuns. Rosie shuddered as she remembered how she had barely recognised her old school friend, how Kate had carried the look of a dog that was regularly thrashed – her once vibrant eyes dead, her skinny arms and legs covered in bruises and welts.

'I do worry she keeps so much stored up inside her, one day it's just all going to have to come out.'

They were both quiet for a while.

Peter knew about the nuns residing at Nazareth House and that there were more than a few bad apples among them. It was knowledge he could do nothing with, and those that could seemed happy to brush it under the carpet. It infuriated and angered him beyond belief, but he knew it was someone else's battle.

'You did a very kind thing, taking her in,' Peter said, as he cast his eye across to Rosie.

'Something she seems intent on repaying me back for tenfold,' Rosie said, nodding at her new dress lying in its protective bag over Peter's arm.

As they crossed over the road and made their way down Grange Terrace, they walked past the front of the tenement where Rosie had lived back when they had met for the very first time, after her uncle Raymond's body had been found at the bottom of the river. Neither of them said anything, but Peter squeezed Rosie's hand as they passed. They didn't want to bring up any kind of remembrance of the man who had caused Rosie such trauma and hurt.

'I have to bring you up to date on Vinnie,' Peter said, knowing that he had to tell Rosie about his visit to Vinnie's cell yesterday. The sooner Gloria got to know, the better.

Rosie looked at Peter, panic and concern on her face. 'You haven't done anything, have you?'

Peter let go of Rosie's hand and instead wrapped his arm around her shoulders and squeezed her to him.

'Not in the way you're thinking,' he laughed.

As they turned down Belvedere Road, Peter asked Rosie if she had heard the news that they were widening the scope of conscription.

'No,' Rosie said, 'I haven't.' She looked embarrassed by her lack of knowledge.

'It's only just happened,' Peter explained. 'Parliament's just sanctioned the changes, so I'm not surprised you haven't. It always takes these things a while to filter through.' He took a breath and explained. 'The long and short of it is that all men under the age of fifty-one now have to do some kind of military service.'

For the briefest of moments Rosie panicked. Peter was forty-three. 'That doesn't mean you're going to be called up?' The words came out as soon as she thought them, but she reprimanded herself. 'God, I really am being thick today. Obviously they can't call you up, because you're in a reserved occupation.' Rosie snuggled into Peter's chest as a car passed and sounded its horn at a couple across the road who waved back their greeting.

Peter was just about to say something when Rosie perked up.

'Sorry, you were saying? Vinnie?'

Peter paused for a moment as if gathering his thoughts. 'Yes, Vinnie. Well, when I heard this, it gave me an idea.'

'Go on,' Rosie said, knowing that what Peter was about to tell her was going to bring Gloria tidings of great joy.

'Well, it was all quite straightforward,' he said. 'I merely pointed out that he had two alternatives.'

Peter briefly explained the choices he had put to Vinnie, who had sensibly opted to take the free rail ticket down to Portsmouth. Peter's somewhat sanitised telling of the time he had spent with Vinnie yesterday ended with the reassurance that Vinnie was now under the command of a very good friend of his, and should Gloria's soon-to-be-ex-husband go AWOL, Peter would be the first to know.

'Not that I think he would have a lot to come back for,' Peter said, before explaining that Vinnie's live-in girlfriend had also washed her hands of him after she had been shown the very detailed police statements.

'I actually think,' Peter reflected as they neared the turning to Tunstall Vale, 'that there was a part of her that was relieved. She was certainly pretty adamant that I pass the message on to Vinnie that she no longer wanted anything to do with him.'

Rosie stopped Peter, reached up and took his face in her hands, then kissed him full on the lips.

'DS Miller,' she said, 'you are the best! And a genius strategist. And I love that Vera's pastries were part of your cunning plan!'

Peter felt as proud as Punch. He had never been able to chat to anyone about his occasional forays into what he called his 'alternative policing methods'.

'This is the best Christmas present ever for Gloria.' Rosie planted another kiss on his lips. 'Thank you!'

As they continued on their way, Peter's feeling of worthiness soon diminished and was replaced by a slight nervousness. *He should have said something when he'd told Rosie about the new legislation.* It would have been the perfect opening to start the conversation he knew he could no longer avoid.

Peter opened his mouth and was just about to speak when Rosie suddenly looked at him.

'You'll take care of yourself when I'm away, won't you?' All the talk about conscription and trips to Portsmouth had suddenly made her think how terrible it would be if Peter were to be taken away from her.

'I know I shouldn't say this,' she hesitated, 'and I know we haven't been courting for all that long, but if anything ever happened to you, or you weren't here for any reason, I think life would be unbearable.'

They had just reached the gate that led onto Brookside Gardens and were now standing looking at each other.

Peter saw that Rosie's eyes were wet with emotion.

'I love you,' Rosie said simply. It was the first time she had said the words, although her actions had already told him what she felt many times. 'And,' she added, 'I never want to be parted from you.'

Peter looked down at the woman who had stolen his heart from the moment they'd first met.

'And I love you too, Rosie. So very, very much.'

As they kissed for a moment, Peter felt awash with a terrible guilt. Why did love always seem to come hand in hand with hurt?

They walked in silence to Peter's front door. Once they were in, Rosie turned to him.

He switched on the hallway light and could see that her eyes were sparkling and her face was a picture of pure happiness.

'You know what?' she said with a half-smile.

Peter traced the outline of her face with his finger. 'What?' he whispered into her ear whilst untying the belt on her grey mackintosh.

'I think Kate is right,' Rosie answered, her voice soft. 'Let's pretend this *is* Christmas Day.'

Peter murmured his agreement as he slid his free arm inside her coat and around her waist.

'So,' Rosie said, her lips grazing Peter's neck, 'what would we do if it was just the two of us?'

'Well,' Peter answered without hesitation, 'first of all, you'd *have* to put on your special Christmas dress.'

His face was deadly serious as he handed her the clothes bag.

Rosie's eyes twinkled as she took the dress without saying anything and went upstairs to change.

Peter took off his coat and went straight into the small but cosy living room with its well-worn armchair and sofa littered with cushions. He switched on the side light and quickly knelt down and grabbed the matches by the hearth to start up the fire that he had stacked up with kindling and coal before he'd left that morning.

He then went back out into the hallway and shouted up the stairs.

'How about a spam sandwich in lieu of a roasted chicken?'

He could hear Rosie's gentle laughter as she opened the bedroom door.

'Give me spam over chicken any day!' she shouted back down the stairs.

Five minutes later the fire was blazing and Peter had quickly slapped together two spam sandwiches, which he had cut into triangles and put on a plate in an attempt to make them look more enticing.

He was just pouring them both a glass of brandy when Rosie walked through the doorway in her new red dress.

Peter stood and stared.

'Happy Christmas,' Rosie said, as she walked across and took her drink.

'Happy Christmas, Rosie,' Peter said, kissing her gently on the lips.

Peter knew then that what he had to tell Rosie would have to wait until she got back.

This evening was just too perfect to spoil.

Chapter Thirty-Three

Christmas Eve 1941

The next morning, as Peter walked into town and made his way to police headquarters, his mind kept swinging from untamed thoughts of Rosie, and the rather magical and very passionate night they had just spent together, and the letter now tucked neatly into his coat pocket.

Images of Rosie practically flying out the front door, determined she was not going to be late for work, then rushing back up his short front pathway, swinging her boxed gas mask over her shoulder and kissing him one last time, suddenly sprang to mind. He had seen in her eyes the anguish she felt at leaving him, and he had also felt it in her farewell kisses.

'I'll miss you,' he had told her. And had meant it – so much more than she could realise.

'Damn it!' Peter said aloud, his words creating a mist as his breath merged with the icy cold air.

He should have just spat it out last night. Told Rosie the truth. He really should have told her as soon as he'd had his conversation with Toby a week ago. It was only fair. He and Rosie had sworn to each other there would be no more secrets – no more lies.

As he walked into the centre of town, he looked about him and felt a fresh wave of anger and frustration. The place was slowly being razed to the ground, brick by brick, by the constant drop of Hitler's bombs. He noticed the shopkeepers' valiant attempts to make their window displays as decorative as possible considering the scarcity of available goods, and how this contrasted with the increasing amount of black being worn by those grieving the menfolk who were never coming home.

He knew this year there would be hundreds of people unable to spend Christmas in their own homes as those were now little more than heaps of bricks and rubble. And he also knew that thousands of children would be spending this special time separated from their families, having been evacuated to live with complete strangers.

It was all of this that made Peter certain that what he was going to do was the right thing.

If only he didn't have Rosie in his life.

But he did, and it was because she was in his life that doing what was right was making him feel so bloody awful.

'*Damn it! Damn it! Damn it!*' he said, as he posted his letter and strode to work.

'Gloria! Gloria!' Rosie couldn't stop herself from shouting out above the hordes of flat-capped heads as she spotted Polly's bottle-green headscarf bobbing next to Gloria's thick brown curls, which had been heaped up into a bun.

Rosie had practically flown back to her flat from Peter's, changed clothes, and was back out her own front door in record-breaking time. Aided by the fact she was wearing lace-up boots and not heels, she'd managed to make it to the main gates of Thompson's by twenty-past seven, thereby giving herself a few minutes' breather as she scrutinised the first batch of workers disembarking from the ferry that was now bobbing about energetically on a frothing River Wear.

On hearing Rosie's distinctive voice, Polly and Gloria both looked up, worried at first until they saw Rosie's smiling face and frantically waving hands straining to be seen above the influx of shipbuilders.

'Looks like Rosie had a date last night,' Gloria said with quiet humour. Polly chuckled. They all now knew when Rosie had been out with her detective as she always turned up at work with traces of make-up on her face.

'Hi!' Rosie couldn't contain her excitement as both women reached her and the three of them were carried by the moving mass of workers to the timekeeper's cabin.

'Sorry, Polly, but do you mind if I grab Gloria for a moment and we catch you up?' Rosie asked as they grabbed their timecards off Alfie, who had managed to find a little Christmas tree and put it in his cabin window. A metal star that one of the platers had cut out of some scrap metal adorned the top.

'Course not,' Polly said, throwing Gloria a curious look before becoming lost in the crowd spilling into the main yard.

'What is it?' Gloria asked as Rosie pulled her into one of the prefabs that was used as a storeroom but was currently empty, giving them a respite from the early-morning melee.

'Vinnie's gone!' Rosie exclaimed, her face animated.

'Gone?' Gloria was confused. 'Gone where? I thought they were still holding him?'

'He's gone for good!' Rosie said. 'Conscripted. Back into the navy.'

Gloria stood and stared at her boss in disbelief.

'I don't understand. Vinnie would never do that,' she said as Rosie hoicked herself up on to the wooden counter.

'The number of times I had to listen to him mithering on about how he had "done his bit" and they could "bugger off if they tried to drag" him into this war.'

Taking a deep breath, Rosie told Gloria what had passed between Vinnie and Peter in the police cell, although her version was even more sanitised than the one Peter had related to her.

As Gloria sat and listened, her expression changed from confusion to surprise to jubilance, before it finally crumpled as she burst into tears.

'Oh my God, Rosie,' Gloria couldn't hold her emotions or her sobs in, 'this is fantastic news. I can't believe it. So he's in Portsmouth now?'

'Yes, and if he takes one step off base and goes AWOL, he'll be court-martialled and Peter will be informed straight away.'

Rosie jumped down off the counter and went over to Gloria, bobbing down so that she was at eye level with her.

'You're *free*, Gloria!' she said. 'You're finally free of that *bastard*!'

Gloria looked at her friend and started laughing and crying at the same time.

By three o'clock Rosie had completed a half-shift, handed over the reins to a very happy Gloria, hurried back to her flat, changed for the second time that day, and with weary limbs lugged herself and her overstuffed carryall the quarter-mile to the railway station just in time to catch her train to York, from where she would catch a connecting local service to Harrogate.

Within minutes of leaving the station, Rosie's eyes had become heavy as she enjoyed the comfort of the cushioned seat. Next to her was an old man who had fallen asleep within minutes of getting settled into his seat; the rest of the carriage appeared to be taken up mainly with army, navy and air force personnel.

Finally, she could rest and simply be alone with her own thoughts.

She felt a lovely warm glow as she recalled telling Gloria the news about Vinnie. It had been a Christmas gift to surpass all others. The news had transformed Gloria. She'd been like a different woman – more relaxed and contented than Rosie and the rest of the women had ever seen her. And there was no need to say why. Gloria had been relieved of the heavy and worrisome burden she had become too used to carrying around with her for too long. Now, finally, it had been taken off her. For good.

Rosie felt her heart swell as she thought of Peter, and how it had been thanks to him.

Looking out of the window at the miles of unspoilt landscape, Rosie marvelled, as she always did when she ventured out of her hometown, at the breathtaking beauty of 'England's green and pleasant land'. And as she allowed her eyes to close, her mind drifted back to Peter. His touch. His smell. The way he made her feel. She had never felt this way about anyone ever before. This past month she'd had to pinch herself – numerous times – to remind herself that what was happening was real. And true.

She was in love with Peter, as he was with her. Neither of them could deny it or try and hide it. She had never dared to hope that she would fall so deeply in love with someone – and would want to be with that person for the rest of her life. She knew that he would be there for her through thick and thin – something she had never had – and he knew that she too would be there for him during all of life's inevitable ups and downs.

It was only now that she had met Peter and had experienced that incredible closeness – the emotional intimacy as well as the physical – that she realised just how alone she had been.

And now – hard though it was to believe – she didn't have to be on her own any more.

Chapter Thirty-Four

Christmas Day 1941

'Mammy! Daddy! Look!' Lucille's jubilant cries had Tramp sitting up alert in her basket and the puppy racing round the rug, snatching up pieces of wrapping paper and shaking her catch from left to right for all her worth.

Last night Lucille had tried her utmost to stay awake in an attempt to catch a glimpse of Father Christmas, but, like most children the length and breadth of the country, she had failed. Her disappointment, though, had soon been overtaken by her joy at seeing that Santa had left behind a stocking stuffed with presents and not a bag of coal, as had been threatened if she was naughty – although it was something the rest of the Elliot household would have been glad to see at the bottom of Lucille's bed, since all fuel was now being rationed.

Having got the fire going before allowing Lucille to drag her Christmas stocking down the stairs and into the kitchen so that she could open her presents on the rag rug by the warmth of the range, Bel and Joe were soon joined by Agnes and Arthur, and then, finally, by Pearl after she'd had her usual morning smoke out in the backyard.

There was only one member of the household missing and that was Polly, who had opted to work a half-shift along with the rest of the women welders. She'd been up and out at seven o'clock sharp, as soon as Gloria had arrived and dropped off Hope, who was now sleeping soundly in Lucille's old crib.

As everyone sat around the kitchen table, all blurry-eyed and sipping on steaming cups of tea, Lucille proudly held up each of her presents as if they were trophies she had won. Bel had been eternally grateful that Gloria had told her about a small, hidden-away second-hand shop down one of the side streets in town. It was where Gloria had got her Silver Cross pram and where most of the toys that Lucille was now waving in the air had been purchased.

There had been some deliberation as to what to wrap the presents in as paper was now a precious commodity due to the country's wood-pulp supplies coming from places now under Nazi control. They had ended up using Arthur's old newspapers and colourful bits of ribbon, and they were pleased to see that this had by no means lessened Lucille's excitement on opening her gifts.

Lucille's joy that it was Christmas Day permeated the whole of the Elliot household. Even Pearl appeared loath to leave the happy atmosphere, the warmth of the roaring fire and the carols blaring out of Arthur's wireless for her shift at the Tatham. Once there, however, she was, as she was apt to say, 'happy as a dog with two tails' as the festive spirit meant she was being bought so many drinks by her regulars that she had to chalk them up on the tab board.

Ronald was the surprising star of the day after managing to get hold of a whole chicken, which Agnes had delightfully accepted with no questions asked. Most of her neighbours were making do with bacon, or a bit of ham, although it was still going to be slim pickings considering the number of people she had to feed today, which, on top of those living under her roof, also included Gloria, Ronald and Arthur's friend, Albert.

'I'll be back in an hour or two!' Joe's voice shouted through to his mother as he pulled on his coat ready to go and see Major Black. He grabbed hold of Lucille, who as always was demanding his attention, and held her aloft, causing her to emit a mix of screams and giggles while he told her to be good until he got back.

Agnes had also invited the Major to spend Christmas with them, but wasn't surprised when Joe told her that the offer had been 'most gratefully received', but had, all the same, been declined.

'Tell him there's more than enough to go round if he changes his mind!' Agnes stuck her head out of the scullery, where she was peeling what felt like a never-ending amount of potatoes and carrots, still thick with mud from Arthur and Albert's allotment.

Bel walked Joe to the front door with Hope cradled in her arms; she was now wide awake, her huge blue eyes taking in all the sights around her.

'Send our Christmas wishes to the Major,' Bel said as Joe gave her a gentle kiss at the door.

As Bel watched Joe hurry off up the street, his walking stick striking the pavement, she was glad he had found a good friend in the Major. As a veteran of the First War, he had experienced his fair share of war atrocities, not least the trauma of losing both his lower limbs in battle. Bel knew there was so much Joe hadn't told her about what had happened out in the desert, and that he probably would never be able to confide in her about his eighteen months on the front line, but she knew Joe talked to the Major. And she was sure it was no coincidence that since he'd come to know Major Black and joined up with the Home Guard, his terrible night terrors, which used to wake the whole house, had abated.

Walking back to the kitchen and into the scullery where Agnes was busy peeling and chopping the veg, Bel prepared a bottle for Hope.

'How you feeling?' she asked. She didn't need to say any more. They both knew that today was going to be a mixed bag for them all. This was their second Christmas Day without Teddy, but their first knowing that there would never be another with him. Agnes looked at Bel and her eyes spoke of the terrible heartache she was feeling and trying desperately to hide. Agnes knew she wasn't the only mother in the country to be feeling so bereft today, but it didn't make her pain any the less. Last week they'd all listened to the latest news about the war in North Africa and Rommel's retreat, but it had not given them cause for jubilation, only a sense that perhaps Teddy's life had not been sacrificed in vain.

'Keeping busy,' Agnes said simply, as she reached with her free hand to gently squeeze her daughter-in-law's arm. She knew Bel's grief over Teddy's death had been overwhelming, just as she also knew that since Bel and Joe had grown close and fallen in love, Bel had continued to battle feelings of guilt.

'But it's like I always say, "our lives must go on,"' Agnes said, looking at baby Hope and smiling a little sadly. 'And, you know, Teddy would want us to be happy and to make the most of our lives.'

She could see tears starting to show in Bel's eyes.

'I just thank God that Joe made it home in one piece,' Agnes said. She would never admit it, but sometimes she was glad Joe had been injured, as there was no way he'd ever be sent back out to the front line.

'And,' she continued, looking through to the kitchen where Lucille was forcing the puppy to do a little jig to music on the wireless as Arthur watched and chuckled, 'I really don't know what I would do if I didn't have you and Lucille and Polly. I really don't.'

Bel couldn't stop a tear falling down her cheek as she gave her mother-in-law a big hug with her free arm.

It was the first time she'd realised that Agnes needed them as much as they needed her.

As Arthur watched Lucille playing and making Pup do a doggy version of the hokey-cokey, he chuckled at the little girl's mischievousness. He remembered Tommy around the same age. Flo had always done her utmost to make Christmas extra special for their grandson. Trying her hardest, Arthur had always thought, to make up for the fact that Tommy didn't have a ma or da with whom to share the most exciting day of the year. Flo would some-how conjure up a feast and a stocking stuffed with toys, even when they could ill afford it.

Watching Lucille collapse in giggles with Pup, Arthur wished that Tommy had also enjoyed that same sense of innocent, gay abandon. But with Tommy there had always been an underlying seriousness – even when he was a toddler. Tommy had his father's looks and strong physique, but he had unfortunately inherited his mother's deep sensitivity. And it was that which caused Arthur concern, especially now he was so far away from home.

Tommy's mother had taken her own life after she'd been unable to get over the death of her husband in the First War, and as Tommy had grown up it was clear that he too had that same emotionally sensitive streak, which often caused him to withdraw and suffer dark moods.

Arthur had hoped that his grandson would find himself a wife, and when Polly had come along and made his grandson happier than he had ever seen him before, he had thought it the answer to his prayers.

Arthur's eyes started to feel heavy and he tried to keep them open as Lucille toddled off to wake up Tramp, who was happily snoozing by the side of the range. The warmth of the fire and the early Christmas Day excitement won over, however, and Arthur closed his eyes, allowing himself to indulge in a little mid-morning snooze. As he felt himself starting to drift off, as always, whenever sleep came for him, Flo appeared by his side.

'Eee, pet, keep yer eye on that grandson of ours,' Arthur asked her. 'Keep him strong, my love. Keep him safe, and bring him back soon.'

'No rest for the wicked then?' Jimmy shouted over to the women welders as they huddled around their five-gallon barrel fire at the start of the half-shift they had all volunteered for. The need for ships to be built and repaired as swiftly as possible took precedence over everything, and that included Christmas Day.

'Yer right there, Jimmy,' Gloria shouted back good-naturedly.

'Aye, well, merry Christmas to yer all anyways,' Jimmy waved.

'Happy Christmas!' the women welders chorused back as Jimmy headed over to his squad of riveters.

Like Jimmy and his men, Gloria, Polly, Dorothy, Angie and Martha had all offered to work today's shift. They too had already bandied about the joke that there was 'no rest for the wicked', but in truth no one had been twisting their arms behind their backs when the call had gone out for festive-season overtime.

Gloria had immediately put her name down as she had not relished the thought of being at home on her own, even if it was with Hope, and when Agnes had invited her over for Christmas dinner, she'd jumped at the chance to work and then spend a few hours at the Elliots'. At least it would take her mind off Jack. Lately it seemed that the more they saw each other, the more she missed him when they weren't together.

Polly, of course, would have worked a full shift had her mother not had a fit at the mere mention of it, and Martha had also come to a compromise with her parents, who agreed to part of – but not the entire – Christmas Day being sacrificed. This was a particularly special time of year for Mr and Mrs Perkins as they had adopted Martha during a bleak and bitter Christmas twenty-two years ago, not that Martha was aware of the significance. It had been something Mr and Mrs Perkins had not felt the need to impart to their daughter, although they had told her that she was adopted. Even when Martha was a small child, they had known it was unlikely they would ever be able to pass her off as their own.

Dorothy and Angie had also not seemed keen on spending the day with their respective families. Angie's house was chaos at the best of times, but since her mam had been doing more overtime – or rather, seeing her fancy man on the sly – it had grown worse. Dorothy, on the other hand, couldn't bear the awkwardness of sharing the day with her mother and stepfather and her four younger half-sisters. They would both have probably signed up for the whole day had they not decided to get themselves togged up and go out on the town after work.

Hannah had asked her boss, Basil, if she too could work on Christmas Day. He had chuckled and ruffled Hannah's thick mop of black hair like she was a little child and told her that the office workers – thankfully – had the day off. He had thought Hannah's keenness to work was because she was a Jew, and as such Christmas Day was the same as any other, but what he didn't realise was that Hannah would have wanted to work even if it was the holiest day of the year. She was now doing all the overtime on offer, and was also working on the Sabbath, which, she told herself, was allowed as God would understand why.

'What's everyone having for their Christmas dinner then?' Angie asked, moving from one foot to another and gently clapping her gloved hands together. It was cold and windy, but there hadn't been even a hint of a white Christmas. Not even a slightly frost-coated one.

'To be answered during the break!' Gloria declared, picking up her welding helmet and motioning the rest of the women to follow her. 'To the fitting-out quay!' she commanded, as she led the way across the yard.

Rosie had put her in charge while she was away and Gloria was keen to do the best job possible, helped by the fact that she felt on cloud nine, and had done since yesterday morning when Rosie had relayed the wonderful news that Vinnie – the bane of her life, the man who had caused her so much physical and emotional pain for so many years – was now out of her life. Permanently.

She had reported the good news to the rest of the women welders over lunch and Dorothy had let loose with an uncontrolled 'Hurrah!' that had caused a fair amount of good-humoured ribbing from the men at the neighbouring tables.

Gloria, however, had to wait to tell Jack until after Christmas, as they'd agreed he was to spend it at home with Helen. The decision to do so had gone a long way to assuage Gloria's feelings of guilt towards Helen, which had become greater on learning how emotional she had seemed when Rosie had gone to thank her on behalf of the women. Gloria's love for Jack, and his love for her, had come with a price to pay. Gloria was paying hers with guilt.

Hopefully, though, Gloria told herself in an effort to ease that guilt, Helen and her father would be sitting in front of a nice warm fire, exchanging presents and getting ready to enjoy their family Christmas dinner together.

'Darling, can you get Geraldine and Frank a glass of the red, please?'

Jack nodded in agreement. He would have spoken, had he thought he'd be heard over the loud music and the chatter that had been steadily increasing in volume as the day had progressed. Any hope of simply enjoying a normal family Christmas and spending some time with his daughter had been quashed from the moment he'd opened his eyes in the comfort of the back bedroom, where he now slept without any objections from Miriam.

As soon as he had woken up he had heard the beginnings of a whirlwind of activity. Poor Mrs Westley. She, along with a couple of local girls who had been brought in to help, had barely had a minute's rest as Miriam had ordered everyone about and organised what was amounting to be the event of the year. Miriam had even jokingly called it 'Christmas with the Crawfords'. It was as though she had purposely invited everyone they knew, or rather *everyone* who was *someone*.

After Jack got up, he'd tried to suggest that he and Helen go for a Christmas-morning walk around Roker Park, and perhaps, if the weather wasn't too awful, have a stroll along the promenade. They mightn't be able to get down to the beach as it had been sprinkled with landmines and cordoned off with rolls of barbed wire, but they could still walk along the clifftops and look out to sea. But Helen had been too busy, running around getting herself ready for a breakfast date at the Grand with some naval officer billeted there.

Jack had asked Helen about him – had actually been quite glad she was going out socialising, as she'd seemed too focused on work lately and he'd been worried she wasn't going out and doing what other young women her age did. He had tried to find out more from Miriam about the mystery man from the Admiralty, but she had simply brushed it aside with some flippant comment about it being a 'short-lived dalliance' that wouldn't last two minutes. Jack had thought Miriam might have shown more interest, since Helen wasn't one to go out much.

'So, Jack – ' it was their neighbour two doors down, who was well known in the banking world and came from what Jack called old money ' – how's life treating you at Crown's?'

Jack forced a smile on his face as he began his now well-worn spiel on all things shipyards and the war. He knew it wouldn't be long before they asked him about his trip to America, about the SS *Tunisia*, which he'd been travelling on when it was sunk by enemy aircraft just off the west coast of Ireland, and about what it was like to nearly drown in the North Atlantic.

He had started to feel like a performing chimp in a circus whenever he was forced to attend any of Miriam's fancy social dos or be part of her determined effort to throw the town's best dinner parties.

When the call went out that dinner was to be served, Jack presumed that he would be next to his daughter, but when he sat down at the bottom end of the table he found himself next to two of the town's bigwigs. Jack had looked around for Helen, only to see her pulling up a chair halfway down the table.

313

So much for spending time with my daughter, Jack thought to himself.

Jack watched as Helen lit up another cigarette. It concerned him that she seemed to be smoking an awful lot lately, and even though she was smiling as she conversed with the woman next to her, she seemed to have a sadness about her.

'This year . . .' Miriam's voice broke the chatter. She was standing at the top of the table, gently tapping the side of her wine glass with a silver knife. 'This year,' she repeated, and her guests fell quiet, 'I have decided there has been far too much misery and warmongering and that we need to have a very special Christmas celebration in defiance of that horrible little man, Hitler.'

There was a resounding murmur of agreement.

Miriam then took a deep breath and looked down the table at Jack.

'But what makes this year so very special is that I thought I had lost the man I love. My husband. Jack Crawford.'

There was a deliberate pause.

'A husband I not only nearly lost the once when his ship was bombed at sea and we didn't know if he had survived.'

Jack was now feeling very uncomfortable. Miriam knew he could only really abide these parties if he kept a low profile.

'But,' Miriam continued, her voice becoming thick and emotional, 'a husband I nearly lost a *second* time when we had no idea whether or not he would come out of his coma.' Miriam again looked down the table at Jack. 'So, I'd like to raise a toast to my husband. The one I thought I had lost, twice, but who thank the Lord, I now have back. *For keeps.*'

There was a loud consensus of 'Hear hear's and lots of clinking of glasses. Jack felt himself bristle. He had been getting more and more of his memory back of late, which he knew could only be down to the amount of time he was spending with Gloria, as well as with Arthur. It was as though his memory was being teased out bit by bit – like a tight knot that's hard to unravel at first, but once loosened a little, it gets easier and easier, until, before you know it, the knot has gone.

Jack understood enough now to know that Miriam did not mean a word of what she had just said. That she had never really loved him, she had only *wanted* him. As though he were her property. Her possession. But it was the way she'd said the words 'For keeps' that had made him bristle and gave him an odd feeling of being trapped.

After dessert had been served and consumed, more toasts followed, mostly along the lines of 'Victory shall be ours!'

Jack raised his glass, but couldn't help wishing that he was working at the yard to bring the country closer to 'victory', rather than simply toasting the idea of it.

As Helen pulled out another cigarette from her packet of Pall Malls, the guest next to her said something and she forced a smile on her face and asked her to repeat the question. Luckily, she didn't have to answer it as her mother had stood up and was chinking the side of her glass with a knife, demanding attention.

Looking at her mother and listening to her little speech, Helen had to silently congratulate her on her performance. The woman knew how to put on a show, that was for sure. And she seemed to do it so seamlessly. Helen, on the other hand, was struggling. She had struggled not to show her true feelings towards her father and had known she would say something if she had taken up his offer of a Christmas walk. She would have preferred to have been at work, had she not known Gloria and the rest of the women welders would be there. Mind you, even if they hadn't been there today, her mother wouldn't have allowed it. She couldn't be seen to have her daughter working in the shipyard, of all places, on Christmas Day. What would people think?

And so she was having to endure this fiasco. This extravaganza of a show her mother was putting on.

She knew her mother had something up her sleeve, although she had not deigned to tell Helen what it was. Whatever Miriam had planned, it involved making everyone think that she and her husband had a wonderful, happy marriage. That they were the perfect family.

Her mother also seemed to be going out of her way to shower her daughter with lots of attention and gifts, including a new no-expense-spared dress from the young seamstress at Maison Nouvelle. Helen had argued with herself that this was her mother trying to make her feel better, knowing how much she'd been hurt by her father's secrets and lies. His betrayal.

So, why didn't she feel comforted by her mother's kindness?

Her mother wouldn't be putting on a show for her too, would she?

Her love for her daughter was real, wasn't it?

Honestly, Helen thought as she blew out a steady stream of smoke and listened to her mother's speech, *I don't think I can tell black from white at the moment.*

'Bon appétit!' Lily declared, wine glass held high as she sat at the head of the kitchen table, on which lay a veritable banquet. George, Kate, Vivian and Maisie all followed suit, raised their glasses and chorused, 'Bon appétit!'

Much to Lily's delight, Maisie added in the most guttural accent she could muster, 'Joyeux Noël!'

Lily would have normally kept the bordello open on what could be a very profitable day, but she'd decided that this year they all needed a break – even if it was just for the day – so she'd given all the girls a generous Christmas bonus and switched the little red light off after the last client had left on Christmas Eve.

Feeling particularly grateful that Peter hadn't blown the whistle on them last month and that they weren't all now eating some form of indeterminable prison gruel courtesy of His Majesty, Lily had paid through the nose to get the best that was on offer on the black market.

Earlier on, over breakfast, Lily had declared that today was all about being totally *'décadent'*, which meant that by the time they all sat down for a rather late Christmas dinner at six o'clock they had all drunk too much. All of them apart from Kate, of course, who hadn't touched a drop since stepping over the threshold of the bordello – the day when her old life had ended and her new one had begun.

Kate had no qualms about being the only sober person in the house as it gave her the chance to keep popping back up to her little attic room to work on her latest creation, although she was only able to snatch the odd half-hour here and there throughout the day as Lily was determined she be a part of the Christmas frivolity.

Most of the day had passed in the usual incessant chatter about everything and everyone, as well as a number of Mae West renditions by Vivian, with George accompanying her on the piano.

Maisie had persuaded George to let her borrow his little red MG to pay a quick visit to Pearl at the Tatham. No one had had any idea that Maisie could drive, and George hadn't been convinced she was telling the truth until he had watched nervously from the front door as she drove down the street changing gear faultlessly.

'Quite the lady driver!' he said to Lily, not bothering to hide his very obvious relief.

Pearl was over the moon when Maisie turned up, looking stunning in a very classy beaded ivory dress that had a dropped waist and made her look like an original Charleston girl – a look enhanced by her sleek ebony cigarette-holder. On seeing Maisie enter the pub, Bill told Pearl to take a break, not that Pearl was waiting on permission. On spotting her daughter, she bellowed across the bar 'Maisie!' and told anyone who would listen that this was *her* daughter.

As usual, Maisie's arrival caused a ripple of interest. It wasn't just her exquisite beauty, however, that turned heads; the dark colour of her skin also caused a few eyebrows to be raised. This was the east end, after all, and the only 'coloured people' they'd ever seen in these parts were the sailor boys from far-flung places on the other side of the world. Pearl clocked the looks and the whispered words but didn't give a toss. She was just chuffed to pieces that Maisie had come to see her and even more so when Maisie pulled out of her large shoulder bag a bottle of whisky and a packet of Woodbines.

Maisie knew this was probably not the most sensible Christmas present to buy someone who had nearly drunk herself into an early grave that night she'd gone walkabouts, but she also knew her mother was never going to be teetotal.

'Eee, thanks, pet,' Pearl said as she inspected her bottle and saw that it was a single malt. She then opened up the packet of cigarettes, pulled two out, gave one to Maisie and shoved the other in her mouth.

'These are on the house!' Bill's booming voice could be heard behind them. They both automatically turned to see

Pearl's boss towering over them with two large brandy glasses.

'Ah, thanks, Bill, that's very kind of you.' Maisie flashed a smile up at Bill as she took the drinks from him. Bill wasn't Maisie's biggest fan as he'd been there when she had revealed herself to Pearl at Bel's wedding reception, but everyone appeared to have made their peace. Besides, Pearl seemed happy enough and that was all that mattered to Bill, who was a bit soft on the woman, not that he would ever admit it to anyone – least of all Pearl.

'Hope you're gonna share that later on?' Bill joked, eyeing up the expensive bottle of Scotch.

'Ha! You'll be lucky to get a sniff!' Pearl shot back, before picking up the bottle and handing it to Bill. 'Shove it behind the bar, will ya?'

After Bill left, Pearl took her brandy from Maisie.

'Well, merry Christmas, pet.' Pearl raised her glass.

'Merry Christmas, "Ma"!' Maisie said, gently chinking Pearl's glass.

They were both unusually quiet, aware that this was actually quite a special moment.

Pearl could never have imagined that she would be sitting there with the daughter she'd thought she would never see again – and on a Christmas Day of all days.

Maisie had also never envisaged a time that she would ever be with the mother she had never known, and whom she had both wanted and hated in equal measure.

'Our first Christmas,' Maisie said, her words spoken quietly and without her usual air of confidence.

'Aye,' Pearl said, 'our first.' She looked at her beautiful daughter and still couldn't quite believe she was her own and, moreover, that she was with her now.

'But not our last,' she added, taking a long drag on her cigarette.

Ten minutes later, when the pub started to heave and Bill was clearly in need of an extra pair of hands, Pearl returned to the other side of the bar. Maisie nipped across the road and paid a very quick visit to her sister and her little niece, whom Maisie had grown quite close to, even though she was not overly fond of children.

Bel was pleased to see Maisie, who had politely declined Agnes's invitation to Christmas dinner. She knew her sister would stay just long enough to wish everyone a happy Christmas and to give Lucille her present – a beautiful, blonde-haired doll that far surpassed all the toys Santa had brought her.

'I'll pop round before the New Year,' Maisie said as Bel saw her to the door and they gave one another a hug.

Bel watched her half-sister walk across to the bright red sports car, which had attracted a growing number of local children during its time parked up outside the pub. Bel laughed as Maisie tried to fend off dozens of questions from the youngsters as she climbed into the driver's seat and gracefully drove off back to her other life, and her other family, at Lily's.

Later on, as the day was drawing to an end, after they had enjoyed their coq au vin Christmas dinner and George had insisted they listen to the King's Christmas speech, Maisie, Vivian and Kate retired to the back reception room and started thumbing through the latest edition of *Woman's Weekly* and some old copies of *Vogue*, leaving Lily and George to enjoy a quiet drink together in the kitchen.

'I wonder how Rosie's getting on with the Rainers and Charlotte?' wondered George as he puffed on a cigar.

'Mm,' Lily said, swirling her Rémy round in an oversized brandy glass, 'I don't think there'll be any problems with Hillary and Thomas. But I think Rosie might struggle a bit with Charlotte. She's getting to that age. No longer a child, but not yet a woman.'

'I don't know about that, but judging by the letters Rosie showed us, I think she wants to come home,' George said.

'Mm,' Lily repeated. 'Home's where the heart is and all that.'

'Could be that,' George agreed, 'or it could be she's not happy where she is. Boarding schools are funny old places. I should know.'

They sat in thought for a moment before Lily spoke again. 'If you're right, *mon cher*, and little Charlotte is not happy in Harrogate, then I don't see why Rosie doesn't just bring her home. She'll even be able to afford that posh school down the road, which is where she was hankering to put her in the first place.'

'Yes, my dear, but that was before we went to war.'

'I know, George, but I think she's being overprotective. It's not as if she's a "bairn". She's old enough, and must be clever enough with the education she's had, to get herself to a shelter if there's an air raid.'

George nodded his agreement. A part of him wondered, though, if Rosie's reticence about having Charlotte back home was more to do with a worry about her sister finding out about the bordello – and Rosie's long-standing connection with it.

'*And*,' Lily said, 'Rosie's got Detective Sergeant Perfect to give her a bit of guidance.' As always when Peter was mentioned, Lily's voice became truculent.

'You're still not warming to him then?' George asked. He still couldn't quite work out why Lily was so against the man. From what he could gather, he seemed a decent chap, and was certainly making their Rosie happier than they had ever seen her.

'Well, for starters he's twice her age,' Lily said, 'and let's face it, the lives they lead couldn't be more different. Chalk and bleedin' cheese. He's on one side of the law and she's on the other. Opposites may attract, for a while at least, but once the shine's worn off ...'

George let the sentence go unfinished. He knew Lily would get to the real reason she wasn't happy about Rosie's love affair.

'I don't trust the man,' Lily declared. 'I've never trusted a copper in my life and I'm not going to start now. My old bones just feel like there's heartbreak on the horizon.'

George sighed resignedly.

'Well,' he said, getting up and walking round to where his fiancée sat, then gently massaging her neck from behind, 'why don't we get those old bones upstairs and start talking about this wedding we've got planned?'

Lily immediately felt herself soften as George worked his magic on her tense muscles.

'She'll always have us,' said George, 'even if it all goes pear-shaped.'

Chapter Thirty-Five

Boxing Day 1941

'Were you out late last night, Georgina?' Mr Pickering asked his daughter as she joined him for breakfast.

Mr Pickering knew that his only daughter – and, indeed, his only offspring left living at home – had spent a good part of Christmas Day working. Not that he minded. The Pickering household had not celebrated Christmas for many years now, not since Mrs Pickering had been taken from them.

'And my powers of deduction tell me that you weren't attending some carol service or late-night Mass,' Mr Pickering added, looking over his half-moon spectacles as his daughter grabbed a slice of bread off the table and went and knelt by the open fire so she could make herself some toast, something she had always enjoyed doing as a child.

Georgina laughed into the dancing orange and red flames of the coal fire, enjoying the heat on her face and body. 'I think you'd be more worried about me if I *had* been sloping around in some church, eating the flesh of Jesus and drinking his blood, or worse still, massacring one of his hymns with my very badly tuned pipes.'

'Ha!' the old man blustered, ignoring his daughter's habit of using quite distasteful imagery – something she was particularly wont to do whenever religion was the topic of conversation. 'They're only "badly tuned" because they've been left to go to rack and ruin. I remember when you were a little girl, if you weren't arguing with your brothers or running about the house, you'd be singing.'

Mr Pickering suddenly felt a pang of nostalgia. A hankering for the days of old, when the house was full of life – when his Hilda would sing along with her daughter, or chase their boys from room to room, making them scream with excitement.

'Well, that was then and this is now,' Georgina retorted a little too sharply.

Knowing he had caused his daughter pain by mentioning the past, Mr Pickering quickly changed tack.

'So, come on, tell me your findings, Miss Holmes, or should I say Mademoiselle Poirot?' Mr Pickering cajoled, steering their chatter back on to safe ground with their familiar banter.

'Just don't call me Miss Marple! I'm not an old spinster yet!' Georgina interrupted in mock outrage as she pushed herself up from the fireplace and made her way across to the big dark wooden table with her piece of toast in hand. She sat down in the high-backed, leather-upholstered chair opposite her father and helped herself to the smallest knob of butter and a scraping of marmalade. Mr Pickering wanted to tell his daughter to have more, but stopped himself. Georgina hated being fussed about. And he had to stop treating her like a child. She had turned twenty-one this year and had a wise head on her shoulders despite her relative youth.

Mr Pickering poured himself another cup of tea and a fresh cup for his daughter, pushing it towards her along with the milk jug. Georgina looked at her dad and smiled her thanks as she added a splash of milk.

'Actually, the past few days have been very insightful,' Georgina began, thinking about the research she had been doing, which had taken her to places she'd not normally have gone to. First off, she'd visited the town's Jewish quarters and found everyone very friendly and, more importantly, very talkative. As a result, it hadn't taken her long to find out what she needed to know.

And she had been surprised at how much she had enjoyed spending time across the water in Monkwearmouth, otherwise known as the Barbary Coast. It was known to be one of the poorest areas of the town, but she'd found it full of colour and life. And because there was so much activity there, as well as being so densely populated, she'd been able to blend in well. It hadn't taken her long at all to get what she needed, helped by the mother of the young welder called Angela not being as discreet as she probably should be.

But it had been at the town's library, where she loved to go regardless of whether she was working or not, that she had found some really interesting information about a couple of the women welders. It was amazing what you could find out simply by looking through the newspaper archives, or having a browse through the births, marriages and deaths.

It was a true saying – if you dig deep enough you'll find something. And sometimes you didn't need to even dig that deep; sometimes it was enough just to scratch the surface of most people's lives to find something of interest.

Georgina hated to admit it, but she had begun to enjoy what she and her father called their 'snooping' work. They had only branched out into this area when Georgina's two brothers had signed up and joined the navy. Surviving without the two main breadwinners of the household meant that beggars couldn't be choosers. And as much as they would have preferred to be investigating some company wrongdoing or helping those who had suffered an injustice, they had been forced to take on less salubrious work. The kind of work people like Mrs Crawford hired them to carry out.

'Out of the six women your Mrs Crawford wanted "looking into", I've made good headway with five of them,' Georgina told her father.

Normally, the pair of them would talk through Georgina's findings with very little enthusiasm or joy. Today, though, Mr Pickering could tell there was something that had caught his daughter's interest, perhaps even her imagination.

'They are quite an eclectic mix of women,' Georgina said, taking another bite of her toast.

'Pray tell more,' Mr Pickering encouraged. He loved to see his daughter's enthusiasm piqued. It kept her busy, or more importantly, it kept her *mind* busy. And he knew that this was what his daughter needed. He just wished there was a way of using her brain for more high-minded matters.

While Georgina chatted away, relating her findings as they ate their breakfast, Mr Pickering could see why his daughter had become so intrigued by this latest assignment. This was a truly diverse group of women. What she had unearthed was interesting, but for him what was more fascinating was the work they were doing, and where they were doing it. It made him wonder why Mrs Crawford wanted to get one over on them. Surely these women were to be revered. They were breaking their backs trying to help win the war. Everyone knew that if it wasn't for the country's shipyards, they'd be in trouble.

But his was not to question why Mrs Crawford had asked for their help. It was work, and work meant money and money meant they got to keep a roof, albeit a leaking one, over their heads.

'There's only one of the women I've not really had a chance to look at,' Georgina said. 'And that's the women's immediate boss, a young woman called Rosie Thornton.'

Georgina paused for a moment. When she'd first read the name it had rung a distant bell in her memory, but she was still none the wiser as to why.

'She's been away these past few days, so I've not had a chance to really do any digging.'

Mr Pickering pushed his chair out and stood up slowly. His body was failing him and it was always at its lowest ebb in the morning. Georgina jumped up to help him, but was immediately shooed away.

'Don't fuss,' he said good-naturedly, despite the sharp shooting pains coursing through every limb, 'or else I'll start fussing over you and then there'll be another war on!'

Georgina smiled, but she was no fool. Her father was in pain and that in turn caused her to hurt.

'Right, I'll get cracking on this Rosie woman,' she said, giving her father a quick hug and a kiss on his stubbly cheek.

As Mr Pickering watched his daughter leave he knew that if there was anything to find then his daughter would undoubtedly find it.

Mrs Crawford would get what she wanted.

Chapter Thirty-Six

Monday 29 December 1941

Rosie had to stop herself from running to Lily's. She had purposely chosen to walk, even though there'd been a tram she could have jumped on that would have taken her most of the way, but her body felt infused with a nervous excitement that only physical exertion could get rid of.

She should have been shattered as she'd hardly had time to breathe since returning from Harrogate. Since stepping off the train late last night she felt that she'd been chasing time. She had a sudden mental image of one of the pictures she remembered seeing in her favourite bedtime book when she was a child. It showed Alice in her blue and white pinafore dress chasing the White Rabbit, who was clutching a huge pocket watch. That's how she felt, desperately trying to snatch at time and make it slow down, or best of all, stop for a while so that she could gain some ground on it.

'Charlotte, Charlotte, Charlotte!' She spoke her thoughts aloud safe in the knowledge that no one could hear her, and even if they could, they would not be able to see her, not in the blackout.

'What am I going to do with you, little sis,' she muttered away to herself as she strode up Burdon Road, past the museum and along the perimeter of Mowbray Park.

Rosie had extended her stay with the Rainers an extra day as she had been so concerned about Charlotte. It was as if she had changed overnight, or at least since she had seen her last a couple of months ago. She had gone from the little sister she knew and loved to someone she hardly recognised any more, full of anger and petulance. It was so unlike Charlotte. She'd tried to chat to her about it but didn't feel that she had got to the bottom of it.

Charlotte had told her that she was fed up with school and wanted to come back home – that at fourteen she could leave school and get a job. Rosie had tried to keep the anger out of her voice as she'd told Charlotte that working wasn't exactly a barrel of laughs either, and that she'd be on pennies, with little hope of improving on that as she got older.

Her argument had been beaten down by Charlotte pointing out that Rosie hadn't done too badly working as a welder and had managed not only to have a decent standard of living herself, but also to pay her boarding fees.

Rosie was in a no-win scenario as she couldn't tell Charlotte how wrong she was, nor could she tell her how she had really earned the money to be able to afford to keep her in school.

When Charlotte had admitted on the evening before Rosie left that she wouldn't mind staying on at school, but only if she could go to one in Sunderland, Rosie had been slightly relieved but also rather perplexed.

Was this simply down to the fact that Charlotte was homesick and wanted to be near the only family she had?

Whatever the reason, it was making Rosie's head spin with ideas and possibilities. She would love to have Charlotte back home. She could do it financially, and the threat from their uncle Raymond was now no more – there was just the one fly in the ointment, and it wasn't, as she had been making out to everyone, the fact that the town lived under the constant threat of Hitler's Luftwaffe.

The real reason was the bordello.

If Charlotte came back to live here it would be nigh-on impossible to keep her in the dark. She might be able to for a little while, but not long term. Not a chance.

But if the business became legit?

Rosie was snapped out of the thoughts racing around her head by the blaring of a horn as she went to cross the road. She stepped back onto the pavement, dug around in her bag and pulled out her little electric torch.

'God, you'll be no good to anyone dead,' she muttered as she made her way safely across to the other side of the road.

'That's the only possible option,' Rosie said aloud as she headed to West Lawn.

The idea had been festering in her head for some time now. Perhaps tonight was the time to give it some air.

'Ah, *ma chérie!*' Lily tottered down the hallway to greet Rosie as she walked through the front door. She gave her a surprising hug as well as the usual two kisses – one on each cheek.

'Honestly, Lily, I've only been gone a few days,' Rosie said, shrugging off her coat and hooking it onto the stand by the door.

'I know, but we were expecting you back on Saturday. And it's now Monday!'

All of a sudden, Rosie felt like a young girl being reproached by her worried mother.

'Rosie!' George came out of the reception room, which sounded lively and busy with girls and clients and Mary Martin singing 'Kiss the Boys Goodbye' playing on the gramophone. His ornate ivory walking stick struck the tiles loudly as he strode, slightly off-kilter, towards her. He too gave her a big hug, rather than the usual kiss on her hand.

Rosie laughed. 'Either you two have been on the brandy or Christmas has made you both sentimental.'

She headed towards her office in the front room.

'Come on, let's have a belated Christmas drink, or an early one for the New Year,' she said, stepping into her favourite room in the entire house. Thick, floor-to-ceiling plush velvet curtains, Persian rugs and a mix of Louis XIV-style furniture – including her huge cherrywood desk – filled the room. She had also recently purchased a huge mahogany cabinet where she now kept her growing number of files, ledgers and boxes of paperwork.

Rosie went to fill three glasses with the top-notch French brandy she kept in a crystal decanter on top of her desk.

'So, tell us all about Charlotte and dear Hillary and Thomas?' Lily said, taking her glass from Rosie and settling herself down on the chaise longue with George. Neither Lily nor George had ever met with Rosie's little sister or the couple who had kept an eye on her over the years, but they still felt as though they knew them.

'Mr and Mrs Rainer were lovely, as always,' Rosie said. She had never got used to calling them by their first names, and they had given up insisting she try.

'They're both getting on a bit, though,' Rosie said thoughtfully.

'How old are they now?' George asked.

'Gosh, I reckon they must be in their late fifties, early sixties,' Rosie said. She had her drink to hand but so far hadn't taken a sip.

'Blimey, ancient then!' Lily laughed, slipping back into her native cockney.

Rosie smiled.

'I guess what I'm really trying to say is that they're getting too old to cope with Charlotte.' She finally took a drink, enjoying the burn down her throat.

'We were wondering how you were getting on with Charlotte,' George said, his face serious. 'Especially after the letters you showed us.'

'Well,' Rosie felt her energy drain a little now that she was sitting down, 'take those letters and times them by ten.'

'That bad?' George empathised.

'Bring the girl back home!' Lily declared, putting her glass down on the little nest of tables. 'Where she belongs!' she added as she pushed herself off the settee and walked over to the desk to take a cigarette from the packet of Gauloises that was kept for clients, although Lily seemed to be the only person ever to smoke them.

Rosie looked at Lily and then at George, who, she thought, had started shuffling about a little uncomfortably.

'It's not quite that easy, Lily,' Rosie said, a little exasperated. 'I can't just haul Charlotte out of her school and swing her back here willy-nilly.'

'Why not?' Lily said, lighting up and blowing out a stream of smoke. 'It makes perfect sense to me. Charlotte's clearly not happy. She's said she wants to come back to her hometown. To be with you. And Mr and Mrs Rainer are clearly knocking on a bit now. And you can easily get her into another school here. That posh one up the road would be perfect. You might even save some money as Charlotte probably won't be boarding. Not if she lives with you.'

Lily took another drag of her cigarette. 'It's a win-win situation.' Her words were emitted with another trail of smoke.

'Yes, but what about all the air raids we've been having?' Rosie argued.

Lily rolled her eyes heavenward.

'Then move somewhere out of town. Nearer here. Hitler doesn't seem to give two figs about our neck of the woods. She'll be safe as houses. And if you're near here, she can come and shelter in the cellar if there's a raid. You don't get much safer than down there, that's for sure.'

Rosie opened her mouth to speak, but nothing came out. She looked across to George and saw by the look on his face that he knew exactly what she was really concerned about.

Lily caught the look and swung round to George.

'Am I missing something here?' she asked, standing with one hand on her hip and the other outstretched, her half-smoked Gauloise burning between her fingers.

Rosie threw a slightly desperate look over at George.

'Lily,' George said, patting the space on the chaise longue next to him, 'come and sit back down.'

Lily acquiesced, sitting down and picking up her glass.

'I think what Rosie may be a tad concerned about – ' George cleared his throat ' – is about Charlotte finding out about the bordello.'

There, he had said it. He was amazed Lily hadn't considered this before. Sometimes she could be the most astute woman he had ever known, and certainly the most business savvy, but often when it came to more personal matters, she could be considerably way off the mark.

Lily looked from George to Rosie as if they had both just slapped her in the face.

She immediately stood back up, marched over to the desk and stabbed her cigarette out aggressively in the ashtray before pulling another from the packet.

'So, I see ...' Lily was now in full cockney twang.

'Ashamed, are you?' She lit her cigarette.

'Ashamed of this place?' She waved her outstretched arms dramatically around the splendour of the room.

'Ashamed of me and George?'

Rosie leant forward in her chair. 'Of course, I'm not ashamed of you and George!' she interrupted Lily's rant.

'But you *are* ashamed of your life here?' Lily asked, staring at Rosie, demanding the truth.

Rosie stuttered. 'It's not that I'm ashamed ... it's just I don't want Charlotte to be a party to it.'

'Gawd, Rosie, you make it sound like we're going to put her to work here!' Lily was now almost shouting.

'No, I don't mean that.' Rosie was getting confused. This conversation was not going the way she wanted it to go. Lily's reaction had thrown her. She had thought Lily would understand how she felt about Charlotte knowing about the bordello.

'So, let me get this right,' Lily said, tapping her cigarette on the side of the ashtray. 'You honestly expect Charlotte to go through her life in blissful ignorance as to how you have not only managed to keep her out of the workhouse, but have also given her the best education a girl could want? Hmm. Charlotte's going to sail through life believing that you managed to do and pay for everything you have done on the wages of a shipyard welder?'

Lily stomped over to get her drink.

Rosie was rigid, staring at Lily, beaten for words.

George reached to take hold of Lily's hand in an attempt to subdue her. He had only seen her like this a few times, but he knew the more fired up she became, the more she said. And the more she said, the more she regretted saying.

'No, George,' Lily said, pulling her hand away, 'this needs to be said.'

She turned back to Rosie. 'Or did you think your detective was going to suddenly whip you and Charlotte away on his white charger and take you off to live some kind of perfect and unblemished existence?'

At the mention of Peter, Rosie felt herself fire up.

'No!' Now it was Rosie's voice that was raised. 'I don't expect that! But perhaps you're right about one thing. Perhaps I am a little ashamed of what I have done. But the long and short of it is, I don't want Charlotte to find out. I don't want her to be involved in the kind of life I've had to live. I want her to have the best. To live a good life.'

Lily banged her glass down.

'And we don't live a *good* life?!'

George stood up, knowing that now was the time to intervene – before the locking of horns.

'You're twisting everything I'm trying to say!' Rosie said. She had never fallen out with Lily before and she had certainly never had what was now amounting to a full-scale argument with her.

'Well, then,' Lily said, 'tell me what you're *really* trying to say.'

Lily looked at George, whose pleading face made her calm down a fraction. But only a fraction.

Rosie sat up straight in her chair.

'I've been doing a lot of thinking,' she said, watching as George gently guided Lily back to the chaise longue. 'And I was hoping that we could try and go legit. You know, like we talked about before all that awfulness with Peter.' Her voice dropped, although her guilt sounded out loud and clear.

'That "awfulness with Peter" that nearly landed us all in jail?' Lily couldn't help but have a stab at Peter. She realised as she said it that it was really him she was angry with.

'Yes,' Rosie said quietly. Her head felt so confused. So tired. She had tried to bury the guilt she had felt over that whole debacle, which had been her fault. But she had to say what had been going through her mind for a while now. 'I want us to make the business legitimate.'

This was what she had wanted to talk about from the off, but Lily had sidetracked her.

This was the answer to her problem. And not only that. Not only could she then bring Charlotte back home to live, but she would also be able to tell Peter that she was a *proper* businesswoman and not the part-owner of a brothel.

She *could* live a normal life.

Lily looked at Rosie and her face softened.

'Oh, Rosie,' she said, 'for someone who has experienced some of life's hardest knocks, you really are such a dreamer—'

'Which is no bad thing – at all,' George butted in. It was the first time he had spoken and Rosie and Lily both looked at him. 'I think it's wonderful to dream,' he continued. 'And I hope you never stop.'

Rosie looked at the man who was the nearest she would ever get to having a father again, and said, 'So why do I sense there is a "but" coming?'

George's smile was sad.

'Yes, I'm afraid there is a rather large "but".' He paused. 'You see, my dear, I don't think Lily and I made it clear that day we were all talking about buying next door and starting up the Gentlemen's Club. I remember we did mention going legit, but we were all so excited and it was a busy day, and we didn't sit down and talk about it as perhaps we should have.'

George took a breath and straightened his back. 'I think you may have got the wrong end of the stick, my dear. What we should have told you was that there is a way we can start to build up a more legitimate business infrastructure by siphoning money off Lily's, as well as La Lumière Bleue, and using it to build up the Gentlemen's Club, which, of course, is all above board, and perhaps also start to build up a property portfolio. Bricks and mortar, my friends in finance tell me, is the next big thing.

'All of this, however, will take time – years, I'm afraid.'

Lily looked at Rosie and saw the look of desolation on her face. Her heart softened immediately.

'*Ma chère*,' she said, 'there's no way we can make the actual bordello a legitimate company. Not unless the government changes the law, which I doubt will happen in our lifetime.'

She made her way over to Rosie, wanting to give her some kind of comfort, to tell her that everything would turn out all right in the end. She wanted to say so much to Rosie, who she could tell was floundering around at sea at the moment, unsure which way to swim to shore. But most annoyingly of all, she knew the reason why their Rosie was floundering in unknown waters.

It was all down to that damned detective.

Seeing Rosie slump, defeated, in her chair, Lily went over and gently put her hands on her head and pulled her close.

Rosie could smell the mix of Chanel N° 5, cigarettes and brandy. It was strangely comforting.

'We'll sort something out,' Lily promised, although, at that moment in time, she had no idea how – *other than to string up that bloody detective.*

Life had been just fine and dandy before he'd come along.

Chapter Thirty-Seven

'Everything all right at the yard?' Bel asked, pouring herself a freshly brewed cup of tea from the pot she had just placed on the mat in the middle of the kitchen table.

Polly was back late, having done a few hours' overtime, and was helping herself to some leftover panackelty that was keeping warm on the range. This was a part of the day they both enjoyed, when their work was done and the house was quiet. Agnes and Arthur had headed off to bed within half an hour of each other, Joe was out doing his duty with the Home Guard, and Pearl was working at the Tatham. It was the only time of day that the two women could sit down together and have a good chat.

'Yeah,' Polly said, putting her plate down on the table and going off to get some cutlery, 'you know – the usual. So much to do and so little time to do it.' She came back armed with her knife and fork. '*Brutus* is coming along nicely, though. Starting to look like she's finally getting a bit of meat on her bones.'

Bel let out a little chuckle. Polly always talked about the ships they were working on as though they were real live beings. 'Glad to hear it. We want her nice and strong, don't we?' she joked.

'Did you see Gloria tonight when she came to pick up Hope?' Polly asked as she started to tuck into her supper, which was barely warm.

'I did,' Bel said, taking a sup of her tea. 'She actually stayed for a quick cuppa for a change. She seems so much more relaxed now that Vinnie's out of the picture.'

'Yeah, she is.' Polly forked up a heap of fried onion, potato and bacon. She always came in from work ravenous. 'One less thing for her to worry about,' she added through a mouthful of food, 'and let's face it, she's got a pretty long list on the go.'

'From what Gloria said, I think Jack was a bit disappointed he didn't get the chance to knock Vinnie from here to kingdom come. I was surprised when she said she'd only got to tell Jack the other day. Did you know she's not seen him at all over the Christmas break?'

'I know,' Polly mumbled, washing her food down with a big glug of tea. 'Gloria thought it'd be a good idea for Jack to give his undivided attention to Helen. You know, with it probably being the last one he has at home with her – as a family.'

'Before they drop their bombshell,' Bel mused.

Polly continued to eat, while Bel sat deep in thought.

'It was all a bit pointless, by the sounds of it, though,' Polly said, now starting to scrape her plate clean.

'What was pointless?' Bel asked.

'The whole "Jack having a happy family Christmas with Helen" malarkey.'

'Oh, yes.' Bel leant forward so as to feel the heat of the fire on her face. 'Gloria said Jack hardly got to speak two words to Helen. A load of fancy, hoity-toity guests over for Christmas dinner and then another right old knees-up on Boxing Day.'

'Well,' Polly said, 'at least Gloria tried to do the right thing. I think she's been feeling a bit guilty about Helen, to be honest.'

'Really?' Bel asked. 'Why, I thought Helen was the devil incarnate. Or at the very least the Wicked Witch of the West. "Cold and calculating and devoid of all feeling", I thought was the general consensus.'

'I dunno,' Polly said, 'I guess Gloria's just feeling bad because she knows how much Helen loves her dad, and that, whatever happens, it's going to break up the family.'

'But,' Bel said, 'she'll still have her dad, won't she? It's not as if he won't love her any more. And from what I know about Jack, you couldn't get a more perfect father. She's actually a very lucky girl.'

Polly took her plate and cutlery into the scullery, put them in the sink and came back and sat down.

'That's your way of looking at it, Bel,' Polly said. 'Somehow, though, I don't think that's going to be the way Helen does. Nor Miriam. God only knows what they'll do when Jack and Gloria finally come clean.'

Bel stretched her legs and sat back, letting out a big yawn.

'It's Hope that's going to be the biggest shocker, though, isn't it? It won't just be a case of, "I'm so sorry we've fallen in love and I'm leaving you, dear Miriam," but, "And by the way, we've had a baby together!"'

'Oh, *don't*, Bel! When you put it like that it makes it sound awful!' Polly reprimanded, before asking, 'Did Gloria say anything to you about when they're going to tell Miriam?'

'Sometime in the New Year,' Bel said, looking across at Polly and seeing how shattered she was. 'She says she feels like she's been caught up in a hurricane this past month, and they just need a few weeks to catch their breath. Especially after all this upset with Vinnie.'

'At least Vinnie's gone,' Polly said, stifling a yawn, 'and there'll be no more shenanigans about Hope now he finally knows that he's not the father.'

'Mm,' Bel agreed, then shuddered. 'Just think, having someone like Vinnie as your father?'

Polly nodded. '*Not* a nice thought.'

As they'd been chatting, Polly's tired mind had wandered a little and for the first time ever she imagined what Tommy would be like as a dad. Of course, he'd be the best da in the world.

Her thoughts, however, were accompanied by a now familiar, painful pull in her chest. She missed him so much.

Chapter Thirty-Eight

Gibraltar

Tuesday 30 December 1941

Tommy was sitting on his bunk bed with just an electric torch for light and a sheet of paper. He knew the other men he shared this small dormitory with weren't all asleep, although there was the usual deep rumbling of Rodders' snoring, which was a constant source of either complaint or comedy amongst them all.

When they had all arrived here, none of them could quite believe anyone could make such a racket when they were asleep and they had all expressed their deepest sympathies for Rodders' missus. They'd joked that since he'd been sent overseas his wife was probably getting the best night's kip she'd ever had; they all knew, though, that Mrs Rodders would probably give anything to have her man snoring away next to her all night long, safe in the knowledge that he was alive and well.

None of the specialist diving team Tommy was a part of had told their loved ones just how dangerous their job was, but they all knew their families were probably well aware of it. It didn't take a genius to work out that pulling limpet mines off the bottoms of boats was not the safest job in the world.

Tommy let out a quiet sigh as he unscrewed the top off his pen. Polly had sent it to him when he was doing his fortnight's training in Portsmouth. He'd got it the day he left for the Rock and every time he held it he felt that she was near him. He kept it in his bedside-cabinet drawer along with Polly's letters, which, after a year of writing to each other, now made quite a pile.

In a strange way, they'd got to know each other more since he'd signed up and been shipped abroad. He'd realised fairly early on during their long-distance correspondence that it was easier to say how he was feeling on paper than to actually speak the words. They had even developed their own code and every letter or postcard was always signed off with a coded 'I love you for ever'.

As Tommy looked out the small round window at the clear, star-speckled night sky, he couldn't help but feel a little despondent. This war did not look like ending any time soon, and he wondered just how long 'for ever' might be.

When he'd first come out he'd often worried that Polly would tire of waiting for him, but the more they wrote to each other, the more his paranoid thoughts about her finding some other bloke were pushed aside. Her letters, just like the last one she had written to him, might be full of all the goings-on at the yard and at Tatham Street, but there was always an overriding sense of love in her words to him that could not be disguised and which left him in no doubt that her feelings for him were true and steadfast.

Dear Polly . . .

Tommy started to write slowly. He always tried to make his writing the best he could.

As always, I hope this letter finds you and everyone we know well.

This was the way Tommy always started his letters. He paused for a moment before starting to write again.

I just want you to know how proud I am of you. I haven't wanted to tell you before in case you think I'm a right softie.

My mates are always pulling my leg about how much I go on about you – and how I'm always telling them that you are 'building ships that are saving our backsides'. They keep ribbing me that I'm telling porkies and that 'my Polly' sounds too perfect and that you are really just 'a figment of my imagination'.

But it doesn't matter to me whether they believe me or not. I know you are real. And I know you are mine!

Anyway, there's not much to report at this end. Nothing for you to worry about. I just need you to look after yourself and make sure you get to the nearest air raid shelter as soon as the sirens start up.

It's good to hear that Arthur's doing well and keeping Agnes well stocked up on fruit and veg – and fish, of course! I know I've said this a few times before but I am so eternally grateful to your mam for taking Arthur under her roof. She really is the best. Tell her I'm missing her gorgeous stews and dumplings!

Tommy had nearly reached the end of the page.

Talking of your ma, I know she will hate me for writing this and a part of me thinks I should tell you to do the complete opposite – but keep building them ships!
And keep sending them out into that great North Sea.

I am so very proud of you and you must keep doing what you have always wanted to do (even before this war).

You are a shipbuilder! Just like your brothers, and your dad and his dad before him.

I can't stress just how very proud I am of you.

After signing his name and putting a kiss next to it, he added, in capitals ILYFE. He then folded up the letter and put it carefully into an envelope and then under his pillow.

As he lay down on his bed, he hoped he had managed to say what he wanted to say in a way that wouldn't sound at all ominous.

He knew Polly would be a little surprised to read what he had said about her working in the yards. He had often tried to put her off working at Thompson's simply because it was dangerous work at the best of times, never mind when the country was at war.

But lately, and particularly since he had been told about his team's next mission, he realised that Polly's work would be invaluable should anything happen to him.

His squad commander had not minced his words about the next covert operation they were presently training for. He had not said anything directly to them, but had suggested they all send their loved ones letters. He didn't need to say any more. They had all understood.

There was no way that Tommy was going to say anything that might in any way worry Polly, and he hoped his letter would come across as normal, but he also hoped that should anything happen to him, Polly would reread his words and she would put on her overalls, go to work, pick up her welding rod and carry on.

Tommy knew Polly and he knew that it would be Thompson's, as well as her closely knit group of women welders, that would ultimately save her and keep her going if he was no longer there.

Chapter Thirty-Nine

Brookside Gardens, Sunderland

New Year's Eve 1941

'God, it feels like I haven't seen you for ever!' Rosie put her arms around Peter as she stood on the threshold of his home.

Peter kissed her for a long time as they stood there, letting in the cold night air.

'It's been longer than that – seven days and ten hours exactly.' Peter smiled down at Rosie's face. It was a face he thought he would never get tired of looking at, talking to or, like now, kissing.

'I'm so sorry about last night,' Peter said as he drew Rosie into the hallway, shut the door and helped her out of her winter coat.

Rosie dismissed the apology with the shake of her head. 'Was it awful?' she asked, her face now deadly serious.

'It was,' Peter said honestly, 'and just so terribly tragic.'

Rosie and Peter had meant to be meeting up the previous evening, but Peter had been called to an accident that had shocked the whole town. Two trainee pilots from the nearby RAF Usworth had collided mid-air directly over the Ford Estate. It had been carnage and the four crew members had been killed instantly.

Rosie gave Peter a big hug. She would not have wanted to deal with the aftermath of such an accident.

'Gloria was telling us about it today at work. She said the whole estate was in shock. One of the planes landed in someone's front garden. It was a miracle no one else was killed. I think it really shook Gloria up.' Rosie followed Peter into the kitchen, where he had already set up a tea tray of cups and saucers and a plate of biscuits. He put the kettle on to boil.

'Oh!' Rosie jumped. 'God, how could I forget.' She took a dramatic intake of breath. 'Gloria was completely overwhelmed by what you did for her. With Vinnie. She can't thank you enough.'

Peter smiled. 'How's her head? Is she fully recovered now?'

'Yes, yes, she's fine, thank goodness, though I think she's just so relieved Vinnie's now out of the picture. She's been so much more relaxed. She took over the reins while I was away and did a great job by the sounds of it.'

Rosie pulled out one of the light iron-framed chairs from under the Formica kitchen table and sat down.

'She also says that Jack seems to be getting his memory back – slowly but surely – which must be a massive relief. He went through a stage of being really tired. I think it was starting to worry her, but from what I've picked up it seems like he's getting back to his old self.'

Rosie also knew that Gloria had been particularly relieved to hear that Jack was now back in the spare room and no longer sharing a bed with Miriam.

Rosie took a deep breath and smiled.

'It's lovely to be here. *With you*,' she added quietly. 'And, there's so much to catch up on!'

'I know,' Peter agreed, trying his hardest to sound casual when really there was only one conversation he wanted – no, *needed* – to have with Rosie this evening. He knew he couldn't put it off any longer.

The kettle came to the boil and Peter poured the steaming-hot water into the pot.

'So, tell me about Charlotte and the Rainers. What was your Christmas Day like? Did you manage a trip into Harrogate?'

As Peter stirred the tea and let it brew for a short while, Rosie started to tell him all about Charlotte and her worries about her little sister, who had not seemed herself and who was adamant she wanted to come back home.

Peter forced himself to concentrate, but it was hard; he was feeling more nervous by the minute about what he had to tell Rosie.

'So,' Peter said, pouring out their cups of tea, 'what do you think is really going on with Charlotte?'

Rosie paused for a moment. 'I'm not sure. All I know is that she's fixed on moving back to Sunderland.' She took her cup, but didn't make any signs that she wanted to go and sit in the lounge, so Peter sat down with her at the little kitchen table.

'Well, if she's anything like her big sister, you're going to have a battle on your hands!' Peter said, before adding in a more serious tone, 'But joking apart, would it not be possible for her to come back here to live?'

Rosie slouched a little and took a drink of her tea. She had been dying to see Peter, had missed him terribly, but most of all she'd had it in her mind that when she saw him she would be able to tell him that she – or rather the bordello – was going legit. She had played out the scene in her head: how she would sit with Peter just as she was now and tell him all about her plans to become a bona fide, upright member of society.

But after her very animated discussion with Lily and George the other night, that plan now looked ridiculously delusional. She'd been given a shot of reality and it had caused her to come crashing back down to earth. It had smashed her dreams not only of living a 'normal' life, but also of being able to bring Charlotte back home.

'If only it were that simple,' Rosie said, reaching for the comfort of one of the assortment of biscuits Peter had laid out on the plate. She looked at Peter. It was time to be honest and open. She couldn't keep avoiding the subject of the bordello. It was a part of her life; a big part. A part he knew about – that had caused him a great deal of shock and distress – but he had accepted it and she didn't feel that he judged her for it. If he did, she wouldn't be with him now.

'Go on, tell me what's going on in that beautifully complex head of yours,' Peter cajoled, topping up both their cups.

Rosie took a deep breath.

'If I allow Charlotte to come and live with me – that's if I manage to get her into the Sunderland Church High School …'

Peter nodded. Rosie had mentioned to him in the past that this was where she had initially wanted to send Charlotte.

'… I know Charlotte will pass the test they make you do there, but they don't always have places. Sometimes there's a waiting list.'

Peter took a biscuit. His stomach was starting to growl. He hadn't really eaten all day, probably because he'd been on edge.

'But if she does come here …' Rosie seemed to be struggling to get her words out and Peter forced himself to concentrate.

'It's inevitable …' She paused.

'Well, it's inevitable that she's going to find out about Lily's.'

There, the words were out.

349

Peter looked at Rosie. This was the first time she had opened up like this. She might have chatted a little about Lily and George, and, of course, Maisie and Vivian, but she had never really discussed the bordello itself. Peter silently reprimanded himself. He should have realised that was the problem from the start. It really had nothing to do with the air raids Hitler was subjecting the town to. Rosie probably wanted Charlotte here as much as her sister wanted to come back home. But, of course, Charlotte was no longer a child – it would be practically impossible for Rosie to keep the bordello a secret, not with the number of hours she spent there. On top of which, Lily, George and Kate were all like family to her. How could she keep them separate from her sister?

'I thought,' Rosie said, 'somewhat foolishly it now appears, that there might be some way of *legitimising* the business, if you know what I mean.'

Peter nodded. He knew they were in unknown territory here and he was aware he had to tread carefully. But he also felt that time was short and this was a topic he had been more than eager to discuss with Rosie for a while now.

'Well,' Peter considered, 'I agree, I can't see a way that Lily's could possibly become legitimate unless there was a change in the law. And I can't see that happening any time soon.'

They were the same words Lily had said to her the other night. For the second time in as many days, Rosie felt incredibly stupid. She was just about to say something when Peter leant forward and took hold of her hand.

Peter knew Rosie was unhappy, but he had to get his concerns out now. God, there was so much to talk to her about this evening and he hadn't banked on having this conversation into the bargain.

'I've wanted to say this to you for a while now.' Peter paused a little nervously. 'But your involvement with Lily's does worry me.'

Rosie pulled her hand away quickly. She didn't like the way this conversation was going.

'What do you mean my "involvement with Lily's does worry" you?' Rosie asked coldly.

Peter knew he couldn't back out now. He had to spit it out.

'I just keep thinking—' Peter went to take hold of Rosie's hand again but she moved it away as soon as she realised what he was trying to do.

'You just keep thinking what?' Rosie repeated.

'I just can't help thinking that if I found out about Lily's then it wouldn't be hard for others to as well.'

Rosie stared at him. This evening was not going at all as she had expected. She had hoped that Peter might be able to help her with her dilemma about Charlotte. Not make it worse.

'And?' Rosie asked harshly.

'And if they do, there's a good chance they won't hesitate to report you. And if they do that ...' Peter knew he didn't need to say any more.

Rosie could feel the anger and hurt rising up in her and Peter could see the look of fury on her face and knew he had to jump in now and try to quell an almighty flare-up.

'I think I'm just trying to say that it worries me,' he said, trying his hardest to convey the deep concern he felt.

Rosie looked daggers at him.

'So, what do you suggest I do?' Her words were hard and biting. '*I know*,' she said, answering her own question, making a show of holding her chin between her finger and thumb as if she were deep in thought. 'I'll just get up and leave the bordello. Leave behind all the money I have worked so damned hard for. I'll just give it to Lily and tell her, "Here, you have my share, I'm off."

'And when she asks me why, I'll tell her, "Oh, I'm a bit worried someone might find out about us and report us." As if that hasn't ever been a worry before. As if that isn't always in the backs of our minds … Oh, and then I'll just haul Charlotte out of school and tell her, "Sorry, Charlotte, but you know all that work you've done so far, all those lessons you've had, and all those qualifications you are about to get, well, forget it, I can't afford to put you through school any more, so get down the Labour Exchange and sign yourself up for some mind-numbing job that will pay a pittance and keep you in poverty for the rest of your life!'

By the time Rosie had finished her tirade, she was out of breath and shaking, and Peter was wishing, desperately, that he could snatch back the words he'd let tumble from his mouth so thoughtlessly.

'Rosie,' Peter's voice was almost pleading, 'I'm so sorry. I didn't mean to upset you. I just … I just …' All of a sudden he didn't really know what he was trying to say. What he had really wanted to say was that he wanted to marry her, wanted them both – and Charlotte – to live here, under this roof. As a family.

But he couldn't.

Not any more.

He had made his choice.

'I just want you safe,' he finally managed.

'Safe? *You* want *me* safe?' Rosie was incredulous. 'Well, if that's what *you* want, Peter, you shouldn't have come and found me that day after the christening. You must have known then that you were jumping into something with someone who was as far removed from safe as you could possibly get. So, if that's what *you* want, then let's make no bones about it, you're not going to get it.'

Rosie stopped for breath. She was so angry, yet she was more upset than anything. The past week had been all topsy-turvy. She'd gone from being as high as a kite to feeling the lowest of the low. She was worried about Charlotte, worried about having to tell her about Lily's, and then her dreams of going legitimate and living as near a normal life as possible had been smashed to smithereens by Lily and George's reality check the other night.

'I'll never be *normal*, Peter.' Rosie spoke with unusual bitterness. 'And you'll never make me *normal* or *safe*, so if you don't like it – tough, you know where the door is.'

Peter saw the confusion of emotions cross Rosie's face. He pushed back his chair and went round to pull Rosie up so that she was facing him, then he put his arms around her and held her close to him.

'I thought you loved me for who I am?' Rosie said, her voice breaking with emotion, but muffled as her face pressed into his chest.

'I do,' Peter said. 'I do.'

He put his hands on her shoulders and made her step back so that he could look her in the eyes.

'I would never change you for all the world. You have to believe me on that,' he said in a steely voice. 'And I love you more than anything else in the world.'

Rosie looked into Peter's dark blue eyes and knew he meant every word he said.

He pulled her in close again and they held each other for a while. Then Rosie looked up at Peter and they kissed.

'I'm sorry for being a blabbermouth and speaking without thinking. I just love you so much, I worry about you. I don't know what I'd do if anything happened to you.' Peter kissed her again.

'I know,' Rosie said softly; her anger had disappeared as quickly as it had appeared. 'I don't know what I'd do if anything happened to you either.'

Peter felt that awful pull of guilt in the pit of his stomach yet again.

'I think we may have just had our first proper bust-up,' Peter said, trying his hardest to be light-hearted. 'You know what?' he said, with a smile.

'What?' Rosie asked, still enjoying the feeling of being in his arms.

'I think I've drunk enough tea today to sink a ship. I think we should go and have a proper drink to see in the New Year.'

Rosie stepped back. A wide smile now on her face.

'I can't believe I nearly forgot – it's New Year's Eve!' Rosie said, breaking free from his embrace and bending down to pick up her handbag and gas mask. 'Come on then,' she said, turning to leave the kitchen. 'What're you waiting for?'

As Peter went to fetch their coats, his heart started to pound. He knew he couldn't use this upset as another excuse not to tell Rosie what she needed to know.

As Rosie and Peter walked the half a mile or so to the Victoria Gardens, just off the Ryhope Road, they chatted more calmly about what Rosie should do in regards to 'the Charlotte situation', although Peter's mind was very much on the imminence of the bombshell he was about to drop.

'From what I'm hearing,' Peter said, 'there's a problem at school, otherwise why would she suddenly want to come back here? My instinct tells me you need to find the source of Charlotte's unhappiness and then look at what you're going to do. It may be the problem can be sorted

and she ends up staying at her all-girls boarding school –
in which case you're worrying unnecessarily.'

They both moved to the side to allow an elderly couple
to pass them.

'However,' Peter continued, 'if the problem can't be
resolved, and there doesn't appear to be any other option,
bar bringing Charlotte back home, *then* think about
whether or not you should tell her about Lily's.'

Rosie listened as they walked.

'Don't worry about something that might not happen,'
Peter said, quoting the well-worn adage.

'I know,' Rosie sighed resignedly. She was thoughtful
for a moment before looking at Peter and smiling. 'You're
right. I'm all paid up until the end of term, so the soonest
Charlotte could leave is March.'

'Which,' Peter said, finishing off her thought process,
'gives you plenty of time to work out what to do.'

As they turned into Villette Road, Rosie looked at
Peter. 'I'm sorry for flying off the handle earlier on.
I know you're just trying to look out for me. And the
stupid thing is, if you weren't bothered, I'd hate it more
because then I'd think you didn't care.' She tightened
her belt, and seeing that she was cold, Peter put his arm
around her shoulders and pulled her to him to give her
some protection from the chill of what was fast becoming
a very bleak midwinter.

'I feel like I've been in a whirlwind these past few
weeks,' Rosie admitted. 'To be honest, my head feels all
over the place. And it's all your fault!' she laughed as she
gently elbowed him.

When they reached the pub, Peter opened the door to
allow Rosie to go through first. As he followed her into
the loud and very busy lounge bar, he felt that if there was
ever a time for a drink, then it was now.

When they'd settled in a relatively quiet corner of the pub, Rosie raised her glass.

'Here's to the New Year!'

'The New Year,' Peter agreed, following suit.

'And may it be a happy one,' Rosie said, 'with no more dramas!'

Peter felt his heart sink.

'If only!' he said, forcing himself to sound jocular.

Chapter Forty

Peter looked at Rosie's face, which seemed so happy, so expectant and so full of life. As she took a sip of her drink, he watched as she gazed around the bar that was now getting so full there was hardly room to move.

'Rosie ...' Peter could feel his heart thumping in his chest.

Rosie brought her attention back to the man she loved. The only man she had ever loved.

'I've got something I have to tell you ...' Peter could feel his mouth had suddenly become dry. 'Something I should have told you before now, but haven't.' He took a quick drink of his pint.

Rosie knew immediately by Peter's tone that 'something' was not right. That 'something' sounded serious. Very serious.

'What?' Rosie demanded.

Peter opened his mouth to speak, but everything he'd planned to say seemed to have become jumbled up in his head.

'I'm so sorry, Rosie,' Peter said. Rosie looked at him and realised for the first time how pale and tired he was.

'Stop it, you're starting to worry me,' she said nervously. 'Are you poorly?' she asked, fearful for a moment that he was ill.

'No, no,' Peter was quick to reassure her. 'I'm fine. Honestly. Fit as a fiddle.'

Rosie felt herself instinctively sit back, as if wanting to put some space between the two of them, knowing she was about to be dealt a terrible blow.

Peter responded by leaning forward, not wanting to lose her, yet knowing it was inevitable.

'I'm sorry, Rosie. There's no way around this, so I'm just going to come out and say it straight. I have to leave you. For a while at least.'

'What do you mean?' Rosie didn't like the way Peter was looking at her, nor the words coming out of his mouth.

'I-I ...' Peter stuttered. 'God, where do I start? There's so much I can't tell you. I have to go away for a while. I have to leave you ... and I'm so sorry.'

'What do you mean, you "have to leave" me?' Rosie spat the words out. The anger that had been quelled earlier on in the evening was beginning to rise back to the surface. 'What? Are you saying you don't want to be with me any more?'

'God, no, Rosie!' Peter couldn't get the words out quickly enough. 'Of course I want to be with you!' He reached to take her hand across the small round bar table they were sitting at. He was glad she didn't pull away from his touch. The pub was getting noisier now as everyone started to wind themselves up to the big count-down to midnight.

He raised his voice.

'I've always wanted you. And always will!'

Rosie looked at him. 'So then why are you leaving me? I don't understand.' Her face was taut and confused.

'Oh God, I should have told you all this before now,' Peter said, knowing that if he had just told her more about Toby's visit and what they had discussed, this would not be coming as such a shock now.

'I've signed up,' he said simply.

'I don't understand, Peter. You're a reserved occupation. They can't make you do this.'

For a moment Rosie felt as though everything would be all right. That this was just a silly misunderstanding that would be sorted out in no time.

Peter looked at the desperate hope in Rosie's eyes and felt even more terrible than he had already.

'Rosie, nobody's *making* me do anything. I *asked* for this.' Peter's words came out as a betrayal.

'What do mean, you "asked for this"?' Rosie said. 'You mean you volunteered?'

Peter nodded slowly. 'I'm sorry, Rosie, but, yes, I did. I wanted to tell you about it when an old friend of mine called Toby dropped by a few weeks ago. I think I might have mentioned it, but only briefly. It was the day poor Gloria was attacked.'

Rosie racked her brains. She still couldn't quite believe they were having this conversation.

'I think I vaguely remember,' she said. 'Yes, I do. We were at Vera's and I'd just got some pie boxed up to take to Gloria at the hospital. Yes, I remember now. I remembered when I was getting ready to go to the hospital that I hadn't asked you about him … I remember telling myself to ask you next time we saw each other, but I forgot.'

'Of course you forgot, there's been so much going on of late.' Peter stretched over to move a blonde curl away from Rosie's eye. She didn't move an inch but kept looking at him, a furrow now developing in her brow.

'After that we didn't manage to see each other until just before you went away … And then you wore that red dress. It was just such a perfect night, I didn't want to spoil it.'

Peter looked at Rosie, but her face was unreadable.

'I've been asked to go down south to become part of a new government organisation,' Peter explained, 'to help the war effort. They recruited Toby while he was working for the BBC as a war correspondent. Anyway, he thought I'd be of some use and so he came to ask me if I'd be up for it.'

Rosie was staring at him.

'And?' She felt like shaking the words out of him. She was struggling to take on-board what Peter was telling her.

'I can't really say much more than that. I'm so sorry.' Peter dropped his voice so the couple next to them couldn't hear their conversation, not that they looked at all interested in anyone else as they were happily whispering sweet nothings in each other's ears.

'All I can say is that …' Peter spoke quietly, ' … is that they need people with various skills and who have experience in certain areas.'

'I don't understand.' Rosie's expression was a mix of confusion and shock. 'I thought you were needed here with the Borough Police?'

Peter squeezed her hand gently. 'They can manage without me.'

'And the Home Guard?' Rosie was starting to sound desperate. 'You've said yourself they need more men with some kind of policing or military experience?'

'That was the case to start with. But the Home Guard is now much stronger than it was. There's a lot of young blood there – miners, shipyard workers, farmers. They're young and keen and physically fit. They don't need me.'

'But *I* need you!' Rosie said. The words were out before she knew it.

'Rosie,' Peter couldn't help but smile in spite of the seriousness of the situation, 'I don't think you've ever needed anyone in your life. You're the least needy person I've ever known!'

Rosie wanted to scream, *I do need you!* She needed him to make her feel the way he had made her feel this past month. She needed him because he made her happy.

'Where's this "organisation" based?' Rosie snapped.

'It's dotted all over really. Toby's up in Scotland, but I think they want me down in Guildford.'

Rosie didn't know anything about Guildford. Nor was she entirely sure where it was in the country, other than hundreds of miles down south.

'Guildford?' Rosie asked.

'It doesn't really matter where I'm going,' Peter said. 'I'm not sure how long I'll even be there. I'll spend a few weeks there to start with, then I'll probably have to go to London, but I'm not sure where I'll be placed after that. The main point is …' Peter took a deep breath.

Rosie's mind was working nineteen to the dozen. She could feel the energy drain out of her. 'They're not sending you overseas, are they?' She was staring at him, demanding more answers.

Peter paused.

'Yes, it's likely.'

'When?' Rosie demanded. 'When do you go?'

'Things are happening quicker than I'd expected, so probably quite soon,' he admitted.

'*How* soon?' Rosie asked.

'In the next week or so,' Peter said quietly.

Rosie felt the panic rising inside her.

Peter was leaving her.

'How long? When will you be back?' she asked, her voice practically a whisper.

Peter knew Rosie deserved an honest answer, even if it hurt.

'Not until we've won this blasted war,' he said.

'I'm sorry,' Peter said again.

Rosie looked at him and that was when she knew. That was when she knew why Peter had struggled to tell her this. Why he had put off telling her.

He didn't know if he was coming back!

It was only then that the reality of what he was trying to tell her really hit home.

'You're not coming back!' Rosie felt as though she had just been punched hard in the stomach. She felt nauseous. She wrenched her hand away from his. She felt herself go cold. Numb. And yet the anger was there. Anger that Peter had not been truthful with her before now. Anger that he hadn't even discussed this with her. Anger that he was going and might never come back. Anger that he was leaving her … That she would not be able to be with him. To feel his arms around her … To lose herself in his kisses and his caresses … Anger that she was having his love and his friendship and his care ripped from her. Ruthlessly. Suddenly. And without any guarantee that she would get it back.

'Damn you, Peter!' Rosie said, abruptly pushing her chair back and standing up.

'Damn you!' She stood, glowering down at him.

And then she grabbed her coat and gas mask off the back of her chair, turned around and pushed herself through crowds of revellers until she found the exit. She almost tumbled out onto the street. Pulling on her coat and throwing her gas mask across her shoulder, she started running down the street. Angry, frustrated tears started streaming down her face.

She didn't care that it had started to rain or that she could barely see where she was going in the blackout.

She didn't care about anything, other than the unbearable pain in her chest and the hurt that was crushing all the life and love out of her heart.

*

Peter knew it was pointless to follow Rosie. She was too hurt, too angry. He cursed himself. He should have told her sooner, although deep down he knew he had purposely held off telling her until the last minute. Selfishly, he'd wanted to continue enjoying the wonderful lightness of being they had when they were together for as long as he possibly could.

He knew Rosie, and knew this would be her reaction. He knew she would see it as a rejection. And he knew that if someone hurt her, she ran. He knew that he could have tried to sugar-coat the bitter pill he had just forced her to swallow; he could have made out that the war would be over before they knew it, and then they'd be back in each other's arms. But that wouldn't have been fair. And, anyway, it would have been a lie. This war was far from over. People believed that just because the Americans had joined the fray victory was on the horizon. But that simply wasn't the case. Hong Kong had just fallen to the Japanese, Russia was in dire straits and the situation in North Africa was precarious to say the least.

On top of which, he knew that where he was likely to be sent, there was a good chance he might not make it back in one piece. Toby had been brutally honest with him and told him that most of those they sent behind enemy lines did not make it back. It was unfair to give Rosie unrealistic expectations. In all the time they had been together, the difference in their ages had never been an issue. Now it was. He was twice Rosie's age. He'd had a life. If it was taken from him during this world war, then it would be a sacrifice worth making.

As Peter sat and finished his pint, oblivious to the hubbub of joviality around him, he knew he'd have to decide whether he should go and see Rosie before he left – tell her that he loved her and that he was sorry – or simply let her be. Let her stay angry with him. Would that make it less painful? Was letting her go the kindest option? Would seeing him again simply make it worse?

Of course, he knew what *he* wanted to do, but what was best for Rosie?

At this moment, he really didn't know anything, other than he had never felt so wretched in his entire life.

Chapter Forty-One

'Oh, *mon Dieu!*'

Lily had hurried out of the back parlour where she had been mixing with the evening's house guests when she'd heard the front door slam. She'd been greeted by the sight of Rosie standing in the hallway, dripping wet, tossing her gas mask and her bag down on the parquet flooring, then trying to pull off her grey mackintosh, which was wet through.

'*Ma chère …*' Lily tottered down the long hallway. It wasn't until she was up close that she saw the devastation etched into Rosie's face. Her mascara had run down her cheeks and her blonde curls were plastered to her face.

'What on earth's wrong?' she asked, as she watched Rosie wrestle with her gaberdine before finally wrenching it off and chucking it to the floor in anger.

'Here, *ma chérie.*' Lily reached out and took Rosie's hand, gently manoeuvring her towards the front reception room. As she did so, George and Maisie appeared in the hallway. They had also heard the door slam and had seen Lily make her excuses to the brigadier, with whom she'd been chatting, before bustling out of the room.

As Lily opened the heavy oak door and guided an overwrought and very wet Rosie through to what had become her office, she gave George a look that said he was to follow her. She then turned her attention to Maisie and asked if she could fetch a towel.

'Come on,' Lily commanded, 'let's get you in front of the fire and warm you up.'

She guided Rosie to one of the armchairs next to the fireplace. She was glad she'd told Milly to get all the fires going because it was New Year's Eve and she'd wanted the bordello to be as warm and cosy as possible as they were expecting a full house that evening.

Rosie slumped into the chair as Maisie hurried in. She knew better than to stick around and left as quickly and as quietly as she had come. George was hovering behind Lily, uncertain as to what to do or say. He had never seen Rosie so openly distressed.

'Be a dear and pour us a couple of brandies, will you, George?' Lily asked before turning her attention back to Rosie, who was now sitting with her hands covering her face. Her shoulders were juddering as she cried silent tears. Lily put the towel around her shoulders and sat down on the leg rest that was next to the leather armchair.

'*Ma chère*, has anyone hurt you?' Lily asked, checking Rosie out but not seeing any signs of an attack or any kind of physical mistreatment.

George squeezed Rosie's shoulder, and held out the glass of brandy. Rosie's hand was shaking as she reached out to take it.

'Is it Peter?' Lily asked, gently.

Rosie nodded before taking in a deep, juddering breath.

'He's leaving me,' she said simply.

Lily looked at George, who was pouring out a second glass of brandy. Her mouth pursed, and she shot him another loaded look as he came over to give her her drink. George knew exactly what Lily was thinking.

Lily sat, drink in both hands, leaning forward, looking at Rosie, who was now staring into the blazing fire.

The music next door was filtering through, as were the sounds of lively chatter and laughter. Vivian's mock Mae West accent could be heard asking for requests for the next record to be played on the gramophone.

'*Ma chère*, what do you mean, he's leaving you? Has he ended the affair?' Lily asked, trying to keep the growing anger out of her voice.

This, Lily realised, must be what it feels like to be a mother, to watch your child's distress and not be able to do anything about it.

'He's going away,' Rosie said, her voice trembling. 'He's going away. And he's not coming back!'

'Oh, *ma chère*.' Lily reached forward and held Rosie's distraught face in her hands. The rain and the tears had washed off her make-up, and the tiny scars were clearly visible. Seeing them added to Lily's ire.

George had seated himself in the other armchair. Comprehension showed itself on his face as he put both hands on the top of his ivory walking stick and leant forward, his attention focused entirely on Rosie.

'Is this to do with some kind of war work?' he asked quietly. Lily turned her head and threw him a questioning look.

Rosie nodded, taking a big glug of her brandy.

At that moment George had a good idea of what had happened. Peter would not have been called up under the new conscription rules, so he must have volunteered.

'Where's he going?' George continued to question Rosie, fishing out the reason for her distress.

'Guildford … London … abroad …' Rosie took another sip of her drink, wanting to escape this terrible pain she was feeling.

It was then that George understood, although he had no idea what to say to make Rosie feel better.

'We promised we'd be honest with each other,' Rosie started to ramble. She looked at Lily and then at George. Her eyes were red and bloodshot. 'That we'd tell each other everything. We promised each other at the very beginning ...' Her voice drifted off as her mind returned to that very first time they had made love.

'He should have told me!' Rosie said in frustration. 'I could have talked him out of it. Got him to stay here!'

George tentatively asked Rosie what it was that Peter had signed up to do, but he could see that she wasn't sure. He listened intently as she mumbled something about a friend of his called Toby and how Peter had 'the skills they needed'.

George and Lily listened to Rosie as she talked, sometimes a little incoherently, about the events of the night. Neither of them said much, knowing that words weren't going to help. Rosie was losing the love of her life after just finding him. She was angry and upset. She just needed a shoulder to cry on, a gentle hug, a sense of empathy. They knew there was no quick fix for this heartache. All they could do was be there for her.

After Rosie drank her second glass of brandy, her energy was spent and her emotions exhausted. Lily tried to convince her to stay over for the evening, but Rosie insisted that she wanted to go back to her own home, so George drove her home.

He insisted on accompanying her into her flat and making her a cup of tea, but by the time the kettle had boiled, Rosie had fallen asleep on the little settee in her living room.

George found a blanket and put it over her before leaving and driving back to the bordello with a heavy heart.

*

When George walked back into the front office, he found Lily puffing away furiously on a Gauloise. Judging by the empty packet and the near to overflowing ashtray, she had been chain-smoking since he'd left. He barely made it halfway across the room before he heard the words he'd known Lily had been desperately holding back all evening.

'I knew it! *Just knew it!* I said that man would bring Rosie heartache and sure enough, he has. The man's barely been in her life two minutes and yet he's tipped her world upside down, ripped the poor girl's heart to shreds and is now just sauntering off – happy as you like – oblivious to the carnage he's left behind.' Lily puffed and blew out gusts of smoke.

'God, I wish *Detective bloody Sergeant Peter Miller* was stood in front of me now so I could strangle him with my own bare hands!'

George knew not to say anything until Lily had got everything off her chest. And he was more than aware that there was lots to unload. This had been brewing for a long time – since the day Rosie had first mentioned that she had bumped into Peter down by the docks back in February.

'That man's been trouble from the start!' Lily took a deep drag on her cigarette as she paced up and down.

George went to top up his drink and then sat down in the armchair by the fire. The party in the next room was now in full swing, and he could hear the kitchen door swinging open and shut as Milly took plates of sandwiches into the reception room and brought empty ones back out to refill with more nibbles.

As he continued to listen to Lily as she verbally massacred Peter and damned him to an eternity of purgatory, he allowed himself a cigar. It was nearly the New Year, after all.

It took until he was just about halfway through the cigar before Lily finally ran out of steam.

'I know you're angry, Lily,' George said tentatively. 'As am I. We love Rosie to bits. She's the most amazing, wonderful, kind-hearted and hard-working woman I know and she really does not deserve this terrible heartache she's presently having to endure … God knows she's been through enough in life already.'

Lily sat down in the armchair opposite and sighed. 'I agree.'

'Her mother and father died,' George continued, 'or rather were *killed*. Then there was all that awfulness with her uncle … She's worked her socks off at that shipyard and here to keep her little sister out of the workhouse. A sister, I hasten to add, who now appears to be going off the rails.'

Lily listened. All of a sudden she felt worn out. The dramatic turn of events, on top of all the preparation she had done during the day to make the New Year Eve's celebration a successful one, had caught up with her.

'And during it all,' George continued, 'she's never enjoyed the love of a good man – or *any man* for that matter – or enjoyed the frivolousness of being in love. Until now.'

Lily made a huffing sound. 'And boy oh boy, did she not half pick the wrong bleedin' bloke to fall hook, line and sinker for.'

George looked at the clock and saw they only had about ten minutes before they would have to show their faces next door for the great countdown to midnight.

'But – ' George took a deep breath, knowing that what he was going to say next was not going to be met with such agreement ' – Rosie has chosen a man who is fundamentally a good man. He has not messed our Rosie about

370

intentionally. From what I've gathered, the man's as besot-
ted with Rosie as she is with him.'

George paused.

'But,' he looked at Lily, who had got up and pulled
another Gauloise out of the packet on the desk, 'he has
done something which I believe to be incredibly selfless
and also very brave. He has forsaken his own needs and
wants and desires, to help his country. Our country. This
wonderful country of ours that is in danger – that could
soon be ruled by a certifiable madman. I, for one, have to
commend Peter. It is terrible for our Rosie. She's not had an
easy ride out of life and it looks like she's still being dealt
a pretty bad hand, but she's going to have to do what she
always does, and that's dust herself down, get up and get
on living this life the best she can.'

Lily looked at George. She knew he was right but she
would never admit it. She was still too angry. She made a
show of taking the glass stopper out of the decanter and
splashing more brandy into her crystal tumbler.

'Well,' she said, taking a sip, 'I still don't like the bloke.
Never have, never will.' She sat back down in the armchair. 'But what really gets my goat most of all is that I
know Rosie. And I know that once she's calmed down and
lets go of her anger, she'll forgive Perfect Peter and then
pine for him. She won't show it, of course. But I know for
sure our girl will think about that bloody copper every day
until he comes back.'

George looked at Lily and took a swig of brandy.

'If,' he said solemnly, *'if* he comes back.'

George still kept an ear to the ground and had con-
tacts from his service in the First World War, and piecing
together what Rosie had said, it looked as though Peter
had signed up with Churchill's so-called 'Secret Army',
the SOE (Special Operations Executive), and if that was

371

the case, the chances he would return weren't high. Covert operations carried out behind enemy lines were dangerous, to say the least. Rosie had mentioned a while ago that Peter's mother hailed from Bordeaux and that French was his second language, so it didn't take a genius to work out that Peter's linguistic skills, combined with his experience as a detective, could be put to good use.

'I just hope that when Detective Sergeant Peter Miller does leave, Rosie will forget about him,' Lily said, breaking through his thoughts.

'I agree, but knowing Rosie, I doubt very much that'll be the case,' George said, just as Maisie came bustling into the room and demanded that they both cheer up and get themselves next door to see in the New Year.

Chapter Forty-Two

'Ah, just the person!' DS Neville Grey shouted out as soon as he spotted Peter coming into the main entrance of the Sunderland Borough Police headquarters. He took his hand off the receiver of the black Bakelite and put on his best speaking voice. 'Yes, sir, Detective Sergeant Miller has just walked into the building. I'm going to hand you over now.'

Peter looked at his colleague and knew by his tone of voice that there was top brass on the other end of the phone.

His time had come.

Walking round to the other side of the counter, he took the phone off DS Grey and introduced himself.

'DS Peter Miller here. How can I help you?' It was just a formality as Peter knew exactly how he could help the Chief Super who was calling from Guildford Police headquarters. The call, however, had come earlier than expected. The correspondence he had sent off just before Christmas had obviously been received and dealt with quickly. Certainly more speedily than anticipated.

DS Grey pretended to busy himself, but was listening intently, although the only words he caught were Peter saying, 'Yes, sir ... No, sir, that's no problem ... Of course,

373

sir. I will be there at twelve hundred hours … Yes. Thank you, sir. Good day.'

When Peter put the phone down, DS Grey asked, 'Everything all right there, Peter?'

Peter nodded as he looked under the counter, where he knew the stationery was kept.

'Yes, thanks, Neville. Listen, I've got to go back out again.' Peter took a piece of paper and an envelope from one of the drawers, folded them up and put them in his inside pocket. He looked at his watch.

'You'll be off shift by the time I'm back, so give my regards to the family. Wish them all the best for the New Year.'

DS Grey said he would and put a hand up to signal his farewell.

Peter knew he would not be seeing Neville, or any of his other colleagues with the Borough Police, for a good while, if at all; nor those men he'd got to know in the town's Home Guard. Apologies about his sudden departure would be made tomorrow – after he'd left – by those higher up the chain of command. It had been agreed with the Chief Super that Peter was to leave without any kind of ceremony as the least fuss made, the better.

All he could think about now was Rosie. Since she'd left him in the pub on New Year's Eve, he'd desperately wanted to go to her, to spend one last night with her, but he had argued with himself that although that was what *he* wanted, was that really fair on *her*? Should he not simply let her be?

Now he'd got the call, he decided to compromise. He would write a letter, give it to Kate and ask her to give it to Rosie, who he knew was always at the bordello on a Friday evening. It would be up to Rosie what action she took.

She could either see him one last time before he left on the train tomorrow – or not.

It was almost dark by the time he reached the Holme Café. It was nearing the end of the day's trading and the customers were leaving in dribs and drabs, enabling Peter to grab a quiet table in the corner near to the window.

He reached into his inside pocket and pulled out his fountain pen and the sheet of paper and envelope he had taken from the station. He sat there for a while, thinking, pen posed. The young waitress took his order and had returned with his pot of tea before Peter finally began to write. He didn't stop until he had reached the end of the page. By the time he signed off *With all my love for ever, Peter*, his hand was shaking.

Had the blackout blinds of the tea shop not been drawn, he would have seen one of the nuns from Nazareth House walk past the window.

He would also have seen that the robust-looking older woman, dressed from head to toe in a traditional black habit, stopped for a moment outside the Maison Nouvelle before straightening her back and entering Kate's little boutique.

If Peter had observed all of this, he would undoubtedly have wondered why a nun would need the services of a seamstress, or indeed have any reason whatsoever to enter such a shop.

And if Peter had left the café just one minute earlier, he would have seen the same ruddy-faced nun stepping out of the Maison Nouvelle before striding back in the direction of the town centre.

When Peter walked into the Maison Nouvelle, it took a few moments for his eyes to search out Kate and find her standing behind her workbench. She was so small and was standing so still he hadn't seen her straight away. She could have easily passed for one of the mannequins standing in the corner of the shop.

'Kate?' Peter felt a moment's concern. Kate was staring ahead, as though in some kind of trance. 'Kate, are you all right?' Only then did Kate's dark eyes come back into focus and she looked at Peter as though she had just realised he was there.

'Peter,' she said, but her voice was low and quiet.

'Are you all right? You look like you're in another world there.'

'Yes, yes,' Kate said, 'I'm fine. Is there something I can help you with?'

Peter looked down at his hand, which had been clutching his letter to Rosie since he had left the tea shop.

'Yes, yes, there is. And I hope you don't think it's an imposition,' Peter said with a slightly embarrassed smile as he held out the letter. 'I wanted to ask if you wouldn't mind giving this to Rosie on my behalf, please?'

'Of course I will,' Kate said without hesitation. She put her hand out for the letter but still did not move from where she was standing. Peter stepped forward and, leaning across the wooden bench, placed it in her hand.

'Thank you, thank you so much. That means an awful lot to me. It really does,' Peter said before turning and walking back towards the shop door.

As he left, he looked back at Kate, who was still rooted to the spot.

It had not occurred to Peter that it was odd Kate made no effort to move from where she was standing, and he didn't know her well enough to think it strange that she didn't come from behind her worktop to welcome him, or that she didn't offer him a cup of tea.

If the light had not been so dim, and if Peter had walked around the counter to give Kate his letter, he would have noticed not only that she was trembling, but that pooled around her new black leather Mary Jane shoes was a small puddle which had formed while her previous visitor had been in her shop.

As soon as Peter had shut the door behind him, Kate stuffed the letter he had given her into her skirt pocket and then turned and went into the back room. She cleaned herself up as best she could before retrieving the mop and bucket from their place by the back door and wiping down the floor where she had been standing. She then grabbed her bag and gas mask, checked everything was safe and secure in the shop, and locked up.

Glad of the darkness, she hurried back to the bordello, letting herself in with her front-door key and making sure she was as quiet as a mouse. She did not want to speak to another living soul.

Heading straight for the kitchen, she stood for a moment at the door, which was slightly ajar, and listened. It was quiet and, therefore, most likely empty. If Milly was cooking or clearing up she usually had the wireless on. Kate slipped through the door and headed straight for the walk-in larder. Rummaging around on the shelves for a short while, she finally found what she was looking for – the cooking brandy. As she quickly left the kitchen she heard the low murmur of chatter and Vera Lynn's voice crackling slightly as the gramophone played 'We'll Meet Again'.

As soon as she reached her room in the attic, she uncorked the brandy and took a swig straight from the bottle. She then closed the door firmly behind her, sat down on the edge of her bed and took another, longer swig. Her face was without expression or emotion.

Kate stayed there, staring straight ahead into nothingness, taking regular swigs of the cheap brandy.

By the time she passed out, the bottle was half-empty.

Chapter Forty-Three

Peter hadn't expected to sleep at all and he was proved right. He had tried to keep himself busy. There was certainly plenty to do – he had to pack, and then he had to tidy up the house in anticipation of it being left empty for an uncertain period of time. Normally he would have put on the wireless whilst doing any kind of mundane task, eager to catch the BBC home news, or any other snippets of information about the war, but this evening he could not risk it. Rosie might knock and he might not hear her.

Earlier on in the evening, shortly after getting back from seeing Kate, he had nipped next door to see his neighbour and ask if she would be so kind as to keep a spare key for the house. He had tried to be as vague as possible about where he was going and for how long, but it was hard as Mrs Jenkins was not only a chatterbox, but also a bit of a nebby-nose who liked nothing more than to grill whoever she was talking to. Peter had thought in the past that she would have made either a good copper or a journalist.

During his time talking to Mrs Jenkins, Peter had refused the offer of tea and repeated offers to come in out of the cold. Instead, he had remained chatting on the doorstep, terrified he might miss Rosie should she turn up.

As the night wore on, he kept doing slow, methodical laps of the house, going from room to room, checking and rechecking that all the electrical appliances had been unplugged, and making sure the place was spick and span; he did so constantly alert for any sound outside the house that might signify that Rosie was walking up the gravel path, or knocking on the door. Indeed, he had kept the front door ajar until it was late, only then reluctantly closing it.

He had considered taking one of the chairs from the kitchen and putting it outside so that he could sit on it, and watch for Rosie's arrival through the little wooden gate at the bottom of the private road. If he had been able to do so without arousing the suspicions of his neighbours, he would have happily done it – in spite of the bitter cold.

By midnight Peter had been forced to accept that Rosie was not coming – even though he had been convinced that she would. The letter he had written to her had been from the heart. It had also explained that he had to leave much sooner than expected, and that he had to catch the twelve o'clock train to Guildford tomorrow.

In the early hours of the morning, Peter toyed with the idea of walking to her flat and knocking on her door – he had been on the verge of doing so, before he managed to stop himself. *If she had wanted to see you, she would have come,* he'd told himself.

It had even gone through his mind that perhaps Rosie had not received the letter, but he had dismissed this as wishful thinking. He knew Kate adored Rosie and would do anything for her.

There was no reason why she wouldn't give Rosie the letter, was there?

When Rosie turned up at the bordello it had just gone seven and she caught a glimpse of the back of Kate hurrying up the stairs. Probably, Rosie thought, to get on with one of her own 'projects'. Kate now had so much work on at the shop that anything personal she wanted to spend time on had to be done of an evening in her free time.

Rosie went into her office and settled down at her desk, where she worked undisturbed for the next couple of hours. Lily and George were out at the theatre, and Rosie knew she wouldn't see hide nor hair of the other girls as they were all, understandably, giving her a wide berth. She was being a real cow at the moment, but she couldn't stop herself. She felt constantly swamped by anger and irritation. She'd managed to just about keep a lid on it at the yard, but she knew her squad were aware that something was up, and she knew she'd have to tell them all at some stage; at the moment, though, she just wanted to stew in her own misery and ill-temper.

She hadn't, however, succeeded in being quite so cordial with some of the girls at the bordello and had snapped at a few of them over the past couple of days. She knew it wasn't fair, but a part of her didn't care. Her whole future had just crumbled in front of her very eyes, and she had not the least desire to try and pretend that her life was tickety-boo.

Yesterday she'd overheard Maisie chatting to Vivian, saying that she was not in the least bit surprised by the breakup. 'Rosie must have been mad to think she could have a normal relationship – *and with a copper of all people.*' It had brought home to Rosie that, much as she hated to admit it, Maisie was right. Her life had never been 'normal' and would never *be* normal.

When the grandfather clock at the end of the hallway announced that it was nine o'clock, Rosie gave up trying to concentrate any more. Her mind seemed unable to focus on the rows of numbers in front of her, and instead kept going over every word Peter had spoken to her on New Year's Eve – and over the conversation she'd had with George last night, when he'd spoken to her about the kind of war work Peter had obviously signed up for.

George had stressed to her that the country needed men like Peter, with his language skills and the knowledge that came from being a long-serving detective. Logically, she knew George was right and that she should be more understanding.

She wished more than anything that she could be like Polly, who had been so understanding when Tommy had joined the navy despite being in a reserved occupation. She had given him her blessing, told him she understood his need to go to war, and promised to wait for him.

But she just couldn't bring herself to do what Polly had done.

All the logic and reasoning in the world could not shift this anger she was feeling.

In frustration at her inability to concentrate, Rosie slammed closed the red leather-bound accounts ledger. She sat staring at the fire, which was dwindling and needed another boost of coal. She pushed her chair away from her desk and stood up. She walked towards the fire and picked up the little brass shovel lying on the hearth. She was just about to stab it into the coal bucket and give the fire the sustenance it needed, when she suddenly changed her mind. Dropping the metal scoop back into the scuttle, she turned and walked across the room, opened the heavy oak door and stepped out into the hallway. Grabbing her mackintosh, but leaving behind her handbag and gas mask, she slipped out of the front door and hurried down the narrow path and through the gate.

Rosie told herself that she just needed a little fresh air; that she was tired and needed waking up so that she could go back and concentrate on her bookkeeping.

She kept telling herself that until she reached the end of Tunstall Vale.

When she crossed over Tunstall Road, though, and started walking down the short stretch of cobbled lane that led to Brookside Gardens, she couldn't kid herself any longer.

Her heart was banging in her chest as she stopped at the little wooden gate. It was pitch-black and she couldn't even see to the end of the row of thirteen terraced houses, although it didn't matter, she could have walked blind-folded to Peter's home.

Every nerve in her body was telling her to click up the latch, walk through the gate, and go and knock on Peter's door.

A minute passed as Rosie stood there in the darkness, her hand on top of the gate.

She so wanted to open it, but it was as though there was an invisible line there that she could not cross. She just could not bring herself to walk through the gateway and go to Peter.

Her anger wouldn't allow it.

Peter was leaving her, damn it! And in doing so he was taking all her dreams with him. Dreams she had not even allowed herself to have until he had stepped out from the shadows and kissed her for the first time on the afternoon of Hope's christening.

He hadn't even allowed her to enjoy those dreams for long – barely six weeks – before he had snatched them back off her.

Rosie looked up to the cloudless night sky and gave a heavy, exasperated sigh.

Then she turned around and walked away.

Away from what had once been her dream.

Away from what had been her hopes of a normal life.

Away from Peter.

Chapter Forty-Four

When Kate woke the next morning, her head felt like it was going to explode and her face felt sticky. When she sat up and looked at her pillow she realised she had been sick in her sleep. She was filled with shame. Terrified that the others would know of her humiliation, she forced her body to stand up. Combating waves of nausea, she began to clean up the evidence of the previous night's stupe-faction. If Lily knew what she had done, she'd be beside herself. Lily had made Kate vow never to touch another drop again after she had taken her under her wing – it had been Lily who had helped her get through the awful withdrawal she had suffered coming off the drink. It had been Lily who had seen her through what she had told her were called the 'delirium tremens', which had felt more terrible than all the beatings she had suffered at the hands of the nuns.

As Kate splashed her face with water from the bowl on her dressing table, she felt angry with herself that she had let Sister Bernadette have such an effect on her. Why had she just stood there and said nothing as the nun had verbally crucified her, hissing that she was the 'devil's child' and doing 'Satan's work' by dressing women like whores?

It hadn't been the nun's words, though, that had upset Kate – she had become accustomed to accusations of being intrinsically evil and that she'd been 'spawned by Jezebel', just like she had become accustomed to all the different kinds of punishment she'd had to endure over the years.

No, it had been the old nun's actual physical presence that had caused Kate such trauma. This was the first time she could recall coming across any of the Poor Sisters of Nazareth who had brought her up. Kate had not had any dealings with the nuns since she'd left Nazareth House. She might well have seen them during her time on the street, but if she had, she couldn't remember. Being so close to the woman who had caused her such misery when she was so young, and who had inflicted such terrible violence on her, had made Kate so petrified that she had lost control of her bodily functions.

She had felt like a child again. Terrified. Vulnerable and helpless.

And it was this that was now making Kate feel full of self-reproof, because she was no longer any of those things. She was not scared, defenceless or powerless.

After Kate dried her face, she pulled off the clothes that she had been wearing yesterday and which she had slept in. As she quickly tossed her skirt into the wicker basket that she used for her dirty laundry, Kate spotted an envelope peeking out of one of the pockets.

'Oh no!' Kate spoke the words aloud.

'No, no, no, no!' she repeated.

She had a sudden image of Peter coming into the shop.

Handing her the letter.

To Rosie.

She felt another wave of nausea that caused her to double over and dry retch.

She had been so wrapped up in her own thoughts and in her self-destructive behaviour, she had forgotten all about Peter's letter!

She had promised to give it to Rosie last night. It must be important. She – indeed, the whole bordello – knew of Rosie's heartache and that she and her detective were no more.

God, how could she be so utterly selfish?

Kate looked around and found her watch. She was shocked to see how long she had slept. It was nearly eleven o'clock. She never slept in this long. Kate stepped towards her wardrobe, flung open the doors and pulled on the first items of clothing she could reach. Her head was still pounding and her mouth felt as dry as cardboard as she pulled on a skirt and jumper and stepped into a pair of flat shoes.

She then bent down and took the envelope out of the pocket of her crumpled skirt. Grabbing the purse and gas mask she had cast into the corner of the room, she ran down the stairs, grabbed her winter coat from the stand, and slipped out the front door.

Lily was just coming out of the kitchen when she saw Kate disappearing into what was turning out to be a rather cold but surprisingly sunny winter's day.

It took half an hour of running and jumping on and off buses and trams before Kate made it to the huge metal gates of Thompson's. It was the first time she had been over the River Wear in many, many years. She avoided going over to the north side as much as she could because it always brought with it too many painful memories, for it was on this side of the river that she had been brought up when her mother was alive. A time when she had been happy.

As Kate stood at the entrance to Thompson's, she suddenly realised she had no idea what to do next. How on earth could she hope to find Rosie in what looked like, from where she was standing, a concrete jungle of metal and machinery? The place was immense and as intimidating as it was expansive.

'Are you all right there?'

Kate looked around to see where the voice had come from.

'Here!' the voice sounded out again. 'Look to your left.'

Kate obeyed the instructions and found herself looking at the face of a blond-haired young lad peering out of a window in what looked like a cabin at the side of the entrance.

'No!' Kate shouted up to the curious face. 'I'm not all right! I need to find Rosie Thornton. She's one of the head welders.'

Kate didn't say any more as the face suddenly disappeared.

Seconds later, Alfie was standing in front of her.

'Aye,' he said in his broad north-east accent, 'I know Rosie. Everyone here knows Rosie.'

'Good,' Kate said. 'I need to see her. It's an emergency.'

Alfie took another long look at Kate and decided that she could be trusted.

'Do you want me to go and get her for you?'

'Oh, yes – yes, please!' Kate felt a flood of relief.

'If anyone tries to come or go,' Alfie said, 'you have to tell them to wait here until I'm back.'

Kate nodded and watched as Alfie started to hurry across the yard, jumping over mounds of chains, dodging rivet heaters and catchers, then stopping to allow a line of cranes chug past, all swinging huge metal plates from their arms.

Kate didn't have to wait long before she saw Alfie reappear with a worried-looking Rosie.

'Is everything all right? Has something happened?' Rosie looked at Kate and thought she didn't look well. 'Are you all right, Kate?' Her voice was full of genuine concern.

'Yes, yes, I'm fine. I just feel awful because I should have given you this last night.' As she spoke, she handed the letter over to Rosie, who took it and stood looking at the writing on the front of the envelope. There was just her name, but she knew straight away whose handwriting it was.

'I'm so sorry, Rosie,' Kate repeated, unsure as to what to give as an excuse. 'I should have got it to you earlier.'

She stood and watched as Rosie tore open the envelope and read the letter.

Kate stared at her friend and thought she saw tears forming in her eyes, but it was hard to tell as her face was so dirty and her eyes looked bloodshot anyway.

'Is everything all right?' Now it was Kate's turn to ask.

Rosie's head jerked up.

'Yes, yes, everything's fine, Kate, but I need to go somewhere. Are you all right getting yourself back home?' Rosie knew Kate rarely ventured this far afield.

'Of course,' Kate said, desperately hoping that nothing had been spoilt by the late delivery of her letter.

'Alfie, will you cover for me?' Rosie asked. 'I won't be long.'

'Course,' Alfie said. 'Mum's the word 'n all that.'

By the time the words were out of his mouth, Rosie was running up the embankment.

Peter stood on the platform as his train pulled in.

He waited until everyone who was boarding the train had got on, his eyes trained on the wooden flight of stairs that led down to the main platform.

He had put the time of his train in his letter. There was a chance that Rosie might come. A slim chance. But a chance nevertheless.

If she turned up now, they could at least hold each other one last time.

Rosie ran as fast as she could, considering she was wearing heavy steel-toecapped boots, looking over her shoulder to see if there was a bus or a tram she could jump on to help her race against time.

Deep down she knew that it was a race she was never going to win, but she didn't care.

She was going to run it regardless.

As she neared the end of Dame Dorothy Street, she tried to convince herself that there was the chance that luck, for once, would be on her side, and Peter's train would be either delayed or running late.

In which case, she might make it.

She might get to see him one last time.

As she turned left and ran across the length of the Wearmouth Bridge and onto Bridge Street, she could feel her chest burning as her breath became more laboured. Her legs felt like jelly yet she forced them to keep moving. To keep running.

She was so angry with herself.

Angry for not going to Peter last night.

For turning back.

For being so bloody stubborn.

Rosie didn't think she had hated herself this much ever before.

'You're your own worst enemy, Rosie Thornton!' She spat out the words as she dodged a woman pushing a pram, and an elderly couple walking away from the town centre.

The pavements were getting busier the nearer she got to the railway station. Looking behind her to check it was safe, she dropped down off the kerb and started running along the side of the road. Anything to get her there in time.

The words Peter had written in his letter kept circling around in her head.

I love you ... always will ... Please understand.

But it was the last paragraph that had made her want to weep.

I will try my damnedest to get back to you, but, if I don't, he had written, *you are young, and you must allow yourself to love again.*

She wanted to see Peter now so she could scream at him that she didn't want *to love again*!

That he was the only one for her!

That he had to come back to her!

Turning into Athenaeum Street, she saw the entrance of the train station.

Rosie heard the blaring of a car horn and she jumped back onto the pavement, but as she did so she tripped and fell, her hands and knees smacking hard against the ground. She felt people staring at her as she pushed herself up and ran the last hundred yards.

As she reached the entrance to the railway station she heard the blast of a whistle and the hissing of a train. She flung herself towards the guard standing next to the barrier.

'Guildford ...' Rosie could barely speak, she was so out of breath.

The elderly guard put his hand to his ear.

'Guildford?' Rosie shouted with her last bit of energy.

The grey-haired guard shook his head.

'Sorry, pet. It's just leaving the station now.'

'*Please*, can you let me through anyway?' Rosie begged.

Seeing the look of desperation on her face, the old man ushered her through, knowing it was fruitless, but doing it all the same.

Rosie could hardly see through all the steam as she blindly thudded down the two flights of stairs.

But it had all been for nothing.

By the time she reached the platform, the train was steadily chugging its way out of the station and all Rosie could do was stand forlornly and watch it go.

Chapter Forty-Five

Monday 5 January 1942

'We're all here for you.' Gloria spoke into Rosie's ear as she hugged her hard.

Polly, Dorothy, Angie and Martha all wanted to do the same, but didn't. Gloria was the only one who could get away with such a public show of affection. Instead they simply waved their goodbyes with sad smiles on their dirt-smeared faces.

The women welders had all witnessed their boss's raw heartache with their own eyes when she had returned from the railway station on Saturday afternoon. She had arrived back at work looking ready to drop and she had clearly been crying as her eyes were red and puffy and bloodshot. None of them had ever seen Rosie like this before. Gloria had quickly taken her off to the canteen for a cup of tea, and Rosie had told her through gut-wrenching tears what had happened. Gloria had simply listened as Rosie's anger had been replaced by self-recrimination. They had cajoled Rosie into going to the Admiral, and Dorothy and Angie had managed to put the tiniest of smiles on her face, but everyone knew, Rosie most of all, that this particular love story was unlikely to have a happy ending.

'Thanks, Gloria, what would I do without you lot?' Rosie forced a smile on her face.

'I think you'd manage, but at least we can cushion the blow a little.'

'Anyway,' Rosie said, 'you get yourself off. I've got to go and see Helen about ordering in some new equipment – if I can find her, that is. She never seems to be about when I need her.'

As Gloria hurried to catch up with Polly, she realised just how little Helen had been about since the incident with Vinnie. She was probably just busy. From what Jack had said, she was never at home much these days either, and they'd both surmised that, like Dorothy and Angie, she was probably just out enjoying herself.

'Rosie doing overtime?' Alfie asked Gloria and Polly as they handed in their timecards. They both ignored his question and instead told him what he really wanted to know.

'Kate won't be coming to meet her today, I'm afraid, Alfie!'

They both chuckled, making the young timekeeper blush. When they'd all been in the Admiral on Saturday night, Alfie had made a point of offering to buy Rosie a drink, which she had declined, knowing he could ill afford it on his wage. They had thought he'd done so as he had seen that Rosie was upset on her return to the yard after her dash to the station. However, when he had then tentatively started asking questions about the young woman who had come to deliver the letter to Rosie, they'd realised that Alfie's sudden keenness to socialise with the women was because of Kate.

'So, what're you doing with the rest of your day?' Gloria asked Polly as they waited for the old steamer to drag herself across the river.

'Oh, I dunno, probably help Ma with some of her chores, prepare the tea, see if Bel wants me to look after Lucille for a few hours.'

'Dorothy and Angie didn't persuade you to go off gal-livanting with them this evening?' Gloria joked.

'No chance!' Polly laughed, as they made their way onto the ferry. 'I don't mind going to the flicks with them, but other than that, I don't think so. They're scary them two when they're out. I actually feel sorry for any blokes they set their sights on.'

Both women laughed and chatted away as they made their way back to Tatham Street. The conversation steered towards Rosie and their concern for her broken heart.

'I just keep thinking how awful it must be that she has absolutely no way of getting in touch with him. She doesn't even know where in Guildford he's based, or how long he's going to be there,' Polly said. 'If that was me and I couldn't have any kind of contact with Tommy, I'd be devastated.'

Gloria murmured her agreement. She knew how much she had missed Jack when he was over in America – when she had not even been able to write him a letter – and it made her realise just how lucky she was to have him back. And even more so to have him back for good.

*

'I need to tell Miriam.' Jack kissed Gloria's thick mass of curly brown hair as he spoke to her. They were in their usual meeting place – the small stone porchway of St Peter's Church. Jack had his arm wrapped around Gloria's shoulders, and he had pulled her close, not just to keep her warm, but also simply because he enjoyed the feeling of her pressed to him.

Gloria knew that Jack had made up his mind. There was to be no more putting off the inevitable. Christmas had been and gone – as had the New Year – and Gloria had given her word that they would come clean once the festivities were over.

Jack had been gutted he hadn't managed to spend any time at all alone with Helen, who seemed to have turned into a socialite in her spare time. He'd thought she might calm down after the New Year, but she hadn't.

'The only reason I agreed to put it off this long,' Jack added, 'was because of Helen, and that's been a total waste of time.'

'Mm,' Gloria agreed. She felt Jack sag a little, clearly relieved that he didn't have to fight her on this any more.

Gloria knew herself that it was time. The irony hadn't escaped her that she had been the one who had desperately wanted to tell the truth from the beginning, but there had been so many obstacles in her way she hadn't been able to. Now that the time had come when they could put a stop to all these clandestine meetings and deceit, she should have been rejoicing. Instead, she felt a deep, nervous dread.

'I was thinking of doing it this weekend coming,' Jack said.

Gloria nodded. She knew that Jack needed to tell Miriam on his own, so it was up to him when he felt the time was right. Doing it on a weekend would mean he would be able to catch Helen and tell her separately, as she only ever did half a day on Saturday and always had Sundays off.

'Do you know what I'm looking forward to the most?' Jack asked. He didn't need to say what he was talking about. It was all either of them had thought about for so long now – the time they could finally be together.

'What's that?' Gloria tipped her head to look up at Jack, who was staring out into the darkness.

'Waking up in the middle of the night and finding you next to me.'

Gloria thought that sounded better than anything in the whole world.

Chapter Forty-Six

Tuesday 6 January 1942

Gloria and Polly steadied themselves as they felt the familiar bump of the ferry reaching the north dock.

'God, I'm freezing,' Polly said as she clasped and unclasped her gloved hands. The past few days had been bitter. The loaded granite-coloured skies had let go of the odd flurry of snow, but there was clearly more to come.

'I know,' Gloria agreed, 'and it's gonna get worse, that's for sure. You seem chipper all the same.' She gave her workmate a sidelong glance. 'Which I'm guessing means you've just had a letter from Tommy?'

Polly looked at Gloria with a smile on her face. 'You know me too well!' she laughed.

'How's he doing?' Gloria asked. Her own two boys had just sent her a postcard. It hadn't told her much but it was enough for her to know that they were alive and well; that was all that mattered.

'Well, you know Tommy, he'd say everything was all fine and dandy even if he was just about to take his last breath.' Polly paused for a moment. 'Actually, he said something really lovely.'

Gloria raised her eyebrows. 'Ah, young love, eh?'

Polly blushed. 'No, nothing like that. No, he said how proud he was of me. Proud that I was working at the yard, building ships.'

Gloria had to stop any concern showing on her face. 'Really? That's a turn-up for the books. I thought he was always trying to get you to stop and do something "safer".'

'I know,' Polly said, 'looks like he's finally accepted that his future wife is going to be a shipyard worker. War or no war!'

Gloria forced herself to sound jocular, despite the niggle in the back of her mind.

'Well,' she said with a smile, not wanting Polly to see what she was thinking – that it seemed an odd and rather sudden change of heart on Tommy's part. 'We'll see how you both feel about that when you're married and out here expecting.' Gloria stuck her hand out in front of her stomach to stress her point.

'God, Glor, what's that expression – "Do as I say and not as I do"?'

They both laughed, thinking of how Gloria had worked the cranes during the later stages of her pregnancy when she could barely haul herself in and out of the metal cabin.

As they walked up the embankment to the main gates, Polly lowered her voice. 'Anyway, how are you feeling about everything? I have to say, you seem so much happier now Vinnie's off the scene.' Polly hadn't been the only one to notice the difference in her workmate – all of the women had commented at some point over the past few weeks that Gloria seemed so much more relaxed of late.

'I am,' Gloria admitted. 'I honestly feel like I've had a weight taken off. And it really is all down to Peter for managing to get shot of Vinnie. Jack didn't say anything, but I knew he was just waiting for the chance to give Vinnie what for.'

As they squashed through the bottleneck at the entrance to the yard, they reached out to take their white boards from Alfie. They no longer had to shout out their own personal identification numbers as the young lad knew them by sight.

'And how's Jack?' Polly always asked about Jack, not just because of his importance in Gloria's life, but because she and the rest of the women genuinely cared about him. He had been good as their boss, and he'd kept shtum about what he had seen that night Rosie had been attacked by her uncle.

'Yes, he's good,' Gloria said, 'and he's remembering so much more. It's really helped him seeing so much of Arthur.'

Polly smiled at the mention of the old man, who was now meeting with Jack almost every day and enjoying a bacon bap and a mug of tea at the café just up from the docks.

'I think Arthur's really enjoying it too. I reckon he could spend just about every waking hour reminiscing about the old days. He still misses working on the river and I know there's not a day goes by when he doesn't miss Flo.'

As they made their way across the yard, Gloria let out a sigh. 'But unfortunately, it's not all sweetness and light. There's still one great big looming cloud on the horizon.'

Knowing what Gloria was going to say next, Polly asked, 'You gonna do it soon?'

Gloria nodded. 'Yes, I think the time's come for us to come clean with Miriam. And Helen.'

Polly could hear the guilt in her friend's voice and squeezed her arm as they arrived at their work area to find Rosie, Dorothy, Angie and Martha trying to keep warm around the five-gallon barrel fire. Hannah was just leaving.

'See you at lunch!' she shouted out as she hurried back to the drawing office.

'Morning!' The women's greetings were emitted along with a long trail of icy vapour. There was just enough time to drink half a cup of tea from their flasks before the hooter sounded out and they all trooped off to the SS *Brutus*.

Just before lunch, Rosie stopped working and pulled up her welding mask. The women followed suit, and as they did so they saw movement down by the quayside.

'Fancy seeing Doxford's latest launch?' she asked, nodding her head in the direction of the river.

The women didn't need asking twice. Switching off their machines, they pulled off their leather gloves and followed Rosie as she led the way. Like most others along the river, there was an unspoken law that allowed workers to down tools for a few minutes to watch any newly launched ship head out to do her trials along the north-east coast.

'She's lovely,' Angie gawped as the bow of the ship, flanked by two tugs, came into view.

Like in some monster-sized fashion show, the huge metal lady majestically glided her way down the watery catwalk that was the River Wear. Spectators lining the riverbanks cheered and clapped as they eyed up the town's latest creation.

Gloria looked at Angie and Dorothy. The pair of them had their arms linked as they scrutinised the 400-foot-long beauty shimmering her way through the sparkling, white-tipped waters of the Wear. She could hear the other workers around them comment on the ship's lines and the quality of her finish, weighing her up just as critically as racing men looking over the points of a horse and making their judgements accordingly.

Breathing in the salt air, Gloria looked at the women welders. Her heart went out to Rosie. None of the women had said anything, but Rosie looked terrible. She had dark rings under her eyes, and was clearly not sleeping. The poor girl was one of the bravest, strongest women Gloria knew, and also one of the unluckiest in life and love.

Gloria's eyes wandered across to Crown's, where she knew Jack would be now, standing, like they all were, watching the ship being guided out of the mouth of the Wear. She loved that man so much. Sometimes she thought too much. If, like Peter, he had to suddenly go away, she didn't know how she could cope. Would she, like Rosie, be able to put on a brave face and carry on? She wasn't so sure.

Looking at her friends and feeling that wonderful sense of belonging she had only ever felt since starting work at Thompson's, Gloria suddenly felt sad. She knew this would all soon be taken from her, or rather that she would be taken from them, as there was no doubt in her mind that as soon as Jack told Miriam about their love – and about Hope – her first act of retribution would be to have Gloria booted out of the yard.

It was the price she had to pay. Miriam, she knew, would make it hard for them to gain employment and it was likely they were going to find it hard to survive financially, but that didn't matter. At least she and Jack and Hope could finally be together. As long as they had each other – and Hope had her mam and dad to love and care for her – nothing else mattered.

Chapter Forty-Seven

Pickering & Sons, Bridge Street, Sunderland

When Georgina heard Mrs Crawford greeting her father in the room next door, she felt herself panic a little. Last night she had seen the head welder, Rosie Thornton, in the flesh and it was then that the faint jingle of a bell in the distant recesses of her memory had started clanging. The memory had caused her pain, but then again, any kind of reminiscence about her mother always did.

Rosie's mum and her own mum had been friends.

Georgina could vividly recall her mother's smiling face and the trail of her lavender perfume as she left the house to have what she called 'her tea and chatter' with her friend, Mrs Thornton.

She had dredged her childhood memories and recalled that Mrs Thornton and her family had lived over the river in Whitburn village, and it was only when she came into town every month that she met with Georgina's mother.

Georgina had met Rosie only the once, and very briefly, when Mrs Thornton had knocked on their door and apologised to her mother for having to call off their usual monthly get-together. She remembered hiding behind the folds of her mother's long skirt and peeking a look at the woman and child on their doorstep. The little blonde girl had smiled back at Georgina, and she remembered thinking how pretty she was.

She had recognised Rosie straight away last night. The pretty little girl had developed into a stunning woman, despite the facial scarring, which she had managed to hide well, but not so well that it was indiscernible.

Strictly speaking, Georgina should hand everything she had learnt about the women welders, including what she now knew about Rosie, over to the client. After all, that was her job, it was what she was paid for.

For heaven's sake, Georgina huffed to herself. *Why should it matter that their mothers had been friends?*

'Good day, Mr Pickering, how are you?' Miriam sounded the epitome of politeness. She even surprised herself sometimes as to how nice she could actually be – how easy it was to win people over. 'And how's that lovely young lady who works for you?' Miriam looked around the room as if expecting to come across Georgina lurking in a corner.

'She's very well, thank you,' Mr Pickering said. 'In fact, let me just go and see if "the lovely young lady" has all the information you required.'

Georgina heard her father's chair scrape back on the bare floorboards and she started scrabbling to put her various bits of paper into order. When he opened the door, she looked up and smiled, trying to keep the indecision from showing on her face.

'I'll bring you the file in two minutes,' she said, causing her father to do an about-turn back to his own office.

Miriam counted out the money she owed Mr Pickering. She was paying cash as there was no way she wanted anyone to have even an inkling that she had visited such a shady establishment – never mind employed the services of a private investigator.

As promised, two minutes later Georgina entered the room with her file and handed it over to Mrs Crawford. It was the first time Georgina had really looked at Miriam and she couldn't help but be a little intimidated. The woman was stunning. For her age, at least.

'Here you are,' she said, feeling a ridiculous urge to drop in a curtsy.

'Thank you, my dear.' Miriam gave the young girl a convincing, kindly smile.

In truth, Miriam didn't think the doleful-looking girl with the sad eyes at all 'lovely', and she certainly wasn't like any of the secretaries Miriam had ever met.

When Georgina left the room and went back to her own small office, she flopped back down on her chair behind the square little wooden desk.

She just hoped that she had made the right decision.

Chapter Forty-Eight

Rosie looked at her little alarm clock and forced herself to get out of bed.

Even though she had barely slept a wink, she wasn't tired, or perhaps she was, but just didn't know it. All she did know was that it felt as though she had been stripped of all human emotion, as if physically she was alive and functioning, but her heart had turned to stone.

Four days ago, when she had walked out of the railway station after seeing Peter's train leave, it was as if she had stepped into some kind of emotional void. Nothing seemed to matter any more. And the same thoughts kept going round and round in her head.

She should have listened to George.

God, she should have been proud of Peter – not shouted at him and then run away!

Now she had not only lost the man she loved, but because of her own bloody-mindedness she had missed the chance to say a final farewell to him. She would give anything to rewind the clock, to have clicked open the gate that night and gone to Peter for what might have been the last time.

She kept replaying the fantasy in her mind. How she would have told him that she loved him, how she understood that the war took precedence over their love, but that theirs was a special love, one that no one – not even this war, or even death – would be able to take away from them.

But it didn't matter how many times she imagined that scene, it didn't make it real. If anything, it just made her feel more wretched, more heartbroken, and even angrier at herself. Now she just wanted to curl up in a ball and shut out the world and everyone in it, but she knew she couldn't. People depended on her. Charlotte, her women welders, Lily and the girls. And there were ships to be built – a war to be won.

She had to do what she had always done in her life. She had to keep going.

And so, like she did every morning, Rosie put on her overalls, laced up her boots and pulled on her heavy winter coat. She then grabbed her holdall and gas mask, and opened the door to another day.

Another day of work. Another day to claw her way through.

'Look!' Angie said, her mouth crammed full of corned beef and potato pie. Her arm was stretched across the table and pointing towards the canteen window. The women all turned to see what had caught their workmate's attention.

'Oh dear,' Martha said ominously.

'What is it?' Hannah asked. Her eyesight wasn't the best and her view was obscured by Martha next to her.

'It's the telegram boy,' Dorothy said, her eyes scrutinising the young lad dressed in the familiar navy-blue uniform. They had become known as 'Angels of Death' as so many messages they now delivered were to inform families that a loved one had been killed in action.

A few of the men on the neighbouring tables had also seen the telegram boy disappear into the administration office and a low murmur started to slowly snake its way around the canteen. The women all looked at Polly, who they knew would be thinking about Tommy, and Gloria, whose two boys were also serving in the navy.

'Come on, you lot.' Rosie broke the grim silence. 'Eat up. We've got a hell of a lot to do this afternoon. I don't want you fading on me saying you're knackered and you've no energy left.'

The women looked back at their food and did as they were told.

Five minutes later, when Gloria, Polly and most of the other men and women in the canteen who had family away at war were just starting to breathe a sigh of relief that the telegram was not for them, Helen's secretary came through the main doors. The noise and chatter of the canteen instantly died down as Marie-Anne made her way across the canteen. Dozens of pairs of eyes watched to see if Helen's red-haired assistant was headed for their table.

'She's coming over here.' Polly's voice sounded faint and full of fear.

None of the rest of the women said anything as Marie-Anne made a beeline for their table. In all the time the women had worked there, they had never seen her in the canteen. Rosie took hold of Polly's hand. The telegram might well come to Thompson's rather than the Elliots' because of Tommy's close connection to the yard. On top of which Tommy had started to send his letters care of Thompson's to see if Polly got them any quicker.

When Marie-Anne reached the table, she looked flushed. Her arrival had caused a stir and the attention was clearly unwelcome.

Rosie, Martha, Hannah, Dorothy and Angie stared hopelessly from Polly to Gloria, then up to a self-conscious-looking Marie-Anne.

'Sorry to intrude on your lunch, ladies.' Marie-Anne was the epitome of politeness but her voice was warm and friendly. 'But,' she turned her attention to Rosie, 'a telegram has arrived for you, Miss Thornton, and Harold has asked to see you.'

Rosie looked shocked, as did all the women. She looked at Marie-Anne and seemed to be about to say something, but didn't. Instead, she stood up, her legs shaky, and turned to Gloria.

'Can you take charge while I'm gone?'

Her request was met by a mute nod from the squad's mother hen.

None of the women spoke a word as Rosie followed Marie-Anne across the dinner hall and out of the doors of the canteen.

There was only one thought going through Rosie's head as she walked across the yard and into the administration building.

Charlotte.

The telegram had to be something to do with her little sister.

Please, God, let her be all right! Rosie begged silently.

As she hurried up the two flights of stairs, she could feel her heart pounding. Marie-Anne knocked on Harold's office door and waited for his gruff 'Come in!' before she opened it and stepped aside to let Rosie through.

Rosie heard the door close behind her and immediately felt caged in. She hated being in these offices.

'Ah, Rosie,' Harold said, waving his hand at the chair in front of his large steel desk. He had a cigar on the go and

409

the air was thick with a sweet, oaky aroma. 'Sit down, my dear. Sit down.' He again proffered her the chair with his outstretched hand.

'I'd rather stand, Harold,' Rosie said, trying to keep the panic out of her voice. 'Is everything all right?' she asked. Her voice was strained.

'Yes, my dear. Everything's fine. Or should I say, no one's been hurt. Or worse still, killed! Bloody telegrams – only seem to mean one thing these days.'

Rosie put both her hands on the back of the chair. All of a sudden, she felt zapped of energy.

'Charlotte's all right?' she asked, needing to hear a more definite confirmation.

'Charlotte?' Harold asked, confused.

'My sister, Charlotte,' Rosie explained, searching Harold's face for a hint of what this was all about.

Harold's face lightened.

'No, this is nothing to do with family. Worry not!' He put on his spectacles, reached for the telegram on his desk and handed it over to Rosie. 'Here you are!'

Rosie stepped forward and took the small, slightly crumpled piece of yellow paper.

'From a "Detective Sergeant Peter Miller",' Harold said with a curious look on his face. 'Looks like you're needed down south?' His voice rose at the end, showing he was both perplexed and curious.

Rosie stared at Harold as though unable to understand what he was saying, before looking down at the words, all typed in capital letters. As she started to read, she suddenly felt breathless and sat down on the proffered chair, all the while her eyes remaining glued to the telegram.

She skim-read it once.

Then read it again, more slowly.

*MISS ROSIE THORNTON THOMPSON'S SHIPYARD
NORTH SANDS SUNDERLAND =*

*RAIL WARRANT ISSUED SUNDERLAND TO
GUILDFORD. LEAVES 1500HRS 7 JANUARY. WILL
AWAIT YOUR ARRIVAL = DETECTIVE SERGEANT
PETER MILLER*

Peter had watched helplessly from the window of the
end carriage as the train had left the railway station that
afternoon. He had not been able to take his eyes off the
steps leading down to the platform – had not been able
to give up hope that Rosie would come to see him off.
He had got on the train at the very last moment and hurried along each carriage, looking out of every window,
keeping his eyes trained on the stairs. He had reached
the end compartment and had pulled down the sash
window. His vision had been obscured by the steam rising from the tracks, but he just couldn't give up. And
then, just as the train started to squeal its way out of the
station, he had caught a glimpse of Rosie just as she'd
arrived on the platform. His heart soared as high as the
clouds and then dropped to the depths of despair in the
space of a breath.

By the time he had arrived at his destination, he knew
what he was going to do.

They *had* to see each other. *Even if it was just for one last
time.*

Rosie almost staggered out of the double doors of the admin
building, still clutching the telegram, her head spinning as
she made her way across the yard to see the women.

Harold had sanctioned her leave with the words 'For however long this detective sergeant needs you for, my dear!' He had no idea what was behind the telegram, nor what Rosie's association with the detective was, other than it was obviously important business. The telegram had been sent to the yard, and it was clearly imperative that their head welder be on the three o'clock train to Guildford.

As soon as the women welders spotted their boss, they all pushed up their helmets, switched off their machines and stood like statues watching her approach. They had only been making a pretence of working and had positioned themselves so that they had a direct view of the main office.

'She's got the telegram,' Polly said.

'She doesn't look upset.' Martha's eyes were scrutinising her boss's face.

'That doesn't mean anything,' said Gloria.

'You all right, miss?' Angie shouted out. She couldn't contain herself any more. Dorothy yanked her friend's arm to shut her up. Behind Rosie they could see Hannah bob out of the drawing office. Olly was behind her and they were both hurrying across the yard.

'Yes,' Rosie shouted back, seeing the row of worried faces all staring at her. The noise of the yard was at its normal level, but she could see that the women had heard her by the looks of relief that had instantly appeared on their faces.

'I'm fine,' she said as she reached them.

The women all moved in close so they could hear each other speak.

'The telegram?' Polly asked.

Rosie held it up as if suddenly realising that she was still holding it.

'It's from Peter,' she said, her hand shaking now as well as her voice.

'Rosie, you all right?' Hannah asked as she arrived, out of puff, but as soon as she saw Rosie's face she knew that whatever it was, it was not bad news.

'I'm fine, Hannah.' Rosie looked down at Hannah's upturned face and at Olly, still trying to catch his breath next to her. 'It's Peter. He's sent me a telegram.'

'And?' Dorothy demanded. She was almost bursting with impatience. *'What does he want?'*

'He wants me to go to Guildford.' Rosie still looked shocked, as if she didn't quite believe it.

'Can I have a look?' Gloria asked.

Rosie handed her the telegram. Gloria read it while Dorothy craned over her shoulder.

'Bloody hell, Rosie,' Dorothy said, her eyes wide with excitement. 'You better get a move on. Your train's at three!'

Rosie didn't move.

'Do you think I should go?' She was looking at Gloria.

'Yes!' six voices practically screamed at her all at once.

'Will you be all right taking over?' Again Rosie looked at Gloria.

'Of course she'll be fine!' Dorothy couldn't stop herself.

'We'll behave, miss, promise, cross our hearts and all that,' Angie chipped in, excitedly.

'Of course I will be, Rosie.' Gloria handed back the telegram. A telegram, she thought, that had been very cleverly worded. To an outsider, who didn't know that Rosie and Peter were romantically involved, it gave the impression that Rosie was needed on some kind of official business. Probably war-related. And by sending the telegram to Thompson's, and stating his full official title of detective sergeant, Peter had ensured that Rosie received the telegram straight away and would be given immediate leave – no questions asked.

Rosie took the telegram but didn't move.

'Now go!' Gloria told her.

'Go!' the women all shouted at her.

A tentative smile spread across Rosie's face. 'All right, I'm going.' And with that she turned and started walking across to the main entrance.

Looking down, Polly saw that her boss had left behind her bag and gas mask. She grabbed them and ran after Rosie.

Rosie looked round and smiled again.

'Oh my God,' Dorothy said, as they watched Rosie leave. 'She looks completely shell-shocked. Do you think she'll be all right?'

Gloria chuckled. 'I think she'll be more than "all right".' She turned to look at the women welders still staring after Rosie.

'Well, come on you lot. Enough gawking. Back to work we go! There's ships to be built!'

Chapter Forty-Nine

An hour after Rosie's departure, the women had successfully welded a particularly large patch of metal on to *Brutus*'s immense flank and were taking a much-needed breather. There was a cold fret creeping in from the North Sea, but when they pushed their masks up they all had sweat dripping down their faces. Not surprisingly, they were all desperate to chat about Rosie and this latest and very dramatic development in her roller coaster of a love life with Peter, but Gloria reminded them of Angie's promise to 'behave' – at least until they got to the Admiral after the end of their shift.

As the women turned their faces up to the sky to catch the cool breeze, they were startled by the sudden appearance of Billy, one of the yard's foremen.

'You in charge today, Gloria?' he shouted above the din of the nearby riveters.

Gloria nodded.

Billy stepped forward to be heard more easily. 'The yard manager needs to talk to you.'

Gloria shouted to the women to make a start on the next section, adding, 'I shouldn't be long!' She then turned to follow Billy, who had already started to make his way back down the metal gangway.

Halfway across the yard, Billy pointed Gloria in the direction of the timekeeper's cabin, where she saw Harold chatting to Alfie. The pair of them were jigging from one foot to the other and rubbing their hands in an attempt to keep warm. As soon as Harold spotted Gloria, he waved her over. Only then did Gloria start to feel a little uneasy. She was sure Billy had said it was the yard manager she needed to see – not Harold.

'What is it with you women welders today?' Harold joked when Gloria reached him. 'Your lot are in demand this afternoon. First Rosie, now you!' He had to raise his voice so as to be heard above the clatter of a load of metal sheets being moved from the nearby platers' shed.

'Nothing to worry about, though!' he reassured Gloria. 'You are, however, needed elsewhere,' he added, pointing a gloved hand over to the company car, a black Ford Anglia that was standing idly just outside the gates.

Gloria looked at the chauffeur-driven car, but when she turned back to Harold he was already hurrying off to the administration block. Even Alfie had disappeared into the cabin, where she knew he had sneaked in his own little three-bar electric heater. Gloria's sense of unease grew. If there had been anything wrong with Hope, Harold would have said, surely? Besides, he'd stressed that there was 'nothing to worry about'.

'Over here, Mrs Armstrong!'

Gloria looked up to see that the driver was holding the passenger door open for her.

It took Gloria just a few minutes to hazard a guess as to where she was being taken once the driver turned right at the top of North Sands and started driving along Harbour View. She knew then that they weren't headed for town, but were instead driving in the direction of Roker. Her suspicions were confirmed when the chauffeur turned left onto Roker Avenue, which heralded the start of the coastal road.

A few minutes later they turned left into Side Cliff Road. It was then that her sense of apprehension turned to panic as the very beautiful, end-of-terrace house that was Jack and Miriam's marital abode came into view on the corner of Park Avenue.

After pulling up outside the house, the driver jumped out and opened the back passenger door. Gloria climbed out, suddenly conscious of the dirty overalls she was wearing and her clumpy leather boots. She forced herself to smile her thanks at the young lad who had brought her here. He gestured to the side of the house and the black wrought-iron gate that had somehow avoided being requisitioned by the Ministry of War. It was open in expectation of her arrival. Gloria walked through the gateway, pulling off her headscarf and stuffing it into her trouser pocket. She had no idea what to expect, but knew that whatever it was, it wouldn't be good.

Glancing behind her, Gloria saw the car pulling away. When she looked back round again, she saw the large front door and there – standing in the doorway – was Miriam. She had a drink in one hand and was beckoning Gloria into the house with the other.

'Welcome, Gloria!' she trilled. 'Please, do come in!'

Gloria looked at Miriam and thought how stunning she looked. Her make-up had been expertly applied. Not too much, but enough to hide the imperfections created by age. Her nails were long and had been painted a vibrant, glossy red.

Once Gloria had stepped across the threshold, Miriam closed the thick oak door behind her, leaving Gloria with the feeling that she had just walked into a trap from which there was no escape.

'Come through,' Miriam beckoned, sliding past Gloria and walking across the terracotta-tiled hallway. 'Jack's just in the front reception room. We've been waiting for you.'

Gloria's heart was thumping. Her senses were on high alert. She looked around as if searching for a way out, but knew it was fruitless. She had unwittingly stepped into the arena and like the gladiators of old, she knew she was going to be forced to fight, whether she liked it or not.

'Can I get you a little tipple – a sherry or something – Gloria?' Miriam was now at the mahogany drinks cabinet and was pouring a good measure of gin into the crystal tumbler she was holding.

Gloria shook her head. She looked across at Jack, who was standing by the large bay window that looked out on to the vicarage opposite and over to the park on the right. He had watched Gloria's arrival and seen the dazed look on his lover's face as she had stepped out onto the pavement.

Jack had arrived back at the house just moments before Gloria's appearance. He'd been at Crown's when he'd been told that he was needed urgently at home and had dashed back, worried sick that something had happened to Helen. But when he had rushed through the front door and found Miriam pouring herself a drink, he knew this had nothing to do with his daughter's well-being. Then, when Miriam told him that they were awaiting a very important guest, alarm bells had started ringing loudly in his head.

'Well, isn't this cosy?' Miriam asked, looking at Gloria and then to Jack.

There was a moment's silence before Jack stepped forward.

'Miriam, this is a conversation that you and I should be having on our own.' He glared at his wife.

'Really, Jack?' Miriam asked. 'Why should this be a conversation between just you and me? After all,' she waved her drink in Gloria's direction, 'this affects all three of us, doesn't it?'

Gloria stepped forward, feeling awkward and out of place in her work gear, as if she was some tradesperson who had ventured into a part of the house that was out of bounds.

'Miriam—' Gloria said.

'Ah, she speaks! Finally!' Miriam chuckled, taking a sip of her drink and peering down her nose at Gloria.

'Miriam,' Gloria persevered. 'I want ... No,' she hesitated, 'no, I *need* to apologise to you. You clearly know about Jack and me ...' Gloria paused. She was unsure as to how much Miriam did, in fact, know, and so refrained from mentioning Hope. 'And I just want you to know that I am truly sorry for any hurt – any upset – that this has caused you. I really don't know what to say, other than I am sorry.'

Gloria stopped. She had not been prepared for this. Had never thought she would ever be in this situation. The intention had always been that Jack would have this conversation with Miriam. On his own. It was *his* wife. He was the one who had to tell her. Besides which, they'd both felt that no wife would want to be told by her husband that he was having an affair and have the mistress present to add to the humiliation, would she?

But then again, this *was* Miriam they were talking about, and not your average wife. It was now abundantly clear that she had actually gone out of her way to orchestrate the three of them being together.

'Oh, Gloria,' Miriam's voice was light and sounded sincere, 'that's awfully nice of you to apologise for any "hurt or upset".' She took another sip of her drink and asked casually, 'Just out of interest, what *was* your plan?'

She looked at Gloria and then at Jack, who opened his mouth to speak.

'No, no,' she jumped in before either of them had a chance to say anything. 'Let me guess.' She took a breath.

'Jack,' she smiled over at her husband, 'you were going to leave me – and this house and your daughter – in order to set up home with Gloria here.' Miriam looked at Gloria and forced another fake smile across her face. 'So that you both – *and of course, let us not forget baby Hope* – could then be one big, happy family.'

The mention of Hope's name gave Gloria a jolt and she automatically looked across to Jack, who was staring at his wife.

'I'm guessing from both your silences that I am right in my supposition?' Miriam said, her eyes darting from one to the other.

Gloria didn't know what to say. There was nothing *to* say. They had been worried about telling Miriam – had honestly believed that Miriam had no idea about them – and they certainly hadn't thought she had any idea about Hope.

'Yes, Miriam,' Jack said, 'you're right. That's exactly what we're going to do. I'm sorry that you've found out about Gloria and me – and Hope – before I had a chance to tell you myself, but at least now everything's out in the open.'

He walked away from the window and sat himself down on the sofa.

'I'll pack my bags and leave today. I'm happy for you to divorce me on the grounds of adultery, and it goes without saying that I don't want a penny from you. I came into this marriage with nothing and I'm more than happy to leave with nothing.'

Miriam walked with her drink to where Jack had been standing. She looked out of the window as if deep in thought. When she turned her attention back to Jack and Gloria the butter-wouldn't-melt mask had been removed – along with the pretence of being the perfect hostess.

'Do you really think that I will just stand by and let you two skip off into the sunset – pushing your bastard child in a second-hand Silver Cross pram? Do you? Do you really think that?' Miriam hissed, her face contorted.

The dramatic change in Miriam's demeanour – as well as her language – shocked Gloria, but it was the fact that she knew the make of Hope's pram that really put her on alert. *Had Miriam been spying on her?*

'I hate to say this, Miriam,' Jack said, forcing himself not to react to the fact that Hope had been called a 'bastard', 'but you haven't really got any choice in the matter. And besides,' he added, 'I doubt very much that you would want me within an inch of you, never mind still live in the same house as you, knowing what you know.'

Miriam let out a sharp, shrill laugh that shocked Jack and sent a shiver down Gloria's spine. She had a terrible sense of foreboding.

'Oh dear Jack,' she smiled at her husband the way a mother does when indulging a small, innocent child, 'you never were the brightest button in the box, were you?' She stepped forward, away from the window, and Gloria could see her face start to twist as she spoke. 'I hate to disappoint you – and you, Gloria – but I do, in fact, have a "choice in the matter". A very big choice.'

She paused.

'But anyway, I'm digressing,' she said, turning her attention back to Gloria, softening her voice and resuming her cordial air. 'Do you like working at Thompson's, Gloria?' she asked, taking another sip of her drink.

Gloria eyed Miriam. It was as she had suspected. Miriam was going to tell her that she had just worked her last few hours and that she would never pass through Thompson's gates, or those of any other shipyard, ever again. For a brief moment Gloria worried about Polly, whom she had left in charge, and how they would all manage until Rosie was back.

'I'll take it your silence means that you do?' Miriam said.

Gloria still didn't respond.

'And the rest of the women you work with?' Miriam said. 'They all seem happy working there, don't they?'

Gloria was thrown. She hadn't expected Miriam to start talking about the other women welders.

'Even the little Jewish girl,' Miriam said. 'I know she struggled at first, but since she's moved across to the drawing office, I've heard she's come on leaps and bounds.'

Now Gloria was really confused. The conversation wasn't going the way she had expected. *Why was she talking about Hannah?* But it was the inflection in her voice that was causing Gloria to feel increasingly concerned about what she was to say next.

'And what a strange bunch they are!' Miriam chuckled.

Gloria bristled. 'Miriam,' she butted in, 'if you've got something to say, then just spit it out, otherwise I'm going to get myself off.'

'Oh no, Gloria, you can't go yet,' Miriam said in her little girl's voice, 'it's only just starting to get interesting. You see, I've got so much I want to tell you. And I think you may find it of particular interest. I know I did. Rather fascinating, actually.'

Miriam walked to the cabinet and casually added a splash of gin and a little tonic to her glass.

'For starters, I'll bet you didn't know about your "little bird" – I think that's what you all like to call her, isn't it? And how she's now not just keeping a roof over her own head but her aunt's head as well. You see, it would seem that dear Aunty Rina is a bit of a soft touch and has not been collecting the money she is owed by her customers. Word on the street is that you just need to make up some sob story and the old woman will give you a hug, followed by a quick kiss on both cheeks before telling you "not to worry" and "pay when you can".

'I was just thinking the other day how awful it would be for Hannah if she were to lose her job at Thompson's. Especially as I can't see the little Jewess getting employment anywhere else – refugees like Hannah are usually last in line for any kind of work.'

Miriam put a clown-like frown on her forehead as she looked at Gloria.

'Poor Hannah and Aunty Rina. They'd struggle something rotten, wouldn't they? Probably end up in one of those awful workhouses.' She paused. 'And they won't accept charity, you know? Hannah and her aunty Rina may both look as timid as church mice, but they're as stubborn as mules when they want to be.'

Miriam puckered her lips.

'From a palace in Prague to the slums of Sunderland. That's quite a fall for your little bird … Do you think she would be able to flutter back up?' Miriam asked. 'Or not?'

Gloria could feel her hands start to clench. She'd had no idea Hannah's aunty was up to her neck in debt.

'And "Big Martha" – that's what everyone calls her at the yard, isn't it?' Miriam asked the question as though she really did want to know the answer.

Gloria didn't say anything.

'Well, a little birdie told me—' Miriam suddenly tittered. 'Not Hannah, of course! Silly me, trying to be clever and making a play on words.'

Gloria glanced across at Jack and they exchanged worried looks.

'Martha,' Miriam continued, 'has the most intriguing family history. Honestly, you couldn't have made it up. And if truth be told, I don't know if I would have believed it myself if I hadn't seen the proof with my own eyes.'

At this point Miriam went over to the sideboard and picked up a copy of an old newspaper, which, judging by its yellow colour and old-fashioned print, must have dated back at least a couple of decades.

'Have either of you ever met Martha's parents?' Miriam asked, swinging her gaze between Jack and Gloria. 'I'm guessing by Jack's blank expression that he hasn't, but I'm also surmising that you probably *have*, Gloria – and if you have, then you will agree with me that it doesn't take a genius to work out that Martha is as different from both her mother and father as can be.'

Gloria's mind was working overtime. It was true. She had met both Martha's parents on a couple of occasions over the past year and a half and neither of them bore any kind of resemblance to their daughter. It had flittered through Gloria's head that it was more than likely that Martha had been adopted, especially as she was an only child. Gloria had no idea, though, if Martha knew whether or not this was the case – she certainly hadn't made any kind of reference to it during the whole Pearl and Maisie drama.

'Well …' Miriam said, shaking out the newspaper and turning it around so that both Jack and Gloria could see the front page.

'No offence, Gloria, but you can read, can't you?'

Gloria had to refrain from going over to Miriam, ripping the newspaper from her hand and slapping her around the face.

'Of course I can read!' she snapped.

Miriam put her drink down on the dresser, walked over to Gloria and showed her the front page. Then she walked over to Jack and sat down next to him on the sofa so that he, too, could see the article.

Neither of them had to say anything. The photograph – or rather the mugshot – on the front page alongside the story said it all.

'The similarity is striking, is it not?' Miriam stood back up, leaving the paper on the oval-shaped coffee table.

A sepia photograph of a woman's large, round face, slightly bulging eyes and a half-smile showing off a wide gap between her two front teeth stared up at them all. The rest of the woman's body could not be seen, but it was clear she was of substantial build.

Gloria's eyes were glued to the image of the woman.

She was the double of Martha.

The two words making up the headline and emblazoned in big bold black lettering across the top of the page said all there was to say:

CHILD KILLER!

Gloria vaguely recalled the court case of a woman from one of the mining villages who had been hanged after it was discovered she had killed at least five children – most of them her own – although it was believed she had murdered others. It had taken a while for her crimes to come to light as she had slowly poisoned each of her victims and made a great show of trying to nurse them back to health. Gloria particularly remembered the court case as she had read the headlines when scouring the newspapers for news of Jack's marriage to Miriam all those years ago.

'And if, like me, you thought that perhaps it was just a coincidence that Big Martha looked the same as this monster – ' Miriam pointed to the newspaper in disgust ' – then I'm afraid that would be wishful thinking.' Miriam walked back over to fetch her drink. 'Because you see, I just *had* to know, and a friend of mine who works in the council offices in the births, marriages and deaths department confirmed it for me.'

This was the only lie that Miriam had told thus far, for, of course, it had been Georgina who had unearthed the shocking revelation about Martha's true parentage.

Gloria and Jack were both dumbstruck.

'I know!' Miriam said. 'Words fail, don't they? Imagine finding out that that "thing" there – ' again she pointed down to the article ' – was your mother?' She looked at Jack and Gloria. 'But then again, you would just be thankful you'd survived to tell the tale, wouldn't you?

'Oh,' she said, again pretending that she had suddenly just thought of something, 'you don't think Martha was also fed poison and somehow managed to survive, do you? Mind you, who knows? What's the expression people like to use – "what doesn't kill you makes you stronger"? Well, judging by Martha's incredible physique this may well have been the case for her.'

Miriam tilted her head to the side as if in deep contemplation. 'The thing is, it does make you wonder how Martha might react should she find out about her mother – especially as, for all we know, she may not even know that she's been adopted ... I mean, she's got the strength of half a dozen men rolled into one, but the mind and intelligence of a child – and a backward child at that.'

This, Gloria thought, was where Miriam was wrong. Martha was no one's fool. Her mind was as sharp and as intelligent as the next person's – and she had an uncanny sixth sense. Miriam, however, was probably right in guessing that Martha's parents had not told her that she was adopted, and even if they had, there was no way they would have told her the truth about her birth mother.

'Oh,' Miriam said, 'and can you imagine the reaction from others if they were to find out who Martha's real mother was? How she was spawned by a monster? Gosh,' Miriam faked a tremor, 'I'd dread to think.'

Gloria stared at Miriam. She knew exactly the reaction it would have. Martha would become the talk of the town, something that would send her straight back into the shell she had taken so long to come out of. She would be ostracised, stared at in the street and whispered about behind her back. Martha might be built like a man mountain, but she was an incredibly sensitive soul underneath her huge, physically tough exterior. It would, in effect, destroy her, as it would her mother and father. It would ruin all of their lives in one fell swoop.

'But, anyway,' Miriam said, 'enough about poor Martha. I'm sure her secret's safe with us.' She narrowed her eyes as though to gauge Jack and Gloria's reaction. 'And enough about such *deadly* serious matters.' Again she laughed. 'Oh dear, I really must stop these puns.'

She walked back towards the window.

'Your other two young girls, Dorothy and Angela,' Miriam said, 'they are quite a hoot by all accounts. They say "like father like son", well, I think with these two it's more "like mother like daughter". What is it with women these days? They seem to want double helpings of everything.'

Gloria looked at Miriam, puzzled.

'You look confused, Gloria? But you of all people should understand. Angie's mother, as well as Dorothy's, and your own dear self – you've all got something in common. One's not enough, is it? You all want to have your cake and eat it. And to be fair to you all, you've managed to get away with it so far ... I mean, look at Angie's delectable mother. Can't stop spewing out children, which makes it all the more surprising that the woman finds the time not just for a husband, but for a lover as well – and quite a young, strapping one at that ... I do hope she doesn't get caught out, though.'

Miriam drew breath.

'Have you seen the monster of a man she's married to?'

Gloria hadn't actually seen Angie's dad, but she had seen the marks he had left on his daughter's face after cuffing her for simply not doing the shopping, or making a noise when he was trying to have a lie-in. God only knew what he'd do to Angie's mother if he found out she was having it off with another man.

'And as for Dorothy's mother!' Miriam's voice rose. 'Well, she's taken the whole concept one step further. *The woman's actually got two husbands!* Can you believe it? Couldn't be bothered to divorce the first one, so she just marched straight back down that aisle and married the next one that came along!'

Now this really did shock Gloria. She knew that Dorothy's mother had been married and that the marriage had broken up. Dorothy never really talked much about her father, but from the bits and pieces she had picked up, the impression she'd got was that he hadn't been missed. But, like Miriam had just claimed, did Dorothy's mother then just conveniently forget she was still legally bound and go ahead and tie the knot with Dorothy's stepfather?

Gloria was now convinced that Miriam had employed some kind of private eye. There was no other way she could have got to know what she had.

'You probably don't know the proper word, Gloria,' Miriam said, 'but such behaviour is called *bigamy*, which, if you don't know, is very much against the laws of the land and can mean a spell in prison, or at the very least a hefty fine.

'But more than anything, for someone like Dorothy's mother, who has the kind of social standing that goes with living in any of the houses next to Backhouse Park, even if she got off with a fine, or some kind of slap on the wrist, it's the shame of it all.

'Of course, as it stands now, no one's going to find out. They haven't so far, have they? But,' Miriam sighed, 'you just never know ... What if the information that I have been given finds its way into the wrong hands? Makes you wonder if the new husband would stick around? I'm sure he has no idea his marriage is not worth the paper it's written on ... And then there's Dorothy's four little half-siblings. They'll be just like your Hope. Bastards. Every last one of them. Oh, it just doesn't bear thinking about.'

Gloria looked at Jack, who shook his head in disgust. It was a look Miriam caught.

'Jack, I really don't think you have any right to sit there shaking your head. This is all your doing. You must realise that, don't you?'

Again, Jack refused to bite back.

'But, I couldn't stand here and chat about Gloria's women welders without mentioning Polly, could I, Jack?' Miriam's voice had returned to its sickly sweetness. 'Especially as I know how close you've always been to Arthur – and Polly's fiancé, Tommy. You and I know all about that boy, don't we? I mean, we saw him grow up. He clearly followed in his granddad's footsteps, didn't he? But,' she paused briefly, 'it also seems young Tommy takes after his mother too. Both a little fragile up here,' she said, tapping the side of her head.

Both Jack and Gloria knew well that Tommy's mother had killed herself, unable to deal with the death of her husband, leaving Tommy to be brought up by Arthur and Flo.

'Playing with explosives is hardly the best occupation for someone like Tommy, I'm sure. Still, I guess no one sane would volunteer for such a job. I heard they call what Tommy's doing out there in the Mediterranean a "suicide mission".'

Miriam walked round the back of the sofa and put both her hands on Jack's shoulders. He flinched from her touch.

'Wouldn't it be just terrible if Tommy thought that his pretty Polly had tired of waiting for him, especially as she's working with so many other young men day in and day out ... It would turn that poor boy's mind.'

Jack stood up, his fists balled and his face flushed red with rage.

'This is one step too far, Miriam!' he yelled.

Gloria came over and took Jack's arm.

'Oh, Jack,' Miriam said with a little laugh, 'calm down! I'm sure no such malicious rumours will make it out to Gibraltar. I'm just letting my mouth run away with me ... I *am* naughty.'

Miriam walked back to the drinks cabinet. 'Are you sure you don't want a drink, darling? I know how much you like your single malt?'

Jack glared by way of response.

'And you, Gloria? Sure I can't tempt you? No? Dearie me, I do hate drinking on my own. Still, I think this is quite the occasion, so I will allow myself to indulge.'

As she spoke Miriam poured another splash of gin into her glass.

'Anyway, last but not least – my husband's favourite.' Miriam gave Jack an angelic smile.

'Rosie.'

Chapter Fifty

At the mention of Rosie's name Gloria felt herself stiffen.

'Pretty little thing, shame about that awful scarring on her face, though …' Miriam paused for effect. 'Still, what can you expect if you choose to do a man's job? Comes with the territory, I suppose. Having said that, though, Rosie's not at all mannish outside of work, is she?'

Gloria froze.

'Quite the opposite,' Miriam said, with a smirk on her face.

Gloria felt her heart sink to the pit of her stomach.

No, please don't let her know about Lily's!

Both Gloria and Jack were now staring, statue-like, at Miriam, as though she were a judge who might – or might not – send a loved one to the guillotine.

'I mean,' Miriam said, pausing and taking a dainty sip of her drink, 'it's surprising – considering her facial disfigurement – that a man could even bear to look at her. But, I suppose, with the right kind of make-up you can get away with murder. And let's face it, she must have some good make-up to get away with the rather seedy goings-on I've heard she's been up to.'

She knows! She bloody well knows. Gloria suddenly felt weak and for the first time put her hands on the back of the armchair next to her in order to give herself some support.

'I mean,' Miriam continued, 'the girl's not much older than Helen. How old is she Jack? You should know, you took her on at the yard when she was barely sixteen.'

Jack simply glared hatred at Miriam and didn't answer.

'Oh well, I'm going to guess she's only in her early twenties ...'

Another dramatic pause.

'And what? Seeing a man *twice* her age! Old enough to be *her father*! And from what I've heard, the pair of them haven't exactly been carrying out a chaste courtship. Practically living in sin by all accounts!'

Miriam was so engrossed in her own monologue that she did not see Gloria's look of sheer relief.

Gloria silently thanked God that whoever had been doing Miriam's dirty work for her had not unearthed Rosie's second life.

'So, there we have it!' Miriam raised her glass to the air as if in a toast. 'The women welders of Thompson's shipyard! I've said it before and I'll say it again, "What an odd, hotchpotch bunch of women, eh?"'

There was a moment of silent standoff before Gloria stepped forward and spoke, knowing that Miriam had now revealed everything she'd had hidden up her sleeve.

'Go on then, Miriam,' Gloria said matter-of-factly, 'let's get to the crux of the matter. You've got yourself some pretty good bargaining chips there. What do you want in exchange?'

'What I want,' said Miriam, 'and what I will *get*, Gloria, is that you are going to carry on being a single mother to your illegitimate child. You will not tell another living soul about your sordid affair with my husband, and you certainly will not breathe a word about your bastard's true paternity. If you do all that, every one of your friends' sleazy secrets will remain just that – secrets.

'But if you don't keep shtum about Jack and your bastard baby, I will make sure every one of your women welders are destroyed. I will rip every one of them and their families to shreds. And you will have to stand by helplessly and watch them all suffer, knowing it is all *your* fault. *Your doing.* That *you* did this to them.'

Miriam then turned her attention to Jack, who was standing in disbelief that his wife – the woman he had been married to for more than two decades – was capable of this kind of vile and threatening behaviour.

'And you, Jack,' she said, 'you're going off to Scotland. To the Clyde, to be exact. You are such a hero. And everyone loves you so much. Everyone wants a bit of you, or rather they want what you know about the new Liberty ships. At least that'll be what we tell everyone. I'll be the proud wife, waiting at home for the return of her husband.'

She sighed.

'The joy about you leaving me for the greater good of the country, though, is that I can still claim you as my husband, but not have to so much as lay eyes on you.'

Miriam let out a tinkling of laughter.

'But don't worry about me being left on my lonesome. In these days, those boys in the Admiralty who keep being billeted at the Grand can be so very discreet. So, *I* – like some of the women we've been talking about – can have my cake and eat it.' Miriam finished off her drink. 'So you see, just getting back to what you said before, Jack, I *do* have a choice. Rather a good choice actually.

'And you, Gloria.' The combination of the gin, and the fact that she was coming to the end of her monologue, was making Miriam's tongue loose. 'You should have kept quiet and convinced that husband of yours the baby was his. Then you might have been able to retain some kind of respectability. As it is, you've rather shot yourself in the foot, haven't you? Now you're going to have to face the incessant chattering of the town's gossipmongers. And how they're going to have a feeding frenzy when they hear all about you and your bastard baby – and how you don't even know who the father is!

'Oh, how I would love to be a fly on the wall. You'll never be able to lift your head high again. Just wait until the news does the rounds at Thompson's. You're going to have a rare old time of it. The yard's "bike" – so many people have had a ride, you've no idea who the father is.'

Now it was time for Gloria to let rip a loud laugh that held no humour.

'Well, that's where you're wrong, Miriam. Because unlike you, I don't care two hoots what people say about me. They can say and think what the hell they want – I don't give a jot.'

Miriam's face fell a little. Gloria's reaction wasn't what she was expecting. She felt her anger rise.

'Well, just you remember, Mrs I-don't-give-a-jot,' Miriam spat out her words, 'if you ever let it be known who Hope's father is, or if for whatever reason it becomes known that Jack is that little bastard's "da", as your lot like to say, it won't just be the women who suffer. I'll make damn sure the appropriate authorities are informed, that you're condemned as an unfit mother – and that your baby's taken off you and put in some godforsaken care home.'

As Miriam spoke, Gloria's whole body tensed and her face flushed. She walked slowly and deliberately up to Miriam so that their faces were just inches apart.

'You do that, Miriam,' Gloria's voice was low and menacing, 'you even *threaten* to do that ever again, and I will make sure that every man, woman and child in this entire town and beyond knows that your husband has had a child with another woman. I will make "damn sure" that *you* are never able to lift your head high in this town ever again without a trail of salacious whispers following you. *And do you know what else I will do?'*

Miriam was staring at Gloria, realising too late that she had gone one step too far. She had not intended to say anything about the baby; she had just got carried away. Had wanted to have one last stab.

'I'll take your silence to mean you don't.' Gloria stared at Miriam, before continuing: 'I will make sure that everyone who is anyone knows how you tricked Jack into marriage. How you pretended you were pregnant. How you conned him and dragged him down the aisle faster than the speed of light – and then how you faked a miscarriage. You will be reviled. You will be a laughing stock. "Desperate Miriam Havelock. She had to pretend she was up the duff to get her man." You will never be able to show your face in so-called decent society ever again.'

Gloria took a breath. 'I will personally make it my life's aim to destroy you, so be warned.'

There was a tense silence before Miriam forced out a laugh, but it sounded hollow and unconvincing.

'Oh, you've got me all worried,' Miriam said, walking over to the door and opening it. 'I'm quaking in my boots ... Oh, sorry, no, I forgot *you're* the one who wears the boots.' She looked down at Gloria's footwear and sneered.

'Anyway, time's up.' Miriam walked into the hallway and over to the front door. 'Toodle-pip, Gloria, you best be getting back to your women welders. They'll be wondering where you are.'

Gloria looked at Jack, expecting to see him follow suit.

Miriam laughed.

'Oh, you don't think Jack's leaving with you, do you? Jack's got a train to catch in about an hour, so we've got a few things to sort out. Jack and I have to say our farewells. We are man and wife, after all. So, shoo, shoo, off you go, my dear!'

And with that Miriam let out another coarse, false laugh and opened the front door. 'You didn't really expect me to allow you both to have the pleasure of one final goodbye, did you? Really?'

Gloria panicked and looked at Jack. She hadn't imagined that he would ever be leaving her again – let alone now.

Her mind was whirling with everything that had been said and the consequences of what had just happened. She wanted to say something to Jack, but nothing came out. She gave him a look that she hoped would express her feelings, but it was impossible. Instead, she did the only thing she could do – she turned and walked out the door, and back down the front steps.

When she reached the gate she looked back, only to see Miriam slamming the door shut.

Just as Miriam and Gloria had come to the end of their verbal sparring, and it was clear the theatre being played out in the lounge was drawing to a close, Helen quietly left the spot where she had been standing by the door in the hallway.

Helen had guessed something was up earlier on when she was at Thompson's and had seen Gloria getting into the chauffeur-driven car. She'd hurried back home to find all the servants had been sent home for the day, and that there were just her mother, her father and Gloria in the front room. She had stood rooted to the spot – her ear to the door – and caught just about every word that had been said.

Tiptoeing quickly back up the carpeted stairs, she just made it to the top of the first flight when she heard the door open and her mother's voice saying that her father had a train to catch that was leaving in an hour.

A part of Helen panicked. She had heard her mother telling her father that he was going to work on the Clyde and her heart had sunk. But now her mother was saying he was leaving *today* she felt distraught. She'd hardly seen anything of her dad these past few weeks. Had been purposely avoiding him, terrified she would say something about what she knew.

But now he was going!

And it sounded like he wasn't coming back.

Helen crouched down on the landing, her hands clutching the wooden balustrades like she was gripping the bars in a prison cell. She wanted to run down the stairs and fling herself into her father's arms and tell him she was sorry. *That this was all her fault.* But at the same time she wanted to scream at him that she hated him. How could he have an affair? But worst of all, how could he have another child – *and another daughter at that?* She felt trapped by her own emotions, seesawing between the two camps.

Love and hate. Guilt and blame.

She heard the front door slam shut. Gloria had gone. She could just about make out her mother's voice. She was telling her father that she had packed his bag in anticipation of him leaving. It sounded as though it was there at the front door because Helen heard something soft slide across the tiled hallway. A few moments later she heard someone knock on the door. She strained to hear. It was the driver. He'd come to take her father away. Helen bit her lip. Should she run down, throw her arms around him and tell him she loved him? Or would she only end up slapping him and telling him she hated him?

By the time she had made up her mind, it was too late. She heard her father say something to her mother about Miriam being 'pure venom' and 'tainting' everything she touched.

And then the door slammed closed for the second time and she knew he was gone.

Chapter Fifty-One

Jack got into the black Ford without saying a word and without giving Miriam or the house even a single backward glance. His wife might think she had won, but by God, she would not stop him saying one last goodbye to the woman he loved.

'Take the back route!' Jack told the driver in no uncertain terms.

Jack kept his eyes peeled as they drove down Bede Street and came out on Harbour View.

'Pull over!' he demanded.

As he went to get out, the driver opened his mouth to object but seeing the look on Jack's face knew it would not be a good idea. Mrs Crawford need not know that he had not taken her husband straight to the train station.

Jack heaved his bag out of the car, swung it over his shoulder and slammed the door shut. He watched as the driver continued on his route into town, thinking that it looked as though the young lad had some sense. If he wanted to keep his job he would make out he had safely delivered Jack at the station in time for the three o'clock train to Glasgow.

Jack looked up towards the Bungalow Café. He would bet money on Gloria taking the longer route back to Thompson's; instead of cutting through the side streets, she would have walked along the top of the promenade so she could look out to sea.

'Gloria!' Jack shouted out as soon as he spotted her. He'd been right. She had her back to him and was standing next to the café, looking out at the North Sea.

On hearing her name, Gloria turned around. Her face looked ashen and Jack could see that she was still in shock. Miriam's behaviour had not blindsided Jack as much as it had Gloria. Since getting his memory back – or at least most of it – he had recalled the many years of unhappiness he had spent married to Miriam. He'd recalled how he had become desensitised over time to her manipulative ways and her ruthless, selfish personality. Gloria, however, had not had many direct dealings with Miriam. Of course, she had always hated her for taking Jack away when they were sweethearts, but she had never been privy to the true extent of his wife's narcissism.

'Gloria, are you all right?' Jack asked as he neared her. He dumped his bag down on the pavement and took her in his arms.

'I love you, Gloria. Always have done and always will.' He kissed her head, her face and finally her lips. He could feel the tears roll down her face and he could taste them as they both stood there and kissed.

After a few moments, Gloria pulled away.

'Someone might see us,' she panicked. There were a few mothers with their children and an old couple in the cafeteria. Jack felt a tidal wave of anger against Miriam. She was already controlling them. He didn't think he had ever hated anyone as much as the woman he was ashamed to admit was his spouse.

'Come on, let's walk,' Jack said. 'There's no sin in two friends walking together, is there?'

Gloria wiped her tears away and smiled at Jack. How she loved this man.

Jack looked at his watch. He had precious little time, barely forty minutes, before his train left. 'St Peter's,' he said simply.

Five minutes later they had reached their favourite place. The church always seemed to be so peaceful and calm in spite of everything that might be going on around it.

'We've not got long,' Jack said, putting his bag down and gently putting both his hands on Gloria's shoulders so that he was looking straight at her. He could see the tears starting to form in her eyes. 'Now you listen to me, Gloria Turnbull.'

Gloria smiled. She loved it when Jack called her by her maiden name. It reminded her of when they were young.

'This is not the end. By any means,' he said with much more certainty than he felt. He knew, though, that he had to be strong for Gloria. He was leaving her – yet again, even if it was not his choice – and he worried that Gloria had been through so much already that this might be the last straw. 'I need you to be strong. For Hope's sake,' he said.

Jack suddenly felt a stab of pain in his chest at the thought that he wasn't even going to be able to see his daughter for one last time. This was followed by rage, but his fury against Miriam would have to be saved until later, when he was on his own. For now, he had to make sure Gloria was all right.

'We'll work something out,' he promised, but on seeing the distraught look on Gloria's face, he pulled her close and they stood there, simply holding each other.

'Why is it that we seem to spend all of our time together saying our goodbyes?' Gloria managed to laugh a little through her tears. They had stood in this very place just over a year ago and said their farewells the day before Jack left for America. It seemed only the other day, but also a lifetime ago.

'You're strong,' Jack said. He had so much he wanted to say to her and so little time. 'You're the strongest woman I know,' he repeated. 'You've been through so much and someone like Miriam is not going to defeat you. Do you hear me?' Jack was speaking softly, but there was also an urgency in his voice. He needed to make these few remaining moments count. God knew when he would see or even speak to her next.

'This will not stop us loving each other. No one, not even Miriam, can do that. I'll write to you as soon as I arrive. Let you know where I am.' Jack was looking at Gloria, needing to see that she had not run out of fight. That she would stay strong.

'Yes.' Gloria looked up at Jack. 'That's good. Write to me.' Her head was still reeling, though. It was on overload and she couldn't think beyond this moment and the fact that Jack was leaving her.

Jack looked at his watch.

'Gloria, I have to go now. I'm going to say goodbye to you here. Then I want you to go back to work and carry on. That's what you do. You survive. And then I want you to go to the Elliots' and pick up Hope and give her a cuddle and tell her that her daddy loves her.' Jack's voice suddenly broke with emotion at the thought of his beautiful baby girl.

'I will,' Gloria promised. 'I will.' She wanted to say so much more, but the words seemed to stick in her throat.

'And don't you forget,' Jack said, giving her one last kiss, 'that I love you.'

Gloria looked at Jack and mouthed the words back to him as he turned and left her.

Again.

Chapter Fifty-Two

After Jack had gone, Gloria did something she rarely did – she clicked open the heavy oak door and walked into the church. She and Jack had always stayed within the confines of the small porch entrance whenever they met up. Today, though, she felt the need to sit on her own for a while, and so she found herself stepping across the threshold and into the nave of the little Anglo-Saxon church, with its uneven flagstones and its pretty stained-glass windows, their colour and craftsmanship obscured by the necessary brown tape.

Gloria could hear her footsteps echo as she walked across to the back row of empty wooden chairs and sat down. It was cold, and she felt colder still as she had left the yard without grabbing her overcoat. The place was empty, though, and Gloria was happy to swap the warmth of an extra layer of clothing for what she had now. Quietness.

What now? she asked herself.

But she already knew the answer.

Nothing.

She could do nothing. Other than carry on. Just like Jack had said. This was a battle that, at the moment, she had to accept she had lost. She was caught in a trap, and she just had to stay caught until she could find a way to free herself.

As she looked up at the church ceiling she noticed the beams had been shaped in such a way that they resembled an upturned wooden boat. Had they been designed like that on purpose? As she cricked her neck and continued to stare up at the thick, wooden beams and the large sand-coloured stones that had been used to build this church hundreds of years ago, her life began to fall into a perspective of sorts.

She had to be strong. Just like this ancient church. Just like Jack had told her to be. And most of all, because her daughter needed her to be.

As Gloria pictured Hope's happy little face looking up at her, she remembered how she had given birth to her in the shipyard, and how she had called her Hope because of Jack, and how she'd had faith that he would come back to her alive.

And he had, hadn't he?

Now, she had to keep hoping. Hoping that they would find a way to be together as a family. That this war would end. That all the problems and the troubles her women welders had would also resolve themselves – either that or remain buried, undisturbed as the tombs she could see at the front of the church.

Gloria knew that she could not give up now. Just over five months ago she had thought that she had lost Jack for ever in the depths of the Atlantic Ocean. But she hadn't. He was back and he was well. He had even just about got his memory back. And what's more, they had created a life together.

Gloria stood up and walked out of the church.

She pulled her little wristwatch out of her top pocket and saw that it was just a few minutes to three o'clock. Jack would be at the station now, probably boarding his train.

By the time Gloria had walked across the graveyard and down the North Sands embankment to the front gates of Thompson's, it had gone three.

445

Jack would be beginning his journey.

Alfie waved Gloria through and she headed across the sea of metal and men and walked along the gangway to where she knew the women welders would be working. She saw them before they saw her and for a brief moment she stood and watched them all.

At the start of this day she had only been keeping the one secret. A secret she had been looking forward to tossing away. One that she had thought she would soon finally be free of, after all this time.

But now, she not only had to keep her own secret tightly wrapped up for the foreseeable future, she also had to keep a close guard on those of her friends – the ones they knew about, and those they didn't.

Gloria stood for a moment simply watching her friends.

A tug on the sleeve of her overall snapped her out of her reverie. She looked round and saw Hannah's young face beaming up at her.

'I saw you come in. Thought I'd come and see you.' She just about managed to shout loud enough to be heard above the noise.

Gloria looked down at Hannah and thought about her aunty Rina and the financial burden Hannah now had balanced on her skinny shoulders – never mind the constant worry she had about her parents.

'Come on, let's go and see what that motley crew of welders is up to,' Gloria shouted back. 'I think it may be time for a quick tea break.'

Hannah nodded her agreement and they walked over to where the women were working. Each one was surrounded by a halo of sparkling molten metal. One by one, as though sensing Gloria and Hannah's approach, they looked up.

Polly, Gloria thought, looked so determined when she was welding – always had done, and even more so since her last letter from Tommy. She dreaded to think what would happen to her if Tommy never came home. Worse still, if Tommy ever thought that Polly wasn't anything but a hundred per cent faithful and loyal.

Standing up to her full height to arch her back, Martha spotted her two friends and pushed up her helmet. She towered above the rest of the women as she waved, a big grin appearing on her face, showing off her distinctive gapped teeth. Gloria's heart went out to their gentle giant.

Even if Martha was able to deal with the truth about her biological mother, she knew for a fact she would not be able to withstand the scrutiny and unwanted attention should it become public knowledge.

'Yeah!' Dorothy's voice was loud and shrill against the surrounding din. She was smiling over at them, waving at them with one arm and giving Angie a whack with the other to alert her of their arrival.

Did Dorothy know about her mother's bigamy?

And did Angie know that her mam was playing away from home?

'Where ya been?' Angie asked as Gloria and Hannah reached them.

'What Angie meant to say, Glor,' Dorothy said, 'was, "*My*, you've been a while, Gloria, is everything all right?"'

Gloria smiled at the comedy duo and rolled her eyes in the direction of Polly, Hannah and Martha, who chuckled.

'Can I get a cup of tea down me first, please, before the Spanish Inquisition?' she said.

And with that, they all trooped over to the very tip of the ship's stern, which was jutting out across the river. The noise in the yard wasn't as loud there, but still enough to

447

stop any real conversation, and so they all sat in a row, pouring the tea from their flasks into their tin cups and looking out at the seemingly infinite North Sea.

And as they all sat sipping their hot tea and exchanging the odd word, Gloria thought about Jack and their rushed farewell, and she knew that her feeling of heartbreak would probably stay with her until they were reunited again – whenever that would be.

But she also knew that she was not alone. Far from it. Next to her she had her makeshift family. Her family of friends. They were all here, apart from Rosie, who hopefully would now be on her way to see her lover.

How on earth was she going to chat to them all about what had just happened at Miriam's? About what she had found out?

What should she tell them?

And what should she keep a secret?

At this very moment in time, she had no idea.

Epilogue

'Have a lovely time!' Kate threw her arms around Rosie as she said her goodbyes on the pavement outside the Maison Nouvelle.

Rosie hugged her back.

'So you'll stop beating yourself up now and get on with your next "haute couture" masterpiece?'

Kate nodded. She had been living under a dark and heavy cloud of self-recrimination since the day Rosie had missed seeing Peter off at the train station. Kate had apologised profusely, but hadn't really offered up much of an explanation as to why she had forgotten to give Rosie the letter.

'And Rosie!' Kate shouted out to her friend as she started to walk away. 'You look gorgeous!'

Underneath her grey mackintosh, Rosie was wearing the red dress Kate had made for her Christmas present. It was the first time Kate had seen Rosie wearing it and not only did it fit her perfectly, it really did look stunning.

'Well, if I do, it's thanks to you!' Rosie said, before turning and hurrying down Holmeside, giving one final wave as she turned the corner into Waterloo Place. From there it was a two-minute walk to the railway station.

What a difference six weeks can make, Rosie mused as she crossed the road to Athenaeum Street. She had fallen in love for the first time, soared higher than she had ever thought possible, and then gone into a terrible tailspin – but she hadn't crash-landed. And now, although she had no idea what the future held, at least she was going to be able to say a proper goodbye to the man she loved.

She was actually glad that she hadn't made it to the station that day to see Peter off; if she had she probably wouldn't be going to see him now. She still had no idea why Kate had 'forgotten' to give her the letter. Whatever the reason, though, Rosie knew without a doubt it must have been something serious. Perhaps Kate would be able to talk to her about it when she got back.

After walking into the main entrance of the railway station and picking up her travel warrant, Rosie showed her pass to the old guard who had kindly let her through the barriers last week in her failed attempt to see Peter. She smiled at him and he smiled back, although it was clear he did not recognise her.

'Train to King's Cross from platform one, my dear. Due in any minute.'

As predicted the train arrived within minutes and Rosie climbed aboard and to her surprise, found an empty carriage.

After putting her bag on the rack above, she settled herself into the high-backed cushioned seat next to the window. The train on the platform opposite was just preparing to leave. Rosie watched through a growing cloud of smoke as a couple clung to each other for one last time. The girl was young, as was the lad, who was dressed in a freshly pressed soldier's uniform, clutching a maroon-coloured beret.

Just as the whistle sounded out the other train's departure, a few last-minute travellers jumped on-board. She thought one of them looked the spit of Jack, but immediately dismissed the thought. Gloria would have mentioned if Jack was going away.

Turning her attention back to the people now getting onto her own train, Rosie watched as travellers passed her compartment door and hoped she might be lucky and keep the carriage to herself. She had brought a small paperback book with her in her handbag, not that she wanted to read it but it would be a way for her to avoid any kind of interaction with the other passengers. She had a long trip ahead of her and she wanted to spend the time simply watching the changing landscapes as she made her maiden journey down south.

Rosie let out a long breath and nestled back into her seat. Hearing the elongated screech of the whistle sound out, followed by the clashing of the heavy wooden doors, she felt a thrill of anticipation. She knew the journey she was about to take was not one that a 'normal' person leading a 'normal' life would be embarking upon – yet, all the same, she felt excited. Happy.

She realised the life she led – and had led for many years now – was not 'normal', yet it was also not a bad life. She loved the people who were a part of it – her women welders, Kate, Lily and George, who were as loving and as caring as any parent, possibly more so, and of course, Charlotte.

She loved Thompson's and, much as she had fought it, the bordello as well. It had been Lily's she had instinctively run to that night when she was distraught – where she had sought solace. It wasn't most people's idea of a 'home', but it was *her* home.

As the train lurched forward and Rosie began her journey, she finally understood what she should have known a long time ago – the life she was destined to lead was not to be a 'normal' one.

But, she thought, as the train picked up speed and the thick smog of steam dissipated to give her a clear view from the window of her carriage – *was that really so bad?*

Dear Reader,

I hope you have thoroughly enjoyed this latest instalment of the Shipyard Girls series and will continue to accompany Rosie, Gloria, Polly, and the rest of the women as they battle through their personal ups and downs, whilst enduring all the hardships, dangers, and worries about loved ones that went hand in hand with life on the Home Front during the Second World War.

Faith is what carries the shipyard women through their struggles – a belief that despite such crippling uncertainty as to what the future might hold, all will be well.

And so, I would like to end this book with the wish that you also have faith that whatever is happening in your life will turn out well too – and that faith is accompanied by love, hope and charity.

Until next time.

With love,

Nancy x

Historical Notes

Mrs Florence Collard is working as a welder at Bartram & Sons' yard, and is the first woman to be admitted to membership of the Boilermakers' Society in this district.

Mrs Florence Collard, who worked as a welder at Bartram & Sons' yard, was one of the seven hundred women who worked in the Sunderland shipyards during World War II.

This photograph was published alongside an article in the *Sunderland Echo* on Tuesday 10 November 1942 under the heading 'Women in Sunderland Shipyards'.

Here is a short extract from that article which, in my opinion, shows just how inspirational, brave and resilient these women were.

'... Mrs Florence Collard is working as a welder at Bartram & Sons' shipyard. She is the first woman to be admitted to membership (temporary) of the Boilermakers' Society in the Wear district. Mrs Collard, whose husband is in the Forces, is nothing if not plucky. A Sunderland woman she was bombed out at Plymouth and since returning to Sunderland she has been bombed out here in a recent raid. She was trapped in the kitchen in her home, but rescued. Though suffering from shock she went to her work at the shipyard for the afternoon shift maintaining that "work comes first".'